HECATE

J.B. ROCKWELL

SEVERED PRESS
HOBART TASMANIA

HECATE

ONE

Hecate's probes slid through the sea of wrecked ships, searching for signs of life. *Any* life—human, AI, anything that survived the massacre that occurred here, deep in unsettled space.

Assuming anything did *survive.*

A sobering thought, and one that consumed Henricksen. Drew his eyes to the floor-to-ceiling windows wrapping the front of *Hecate*'s bridge. To the stars and devastation, hoping, *praying* to spot something out there, and finding naught but despair.

Death and wreckage everywhere he looked.

"Farrow," he called, half turning. Flicking his fingers at the fair-haired woman working the station to his right. "What's the word?"

"Checking." Farrow bent her wrists, exposing the comms ports sunk into her flesh, trailing cables connecting her to the panel in front of her. "Wasteland," she reported, voice dreamy, blue eyes hidden behind the Comms visor covering her eyes and forehead, wrapping across her ears. "Some kind of interference..." She winced, adjusting a tiny dial near her temple. "No one sending, though. No one picking up, as far as I can tell."

Well, that's certainly ominous.

Henricksen frowned, eyes flickering to the windows. "Scan. What's out there?"

"Nothing, sir." Duclos twisted in his seat, shaven head painted in the multi-colored lights flashing across Scan's panel, long nose looking even longer in the low lighting around him. "Few blips now and then, but I can't get a solid reading."

"Meaning?"

"Radiation," *Hecate* cut in, serene, AI tones drifting from the overhead speakers, camera swiveling to point Henricksen's way. "It's confusing the probes' sensors. Messing up the scans." A twitch of the camera, taking in Farrow. "Possibly Comms."

Henricksen grunted, thinking. "Any chance it's natural?"

"Doubtful. No planets nearby, and the closest star is still light years away. Sensors aren't picking up any solar particle events."

Ship then. Or weapons. Manmade in either event.

Henricksen didn't like it. Not one bit.

"And the blips?"

"Could be anything. A byproduct of the radiation itself."

"Wonderful," he grunted. "Just fucking wonderful."

Didn't come across radiation often these days. Ships still used radiological weapons—Fleet ships included, at least the larger ones, like the Dreadnoughts—but nuclear drives were old beyond old, bordering on ancient. Phased out a couple of centuries ago in favor of the fuel cells and plasma drives more modern ships carried.

Radiologicals complicated things. Turned this simple little recon mission they'd been sent on into something altogether different. Radiation—enough radiation for the probes' sensors to pick up on—likely meant contamination, a complication Henricksen most definitely did *not* want to deal with.

He stared through the bridge's windows, considering the messed they'd found outside. Lifted his eyes to *Hecate*'s camera sitting just above them, one of dozens scattered across the length and breadth of her warship's body—her eyes on the crew, on everything going on around the ship. "Whaddaya wanna do?" he asked her, because this wasn't his decision. He was captain—*her* captain—and in charge of the crew, but not *Hecate's* master. Nor she his, either.

Hecate considered the question before answering.

Not entirely her call, this time. Technically *Seychelles*—the grey-skinned, smooth-sided Valkyrie cruiser behind them—was in charge of this mission, granted authority over the entire operation by *Brutus* himself. *Hecate* and three of her disc-shaped Aurora brethren detailed to go with her, backed up by a handful of Titans—sharp-sided and sinister, bodies shaped like four-pointed spearheads.

Ten ships in total, sent walkabout on a reconnaissance mission. Ten Fleet cruisers deployed to find out what the hell had happened to those vessels out there. And why no one knew anything *had* happened until it was entirely too late.

"No sense leaving the probes out there," *Hecate* decided, camera adjusting, zooming in on Henricksen's face. "Not sure there's all that much they can do."

"'Spose not," he murmured, dropping his eyes to the windows, considering the drifting wreckage outside. "Fuck it. Recall 'em, Duclos."

Duclos glanced around, blinking in surprise. "But the probes, our orders—"

"Know my orders, Duclos." Henricksen favored the crewman with a flat-eyed stare. Lean face all planes and angles, turned harsh and angry in the bridge's sparse light. Like all the crew, he dressed in *Hecate*'s midnight blue uniform, torch and keys patch a silver twinkle on his shoulder, nothing but the insignia pinned to his collar to set him apart from any of the others.

Commander's insignia, this being an Aurora, not a Dreadnought or Valkyrie. Silver leaves, not the stars Henricksen wanted, and by all rights should already have earned.

"You heard her." A nod to the camera above them, Henricksen's eyes never leaving Duclos's face. "Probes are useless. Radiation's mucking up the scans. Pull 'em back in, Duclos. Now, if you please."

Duclos hesitated, eyes flicking from Henricksen at the Command Post to *Hecate*'s camera watching from above. "Aye, sir," he said softly, facing back around. His hands lifted, reaching for the panels in front of him and froze there, hanging just above it, brow furrowing as he stared at its polyglass surface.

Like he'd forgotten how to work the thing. Or he didn't know quite what to do.

"Umm… Sir?" Another glance at Henricksen, standing at the Command Post dominating the center of *Hecate*'s bridge. "How are we supposed to…"

Duclos trailed off, waving vaguely at the windows. The wrecked ships drifting against a backdrop of black night and stars.

Henricksen quirked an eyebrow, looking a question at the camera.

"Helm," *Hecate* called, AI voice filling the bridge. "Take us in."

"Aye—wait. In?" Shaheen frowned hard at the camera.

Serious young woman, that one. Sepia-toned skin, long, dark hair pulled back and plaited in a tight, regulation braid. Uniform crisp and perfect no matter how many shifts she stood on the bridge.

"In where?" she demanded, looking thoroughly confused.

Henricksen shrugged, smiling, nodding to the cluster of ships in the distance.

Shaheen stared—eyes wide, mouth sagging open. "*There*? Sir. I'm not—I really don't think—"

"No. You don't." Henricksen's smile vanished, face turning stony and hard. "You do what the lady says." A touch of one hand to his temple, tipping an invisible cap to *Hecate*'s camera. "Now take us in, Shaheen. Probes can't pick up squat in that radioactive soup, but maybe those fancy new sensors *Hecate* got installed last month can."

"Aye, sir," Shaheen murmured, throwing an apologetic look at the camera. Slim fingers touched at Helm's panel, bringing the impulse engines to life. A few strokes of virtual keys and *Hecate* slid forward, approaching the cluster of wrecked ships.

Henricksen stared through the windows, watching those vessels draw closer. "Farrow. Send a message to *Seychelles*. Tell her and the others to stay put while—"

"Why don't you let me do that," *Hecate* interrupted. "*Seychelles* is in *charge* of this mission," she reminded him. "I'm guessing she might not like being told what to do."

"AI never do, do they?" Henricksen grunted.

Hecate laughed softly, dulcet tones filling the bridge. "Not generally, no," she admitted. "Which is why I'll *suggest* she stay put."

Henricksen dipped his head, smiling crookedly as *Hecate* opened ship-to-ship comms.

A good ship, this Aurora. His third command and easily his favorite, despite their rough start. Respected *Hecate*. Respected the *hell* out of her. *Liked* her, which he hadn't expected, Aurora AI being sixth generation and nothing at all like the quirky, oft-argumentative eight generation Titans he'd commanded before.

Lucky to have this assignment, Henricksen admitted. *Can't imagine leaving her.*

But he would, eventually. Didn't like to think about it, not after everything they'd been through together, but he wanted those captain's stars. Chased them for so many years.

Commander's billet on an Aurora, though, which meant a captain—once promoted—couldn't stay. Once he earned his captain's stars, *if* he earned his captain's stars...

Henricksen sighed heavily, touching at the silver insignia pinned to his collar. Promotion in the Fleet was never a sure thing—more officers than there were billets on hand, generally, which meant that, with each turn of the crank, a few more got spat out. He'd fought his way to commander. Earned that rank the hard way—through combat rotations and hazardous duty assignments, spilling a fair amount of his own blood on his way to *Hecate*'s chair—but captains…captains tended to stick around and *keep* their postings, so long as they didn't get killed or age out. Screw up so badly that the Fleet had to kick them to the curb.

Results got Henricksen this far. Results and a reputation for working goddamned hard. But no matter *how* good his record, Henricksen was still a pusher kid from the colonies—youth spent running the long haul freighters. An Officers Candidate School graduate from the combat program on Aeleon, not one of those stuck up assholes the Fleet pushed through the Academies on Sosholo or Yunshinshin.

Three commands under Henricksen's belt now. Two eighth generation Titans—*Harbinger*, who died in a collision with a DSR cruiser, and *Vigilant* after that—and now battle-scarred *Hecate,* with close to two hundred years in the Fleet. Three commands and still hustling. Fighting for the captain's stars the Academy boys—with their pedigree, and manners, and lineages stretching back centuries—bought on credit with their rich-ass parents' funds.

Well fuck them. He wasn't done fighting. And he wasn't giving up on his stars.

"Henricksen. *Henricksen!*" *Hecate* called, camera pivoting his way.

"Sorry." He snatched his fingers from his collar, hand dropping to his side. "Thinking."

A pause before *Hecate* answered, camera zooming in tight. "Dreaming of stars, no doubt."

Caught red-handed.

Henricksen ducked his head, face flushing.

Hecate knew him too well. Knew just how *much* he wanted those stars.

"Sorry," he repeated. Hand lifting unbidden, reaching for the devices on his collar before he forced it back down. "So what's the word?" he asked her, in the silence that followed—*Hecate* watching, crew watching, all those eyes focused on him. "What's *Seychelles* got to say."

"We're cleared to go in," she told him. "*Seychelles* advises us to be careful," she added, a hint of a smile creeping into her voice.

"Careful," Henricksen snorted, regaining his composure. Shoulders twitching as he straightened up. "When have I ever *not* be careful?"

"You really want me to answer that?"

"What? That thing on Ephelus again." Henricksen rolled his eyes. "You're never gonna let me live that down, are you?"

"Ephelus. Trisserine. Agdonalo—"

"*You* were as much to blame for those last two as me, you know."

Hecate wisely didn't answer. *Her* decision to move on the DSR before reinforcements arrived. Her guns that chased them off in both cases, making the local constabulary quite happy in the process.

Good team, *Hecate* and he. One of the best in the galaxy, if he did say so himself.

Almost made him want to stay. Almost made him want to give up chasing those stars.

Later, he told himself. *Worry about the stars later. Focus on the job for now.*

"Shaheen!" Henricksen called, turning toward Helm. "Time to intercept?"

"Three minutes, sir. We're on approach."

"Right. Sikuuku!" Henricksen pivoted, pointing at the gimballed Artillery pod bulging roundly from the right-hand wall. The squat, square man stuffed inside it, slouching insouciantly, looking bored out of his mind. Tattoos showed darkly on his red-brown skin, blue-black patterns inked across his nose and cheeks, framed by jet-black hair the color of raven's wings clipped to a soft fuzz on his wide head. "*Seychelles* wants us to be careful. Think you can help out with that?"

"'Spose," Sikuuku shrugged, muscled shoulders rippling beneath his uniform jacket. "Not like I've got anything else to do." He reached for the targeting visor lying abandoned on the Artillery pod's panel, plucked it up with thick fingers and slipped it over his eyes. "Snipe hunt, if you ask me, but it's no skin off my nose if you wanna wave *Hecate*'s guns around a bit."

"Hope you're right," Henricksen told him. "But *something* bad happened to those vessels." He nodded to the drifting ships outside without looking. "DSR bad, I'm willing to bet."

Sikuuku leaned out of his pod and lifted his visor with one finger, considering the scene outside himself. "Yeah. Looks like." A grimace and he knocked the visor back down, ran the pod through a system's check, machinery buzzing and whirring as he pivoted about. "Weapons are hot," he reported. "Anything moves, you just give the word and I'll vaporize it, Commander."

He would—Sikuuku was a damn fine gunner. One of the best in the Fleet, based on Henricksen's experience. Three ships they'd served on together, the last two under Henricksen's command. Had to pull a few strings to get the two of them assigned together this time, but it was worth it. Worth every damned favor Henricksen had to pay off to make it happen.

No one else he wanted sitting in that Artillery station. No other gunner in the Fleet he trusted more than Sikuuku.

"Duclos. How we doing with those probes?"

"Last one's coming on board, sir. Eight's a bit slow."

Henricksen raised his head, quirking an eyebrow at *Hecate*'s camera.

"Missed his maintenance cycle. I'll have the TSGs give him a once-over to see what's going on."

"Tell them to put a rush on it. Last thing we need is a slow-ass, lazy probe."

"Eight's not lazy," *Hecate* chided. "He's just old and needs a little extra attention now and then."

"Whatever." Henricksen flipped a hand, returning his attention to the windows as the drifting ships drew close. "Bunched up pretty tight," he noted, tapping at a panel in front of him—one of five arranged in a semi-circle in front of the Command Post's black, padded chair.

A stroke of the keys cycled the feeds from *Hecate*'s hull cameras, one view replacing another as he scanned the ships outside. A score of them in total—a nice, round number that just didn't feel right.

"Looks like merchanters," he said, hiding his discomfort. "Colony ships, maybe."

"Targeting system's showing minimal armaments," Sikuuku noted. "None of 'em hot, which is good." He touched at a screen, studying the video from a camera mounted on one of *Hecate*'s forward-facing cannons. "Engines look dead. Least, nothing's movin'." Another touch panned the camera, zoomed it in on one ship and another. "If they're colony ships, they probably pulled together like that to make the best use of what they've got." A glance at Henricksen and he pushed the feed to the Command Post, zooming back out. "Put the vulnerable ships in the middle. Armed ones on the outside for protection."

"Stayed that way, too," Henricksen murmured, eyes flicking from the video feed to the windows. "Stayed *here,* far from any colonized planet."

Which didn't bode well for survivors. Dead ships drifting in space…

Ripe target. Fat one, considering the equipment and provisions colony ships carried.

"What the hell happened?" he wondered, toggling the camera controls himself, zooming in on the nearest ship.

Perseid, surprisingly. Star cruiser chassis, retired from the Fleet a good fifty years ago and sold off for commercial use.

Hard to believe the Meridian Alliance used to do that. These days even a wrecked warship was valuable, its body a ready source of parts to refit others. Selling one… heresy even *thinking* about selling one these days. Stupid too, considering all the advanced electronics. Engine systems, weapons systems, the horrifically expensive investment the Fleet made in each and every vessel it commissioned.

Different time, he thought, studying the Perseid on his display. *Few hundred years ago no one thought an old clunker like that was* worth *keeping around.*

"Got anything on it?" he asked, looking over at Scan.

Duclos opened his mouth and closed it, frowning at Scan's panels. "I'm not…" He leaned forward, fiddling with the data feeds, muttering under his breath.

"Duclos!" Henricksen smacked the panel in front of him, making the crewman jump. "Report!"

"Nothing, sir." Duclos twisted, throwing an apologetic look at the Command Post. "I thought for a minute there… but there's nothing. No beacon. Just a dead ship."

"You're sure?"

Duclos flicked his eyes to his panel, clearly *not* sure. But he nodded anyway. Tried to look confident.

"Keep an eye on it. On *all* of them," Henricksen told him, nodding to the ships outside.

"Aye, sir," Duclos murmured, facing around.

Closer in and debris appeared, floating around the wrecked collection of ships. Composite metal, mostly. Sparkling clouds of reinforced glass mixed with glinting bits of metal, dulls shreds of high-durability plastics.

Everything drifting serenely. Floating along with that clutch of wrecked ships.

Dead ships—*Hecate*'s sensors confirmed it. Powered down, no energy signatures showing. No ships' beacons, none of the electronic noise an interstellar vessel typically gave off. Up close, they didn't actually *look* all that bad—scorched in places, pockmarked, a few rents, and tears, and pieces missing here and there, but surprisingly intact. Take the big, orb-shaped ship at the center, for instance. Cepheid science vessel, from what Henricksen could tell. Originally designed for deep space survey. Likely converted to serve as an agro ship or some such. Powered down like all the others, and yet, from here it looked right as rain. Like it should just pick up and go at any minute. Power up its engines and fly away.

"Something's not right." Henricksen shared a worried look with *Hecate*'s camera. "You keep a close eye on Scan, Duclos, you hear me? This place... I've got a *severely* bad feeling about this place."

"Aye, sir. Trying, sir." Duclose leaned close to Scan's panels, pouring through the feeds from *Hecate*'s sensors. "Still having trouble, though. Radiation's screwing with pretty much everything."

"Can you clean up the filters?" Henricksen nodded to the windows in front of him, eyes locked on *Hecate*'s camera. "Like to know what we're dealing with out there."

"I'll see what I can do."

"Sir." Farrow's head turned, blue eyes hidden behind her Comms visor, straw blond hair tucked neatly behind her ears. "Message from *Seychelles.* Valkyrie's compliments, but she'd like to know if we've found anything."

"Have we found anything yet," Henricksen muttered, flicking through the camera feeds. "What's the goddamned hurry? Not like those ships out there are going anywhere."

"Sir?"

"Never mind, Farrow." Henricksen sighed, swiping at the panel to shut it down. Straightened and stared at the windows, the ships outside. "Tell her..."

What? That they were trying? That they couldn't tell shit about those ships because their sensors were screwed? Nuh-uh. Not disparaging *Hecate* like that.

He lifted his eyes to the camera. "Tell her—"

"I told her we need fifteen minutes," *Hecate* interjected. "I fixed the filters, by the way."

She shunted Scan's feeds to the front window and layered them together, added the video from half a dozen cameras to create a single display. Let the feeds run, providing updates in real time.

Henricksen leaned forward, hands braced against the panel in front of him, drinking all that data in.

Sensors still fritzed a bit—lot of radiation out there, the filters could only see through so much—but the scans showed the ships clearly. Picked up damage to that Cepheid he'd missed earlier: a huge hole near the engine ports, radiation leaking from its old-as-dirt nuclear propulsion system, surrounding it in a dense cloud.

"Looks like that's our suspect." Henricksen nodded to silver-sided Cepheid. "AI might still be alive, but the crew..." He shook his head hard. "That much radiation, any crew that made it through the attack'll be dead by now. No way they could survive in that toxic soup."

Didn't explain why those other ships were down, though. Reactor spill was bad, yeah, but space... lot of real estate to play with. No way the reactor on that leaky old tub of a Cepheid took all those other vessels out.

"What the hell is going on here?" Henricksen murmured, frowning at the ships outside.

Duclos snuck a glance at Shin sitting Engineering, sharing a worried look. Shared that look with Shaheen on her far side.

Shin and Shaheen, Helm and Engineering—sing-song names for two joined-at-the-hip crew. Took Henricksen a while to get the two of them straight and *keep* them straight, despite that Shin—with her copper skin and odd, violet eyes—looked nothing at all like dark-eyed, darker-skinned Shaheen.

"Henricksen."

Hecate's voice pulled his eyes back to the front windows. "What? What now?"

"There's something out there."

A blip appeared, flashing on the front windows. Electronic signature glowing ghostly against the glass.

"Ship?" he asked, pulling the scan data to his panel, scrolling through the reams of information on display. "What the hell?" The blip blinked and faded, flared to life almost a kilometer away. "*Hecate?* Your sensors buggy or somethin'?"

"Not sure."

Surprising admission. Not one you heard often from an AI.

Hecate was quiet a moment, running analytics, pouring over every bit of information at hand. Repeated her analysis when the blip blanked and moved again. A third time when it disappeared and jumped almost a kilometer away.

"What's going on?" Henricksen demanded. "Is it the radiation? Is it fucking with things again?"

"No," she told him. "Not the radiation this time."

"Then what? For the luvva god—"

Perimeter alarms lit up, klaxons screaming as the sensors sucked in information, dumping reams of new data into *Hecate*'s systems, sending it all to Scan's board.

"Ships' signatures." Duclos leaned over his panel, sorting like mad. "We've got company!"

"Overlay." Henricksen snapped his fingers, pointing at the front windows.

"On it." A touch at Scan's panel and Duclos shunted the data to the curving wall of glass at the front of the bridge, three dimensional schematic flashing with multi-colored lights as Scan tagged each signature, assigning it to one of the ships outside.

Fourteen ships in total. Fourteen of the twenty wrecked vessels drifting in space. Not a one of them actually moving—not yet, anyway—but live, suddenly. Powered up, when before they seemed stone cold dead.

TWO

"Friendlies?" Henricksen asked, lifting his eyes to *Hecate*'s camera.

"No telling," she answered, adding data tags to the schematic on the front windows, highlighting a dozen in quick succession.

Energy signatures only at this point—no ships' beacons. Not from the Cepheid, the dozen plus one ships around it. Just the telltale signs of engines and armaments powering up, readying themselves for God only knew what.

What the hell are they up to? Henricksen wondered, chewing at his lip. "Farrow. Alert the Valkyrie."

"Aye, sir. Reinforcements, sir?"

Henricksen considered, studying the schematic. The vessels floating serenely outside.

"Sir?" Farrow prompted, visored face turning his way.

"Your call," he said, eyes lifting to *Hecate*'s camera.

"No, Farrow," she answered. "No reinforcements just yet. Tell *Seychelles* we've got ships' signatures and we're investigating. Ask her to stand by."

"Aye." Farrow flicked her wrists, cables snaking from the ports sunk in her flesh to the Comms station at which she stood. A second flick opened a channel to the Valkyrie, Farrow's soft voice murmuring to someone on the other end.

"You sure about this?" Henricksen pitched his voice low so only *Hecate* would hear. "Smarter to just back outta here."

"*Brutus* sent us here to investigate. Look for survivors—"

"*Brutus*'s orders *stopped* at investigate," Henricksen corrected. "*Seychelles* added the 'search for survivors' part."

"Thought you were bucking for captain, Henricksen, not sea lawyer."

Icy undercurrent to *Hecate*'s voice now. A hard tone she used rarely. One that brooked no argument. Accepted no excuses.

"The debris outside indicates those ships ran into trouble. Got themselves pretty beat up in the process. But ships' signatures means ships with power, Henricksen. Could be there's crew out there. An AI in need of rescue."

Henricksen cocked his head, eyes flicking from the windows to the camera. "So why didn't we see them? Why didn't the sensors pick up on those energy signatures before now?"

"Shielding, if I had to guess. Probably shut down everything but the basic functions—atmospherics, environmentals, short range scans. Charged the hull plating to hide the energy signature the ships' systems put out. Pulled in tight to make themselves electronically invisible."

"So, what? They're *hiding* out here?"

"Wouldn't you? DSR drops in on them and tears hell out of their ships. Take what they want and leave the rest stranded." The camera *whirred* softly, zooming in and back out. "You were merchanter once."

"Pusher. There's a difference."

Not much, but there was pride. Pushers were blue collar, unlike those merchanter elitist pricks.

"Semantics, Henricksen. You know what happens." She turned the camera, pointing it at the front windows. "Call for help and maybe the DSR comes back and finishes them off. Hide out here and fix things, maybe they can limp their way to the nearest port. Come out of this with their lives intact."

Henricksen rubbed his chin, thinking that over. "Not like the DSR to leave survivors."

Or ships, for that matter. Usually they took everything, pressing functioning ships into service, chopping the rest up for parts. Destroyed what they didn't need or couldn't use to cover their trail. Make sure no one *else* could make use of the scrap either.

Simple, efficient operations. Say one thing about the DSR: they were champion scavengers. Made the most of the leftovers they came across. Which made the situation here all the more worrisome because it just didn't fit their MO.

"This stinks, *Hecate*. This whole thing stinks."

"No argument here. But if there are people on board, AI that need rescuing…"

"Yeah," Henricksen said softly. "Yeah." He sucked in a breath and blew it back out, scrubbing fingers through his short-clipped hair. "Sikuuku." He glanced at Artillery, catching the gunner's visored eyes. "Not quite sure what's going on here, but those ships out there seem content to sit for now. Anything changes, you see *anything* move, you blast it, understand? Weapons free. Fire at will."

"You sure?" he asked, lifting the targeting visor away from his eyes. "Colony ships out there."

"Yeah," Henricksen said quietly. "Fuckers back at Trisserine looked like colony ships, too. And look what happened to *Bertram*."

Freighter, carrying armaments to resupply the Meridian Alliance depot orbiting above the planet. *Bertram* went nuclear—waylaid and obliterated when the DSR realized they couldn't take him—destroying the payload he carried, and the ship right along with it.

Hecate was en route when the distress call came in. Arrived too late to save *Bertram*, but just in time to blow holy hell out of the DSR ships that took him down. Destroyed three of their ships before the rest vanished, jumping away to hide in deep space.

People on Tesserine were grateful—weapons manufactories down there, figured if the DSR got those munitions, they'd turn them on the surface and kill everyone—which made the Fleet Brass happy. Grateful citizens didn't cause problems, after all. And having a few less DSR ships in the galaxy to deal with… well, that was always a good thing.

Besides, Fleet liked victories. Even Pyrrhic victories, like Tesserine.

"Ship moves, it dies, ya hear me, Sikuuku?"

"Aye, sir. On it." Sikuuku tapped two fingers to his temple and flipped his visor back down. Pivoted the gimbaled Artillery pod, bringing the targeting system on-line.

"Sir." Farrow again, wrists bent, fingers plucking at invisible strings as she navigated the comms channels her visor laid in front of her eyes. "*Seychelles* is asking for an update."

"Stand by," Henricksen told her. "Shaheen. Move us closer to that freighter." He pointed at the ship in question—a huge thing, square sided and oblong drifting a few kilometers off their starboard bow.

"Aye, sir." Shaheen tagged it, nodding, feathering the maneuvering thrusters to adjust *Hecate*'s course and bring her alongside.

"Duclos. Run the sensors in a broad spectrum scan."

"Aye."

"Farrow." A nod to the collection of ships outside. "Try hailing them again."

"Aye, sir. Just need a minute." Farrow's head tilted, lights flashing behind her visor. A flick of each wrist and her fingers started moving, making those odd, plucking gestures as she scrubbed through the channels, searching for open lines. "Nothing," she reported, shaking her head. "Static. Some feedback from the radiation, that's about it. If there are people out there, sir, they're not talking. Or can't," she added, lips twisting. "DSR…" Her head turned, finger lifting her visor to reveal startling blue eyes. "They may have trashed the comms system, sir, before they left those ships for dead."

Translation: there might be people on those ships. *Live* people, for all they knew, looking to them for help.

It fit the DSR pattern. Made sense in a horrible sort of way.

"Damn," Henricksen sighed, rubbing at his face. "God damn." A glance at the windows and he turned his gaze Farrow's way. "Keep an ear to the channels. Let me know if you pick anything up."

"Aye, sir." Farrow dropped her visor back into place, retreating into the comms system's cocoon.

"Henricksen." *Hecate* flashed a screen on the Command Post, shunting a data package to the center panel. "Found something. Your freighter," she explained as Henricksen swiped at the panel, scrolling through the information on display.

"Engines are intact." Henricksen frowned, finding yet another thing about this ship that just didn't make sense. "Why the hell would they—"

"Movement! We've got movement!" Duclos pointed to the windows as the Perseid slid forward, banked hard to port and headed their way.

"Son-of-a—Sikuuku! Blast that fucker!"

"With pleasure." Sikuuku keyed the targeting system, pod slewing around as he gripped the firing sticks with both hands. A squeeze of the triggers and he unloaded on the approaching vessel, spewing out stuttering strings of cobalt blue plasma rounds that kissed the Perseid's hull, scoring the composite metal just as the vessel jumped away.

"Scan! Duclos! Where'd it—"

Perimeter alarms went haywire as the Perseid reappeared—a fast-moving blur of composite metal and burnt out engines plowing bow-first into *Hecate*'s port-side rear quarter.

Short hop, Henricksen's brain registered in the instant before the Perseid hit.

Hyperspace engines primed but minimally loaded, not yet capable of true jump. Turning that ship into an oversized missile that skewered *Hecate* like a spear, slewing her offline.

Henricksen slammed against the Command Post's panels, breath driven from his body in a rush. Grabbed at the nearest panel and held on for dear life as *Hecate* shuddered and shook around him, bridge lights flashing and flaring before cutting out entirely, plunging the room into darkness.

Panels dying with them, silencing the klaxons mid-shriek.

Three seconds—that's how long it took the emergency systems to kick in. Three long, terrifying seconds of pitch black silence: fans dead, heat dead, environmentals completely shut off. Three pulse-pounding, sick with fear seconds before the lights came back on—auxiliary illumination bathing the bridge in a blood-red glow—and the atmospherics soon after.

A puff of cold air ruffled the hair atop Henricksen's head, swirled and stroked at his cheeks. Lights flashed as the Command Post rebooted, panels flickering across the bridge as, one by one, *Hecate*'s stations came back online. He killed the klaxons when they resumed their incessant blatting—hell on the ears, those shrieking sirens, and he didn't need them to know they were in deep shit—and almost wished he hadn't

Without them, he could hear the ship itself screaming. *Hecate*'s chassis groaning as it twisted. Hull splitting, compartments venting their contents into space.

"Damage report!" Henricksen forced his hands open and straightened, wincing at the pain of bruised ribs. Scanned the bridge and found crew scattered across the decking, pitched ass-over-tea-kettle onto the floor.

Scared crew, the lot of them. Wide-eyed faces turned bloody in the red glow of emergency lighting. Farrow crawled around, searching for her lost visor, climbed unsteadily to her feet when she found it and slipped it over her face. Duclos clutched his shoulder, jaw clenched tight as he pulled himself into the seat in front of his station, breath hissing between his teeth as he worked away on the panels. Shaheen...actually, Shaheen seemed to be alright, but Shin just sat in front of her station—hunched over, cradling an oddly cocked hand against her stomach. And to one side, just over Henricksen's shoulder, the familiar sound of swearing—Sikuuku cursing a blue streak as he kicked at the pedals controlling the gimbaled Artillery pod's movements. A pod that, based on the volume and quantity of swearing, stubbornly refused to budge.

"Shit, shit, *shit!*" Sikuuku yelled, voice filled with frustration. "I got no firing solution, Commander. Targeting system's a complete loss. Cannons are pointing—aw fuck, I have *no* idea what the cannons are pointing at, but it ain't at those ships, that's for sure." He punched a panel, flicking at switches, jammed the maneuvering pedal with his foot and bashed at the controls with both fists, but the pod remained stuck. "*God fucking dammit,*" he screamed. "*Move, you piece of fucking shit, move!*"

"*Hecate!*"

"Diagnostics are showing a mechanical failure. I've got a couple of TSGs on their way to the bridge to try and fix it."

"And until then we've got no guns. Fuck. Fuck me," Henricksen breathed, staring out the windows.

Hell of a thing, being defenseless. Especially when there was a hand-me-down, refitted warship stuck in your side.

He called down to maintenance, summoning a couple of techs to the bridge to help the TSGs out. Might just get in the robots' way but many hands made light work and all that and he wanted as many hands up here as he could get. And while he waited, there was the hull damage to consider. That self-same, hand-me-down ship poking rudely from *Hecate*'s side.

He accessed a panel, pulling the feeds from the external cameras to it so he could get a sense for the damaged outside. Video showed the Perseid stuck tight—nose buried up to the bridge pod in *Hecate*'s rear quarter, cracks spidering outward in jagged lightning bolts from the impact point. Splits in *Hecate*'s skin appearing. Fractures that joined and divided, splitting and splitting again.

Not good. Not good at all.

"Shin. Damage report." Henricksen barked.

"Aye, sir." Shin called up the monitoring system, alerts flashing everywhere. Yellow and orange boxes marking damaged areas that remained intact, red boxes flagging compromised sections of the ship. She skipped over the former, focusing on the latter for now. "Hull breach, port side aft. Levels 3 through 8."

"Contained?" Henricksen leaned forward, eyes locked on the back of Shin's head. "*Is it contained, Shin?*"

"Hang on! Hang on!" Shin sorted like mad, swapping one set of data for another. "Aye sir! We lost the compartments in Sector 4, but the blast doors closed, protecting the rest of the ship."

Four. Cargo bay. Barracks on Tier 6.

"Casualties?" Henricksen closed his eyes, bracing himself for the worst.

"Twenty-eight confirmed dead. Med bay's got another sixteen reporting injured." Shin swapped data screens, scrolling through the reports from the lower levels. "Looks like thirty-four more unaccounted for, sir."

Seventy-eight crew, out of a complement of three hundred and twelve.

"Damn. God damn." Henricksen curled his hand into a fist, pounding it against the panel. "*Hecate.*" He raised his head, searching for the camera. "Can you—"

"Movement. We've got movement," Duclose warned as the schematic on the front window lit up.

"Jesus Bloody Christ, what *now*?"

A check of the windows showed the ships outside shifting, thrusters firing as they muscled their bodies around. Henricksen turned his eyes toward the glass and found himself staring down the long nose of a Starstrider—long haul merchanter vessel, not all that different from the cargo pushers he crewed once upon a time.

"Brace!" he yelled, convinced the ship meant to ram them. The Starstrider's engines firing, shoving the ship close. He grabbed at panels, anticipating the impact, but a flash of light and the Starstrider disappeared, flipping past *Hecate* in one of those short-hop jumps.

Reappeared just a second or two later—nose onto a Titan named *Turnbull* waiting with the rest of the Meridian Alliance ships behind them—and collided with the smaller, stationary vessel. Sub-light momentum carrying the Starstrider along at speed, all but obliterating *Turnbull* when it hit.

Scan recorded every last detail of the collision, rearward facing cameras transmitting the horrible scene to the crew. The Starstrider slammed head on into *Turnbull,* burrowing straight through the Titan. Munitions detonating, taking the propulsion system with them. A flare and everything inside the Titan exploded, destroying both ships in a flare of cobalt fire.

"No," Henricksen breathed, watching *Turnbull* die.

A second flash—this one in front of them, glare lighting *Hecate*'s bridge through the front windows—and a second ship disappeared, launching itself into jump. Passenger transport vessel, this time. Blinking out of existence only to reappear a few seconds later with an Aurora directly in its path.

The transport vessel hit hard, but off-center, scraping along the Aurora's starboard side. Tearing most of her hull plating away in the process, exposing the bones of her superstructure beneath.

Puffs of atmosphere, all along the Aurora's damaged side. She jigged hard, turning away from the transport vessel, hauled over and let momentum carry it past.

"What's wrong with them?" Shin whispered, eyes wide with horror. "Why are they doing that?"

"They don't have any choice." *Hecate* threw a data window onto the glass, highlighting several repeating strings of information.

No consciousness on board the transport vessel—that's what that data said. No AI running *any* of the ships out there. No life of any kind inside the Perseid jammed into *Hecate*'s side.

"Drones." Henricksen stared at the camera, shaking his head in disbelief. "DSR droned 'em. Killed off the AI and just...left them."

"*Here,*" *Hecate* said pointedly. "Knowing we'd find them. A trap, Henricksen. They set a trap and we—"

"Waltzed right into it," he said bitterly. "Sneaky-ass bastards knew we couldn't resist."

Under other circumstances, he might have appreciated what they'd done. The complexity of what the DSR had pulled off. But not right now. At the moment he was too damn pissed off.

"Shin. Status."

"Engines are compromised. Life support's holding, but the Perseid sheared through the weapons systems. We've got forward batteries, that's it."

And those slaved to Sikuuku's Artillery pod, which just happened to be stuck.

"What's the status on those TSGs, *Hecate*?"

"Stuck in an elevator with your techs. Crew's trying to fix it. I've got a couple more working their way through the ladderways."

"Wonderful. Just fucking wonderful." Henricksen closed his eyes, scrubbing a hand across his face. "Get those engines on-line, Shin. This is a severely unsafe place to be at the moment. I want *out* of here, understand me? Quick as you can."

"Aye, sir." Shin got down to business, fingers flying as she worked away at her panel.

And outside, the ships kept disappearing, *Hecate*'s bridge flickering with intermittent flares of brightest, bright light as engines ignited, skipping the droned ships away.

Flinging them past her to *Seychelles* and the ships she brought with her. A small fleet, desperately maneuvering, comms filled with chatter as the Meridian Alliance ships shifted about.

The wounded Aurora took a second hit in the middle of all that shucking and jiving—a glancing blow at her center that wiped out her bridge pod, causing her to veer sharply off-line. Ended up in the path of a Titan named *Shylock*—crashed right into the poor bastard, disc-shaped body forced onto one of the Titan's spear points—and stuck there. The two Fleet ships helplessly twined together, forming a nice, fat target that the droned ship plowed into, taking both ships out at once.

"Bastards." Henricksen shaded his eyes as the Aurora's munitions cache erupted, compromised plasma shells popping off like fireworks, destroying all three ships at once. "DSR's too goddamn scared to face us in a *real* fight, so they send these booby-trapped junk heaps after us. Where the hell are they anyway?"

"No telling," *Hecate* told him. "Droned ships. Could be just about anywhere."

"Cowards," he spat, glaring at the ships outside.

Smart cowards—he'd give them that. Smart enough to set all this up and know just how to draw them in, but cowards just the same.

Henricksen hated cowards. Hated anyone too scared or prissy to get their hands dirty once in a while.

"Sir!" Farrow surfaced from Comms, visored face turning his way. "Message from *Seychelles*. She's inbound with the rest of her ships."

"Well, hallelujah! Happy to have the rescue. Shin!" Henricksen called. "Where are we with those engines?"

"Main propulsion's operational. Just," she added, looking around. "Still got that ship stuck in us, but I think we can navigate our way out of here."

"Wonderful! Best news I've gotten all day. Shaheen. Get us out of here," Henricksen ordered as another ship jumped.

That one plowed through two Auroras and exploded, narrowly missing *Seychelles* in the process.

"Is it just me, or is their aim getting better?" Henricksen asked, watching the carnage through one of the rearward facing cameras.

Silence from *Hecate*—not like her at all.

Henricksen glanced up, wondering at that. Decided it might be a good idea to give the Valkyrie a warning. "Farrow. Dial up *Seychelles*—"

"Already done, sir. *Seychelles* sends—" Farrow paused, frowning, wrist flicking in a short, sharp gesture. "Ships inbound."

Henricksen spun, throwing a sharp look at Comms. "DSR or friendlies?"

Farrow held up a hand, shaking her head. Listened a moment and nodded just once. "Meridian Alliance. They're Fleet, sir." She pointed at the windows as a dozen dark disturbances appeared—a swirling void of inky blackness marking a hyperspace buckle, silver-sided warships sliding through in the distance.

Engines lighting, glowing cobalt blue against the dark of space as they raced toward *Seychelles* and her tiny fleet of ships. Toward *Hecate* trapped amongst the droned vessels the DSR had left behind, her own engines stuttering on the edge of complete failure as she desperately tried to escape.

"Reinforcements." Henricksen flicked his eyes to *Hecate*'s camera. "That *Seychelles's* doin'? Callin' 'em in so quick?"

"No," *Hecate* told him. "*Seychelles* sent no summons."

Henricksen shivered, body gone cold all over. "Who?" he asked, but *Hecate*'s camera just stared. Shifted, pointing at the windows as a panel on the Command Post flashed, displaying a long list of Meridian Alliance vessels: *Shiloh* and *Anatolia, Harker* and *Cicatrix,* a whole host of others. Four Titans and six Auroras in total, and following behind them—last to clear the buckle from hyperspace, last name on that list—came a hulking, familiar shape.

"*Gogmagog*."

Henricksen stared at the name on his panel—awed, disturbed, wondering why *Brutus* would send a Dreadnought, especially *this* Dreadnought, to deal with a situation like this. Not that he wasn't grateful—*Gogmagog* come in like a freight train, battered chassis prickling with cannons and conning towers, Fleet-wide comms blaring as he ordered ships out of his way—but it was overkill, sending a bruiser like *Gogmagog* to deal with less than a dozen droned ships.

"What the hell is he doing here?" he whispered. "Why would *Brutus* send *Gogmagog* of all ships?"

"Not *Brutus*," *Hecate* told him. "*Cadmus. Gogmagog*'s *Cadmus*'s boy."

And the Bastions eternally bickering, vying for *Cerberus*'s favor. Sending *Gogmagog* just another part of their stupid turf war. *Cadmus*'s way of muscling in on *Brutus*'s operation and winning some glory points with *Cerberus:* the admiral in charge of the Meridian Alliance Fleet.

"*Seychelles* won't like this," *Hecate* noted.

"No. I don't suspect she would." Henricksen grimaced, caught up in Fleet politics and hating every minute of it. "Personally, as long as we get us out of this in one piece, I really don't care."

Another droned ship shot away as he spoke, slammed into *Ostea* guarding *Seychelles* front quarter and passed right through her, clipping the tail off *Coriolanus* before spinning off into space.

"Shaheen. We need to get moving."

"I'm *trying*," Shaheen growled, voice filled with frustration. "But the engines are screwed to hell and that bastard Perseid is fucking everything up."

"Well then, *un*-fuck it," Henricksen ordered. "Ships out there are suiciding like crazy. Last place I wanna be—"

"Shit, shit, shit! Sir! The Cepheid!" Duclos twisted, pale face drained of all color, slim finger pointing at the silver orb floating outside the windows. "There's—There's something…"

"What?" Henricksen snapped as Duclos trailed off. "What something?"

"Energy signature. Big one. Building inside it."

"Inside it," Henricksen repeated, staring numbly out the windows.

Cepheid. Science ship. Nuclear reactor at its core. Massive amounts of energy. Enough radiation if it blew to kill them a hundred times over.

"Fuck. We're so fucked," Sikuuku said, as a crack appeared around the Cepheid's middle, the two halves of the orb separating, causing the energy signature to spike.

"Shaheen!"

Hecate's body shuddered and lurched forward, main propulsion miraculously coming to life. Slewed hard to port, the Perseid in *Hecate*'s side dragging like an anchor, slowly pulling her around.

"Fuck," Henricksen swore, watching that crack in the Cepheid widen. Releasing a cloud of shining metal objects hidden inside.

Specks like diamond dust at this distance. Glinting in the starlight. Flashing mirror-like as yet another droned ship short-jumped away.

"What *is* that?" Duclos whispered, toggling the camera controls, swapping one video feed for another.

"Don't know, don't care, don't wanna stick around to find out. Shaheen!" Henricksen shouted. "Full power. Now, please."

"I can't—I'm *trying*, god dammit!"

"Fuck trying and just do it, Shaheen, or we're all gonna—"

"Henricksen." *Hecate*'s serene voice cut right through the panic. The noise and voices cluttering up the bridge. She looked at him, and turned her camera toward the windows as a blinding flare lit up the bridge. "Hold on," she told them, a split seconds before a second ship slammed into her, breaking her body in half.

THREE

Henricksen pitched forward, launched clear across the Command Post, landing on the hard, unforgiving floor on the other side. Lay there for a long time, dazed and blinking in the darkness that followed—an inky black terror that went on, and on, and on.

Listened to the crew screaming around him and wondered how many were dying. How many were already dead. If the darkness around him would ever end.

Blood intruded eventually, some indeterminate amount of time later. Emergency lights dousing the bridge in a flickering, fading glow. Environmentals came and went, fans stuttering and stopping, roaring to life before shutting back down and starting the whole process over again. The klaxons—those screaming sirens that Henricksen so hated—squawked intermittently, rising and falling as the power ebbed and flowed. Fires brokes out, prompting the automated systems to kick in, ordering *Hecate*'s crew to the lifeboats as smoke and flame consumed her compartments, filling the bridge with a grey-black haze that snaked and swirled. A river of blood caught in the glow of the emergency power's lights.

Henricksen coughed, blinking as the smoke stung his eyes. Rolled over and pushed to his knees—arms shaking, vision doubling, sight wavering in and out.

Touched at something warm and wet, slithering down his cheek and felt his fingers come away drenched into a tacky, slick substance. Turned his hand over and stared uncomprehendingly at the blood coating his palm.

"Shaheen. Get us out of here," he rasped, gathering his legs under him, shoving to his feet. Swaying once he got there, feeling decidedly unsteady, blinking hard until his eyes grudgingly agreed to focus. "Shaheen!" He tottered around, screams filling his ears—deep-throated shrieks of anger and agony, tinged with panic and fear. "Shaheen," he repeated, coughing on a smoky breath, waving a hand to clear the air in front of his face. "Report!"

Another step and he fetched up against Helm's panel. Glanced down and found Shaheen staring back at him—dark eyes unblinking, neck turned at an impossible angle.

Dead, apparently. Wholly, completely, irrevocably gone.

He stood there a while, trying to understand that. Shuffled his feet—unsteady still, vision threatening to cut out at any moment—and set off into the smoke and blood darkness, following the shrieking noise of screaming to the battered remains of *Hecate*'s Artillery pod, and found Sikuuku trapped inside.

Fenced in, crumpled metal panels pinning him down. Flames dancing all around it, slipping in to eat through the heavy material of the gunner's dark blue uniform. Gnaw at arms, chew at legs.

"Help me," he begged, choking on pain, banging on the pod's remains from the inside.

Henricksen grabbed at the crushed and crumpled metal, tearing at the panels with his bare hands. "Hang on," he grunted, yanking hard, trying to clear the bulky, broken panels away. "Hang on. Just hang on!" he repeated as Sikuuku screamed louder—pissed off, hurting, desperate to get out.

The pod resisted them, being purpose-built to survive a warship's abuse, so Henricksen redoubled his efforts. Tugged and twisted, putting everything he had left in him into trying to bust the pod's broken panels loose. Hands shaking with the effort, veins standing out in his neck.

Nothing moved at first. Not even an inch. And then suddenly, unexpectedly, the panel Henricksen held gave way.

He stumbled backward, completely off-balance, clutching a crumpled square of metal in his hands. Chucked it aside and reached for Sikuuku as he spilled out onto the bridge, knocking them both to the floor.

Henricksen lay there, panting harshly, vision a mess of spiky-edged points of dark nothingness, like starbursts in reverse. Sucked in a smoke filled breath and felt Sikuuku writhe atop him—moaning raggedly, thick arms tucked up against his chest.

He wrapped his arms around him and rolled over, laying Sikuuku flat on his back. Found blood on his face, obscuring the tattoos on his cheeks. More blood on his wrists and ankles, forearms and shins. Raw, blistered flesh peeking through his uniform's burnt remains. Breath hitching in choking gasps. Dark eyes filled with immeasurable pain.

"Hold on," Henricksen said, laying a hand on the gunner's shoulder. "Just hold on. Gonna get you some help."

Sikuuku choked, nodding, as Henricksen yelled into the blood and grey, praying someone would answer. Hoping they weren't all like Shaheen.

"Shin! Farrow!" he croaked, coughing on a smoke-filled breath. "Get over here!"

A sound of scrabbling followed by movement to one side—a dark figure in a dark uniform crawling across the floor. Shin appeared first, wide-eyed and terrified, dark strip of fabric—undershirt from her uniform, by the looks of it—wrapped around her face, covering her nose and mouth. "Sir," she said, coughing lightly.

"Med kit." Henricksen waved to a panel on the wall.

"Aye, sir." Shin scooted across the room and tore the panel away. Hustled back clutching a metal case to her chest and dropped down to the floor.

No sign of Farrow anywhere—Henricksen tried not to think what that meant.

"Morphaux. Single dose," he ordered, shifting to one side.

Synthetic opioid—morphine, but stronger. Less addictive than that old school drug.

Shin nodded, scooting in at Sikuuku's side. Tore the med kit open and dug through the contents searching for the morphaux injector, while Henricksen slid his hands under the gunner's shoulders. Lifting him carefully, ever so carefully. Murmuring apologies as he slowly, painfully, sat the gunner both up.

"Easy, buddy, easy," he whispered as Sikuuku shivered, moaning aloud. "I got ya. I got ya. Shin's got somethin' here to help ya out."

He took the morphaux injector from Shin once she finished loading it. Jammed the needle hard against Sikuuku's shoulder and dropped it to the floor. Wrapped his arms around the gunner after and just held him, cradling his heavy body against his chest while he shuddered and shook, the two of them waiting together for the painkillers to kick in.

Long time before the morphaux took hold, and even then, it only dulled the pain. Sikuuku twitched and whimpered, one hand shaking badly while the other clutched the sleeve of Henricksen's uniform, twisting the fabric until it threatened to tear.

"It's alright," Henricksen told him. "You're alright."

He wasn't—Sikuuku, the ship, pretty much this entire situation was pretty damn far from "alright"—but Henricksen repeated the lie because the crew needed to hear it. Needed that hope to get through this, and come out on the other side.

"There ya go," he said, cradling the gunner's burnt and bleeding body. Holding him close until the trembling eased, and that desperately clutching hand let go. "There ya go, buddy. Just gonna turn ya over to Shin for a moment." Henricksen caught Shin's eye and scooted backward, gently laying the gunner back down. "Bandage him up," he said. "Best you can."

"Aye, sir," she whispered, voice muffled by the cloth covering her nose and mouth, wide eyes locked onto Sikuuku's bloody, weeping arms.

Henricksen gripped her shoulder, squeezing until she looked at him. Nodded once and stood, glancing around to orient himself before walking unsteadily over to Helm.

Pushed Shaheen's body from her seat—murmuring apologies to her corpse, knowing this was no way to treat fallen crew—and flopped down in front of Helm's panel. Pressed a hand to the polyglass surface, and a second when that first failed to convince the system to wake. "Work. Please work," he begged, but the panel remained dark, the system beneath off-line. Nothing but his own blurred, bloody visage reflecting back from the glass. "Dead," he whispered, staring in dismay.

Dead as Shaheen. As countless others scattered throughout the ship.

He turned his head, scanning the bridge around him. Dim lighting everywhere, making it hard to see much of anything, especially with all that smoke hanging in the air. But the stations were obviously—dark shapes in the blood and grey misty, panels empty as Helm's. Not a system on that bridge working, which was hardly surprising, really. Considering the pounding the ship had taken.

The ship.

"*Hecate.*" Henricksen raised his head, searching for her camera. "*Hecate.* What's our status?"

"Engines are offline, Henricksen. Navigation, Artillery—"

"Are dead, and dead, and dead. I get it," he said, waving a weary hand. "We're in a world of shit. Forget the other systems, just focus on getting the engines back online so we can get the hell outta here."

"I can't, Henricksen," *Hecate* said quietly. Voice calm—so very, very calm even now.

Henricksen envied her for that. For that level of emotional control. Some argued AI didn't experience true emotion. That it was all just an output of advanced emulation routines, but any officer who'd commanded a ship would tell you differently. AI—old AI like *Hecate*—understood fear. Felt it, though differently than humans. Buried it, in times of crisis. Glossed it over with that oh-so-calm demeanor. That icy-cold serenity that no human could ever touch.

Scared as shit—that's what that calm voice meant. Worried about her crew. About herself, because she needed to protect them.

"I'm sorry," *Hecate* said in her softest, most gentle voice.

A voice that cut through him, keen as the sharpest knife.

Henricksen's hands fell away from Helm's panel, piling uselessly in his lap. "It's not over," he whispered, klaxons screeching on a last bit of power, sputtering as they died. "It's not over. It *can't* be."

Smoke drifted between them, obscuring *Hecate*'s camera from his eyes. Filling his nose with the stench of ash and charred clothing, burnt skin and melted plastics—a cloying, sickening combination that reminded him of death.

Sikuuku shrieked in agony, screams battering at Henricksen's ears. Shin scrabbled at the med kit for more painkillers, reloaded the injector and slammed the shot against the gunner's shoulder. Cupped his tattooed face between her hands after, murmuring softly until he settled. Finished bandaging his burns once she could touch him without causing too much pain and just sat with him once she'd finished, holding the gunner's hand.

A whir from overhead as the fans kicked in, chugging away at the smoke-filled room. Fresh air poured in, a frosty, hiccupping breeze filtering downward in fits and starts.

Henricksen closed his eyes and tilted his face toward the ceiling, letting the cool air wash over his cheeks.

Environmentals were the most important of *Hecate*'s systems. Her first priority for restoration in any emergency event. There'd been many of those over the years—Henricksen had personally seen *Hecate* parked in spacedock getting repairs more times than he could count—but this time...

This one was worse. Much, much worse than anything they'd been through before.

"Henricksen."

"I know," he said, sighing as the fan overhead died. He lowered his head, eyes drifting to the windows as a flash popped off and yet another ship disappeared.

Just a handful left out there now, including that ominous, silver orb. The Cepheid floated serenely, the cloud of shining, metal objects it gave birth to spreading in a diffuse cloud around it. Sparkling and silver, like starlight and moondust.

"Henricksen."

He glanced at her camera and moved closer to the windows, staring hard at that cloud. Realized it was moving quickly. Not just drifting, *propelled* somehow.

And closing in on *Hecate*. Fanning to either side.

"What is that?" he asked, pressing a hand to the windows. "What the hell are—"

"*Henricksen!*"

He jumped, snatching his hand from the windows, *Hecate*'s sharp, angry tone drawing his eyes back to the camera.

"Nothing you can do about that."

Softer this time. Calm and reasoning. The *Hecate* he knew. The *Hecate* he'd served all these years.

"The crew needs you, Henricksen."

"Crew," he repeated, scanning his eyes across the bridge.

Poor, dead Shaheen lay crumpled where he'd left her. Shin knelt beside Sikuuku, holding tight to his hand. Duclos...almost missed Duclos, sitting still as a statue at Scan. Hands resting on the panel, eyes fixed on the polyglass surface, staring intently, as if expecting it to wake at any moment. And behind him, a shadow, wandering around the bridge. A ghost that resolved into Farrow, clutching her broken visor in one hand.

Crew. *His* crew. Crew that needed him, just as *Hecate* said.

Right now Henricksen had no idea what to tell them. What to *do* to get them out of this mess. "*Hecate,*" he called, eyes lifting to her camera.

"Abandon ship," she said, comms system crackling to life. *Hecate* cast her voice across the ship, speaking to all ten tiers at once. "All crew to the lifeboats," she ordered in her serene, AI voice. And more gently, to Henricksen, "That means you, too, Captain."

"No," he told her, refusing *Hecate*'s orders this one and only time. Refusing the title she gave, because it wasn't his. Not yet. "We're not leaving."

"You don't have a choice."

Henricksen raised his head, staring in confusion. Glanced to one side as the bridge door shut with a sibilant hiss, locking system kicking in as the gaskets sucked tight, sealing the room up.

A *whir* and *clunk* and the mooring bolts burst free—deafening noise in the confined space of the bridge, pod shuddering and shaking as it separated from the rest of the ship.

"No!" Henricksen turned from the windows, moving closer to the camera. "*Hecate*. Please. Don't do this."

"Goodbye, Henricksen," she whispered, fondness in her voice. "You've earned your stars. Don't let anyone take them."

"*Hecate!*"

She ejected the bridge pod with Henricksen still screaming, calling out her name. Emergency beacon kicking in automatically, squawking for attention, calling out to *Seychelles* and *Anatolia*, *Shiloh* and *Centrix* and *Gogmagog,* just arriving. Pleading with them to help as the bridge pod moved away.

They would, eventually—that was the way of things, Fleet left no one behind—but right now those ships were far too busy to worry about little things like lifeboats and escape pods. Danger stalked the stars—deadly and pernicious, random in its intent. The Fleet ships registered the bridge pod's request, logging it for action later, focusing the sum total of their attention on the booby-trapped ships attacking them for now. Slicing through the droned ships one-by-one, until only the Cepheid remained—a silver orb surrounded by a stardust nimbus, like winking grains of metallic sand.

Helpless, purposeless, Henricksen stared through the bridge pod's windows, watching the Cepheid's spawn divide. One cloud of shining objects becoming two, then many, gaining speed as they moved away from their host.

Surrounded *Hecate*. Moved past her to the other Meridian Alliance vessels.

"No," he breathed, filled with sudden fear. Overwhelmed by a sense of foreboding. "No, *Hecate!*" he yelled, beating at the windows. Screaming her name over and over as *Gogmagog* opened fire, targeting the Cepheid with every last one of his cannons.

Missiles released, sliding silently through space. Struck the Cepheid on one half moon side and the other, pounding through silver-sided hull plating, exposing the nuclear reactor inside.

"Run," Henricksen whispered, palms pressed to the windows, eyes locked onto *Hecate*'s shredded shape. "Get out of there," he begged.

But *Hecate* never ran from anything. Not once in her two centuries of life. And with her engines crippled, she *couldn't* run, even if she'd wanted to. Instead, she just floated there, alone and all but helpless as the Cepheid's silver sphere bulged, metal skin melting, hull plating shredding as the reactor inside it overloaded and catastrophically failed. Creating a vast shockwave that spread outward in a wave of destructive energy.

Roaring over *Hecate*. Destroying her in an instant.

"*Hecate.*"

Henricksen stared at the stars, feeling cold—impossibly cold, incredibly empty—now that *Hecate* was gone.

Ten seconds later, the shockwave reached them, its energy largely dissipated, bled off in huge chunks as the ring expanded, traveling across the stars. The force that obliterated *Hecate* bumped her bridge pod almost gently, rocking it like a deep ocean wave before continuing on to parts unknown. Carrying the shredded remains of *Hecate* with it. The debris from the Cepheid, the other dead ships that stayed behind.

And all the while, the emergency beacon kept shrieking, calling out to the Valkyrie, the Titans and Auroras, that hulking Dreadnought *Gogmagog* who'd destroyed the Cepheid, dooming *Hecate* to death.

But *Gogmagog* never answered. Instead, it was *Seychelles* who eventually came to get them, *Gogmagog* having lost interest in the entire affair once the fighting ended. He stuck around long enough to blast through the last of the droned ships, chewing the dead vessels and any sizeable chunks of wreckage into teeny-tiny bits of space junk before spooling up his hyperspace drives and jumping back to whatever Fleet base spawned him. Taking his entourage with him. Leaving *Seychelles* and crippled *Ostea*, *Hoarfrost* and *Timpani* and *Coriolanus* with his missing tail to finish the mission.

Search for survivors. Bring *Hecate*'s remaining crew home.

FOUR

Henricksen slammed the door to his borrowed barracks quarters, kicked over a chair and threw the reader against the wall.

The device hit and rebounded, blanking as soon as it clattered to the metal decking, shock resistant case dented heavily on one side. Powered down and lay there, doing a pretty decent impersonation of a doorstop.

Apparently "shock resistant" didn't mean "throw resistant". Engineering specs failed to account for the devices being chucked in anger and fits of despondent, despairing rage.

"Well, that was brilliant." Henricksen folded his arms and leaned against the door, shaking his head in disgust.

Venting his frustration on an innocent piece of electronic equipment... not exactly his proudest moment. Hopefully the damn thing wasn't broken.

"Probably dock my pay if it is," he muttered, pushing away from the door.

Voices in the hallway made him glance over his shoulder, ears perking as the loud, jocular tones of the group of people out there dropped to a whisper. Footsteps slowing as they approached his quarters, speeding up as they hurried on by.

Officers' quarters, this section of the station. Most of them junior—ensigns and lieutenants waiting for their ships to pull in so they could take up their new assignments. Young, all of them. Skittish around the hard-eyed, scar-faced, scowling senior who'd come among them—angry when he arrived here, angry ever since.

Scared, the lot of them. Shied away whenever they happened to cross Henricksen's path. Avoided him like the plague in the mess hall, slinking away in terror whenever he entered one of the common spaces where the junior officers liked to hang out. Hardly dared to even *look* at him because they knew Henricksen's reputation. The rumors about what had happened to his last ship.

Infamous—that was Henricksen. No mistaking the grim-faced officer in the dark blue uniform. Torch and key patch on his shoulder a reminder of the AI he'd left for dead.

"Hell of a legacy," he muttered, eying the grey walls around him. The cheap plastic-and-metal, overly utilitarian barracks furniture crammed into the tiny room.

Depressingly dull, the lot of it. "Thrifty", if he was feeling generous. Exceedingly military either way. And the quarters themselves... tiny spaces compared to his berthing on *Hecate*. The smallest room he'd inhabited in a long, long time.

Since I was one of them, he thought, listening to the junior officers' voices fading as they moved down the hall. *Since I was stuck in one of those four-bys the enlisted all envied because at least you didn't have to hot rack it like they did in the barracks bunks.*

Hard to remember those days, sometimes. What it felt like to be that young and unblooded. Wide-eyed and naïve about the universe. Was a time when he too stood in awe of the senior officers. The battle-scarred, grey-haired men and women who'd seen so much war.

Scared of them as an ensign. Scared of ending up like them. Of turning that cold and hard.

But life happened. And death. Nearly twenty years he'd served in the Fleet, and cold, hard, well that just sort of came with the territory. As inevitable as time.

Still...

He bowed his head, touching his shoulder. Fingering the torch and key patch.

Hard to believe he'd ever been that innocent. Then again, maybe he never was. Pusher kid, after all, and pushers saw their fair share of death. Lost crews on the shipping lanes to DSR and pirates. To the scavengers that preyed on the freighters way, way out. Father went that way. Mother too, eventually, leaving Henricksen to raise himself.

Learn the ropes. Earn his place among the stars. Fight his way through the pusher ranks to that shit Officer Candidate School on Aerelon. *Keep* fighting until he clawed his way to *Hecate*'s commanding officer's chair.

Gone, he reminded himself, rubbing wearily at his eyes. Hecate*'s gone now.*

And Henricksen's assignment with her. That was the problem. The source of his current foul mood.

"Dammit," he sighed, casting his eyes across that depressing-as-all-get-out room. "God fucking dammit to hell."

He pushed away from the door, forgetting the junior officers in the hall for now. Stalked across his tiny room and scooped the dented reader from the decking. Keyed it on—silently relieved to find it still working—and settled into a chair in front of a desk shoved in the far corner.

Sat there for a long time, just staring at the screen, thinking of the bar on the opposite side of the station and how he hadn't gotten blind, stinking drunk in a long, long time. Too long, to be honest, considering he couldn't quite remember when that last time even was.

Commanding officer assignment came with certain expectations, and getting tipsy with the crew was a definite no-no. Sociable drink now and then was fine, but a drunk and disorderly—no matter *what* the circumstances—was a sure way to torpedo his career.

Later, maybe.

Once Sikuuku made his decision. To celebrate his new assignment.

Speaking of which...

A touch of the reader's screen and Henricksen pulled up a file. Scrolled through a roster of ships' listings, searching for a billet, *any* billet that, by some miracle, he might have missed.

"Nothing," he muttered, reaching the end of the roster. "Nothing, and nothing, and more nothing." He tossed the reader aside, lip lifting in disgust. Leaned back and stared at the ceiling, fingers knitted together behind his head. "I'm fucked. Twenty years of service and I'm well and truly fucked."

A knock at the door did nothing to improve his mood. Didn't want company, especially right now. But a second knock and Sikuuku barged his way in—bottle in hand, smile plastered across his face, looking like he'd already enjoyed a little liquid cheer along the way.

"Drink?" he offered, holding the bottle up.

Still wasn't in the mood for company, but a drink was tempting. Exactly what Henricksen wanted at the moment. "Why the hell not," he decided, hooking a chair over, backing his own up against the wall.

Just two seats in here, plus the desk and a rock-hard couch. Too much furniture, honestly for such a tiny space. Made a tight room that much tighter. Almost claustrophobic with two people inside it, sucking up all the air.

Three long, striding steps and Sikuuku plunked down in the chair across from Henricksen, setting the bottle on the desk beside him. Patted his pockets, looking around for something, smiled and nodded as Henricksen opened a desk drawer and pulled two glasses out.

Dusty glasses. The dregs of the last drink they'd held crusting the bottom.

Sikuuku's smile faded, tipped over and turned into a frown. "Seriously?" He picked up one of the glasses, grimaced and set it back down. "*That's* the best you can do?"

"Princess," Henricksen muttered, rolling his eyes.

He picked up a glass and blew the worst of the dust from the inside. Pulled a scrap of cloth from the drawer—clean, as far as he could tell, left there by the room's previous tenant—and wiped it down for good measure. Gave the second glass the same treatment and held both out for Sikuuku's inspection.

"Better? I can spit in 'em, if ya want. Clean 'em out proper."

Sikuuku grimaced. "Thanks, but I think I'll pass." He snagged a glass from Henricksen's hand, spun the cap off the bottle and filled it halfway. Tipped the container over its mate and splashed a dollop of liquor inside. "Cheers," he said, lifting his drink.

Henricksen pulled his drink to him, cupping it loosely in his hand. Considered Sikuuku's tattooed face sitting across from him—smiling widely, hinting at good news he was just itching to share—and the bandages peeking from beneath the cuffs of his uniform jacket. Bright and white and obviously new. A cocoon of gauze and antibiotic, antibacterial, anti-everything sterile wrappings that engulfed the gunner's tattooed forearms, winding halfway to his shoulders.

More bandages on Sikuuku's lower legs, though he couldn't see them, covering half-healed burns. Scar on Henricksen's face the docs said they could get rid of. Wipe away like an errant spot of paint. Leave his skin soft and smooth, like that scar had never been there at all.

"Piss off," he'd told them when the doctors offered. "I'm keepin' it," he declared, much to their dismay.

Stormed out, leaving shocked looks and muttered questions in his wake, but fuck them. No way in *hell* he was forgetting *Hecate*. Didn't *want* to forget what happened. Didn't *want* their baby fresh skin.

Didn't blame Sikuuku if he went the opposite route, though. Awful scarring from those burns. Twisted, painful-looking. Did a number on his tattoos. Fewer questions at his next assignment if he covered them over. Fewer people stopping. Staring. Wondering at those scars…

"So." Henricksen cleared his throat, spinning his glass on the desktop. "You make your decision yet?"

"Maybe." Sikuuku's smile turned secretive, broad shoulders shrugging.

Henricksen grunted, scooping up his glass. Sat back and studied its contents, conscious of Sikuuku's eyes watching from just a few feet away.

"To *Hecate*," the gunner said softly, holding out his glass. "And the crew we left behind with her."

Henricksen grimaced, fingers curling around the glass. "*Hecate*," he said, choking on the name. Lump forming in his throat. He opened his mouth and closed it, not trusting his voice. Not knowing what else to add. Leaned forward and clinked their two glasses together. Sat back and just held his drink for a while, picturing that last moment, just before the shockwave washed over *Hecate,* obliterating her body. Killing her AI.

Three weeks since *Hecate* died, and two-thirds of her crew with her. Three weeks he'd been stuck here with Sikuuku on this grim-as-death military station watching *Hecate*'s surviving crew trickle away.

Reassigned. Sent off to other ships. One by one, *Hecate*'s crew disappeared, leaving Henricksen and Sikuuku sitting here alone.

Well, except for all those junior officers, of course. Whole ream of them coming and going, faces changing out every few days. And Sikuuku…well, judging by that smile on his face, he'd be shoving off to his next assignment soon. Had his choice of close to a dozen billets, experienced gunners being in short supply and high demand right now.

Lot more gunner billets in the Fleet than captain assignments. Which left Henricksen waiting, and waiting, hoping the Fleet valued him enough to find a place for a him. Walked the station with *Hecate*'s patch on his shoulder—a brand that marked him, advertising exactly what he was.

A soldier with no assignment. An officer who'd survived the death of his ship.

"Congrats, by the way." Sikuuku tapped at his throat, tipped his glass toward the stars on Henricksen's collar.

"Thanks." Henricksen ducked his head, avoiding Sikuuku's eyes.

He should be happy. After all, he'd worked hard to get those captain's stars. Fought, and bit, and kicked his way to that rank.

Load of guilt over it, though. Not at all the way he'd imagined getting here.

Henricksen touched at the insignia, tracing the outline of those captain's stars. Hard-earned and a long time coming, but the rank felt empty. Worthless, without a ship to command. Especially since his last posting involved the complete destruction of an Aurora class warship, the AI inside it, and a good chunk of his crew.

Hard to feel good about that. Impossible to celebrate a promotion with that hanging over his head.

Then again, this celebration wasn't *his* celebration. Bottle of hooch, smile on his face—Sikuuku had an assignment. No mistaking that look.

"So what's it gonna be?" Henricksen sampled his drink and found it to his liking, glanced at Sikuuku, eyebrows lifting in surprise. "Scotch?"

"Uh-huh. Good stuff, too. Not that bathtub swill."

"Where in hell did you find it?"

Sikuuku shrugged, offering that secretive smile again. "Chief," he explained, tapping the anchors on his collar. "I know a few people."

Henricksen grunted, smiling, and left it at that. Better for him if he didn't know who these connections of Sikuuku's were. "Well, thanks for this." He held up his glass. "Exactly what I needed." He sipped at his drink, drained the glass and let Sikuuku refill it. Sat back, taking the drink with him, and drew one leg up, resting his foot on the seat of his chair. Rested his arm on his knee leaving his glass dangling, hanging loosely from his fingers.

Considered Sikuuku a moment, watching him sip at his drink, eyes roaming around the room. "I know you've had offers."

Sikuuku's eyes snapped back to him, locking onto Henricksen's face.

"You gonna go with a Dreadnought or a Bastion?"

Sikuuku hesitated, shrugged and flicked his fingers. "Passed 'em over."

"Really?" Henricksen thought Sikuuku would go with the Bastion for sure. "For what? One of those Valkyries like *Seychelles*?"

"Maybe." Sikuuku slouched in his chair, resting his drink on his stomach. "Still considering my options, actually." He pursed his lips, thinking a moment, eyes flicking around the room again. Emptied his glass and refilled it, sliding the bottle Henricksen's way. "What about you? Any promising leads?"

"None," Henricksen said, resentment returning. He drained his glass and grabbed the bottle, filling it back up.

"Thought you mentioned a Bastion posting?"

"Bastion. Right," Henricksen snorted. "Ops boss. Not my style."

Didn't fancy playing second fiddle on a Bastion, cow-towing to some other, more senior captain.

"What about another Aurora? I know they're commander billets but—"

"Checked. None available. Nor likely will be for quite some time." Henricksen sighed wearily, scrubbing his fingers through his short-clipped hair. "Could probably call in a few favors. Get a posting on a Titan, I suppose."

"Step down, going back to a Titan." Sikuuku sipped at his glass, watching Henricksen from his chair.

"Yeah. Well." Henricksen shrugged, at a loss for words again. Already knew he wouldn't take a Titan even if it was offered. Good ships, solid and dependable. But he'd been there, and done that, had no interest in going back.

Honestly didn't want another Aurora either. Didn't help him, being a captain in a commander billet. Didn't get him where he wanted to go.

"Move up or move out. Fleet's unofficial motto." Henricksen's lips twisted bitterly. He raised his glass and lowered it again without drinking, bowed his head and stared at the contents, swirling the Scotch inside. "Not sure quite sure where I'm going," he said softly, "but it's not out." He glanced up and back down again, shaking his head hard. "It's not out."

Spent most of his life with the Fleet. Had stars on his collar now after twenty hard-fought years of service. No way he was getting out. No way in hell.

"Here, here," Sikuuku said, raising his glass.

They drank together and shared the bottle, finished that round and moved on to another before circling back to the topic of assignments again.

"So. Seriously. What're ya gonna do?" Sikuuku asked him.

"Hell if I know," Henricksen grunted, sipping at his glass. "Been looking over the rosters." He waved to the abandoned reader, the lists of ships' assignments lined up on the display. "Apparently, the Fleet's flush on captain's postings at the moment. More stars than seats to put them in," he explained, with another bitter smile. "Stick me in some station admin job if I'm here much longer." His eyes drifted to the reader again, lying so innocently on the desk. "Should probably just take that Bastion posting. At least it'll be a ship."

Not what he wanted, but better than being bound to a station. Denied the stars for the next god-only-knew-how-many years.

Sikuuku considered him a moment, dark eyes blinking slowly. Bowed his and clasped his glass between both hands, spinning it back and forth, back and forth while Henricksen sat there, staring resentfully at the walls. "What if there was something different?" he asked some time later.

"Different." Henricksen frowned. "Different how? Experimental? Jump jock test pilot assignment or some such?"

"Something like that." Sikuuku glanced up, eyes shining with secrets, lips twitching with a smile.

"You're on to something, aren't you?" Henricksen leaned forward, dropping his foot to the floor. "What is it? What makes you think I'd be interested, or even qualified for this assignment of yours?"

"Dunno," Sikuuku admitted. "Chance to be stationed together, though. Wouldn't mind that." He sipped at his drink, eyes never leaving Henricksen's face.

"You and me."

"That's the thought."

"Huh." Henricksen sat back, shaking his head. "No postings on there for captain and gunner." He nodded to the reader, the ships' listing stored inside. "Unless you're talking about that Bastion."

"Nope. Not a Bastion." Sikuuku knocked his drink back and set the empty glass down on the desk. "Something better," he said, catching Henricksen's eye.

"Better. Really." Henricksen squinted suspiciously, folding his arms. "And just what could be better than being an ops boss on a Bastion?"

Sikuuku barked a laugh. "Wow. That didn't sound bitter at all." He held up a finger and reached inside his jacket, fished around in a pocket and pulled out a reader of his own.

Duplicate to Henricksen's, but less dented. Apparently chief's knew how to treat an electronic device proper.

A touch of his finger keyed the device on. Sikuuku set it down, watching Henricksen's face as he turned the display his way. "That," he said, nodding to the reader between them. "And the chance to keep me around, of course."

He smiled smugly and sat back, folding his arms. Scooped up the bottle and refilled his glass while Henricksen pulled the reader to him and scanned the first page.

"A ship," he murmured, eyes flicking across the display. "*Some* kinda ship, anyway." He was quiet a moment, reading. Raised his head and looked a question the gunner's way.

"Keep reading." Sikuuku waved his glass, crooked smile twisting his face. "I ain't goin' anywhere."

Henricksen frowned, tiring of this game. Tempted to power the damned reader off and just give it back. But it was a ship Sikuuku offered—not one he knew, granted, but a ship just the same. A chance to fly again and escape this dreary station. Get back to the stars. "I'm not committing to anything, you understand."

"Just read, Captain." Sikuuku touched a finger to the reader, sliding it just that little bit closer. "When you're done we can talk about whether you want to sign on the dotted line."

Henricksen hesitated still, feeling oddly, uncharacteristically uncertain. Shoved his misgivings aside and dug deeper into the reader's record, poring over the information inside.

"So?" Sikuuku sometime later, setting his glass down. He reached for the bottle—the contents severely depleted, the bottle itself barely half-full now—but stopped with his fingers just touching it, and pulled his hand back, leaving his glass empty for now. "What do you think?"

Henricksen looked at him, and at the reader, scrolling back to the beginning of the file. "Not sure. Hell, I'm not even really sure what I'm looking at. RV-N?" He pointed to the name written in blocky red letters at the top of the page. "What the hell is that? Never even *heard* of this ship, and now you want me to—"

"Raven," Sikuuku interrupted. "They're calling it a Raven." He touched a finger to the reader, eyebrows lifting in question. Searched through the file when Henricksen passed it to him and brought up the ship's specifications. "Recon Vessel - Non-combat." He glanced at Henricksen, lips twisting in a smile. "'Least, that's how it's classified."

"Raven," Henricksen grunted. "How fitting for Black Ops."

No mention of Black Ops anywhere in that file, but he knew a skunkworks project when he saw one. Only Black Ops would run something like this RV-N.

"I know it's not public, but is it sanctioned?"

"More or less." Sikuuku reached for the bottle, spilling a few swallows into his glass. Did the same for Henricksen's without asking and set the bottle back down. "Government funded anyway. RV-Ns are officially listed as drone sensor ships."

"Sensor ships. Right," Henricksen snorted. "Never mind the laser arrays and high-velocity rail guns mounted under their wings."

"Kinda ruins that whole 'non-combatant' thing, doesn't it?" Sikuuku smiled. "Fleet's dirty little secret," he said, tapping a finger to his nose. "That and the fact they're not drones."

Henricksen glanced up sharply. "*Not* drones."

"Nope." Sikuuku's smile widened. "Chassis spec'd out for a combat AI and four-man crew. Nothing at all droned in that."

Henricksen frowned, scanning through the RV-N's file again. No mention of AI anywhere, much less crew. He shut the reader down, pushed it away and sat back, studying Sikuuku's face. "How do you know so much about this?"

Sikuuku shrugged, setting his glass down. "Friend on the inside. Retired military. Combat retirement," he said, catching Henricksen's eyes. "Lost an arm and a leg during that business on Kantri."

"Nasty," Henricksen grunted, staring right back.

Battle on Kantri was legendary—the last major ground campaign between the Meridian Alliance shock troops and the DSR revolutionaries. Heavy casualties. DSR dug in so deep they almost won it.

Starved them out in the end. Starved their own troops and the planet's inhabitants in the process, leaving hundreds of thousands dead.

A resounding victory, as far as the military was concerned. Broke the DSR so completely that they gave up their attempts at planetary establishment entirely and retreated to deep space. Base of operations in the ass end of nowhere, relocated every time the Meridian Alliance honed in on it. Supply lines run through sympathizing stations using pirates and other unsavories to deliver goods in secret.

Broke the DSR on Kantri, but didn't kill them. Revolutionaries adapted. Survived and kept fighting. Turned to guerilla tactics when head-on combat didn't work, targeting military depots and other strategic assets. Ships when they needed them.

Like that convoy three weeks ago. Colony ships they'd picked clean, cored out and turned them into weapons. Weapons powerful enough to kill a warship like *Hecate*.

Hecate. Henricksen closed his eyes, picturing her. Remember the last time he saw *Hecate* alive.

Hardly seemed worth it, going to all that trouble just to take a few Fleet vessels out. Hard to believe the DSR really thought they could take down a military machine like the Meridian Alliance Fleet with a bunch of half-assed, booby-trapped ships.

"Doesn't make sense," he muttered, pulling the reader to him, flipping through the RV-N's information again. "Black Ops has been running counterintelligence for ages, but the DSR's just about done for." He turned the reader around, sliding it Sikuuku's way. "Why would the Fleet need something like this?"

"Don't know," Sikuuku told him, shrugging again. "Honestly, I don't," he insisted at Henricksen's skeptical look. "Just know it's a new program and they're looking for crew to run a dozen or so ships."

"*New* program." Henricksen's eyes slid to the reader. "So they're not tested. Ravens haven't seen combat yet."

"Not that I know of. Completed experimental trials, though. Kinsey tells me they're ready to go. Program's itching to get them deployed to the field."

"Kinsey. This friend of yours."

"Acquaintance, really. Kinsey…" Sikuuku smiled apologetically, spreading his hands. "He's not really the kinda guy that has friends."

Henricksen frowned, wary once more. "And this acquaintance of yours just *happens* to get in touch with you right after you just *happen* to lose your ship."

Sikuuku ducked his head, staring at his hands. "We've kept in touch over the years. Kinsey…" Another shrug of those burly shoulders, Sikuuku seemed *full* of shrugs these days. "He contacted me a time or two about other opportunities."

"*Other* opportunities." Henricksen folded his arms, giving him a look. "*What* other opportunities?"

"Look," Sikuuku sighed, looking Henricksen right in the face. "I wasn't going to leave *Hecate*. Never even considered it. But, after…after…" He sighed again and leaned back, collecting his thoughts while he looked around the room. "Black Ops." He flicked his eyes to Henricksen, lips twisting in a lopsided grin. "Gotta admit that sounds cool."

"Cool. Right. I'm all about cool." Henricksen scooped up the reader, studying the RV-N diagram in silence. "You already signed on, didn't you?"

Sikuuku's guilty flush confirmed it. Didn't have to say a word.

Henricksen grunted, shaking his head. "Explains why you've been so coy about assignments these last couple of weeks."

"Kinsey came and saw me in the hospital." Sikuuku looked at him, face apologetic. "Got my orders a week after that."

"And since then?" Henricksen prompted when Sikuuku went quiet. "You've got orders. Why the hell are you still here?"

Sikuuku laughed softly. "Nothing ever gets by you, does it?" He leaned forward, elbows resting on his knees, hands clasped loosely together. "Thing is, the squadron needs a captain." He caught Henricksen's gaze and held it. "And I think I know just the right one."

"Really?" Henricksen touched the stars on his collar—intrigued despite himself, worried at the same time.

Secrets weren't his thing. Warship—that's what he wanted, not some Black Ops intel squadron. A captain's billet, a proper one, complete with command.

Wasn't sure he'd ever get that if he signed onto a skunkworks project. Wasn't sure he'd ever get free if he mired himself in this Black Ops squadron.

"Sikuuku—"

"Not goin' if you pass it up." Stubborn set to Sikuuku's jaw. Sharp shake of his head. "Black Ops sounds interesting—not gonna deny that. But I won't work for some stick-in-his-ass Academy grad. Vouched for you with Kinsey. Told me the billet was yours if you wanted it."

Henricksen smiled ruefully. "But he sent you to try to convince me."

Smart then, this man Kinsey. Picked up enough from his discussions with Sikuuku to know he'd be wasting his time coming here himself.

"How in hell does a ground-pounder get involved with Fleet Black Ops, anyway?"

"Connections." Sikuuku twiddled his fingers, gesturing vaguely. "Knew someone, who knew someone—you know how these things work."

Henricksen grunted nodding. Lot of officers made promotion that way. Worked their way into choice billets by having their connections pull strings.

Not the way he liked to operate. Not at all.

"Think on it." Sikuuku drained his glass and set it down, shoving back his chair. "Doc won't clear me to leave station for another week." He wrapped his fingers around a bandaged forearm, grimacing a bit. "Think on it for a few days, then let me know what you think."

Henricksen sighed wearily, rubbing at his face. "I can't promise—"

"Not asking you to." Sikuuku was quiet a moment, watching Henricksen, eyes skipping around the room. "Keep it," he said, when Henricksen offered him the reader. "Bottle, too. I'm sure I'll find another somewhere." He smiled crookedly and tapped two fingers to his temple, stood and turned toward the door. "Goodnight, Garrett," he said, opening it.

"'Night, Akewane," he said distractedly, barely noticing when the gunner stepped into the hall.

The door clicked closed, leaving Henricksen staring at the reader while Sikuuku retreated to his quarters, booted footsteps thumping heavily against the metal decking outside. He checked the time out of habit and found it almost midnight.

Midnight, and his rack still empty. Well past when he should by all rights already be in bed.

But the reader beckoned—his own and Sikuuku's both. Henricksen pulled the one to him, poring over the list of assignments one more time. Gave up partway through and grabbed up Sikuuku's, cursing the gunner for bringing him this problem as he dove into the Raven's data, giving it another thorough going over.

FIVE

Fate decided things, in the end. The Bastion ops boss position filled up the very next day—no great loss, Henricksen really, truly didn't want it—leaving him just two options: the Black Ops Raven assignment that wasn't even officially listed, or a tour as commanding officer on an ancient Titan named *Vertigo*.

No choice at all, really. Black Ops was iffy—questionable whether it would help or hurt his career—but stepping down to a Titan...

Bad move. Especially since he'd *just* made captain.

That's how Henricksen ended up on a military cargo transport. He and Sikuuku both, packed in amongst the crates of dried goods and the cases of ammunition. The spare parts and machinery the Fleet staged at Dragoon—a Meridian Alliance space station tucked way, way out. Far from the nearest planet—Fermi, a rock not even worth terraforming—and just a hop, skip and a jump from the frontier.

"Uncharted space", that vast section of stars, or so the star charts proclaimed. Truth was the Meridian Alliance ran surveys decades ago. Mapped out vast stretches of frontier space in infinite levels of detail, marking the stars, and planets, and all the emptiness in between. Just happened they didn't see fit to *share* those charts with anyone, purposely keeping that knowledge to themselves.

Didn't want anyone dropping in unannounced, after all. Not with Dragoon out there—a staging ground for all sorts of wonky experiments and hush-hush operations. A training ground for elite troops, and now the home of the Ravens: Black Ops' very own stealth ship squadron.

Three days of travel on that bumpy old cargo hauler to get to the space station. Three days of leapfrogging through hyperspace, following a long and confusing to make sure prying eyes couldn't track their transit. And when they finally got there—tired, irritable, bored to tears after being pent up in that no-frills transport with just a worn-out deck of cards to amuse them—they were met by a very young, very apologetic ensign dressed in a conspicuously anonymous uniform.

No patch on his shoulder, no emblems of any type, in fact. Just a snug set of black coveralls, and those ensign bars on his collar. A silver nametag pinned to his chest.

"Taking this whole Black Ops thing a bit seriously," Henricksen muttered, sharing a look with Sikuuku beside him.

The ensign—nametag read Fisker, freckles on his cheeks spoke of some Old Earth, grey-skied ancestry, youth spent on some planet circling a star shining above—braced up hard and snapped off a very smart, very regulation salute. Held it, back ramrod straight, arm angled just so, waiting until Henricksen returned the gesture before dropping that hand to his side and gesturing diffidently for them to follow. "With me, sirs, if you please," he said, dipping his head.

Odd lilt to Fisker's voice. An accent that almost seemed familiar, but wasn't. Not quite.

Henricksen slid a look Sikuuku's way, eyebrows lifting as Fisker about-faced and set off. Caught the gunner staring at Fisker's back with an odd, almost thoughtful look on his face. "Son-of-a-bitch," he murmured, shaking his head. "Interesting place, this station." He set off after Fisker without another word, leaving Henricksen scratching his head, wondering what the hell to make of that cryptic comment.

Docks where the transport dumped them was a huge, echoing place, vaulted ceiling with exposed, composite metal girders rising twenty feet overhead. Metal decking and matching wall panels, a single, wide corridor stretching left and right.

Mechanized cargo haulers roamed everywhere, towing skid pallets piled high with everything from toilet paper to machine parts to the dry goods their own ship had brought. Fisker scanned his credentials at a security door, pressed his hand to a panel to let it read his prints, presenting an eye to the retinal scanner at a prompt.

A flash of green and the door chimed politely, popped open and let Fisker through. After that, things got fuzzy. One monotone hallway leading to another hallway, a labyrinth of drab, grey corridors—metal decking, plasmetal walls, a few polyglass panels here and there—that left Henricksen dizzy and disoriented. Completely confused.

Good thing they had Fisker to guide them. From the outside, Dragoon seemed relatively anonymous—a hulking, bloated stack of cubes piled atop more cubes, creating a massive, floating fortress in space—but inside was a labyrinth of criss-crossing hallways. Blank ends and locked doors and everything grey-on-grey.

And there was a smell to it—that's the one thing, the *only* thing that really stood out in Henricksen's mind. A stale mustiness that stank of oil and machinery, bone-chilling cold and long disuse that greeted them at every turning, growing stronger, more pungent and potent the farther they traveled. The worst of it centered around the vents for the air filtration system, hinting at a rottenness at the station's very center. A deep-seated contagion too difficult to roust out.

Old station, Henricksen thought as that smell wrapped around him.

Old machinery working the filtration system. Ancient ducting piping the environmentals around. Newer sections added on over time, but the core systems still there. Upgraded, augmented, but too bulky and unwieldy, too *expensive* to rip out.

Odd place for Black Ops to set up. Darlings of the Fleet, from what he could tell. Surprised they'd relegate their base to an ancient, creaking station like this. Almost asked Fisker about that when he stopped at the next pressure door— dozens of them on this station, isolating each section from the next in the event of explosive decompression—but figured him *being* an ensign, and low on the food chain, he likely wouldn't know.

"You tracking all this?" Sikuuku asked as they reached their seventh—or was it eighth?—security door.

"Huh-uh. Completely lost."

"Me too," Sikuuku grunted. "Die of starvation if you get lost in here. Speaking of which—you carrying any snacks, Fisker?"

"Sir?" Fisker turned around, blinking owlishly as the pressure door's security panel flashed and chimed, popping open.

"Nothing, Fisker." Henricksen pointed at the door, waving the ensign on. "He's just…" A glance at Sikuuku beside him, lips twitching in a smile, "eager to see our new accommodations."

"Yes, sir." Fisker eyed the gunner uncertainly. "This way. Almost there." He pushed the door open, stepped through and held it, waiting for Henricksen and Sikuuku to follow.

"Sir, he calls me." Sikuuku grunted in disgust.

Chief's anchors on the gunner's collar—senior enlisted and not anyone's "sir".

"Leave it," Henricksen warned, pitching his voice low. "Ensign, remember?" He tapped a finger to the stars on his collar. "Still learning the ropes."

"Even *you* figured out the difference between chiefs and officers—"

"Leave it." Henricksen grabbed his arm and gripped it hard. "Young kid." He flicked his eyes to Fisker waiting patiently on the other side of the door. A slightly confused-looking Fisker who shuffled his feet, obviously wondering what was going on. "Give him time. He'll figure it out." A pat on the gunner's shoulder and Henricksen stepped through the doorway, waving Fisker ahead as Sikuuku fell in at his side.

Still didn't look happy, but he kept his complaints to himself after that. Walked along in silence until Fisker lead them somewhere that looked different. A corridor with a grey length of wall on one side, just like all the others, and the opposite filled with windows. A half wall of plasmetal panels rising from the floor, connecting to triple-thick panes of polyglass reaching to the ceiling above. The view through them uncertain, looking out on a wide expanse of cavernous hangar deck.

"Guess this is it," Sikuuku said, nudging Henricksen in the side.

"Apparently." Henricksen stepped to his right, staring through those panes of glass, taking a good, long look at the hangar on the other side.

Not much to see, actually. Dark in that hangar bay. Light from the hallway spilling through the windows, illuminating the decking just outside. But the rest of it…

Wreathed in shadows. A pitch black void stretching endlessly into the distance.

Fisker coughed politely, smiling when he had Henricksen's attention—a nervous thing, twitching and uncertain, pulling at the corners of Fisker's mouth. "This way, sir." He nodded to the end of the hallway, and a set of stairs leading to a landing outside a sealed door. "I'll wait here until you're ready, sirs," he said, stationing himself outside.

Henricksen left him there, pulled the door open and stepped through with Sikuuku a step behind him, letting Fisker pulled the door closed behind him while he examined the room on the other side.

Control room, from the look of it. Wall of floor-to-ceiling windows on his right, looking out on the hangar deck, banks of monitoring stations in front of them, others scattered about the room, pushed up against the walls.

Trio of lab-coated civilians huddled together on the far side of the room, directly across from the door. Bright white clothing showing ghostly in the control room's dim lighting, heads bowed together as they discussed something on one of the station's panels.

Pinstripe-suited administrator type standing by the windows, back to the door as he considered the hangar deck below.

Henricksen ignored the lab coats—engineers, scientists, some other form of project support crew—and focused on the man in the obviously expensive clothing. Broad-shouldered, barrel-chested, skin the color of the sky at dusk. Feet spread wide as he stood in front of those windows. Back ramrod straight, hands clasped loosely behind him.

Marshal bearing, despite the civ suit. Scars on the back of the man's head, twisting beneath a short cap of salt and pepper hair. Matching scar, though thicker, peeking above the starched collar of an equally pinstriped shirt.

Starch and stiff meant military, and that stance—feet and shoulders in line, hands resting in the small of his back—screamed infantry. Drill sergeant, if Henricksen had to guess. Combat master sergeant, something of that ilk.

Henricksen disliked him instantly. Military was one thing—a life he chose, no other he wanted—but infantry, in his experienced, were a bunch of puffed up pricks. Put more stake in spit and polish than actually getting the job done. Like those Academy grads they churned out of Sosholo and Yunshinshin but without the wealth and privilege.

"This is Kinsey, I take it?"

Sikuuku nodded, looking surprisingly anxious. Grabbed Henricksen's arm as he stepped forward and shook his head hard, making a chopping motion with his hand to warn him not to talk.

Henricksen looked at him, and at Kinsey by the windows. *So that's how it is. Summoned to the king's court and now we wait on his pleasure.*

His dislike of this man Kinsey deepened. He hated stupid, bullshit games.

"Gentlemen." Kinsey pivoted, hands linked behind him, staring at them from across the room.

Strong face on Kinsey. *Hard* face. Wide nose set above lips pressed tightly together. Dark eyes like onyx sitting beneath a creased and scarred brow. He stared at them a moment, letting the glow from control room's empty monitoring stations crawl across his body, flickering across his pinstriped body. Giving them a narrow-eyed, almost disapproving look.

Five seconds he stood there, studying his visitors like he didn't have the faintest idea what to do with them. And then the shoulders eased a bit, and the lips softened, curving into something that almost resembled a smile. "How was the trip in?" he asked in a measured, politely bland voice.

Kinsey stepped away from the windows, offering his hand. Henricksen looked at it, and at Sikuuku, walked across the room and wrapped his fingers around Kinsey's.

Firm grip, fingers clenching tight. Kinsey's eyes locked onto Henricksen's face, never wavering as he pumped that hand up and down.

Challenge in that stare. Kinsey measuring Henricksen, judging him based on that handshake. What Kinsey saw in his eyes.

Pissed Henricksen off, being sized up like some racehorse. Made him want to cold-cock the guy right then and there and drop him to the floor. But he squeezed that hand instead—lean, sinewy, rough with callouses—and stared right back.

Dead-eyed. Closed up. Giving him nothing. Absolutely nothing at all.

That smile again—a quirk of amusement that never quite reached Kinsey's eyes. He squeezed Henricksen's hand and released it, moving a step back. "So you're Henricksen," he said, eyes flicking to the stars on Henricksen's collar. "Heard a lot about you." The smile twitched, turned condescending. Twitched again, changing as he turned to Sikuuku. Taking on life as reached for his hand. Seeming real for the first time. "Good to see you again, Akiwane. How are you feeling?" he asked, pushing at the gunner's sleeve.

Bandages still, hiding under Sikuuku's uniform jacket. Would be for another couple weeks, but the skin beneath was almost healed—scarred and pale and tattoo free, but whole now. A vast improvement over the twisted, bloody mess it was a month ago.

"Fair enough." Sikuuku smiled back, looking pleased that Kinsey cared. "Cleared for duty, which is all that matters."

"True enough." Kinsey's smile widened, showing the whiteness of his teeth. "You've filled him in on what we're doing here?" A nod to Henricksen, eyes never leaving Sikuuku's face.

Sikuuku shrugged uncomfortably, sliding a look Henricksen's way. "What I know anyway."

Which wasn't everything—Henricksen read that in the set of Sikuuku's shoulders. Knew as much from their earlier conversations.

"I suppose you'll want to see them." Kinsey turned his eyes toward Henricksen, smile taking on a cold edge. "The squadron, that is."

"Wouldn't mind." Henricksen kept his tone even, refusing to be baited. Intimidated or cowed. "Seeing as how I'm supposed to be in charge."

Kinsey's eyes flashed—a brief moment of anger, quickly brought under control

Chink in tight-ass's armor. Henricksen smiled in satisfaction, filing that little tidbit away.

"You're assigned to the squadron, Captain." Kinsey stepped in close, getting right in Henricksen's face. "But make no mistake about our roles here. *I'm* in charge of the project."

Henricksen blinked slowly, favoring Kinsey with that dead-eyed stare. "Don't want the project, Kinsey." He nodded to the windows, the hangar deck on the other side. "Just want the birds. Just want to fly."

Kinsey barked a surprised laugh and stepped away, his entire demeanor changing in an instant. "Alright. Just so we understand each other." A flick of his eyes to Sikuuku, before returning his attention to Henricksen. "Come with me," he said, crooking a finger. Turned around and walked stiff-backed to the windows.

Roll to his gait Henricksen hadn't noticed earlier. A hitch in his get-along most wouldn't even pick up.

"Prosthetics," Sikuuku whispered, nodding at Kinsey's back. "Leg. Arm. Partial ceramic skull. Had to rebuild it," he explained, rapping his knuckles against the back of his head.

Henricksen grunted, considering Kinsey standing by the windows. Combat retirement, Sikuuku had said. From the sound of things, Kinsey was lucky to be alive.

Kinsey turned his head, looking over his shoulder. "If you're done whispering about me you can come join me. There's something I think you'll want to see."

Sikuuku flushed guiltily and hurried over, Henricksen lagging just a few steps behind.

The control room windows sat roughly thirty meters up, looking down on the hangar bay below. Couldn't see all that much of it, even from here, the darkness that covered it masking everything, even the area right in front of the windows.

"Ready?" Kinsey looked at him, smiling in that stiffly polite way of his. Reached to one side and flipped a few switches, cutting on a bank of lights.

Spotlights shone down from the ceiling, pushing back the shadows. A cavernous space unfolded—tall enough, wide enough, deep enough to hold a couple of Aurora class warships like *Hecate*. A Valkyrie like *Seychelles* and a few other smaller ships beside.

But it wasn't an Aurora Henricksen spotted below him, nor a Valkyrie either. In fact, the ships sitting on the hangar bay's decking looked nothing at all like any ship he'd ever come across in his life.

Tiny things. Miniscule compared to the Fleet's warships. Barely a third the size of a Titan, small enough to fit inside a Valkyrie's belly. And the shape of them...

Sharp-sided and sinister. Dark on dark, invisible in the shadows. A half dozen knife-blade shapes squatting menacingly on the decking, arranged in a circle with their engines pointing toward the center.

Henricksen studied them, feeling cold all over. Wasn't sure he liked them. Wasn't quite sure he wanted anything to *do* with a ship that look like that.

"So that's them?" Sikuuku stepped close to the windows, nodding to the ships below. "Those are the Ravens?"

Kinsey nodded wordlessly, arms folded, watching Sikuuku and Henricksen both. "What do you think?"

Sikuuku opened his mouth and closed it. Frowned and slid his eyes to Henricksen.

"Not exactly pretty, are they?"

Kinsey scowled, disapproval written clearly on his face. "They're not *supposed* to be pretty, Captain. They're supposed to be *stealthy.*"

"And?" Henricksen folded his arms, copying Kinsey's stance. "Are they?"

"Are they what?" Kinsey snapped.

"Stealthy. They better be, ugly as they look."

Kinsey didn't answer. Kept his face carefully neutral, though his eyes flashed with fire.

"You don't know, do you?" Henricksen's eyebrows lifted. "You burned through a bunch of Meridian Alliance funding making a squadron of stealth ships and you don't even know if they can do their job." He barked a laugh, shaking his head. "Hell of an outfit you talked me into, Sikuuku." He felt the gunner stiffen, saw him flush and drop his eyes. Felt bad about that—hadn't meant to embarrass him—but apologies would have to wait until later. When Kinsey wasn't around. "I trust they can *fly,* at least?"

Kinsey bristled, dark eyes sparkling with anger. "We tested all the avionics. Propulsion engines are solid and we've proved the RV-N can successfully transit jump."

Henricksen waited, knowing there was more. "But?" he prompted when Kinsey stayed silent.

"The systems need tuning." Kinsey stepped close to the windows, looking down. "Burned out the jump drives the first time through. Lost two pilots trying to get them to pass testing."

"Dead?" Henricksen guessed.

"Retired," Kinsey said, looking around.

Which meant disabled. Incapacitated. Broken in some fundamental way that made them incapable of doing their job.

Henricksen shivered. Sometimes dead was preferable. Suddenly this whole project stank. "So the airframe's unstable. That what you're telling me?"

Kinsey shrugged and nodded, gave a sharp shake of his head.

Not quite yes, not quite no. An answer that didn't exactly inspire confidence. Especially since Sikuuku and Henricksen were expected to climb into one of those ugly, pilot-mangling monstrosities down there themselves.

"So what's to stop me from turning around right now and walking out that door over there?" Henricksen stabbed a finger at the portal in question, Fisker standing guard on the opposite side. "Why should I believe you'll ever get that shit-show of a spaceship working enough to actually do its job?"

Kinsey turned around, leaning his shoulders against the glass. "I've got some of the Fleet's best and brightest assigned to this project. Engineers, mechanics, pilots." A pause, eyes locking on Henricksen's. "You."

The compliment caught Henricksen by surprise. Didn't know what to do with it at first, given Kinsey's stiff, disapproving demeanor. The hint of hostility lurking in his eyes.

He considered the administrator a moment, dipped his head in acknowledgment and received a nod from Kinsey in return.

"We've worked out the kinks in the jump drives and mostly have the stealth system up to snuff. But we need pilots to take test runs so we can dial in the rest of the systems and maximize the RV-N's operational capability."

"Maximize its operational capability." Henricksen grunted, lips twisting bitterly. "What kinda military horseshit you tryin' to sell me, Kinsey?"

Kinsey's face blanked, eyes hooding. Turning cold, and flat, and dead. "Nothing shit about it, Captain. The ships will fly. They'll do their job. I just need crew to run them through their paces."

Henricksen looked at him, and at Sikuuku standing to one side. Stepped to the windows and looked down on the squadron of stealth ships squatting on the hangar bay's floor.

"I read your record, Henricksen." Soft voice from Kinsey. Thoughtful, reasoning tone. He moved closer, standing right beside Henricksen, joining him in his study of the hangar bay's occupants below. "You're not one to shy away from a challenge. Those stars…" He tapped a finger to his own collar—stiff and civ, no insignia in sight. "You fought for them. Chose combat assignments over admin billets. Chose the warships over politics to move you up through the ranks." Kinsey's looked at him, head tilting, smile playing about his lips. "I like that about you, Captain. Most officers I work with are stuck up assholes who can't see past this," a touch at his pinstriped suit, "to see this." He grabbed one hand with the other, twisted and pulled, separating his prosthetic arm at the shoulder. "Lost my arm to the Dark Star Revolution." He held the limb in question up, letting Henricksen get a good look. Threaded it back into his sleeve and locked it into place. "Lost a leg too. Part of my brain. More men than I can count." He grimaced, lips pressing in a hard line. "Most of the Fleet thinks we broke the DSR at Kantri, but I'm here to tell you they're wrong." Kinsey nodded to the hangar below, the huge doors—closed now, sealed up tight—filling one wall. "Those bastards are out there, Captain. They're out there and they're plotting—"

Kinsey broke off, eyes widening, flicking surreptitiously to a camera watching from the corner. A deep breath and he shrugged his shoulders, turned around and walked over to a monitoring station, keying the system on. "They'll work, Captain. They *have* to work. We need the Ravens. Now more than ever."

Henricksen frowned, throwing a worried look Sikuuku's way. Saw the gunner shrug and shake his head, tattooed face frowning right back.

"I run the squadron," Henricksen said. A statement, not a question, but Kinsey nodded anyway. "I pull the crews at my discretion."

Kinsey turned his head, showing him one eye.

"I test those ships and find them unsafe, I'm pulling the crews until the engineers and mechanics fix them. *I* do. *My* decision, not yours. You say the Ravens are important and I believe you. But I won't lose crew. I won't kill this squadron just so those stealth ships can fly."

Kinsey pursed his lips, thinking, eyes flicking to the camera in the corner. "Alright. What else?" he asked, turning around.

Henricksen straightened, chin lifting. "I crew one of the ships myself. Me and Sikuuku," he said, hooking a thumb at the gunner. "No goddamn way I'm flying a desk."

Kinsey considered, dark eyes filled with secrets. "*Four* man crews on the stealth ships, not two."

"Alright. Sikuuku here will pick the others."

"I will?" Sikuuku blinked, obviously surprised.

"Anything else?" Kinsey asked him.

"I choose my ship." Important an AI and captain got along. The AI he chose would run the squadron, every bit as much as himself. "Don't wanna end up with some big-brained asshole as a partner."

Sikuuku choked and turned around, shoulders shaking with suppressed laughter.

Kinsey stared at them, face unreadable, eyes flicking from Henricksen to Sikuuku and back again. "Done," he said. "But lose the uniforms."

Henricksen touched *Hecate*'s patch on his shoulder. Protective of it. Loathe to give it up.

"Your days with *Hecate* are over, Captain. Time to get over her and move on." Kindly voice this time. Another chink in Kinsey's armor, this one letting a fleeting look of commiseration slip through. He looked away, tugging at his cuffs and collar, and when he looked back he was all business again. "You'll find fresh uniforms in the barracks, along with everything else you need. I've billeted you in the administrative quarters—"

"No," Henricksen said quietly, and saw Kinsey's face darken, eyes flashing in annoyance. "Appreciate the offer, but I prefer to stay with the crew. Assuming there's room, of course."

Kinsey glared at him, jaw clenched tight. "As you wish," he said, nodding stiffly. "Fisker will fetch whatever you need. Goodnight, gentlemen." He flicked his fingers, dismissing them. Ending their audience just like that. "I'll see you here at 0700 tomorrow morning." A nod and Kinsey turned back to the windows.

Henricksen gathered up Sikuuku and headed for the door, leaving Kinsey standing there, staring through the glass.

SIX

Fisker pushed away from the wall as Henricksen and Sikuuku stepped out of the control room, braced up hard and saluted for all he was worth.

Held that stance for a long time—stiff as a board, eyes almost-but-not-quite looking at Henricksen, hand slanted precisely across his brow, moving not so much as a *whisker* until Henricksen acknowledged him. Tapped two fingers to his temple and told the ensign to stand at ease.

Very prim and proper, this shiny new ensign. Not really Henricksen's style—rank and respect was one thing, but prim and proper smacked of useless posturing and nonsense—but he forgave the formality in this case. Ensigns were *supposed* to be prim and proper. Fleet Academies beat deferential into them. Officer Candidate Schools tried—Henricksen himself suffered through a whole host of instruction focused on knife and fork training—but most of it never stuck. Academy grads, though...took to it like ducks to water. Preened, and postured, and polished themselves blue in the face.

Few years in the Fleet, though, and they lost most of that prim and proper. The over-starched shirts and perfectly creased pants. Fleet expected honor, respect for rank and service. Fleet didn't care much about starch and creases.

Starch and creases didn't win battles. Keep ships from getting blown apart.

"This way, sirs. If you wouldn't mind." Fisker smiled his nervous smile, nodding to Henricksen and Sikuuku both before setting off down the stairs.

Escorted his two charges back down the hallway bordering the hangar deck—wall of windows on the left, plasmetal panels on the right—stopping at pressure door halfway along its length.

Ancient thing, straight on the sides, rounded at the top and bottom. Oversized wheel in the center in addition to the heavy latch, and the security system panel set in the wall to one side.

"Wagon wheel." Sikuuku grunted, sliding a sidelong a look Henricksen's way. "Haven't seen one of *those* in a while."

Old style fitting, phased out a century and more ago. Wheel used to crank the door closed and seal it tight against the frame's gaskets. Heavy latch to lock it and suck everything up tight.

Slow to secure, those heavy, ancient portals. Not what you wanted in an emergency. On the plus side, the system held its pressure, even after a catastrophic power loss.

Surprised Henricksen that they hadn't replaced them, though. Wheels tended to fail. Metal rusted—steel here, not the more modern, composite metal materials adopted across the galaxy fifty plus years ago. Bent and twisted. Got stuck at the most inopportune times.

Fisker shuffled his feet, waving vaguely at the door. "Space was available. And Kinsey—Mr. Kinsey wanted to be close to the hangar." A shrug of his shoulders, making it clear it wasn't *his* idea, and Fisker flashed that nervous smile, keyed into the security system and spun the wheel when it popped. Grabbed the latch and yanked, leaning backward as he hauled the heavy door open. "RV-N staff only," he said, glancing at Henricksen and Sikuuku behind him. "Mr. Kinsey will issue you a security code tomorrow. Only works here, though." He pointed to the security panel beside the door, nodded to the hall stretching on the other side—double doors at the end of it, crossing corridors to the left and right. "And the hangar deck, of course."

Second nod, this one to the wall of windows behind them, the darkened, cavernous space looming on the other side.

Henricksen considered the way ahead, the hangar deck where the RV-N's squatted. "What about the *rest* of the station?"

Fisker shrugged, smile turning apologetic. "Not allowed. You've got the run of the RV-N spaces and the hangar deck, the control room above. But the rest of station…" He hesitated, cheeks flushing beneath the freckles. Looked both ways—up the beside-the-hangar-deck corridor and down—dropping his voice as he leaned close. "Dragoon's carved up into sections. Each one more hush-hush than the last. Not even sure what else is going on here, to be honest. Ensign," he explained, touching a finger to the single gold bar on his collar. "They don't tell me all that much."

"No," Henricksen murmured, sliding his eyes Sikuuku's way. "I suppose they don't."

Sikuuku grunted, offering nothing more than that, while Fisker licked his lips, growing increasingly uncomfortable the longer they stood there in the hall.

"If—if you don't mind, sirs?" He stepped aside, holding the door open as he waved Henricksen and Sikuuku through. Stepped in after—knee bending, foot lifting as he crossed the elevated threshold—and pulled the door to. "This way," he said, stepping around his two charges to move ahead of them. Chattering a blue streak as he gave them the nickel tour of their new home. "Billets for the civilians down there." He flipped a finger at a crossing corridor—one of two coming in from the left, stagger-stepped, matching corridors leading off to the right. "Engineers and science staff," he explained at Henricksen's raised eyebrow look. "Military across the way."

"Barracks?" Henricksen asked him.

"For the enlisted," Fisker nodded. "Suites for the officers. Shared, mostly," he added, eyes flicking to Sikuuku's collar, the tattoos covering his face.

Sikuuku grunted, lips twisting. "Civ *and* military." A glance at Henricksen, offering a crooked smile. "Everyone packed in together. Isn't that nice?"

Surprising, really. Not often the suits and uniforms bedded down together. *Some* separation here, but still…

Interesting. Not what Henricksen expected.

He waved Fisker ahead, ambling along behind him as they worked their way down that long, central corridor—a square-sided, square-cornered tube burrowing deep into the station proper. Blocked at the end by those wide, double doors. Grey everywhere—walls, ceiling floor—and plasmetal and carbon weave concrete. Drab, durable materials stretching as far as the eye could see.

He glanced down a crossing corridor—lefthand side, the hallways on either side of the center thoroughfare set at stagger-steps to each other—and counted a dozen doorways spaced along its length. Thick, heavy looking portals. Same latch-and-wheel construction as the pressure door behind them.

Original station, Henricksen thought, spying the same configuration in the next corridor, stretching off to his right. *Original fittings. Probably easier to add on new spaces than rehab and upgrade this little rabbit warren of rooms.*

Fleet did that, more often than not. Built a small station and added on other sections as they needed them, expand the entire complex over time. But the seed remained, if you could find it. Spaces with old style construction, just like this one. Everything ponderous and durable, almost prison-like in its simplicity. And the smell…

Same smell as the rest of the station, but stronger. More pungent. A touch of damp in the air, like it was seeping from the walls. A stink distinctive to abandoned stations. To spaces left to molder and rot.

Reminded Henricksen of Grandee, that oldest of old stations. A fringe trading post established before the fringe moved a few hundred thousand lightyears outward. Visited that station a few times, back in his pusher kid days. Remembered the day word came across the wire that they'd lost it—explosive decompression, catastrophic compartment failures across the length and breadth of its structures. Core held, but the atmosphere didn't. At least, not long enough to keep the people inside alive.

Grandee smelled just like this place. Henricksen slowed, looking around. *Same taint. Same moldering stink.*

Supposed he'd get used to it—didn't want to, didn't like being reminded of Grandee and all those dead people—but supposed he would, in time. Made him wonder, though, why they'd shut this section of the station down. What prompted the Fleet to open it back up again…

"Hope to hell they kept up the maintenance." He turned his head, eying a crack between two panels—a jagged edged, dark line interrupting the bland greyness of one wall.

"Grim looking place, isn't it?" Sikuuku muttered, pitching his voice low.

"Station." Henricksen shrugged, throwing a look the gunner's way. "Most of them are."

"Enlisted barracks." Fisker smiled politely as Henricksen looked up. "That hallway," he inched a finger at the corridor Henricksen and Sikuuku were currently inspecting. "That's enlisted barracks, sir." He stiffened, face paling as a raucous noise erupted—laughter and raised voices drifting from the hallway in question.

Sikuuku smiled, listening for a few seconds. "Sounds they're having fun."

"Mechanics." Fisker spread his hands—nervous, apologetic, the trademarks of this oh-so-young ensign. "They're a rather… rowdy bunch." A twitch of his lips, hands wringing, eyes flicking down the hall. More laughter—accompanied by a liberal amount of what could only be swearing—and he cleared his throat uncomfortably, spun around and continued on. "This way, sirs." A glance over his shoulder, pointing to the double doors ahead. "Mess hall and rec room are at the end. You and the other RV-N officers are billeted down here." Fisker nodded to the next hallway—the second of the two crossings on their right. Turned the corner and beckoned with his fingers. "Follow me. I'll show you which rooms are yours."

Sikuuku slowed, arms folding. "Thought you said this was officers' quarters."

Fisker jerked to a halt, freckled facing frowning worriedly as he turned around. "Mr. Kinsey..." He paused, fidgeting, glancing up and down the hall. "Mr. Kinsey made special arrangements. This way," he repeated, waving at the hallway with its spoke and wheel doors.

Sikuuku kept staring a moment, shrugged and reluctantly followed. Nudged Henricksen in the ribs when he came alongside him, pointing with his chin at a door to one side. "Airlock at the entrance to this section makes sense given the age of the place. But quarters?" He glanced across the hall, shaking his head hard. "Seems kind of extreme."

Henricksen shrugged, eying one of the doors as they walked by. "Dragoon's no spring chicken. Random depressurization wasn't all that uncommon a hundred years ago." He glanced up, noting the vents above them, equipped with manual cutoff valves. "Airlocks kept the crew safe in quarters until rescue came. Or station operations returned to normal."

"So...what? This is some kind of museum?" Sikuuku looked less than thrilled with the idea.

"Not quite that old." Henricksen smiled. "And if you're worried, don't be. Black Ops stronghold like this..." He gestured at the walls around them. "Probably got the most high-tech backbone infrastructure in the Fleet."

Sikuuku eyed him uncertainly, threw a mistrusting look at the next door they passed by. "That why this place smells like my old uncle's cabin?"

"You'll get used to it."

Sikuuku grunted and kept walking, clearly unconvinced. "Not sure I like stations." A flick of his eyes to Henricksen. "Rather be out there among the stars than trapped in this ancient collection of cans."

Henricksen laughed softly. "You're the one that talked me into coming here, remember? So don't you go getting all weak in the knees and scared just because of a couple of hallways with hatch doors, Akiwane."

"Sir?" Fisker called from the end of the hall. "This one, sir." He pointed to the last door on the right. "This one's yours, Captain." A nod to the door across the hallway. "And the other's for you, sir," he said, offering Sikuuku one of his patented, wanting-to-please smiles.

"For the luvva—I'm not your damned sir." Sikuuku pushed past Fisker and grabbed the wheel on the door to his quarters, spun it three full turns and yanked angrily at the latch to push the door open.

Stood there after and just stared at the tiny suite of rooms on the other side: sitting area at the front with a desk and chair crammed in one corner, couch and two uncomfortable-looking chairs cluttering what little space was left.

Door standing open to the right, leading to an equally tiny bedroom with a cubicle of a bathroom attached. Tight quarters, to say the least. Especially for someone as large as the gunner.

"This is a joke, right?" Sikuuku turned, hooking a thumb over his shoulder. "Fucking shoe box in there."

Fisker ducked his head, bright spots of color blooming on his cheeks. "Sorry, sir. The rest of them are doubles." He waved at the doorways lining the hall. "Chiefs and officers all have roommates. Enlisted are in barracks." A nod to the opposite end of the hallway, eyes flicking to one side. "It's four to a room down there."

Sikuuku still didn't look happy.

"The Captain's rooms are the same," Fisker offered. "And at least you don't have to share."

"This is bullshit." Sikuuku scowled, looking past Fisker to Henricksen. "What'd they give you?"

Henricksen shrugged, eyes flicking to Fisker. "Kid says it's the same setup. Expect it's the same."

Fisker looked at him, pathetically grateful.

Felt bad for the kid. Tough being an ensign—Henricksen should know, he'd been there and hated every minute of it. Also hated seeing people treat like them idiots, even though most of them were at that age.

Not their fault Academy don't teach them how the real military works.

"Open it." Sikuuku lifted his chin, hugging his arms tight to his chest. "Let's have a look."

"You're being ridiculous."

"Open it," Sikuuku repeated, staring stubbornly at Henricksen's face.

Henricksen rolled his eyes. "Fine, ya big baby. 'Scuse," he said, pushing Fisker to one side. Stepped across the hall and spun the wheel on the door to his quarters, moved aside and let Sikuuku take a look. "See? Same as yours." Right down to those hard, uncomfortable-looking chairs. "Not like the ship, Akiwane. Station barracks, which means rank goes out the window. *Everyone* gets a shoebox." He tipped a wink at Fisker, offering a crooked smile. "Even us highfalutin captains."

Sikuuku still didn't look happy. Scowled even harder, not quite ready to give up. "What about Kinsey? What's he got?"

Fisker paled, freckles standing out starkly as he glanced guiltily at Sikuuku's quarters. "I don't—I'm not—"

"Ease off, Chief." Henricksen caught the gunner's eyes, gave a slow shake of his head. "Kinsey's a bureaucrat. They *always* get better quarters. Ain't that right, Fisker?" He slid a look at Fisker, eyebrows lifting in question. Saw the ensign nod and duck his head, dropping his eyes.

"Separate section of the station," he said softly. "Senior administration only."

Henricksen nodded—that was typically the way of things. "I know it's not what you got used to on *Hecate*." Not even close. Sikuuku's shipboard quarters had been twice as large as these. Henricksen's far roomier than that. "But if they get the RV-Ns working properly we won't be spending all that much time here anyway."

Sikuuku held onto his righteous indignation a while longer—stubborn cuss, stubborn as they came—but eventually relented. Dipped his head when Henricksen kept staring, matching him stubborn for stubborn, and shrugged his shoulders, looking slightly less grumpy, but nowhere near content. "Guess I'll get used to it. Like the smell."

"Atta boy." Henricksen flashed a grin, punching the gunner on the shoulder. "Alright, Fisker. What's next?"

"Um, well…" Fisker licked his lips, fidgeting again. "I hadn't—I wasn't really—I thought you'd want to stow your gear, sir." He waved at the rooms on either side of the hall. "Maybe get settled in a bit before—"

"No gear to stow," Henricksen told him. "All went up with the ship."

Not entirely true—they both had personals stashed in storage they hadn't taken with them on that last mission. But the toiletries and uniform items, everything Henricksen brought on board *Hecate* disappeared when she went down.

"As for settling in…" Henricksen threw a look over his shoulder, inspecting the rooms behind him. "I think that's pretty much done." He flashed a grin as Fisker colored, pink skin turning red beneath his freckles now. Turned his head and nodded to the far end of the hallway. "Got a bar in this place, Fisker? Chow hall where we can get something to eat before Sikuuku and I get drunk?"

Didn't really intend to—*wanted* to in the worst way, but he wouldn't. At least not tonight. Bad mistake, getting stinking drunk on the first day of a new assignment. With crew around he didn't even know.

Hell of a way to make a first impression. Likely never live that down.

"I don't—I think…" Fisker gaped in horror. Academy painted a lofty, idealized picture of captains. Never said *anything* about them wanting to get drunk. "Mr. Kinsey doesn't like the crew getting inebriated. Sir." Fisker blushed all over again. Incredibly apologetic. Entirely embarrassed.

Henricksen grunted, sharing a look with Sikuuku across the hall. "Well, Kinsey don't live here, do he? And since he turned the running of the Raven crews over to me, *I* get to say when they're allowed to get drunk. Which is tonight, if I feel like it." He tipped a wink at Sikuuku and saw the gunner start to smile. "Three days on that goddamn freighter with nothing more than water and freeze-dried rations. If *ever* there was a time for drinking, it's now."

Fisker stared disbelieving. "Yes, sir," he said faintly. "If you say so, sir."

"I do, Fisker." Henricksen poked a finger at the ensign's uniformed chest. "I most certainly do."

"Aye, sir." Fisker snapped a salute without thinking, pivoted on his heel—neat as you please, like a little toy soldier on the parade grounds—and waited while Henricksen and Sikuuku closed up their quarters before leading them back down the hall.

"Like to meet the crew," Henricksen said casually, pacing along behind his escort.

Fisker looked around, nodded just once. "Yes, sir. Most of them are in there already, sir." He rounded the corner when they reached the main corridor, waved at the double doors at the far end. "I can roust the rest from their quarters, if you'd like."

"Much obliged," Henricksen told him, dipping his head. "Dinner time anyway." He slid his eyes to Sikuuku. "Good chance to see what kinda crew your man Kinsey lined up for us."

"Not all here yet, from what he told me." Sikuuku's gaze flickered toward him, just as quickly snapped away. "Fleet's fighting him for billets. Gave up enough for six crews but they balked at the rest."

"Did they now?"

Sikuuku nodded, shrugging uncomfortably. "Told me they won't cough up the rest until the chassis' stable."

Henricksen slowed, eyebrows lifting. "So you *did* know the Ravens aren't working yet."

"They *work*," Sikuuku insisted, tone defensive. "They just need a little finetuning. You heard him." He twisted, flailing a hand at the security door behind them. The RV-N hangar and the control room where they'd left Kinsey, looking down upon his kingdom.

"Right." Henricksen snorted. "Like getting them to stop pulverizing pilots."

Sikuuku stopped dead, giving him a dirty look, but Henricksen just flicked his fingers and kept going, following Fisker to the end of the hallway, turning right toward the double doors.

Squared out room on the other, filled with a dozen or so tables. Mess hall, if Henricksen ever saw one. Square tables and squarer chairs—one for each side. Chow line at the back of the room, bar to the left next to a doorway leading to a rec room with more chairs—softer ones, matched to a couple of worn out couches—and a pool table, of all things. Vid system casting flickering images from some action-horror flick on the wall.

Not exactly the best accompaniment for the dinner time meal. But then, neither was the bass thump issuing from the speakers in the rec room's ceiling. Strangled, tinny strains of muted, synth-pop trash music invading the mess hall proper.

"Smells good." Sikuuku sniffed at the air as the aroma of the chow line wafted to them, covering the station's mildew scent. Glanced at the rec room and grimaced, sticking a finger in his ear. "Atmosphere's a bit crappy."

Henricksen grunted, nodding, casting his eyes around the room.

Comfortable space, really. The first room they'd come across on Dragoon across that was any color than grey. Civ and military personnel both in that room, chattering away as they ate their meals. Picked up drinks at the bar and retreated to the comparative comfort of the rec room's stuffed chairs.

Well, military did. Civs collected in the room's front corners. Clustered together, giving the military wide berth. Glanced at the rec room but didn't go anywhere near it.

Henricksen noted it like he did so many things. Filing that tidbit of information away.

"Not bad," Sikuuku admitted. "I've seen better, but—"

"Attention on deck!" Movement in a far corner—chief in coveralls jumping to her feet as she barked out that order, killing the conversations in the room.

Chairs scraped across the floor as military shot up straight. Braced up and saluted the captain come unexpectedly into their midst.

Civvies glanced at each other, looking confused. Shambled uncertainly to their feet and just stood there, not knowing what to do.

Henricksen gave them a pass—civvies weren't required to salute. Swept his eyes across the military as he raised his hand and returned the salute. "As you were."

Crew relaxed, conversations resuming as they sank down into their chairs. Grabbed up beer mugs and abandoned utensils as they finished their meals.

Civvies got caught out again, poor saps. Weren't quite sure why they'd stood up in the first place and now here they were left wondering what had changed. They glanced at each, and at the military around them, making sure the crew *stayed* seated this time before following their lead. Plunked down in their chairs and leaned their heads together, throwing curious looks Henricksen's way.

Henricksen nodded to them, and to the military, pinched Fisker's sleeve between his fingers and pulled him close. "No more of that, ya hear me? Certain amount of formality's required in the military—I know that as well as anyone—but you tell the crew they can drop the whole 'attention on deck' thing from here on out."

Stupid bit of ceremony, in his opinion. Remnant of another time when military protocol included frequent reminders about who was in charge. Well, Henricksen didn't need that. Not his style. Not his style at all.

Fisker blinked, glancing around the room. "Yes, sir. Sorry, sir."

"No more of that either," Henricksen told him. "You're an ensign which means you're gonna screw up. *Frequently.* That's just the way it works."

Fisker's eyes widened, looking surprised, and scared, and slightly indignant, all at the same time.

Henricksen let go of his sleeve, looking Fisker up and down. "Beauty of being an ensign is no one expects you to do much of anything right. I'll tell you when you need to apologize, Fisker. 'Til then, you just drop the sorries."

"Aye, sir," Fisker mumbled, glancing at the crew scattered around the mess hall. "Food, sir?" He waved at the chow line across the room. "Beef and bell peppers tonight."

"Sounds good."

It didn't actually—"beef", in Henricksen's experience usually turned out to be some kind of brown-dyed soy mess—but Fisker had enough going on. He didn't need a grumpy captain telling him the food they served was most likely crap.

"Lead on, McDuff."

Fisker glanced down, eying the nametag on his chest uncertainly. Flashed an equally uncertain smile at Henricksen and set off, weaving a wandering path between the mess hall's tables as Sikuuku and Henricksen followed behind.

"Severely young ensign." Sikuuku touched Henricksen's arm, nodding at Fisker's back.

"Noticed that." Henricksen nodded.

Academy grad, if he had to guess, but without the usual Academy swagger. Just a wet-behind-the-ears junior officer scared spitless at a Black Ops assignment. Not the usual route for an ensign—OCS or otherwise. Ship, usually, not a station.

Hardly seemed fair, placing Fisker here so soon after graduation. Secret squirrel base like Dragoon was no place for an ensign. And Kinsey was a prick.

"Give him time. Great thing about ensigns is they're malleable." Henricksen smiled crookedly. "Not grumpy and set in their ways like you crusty old chiefs."

Sikuuku laughed softly, eyes flicking from Henricksen to the crew sitting at the tables around them. Watching them. Voices dropping to whispers, hands lifting to cover their lips as Henricksen and Sikuuku walked by.

Same drill with every new assignment. Scrub the smell out of the air and this could be any station. Any ship in the Meridian Alliance Fleet.

Except for those uniforms, Henricksen thought, eying the tables of crew to either side.

Dark uniforms here, every last one of them. Not the civvies in the corner, of course, but the rest of them...

Black on black like Fisker. Not a ship or station patch among them.

Henricksen touched at his shoulder, tracing *Hecate*'s torch and key with his finger. That patch marked him as different. Made him feel suddenly, unreasoningly conspicuous in his midnight blue uniform, ship's designation picked out in gold thread.

"New kids on the block." Sikuuku grimaced, sharing a look with Henricksen. "Hate being the new kid."

"No one likes being the new kid," Henricksen murmured, scanning the room.

Most of the crew wouldn't look at him. Glanced away quickly if they happened to catch Henricksen's eye. Even the civvies tucked up in their corner by the double doors.

Hint of suspicion there, actually. In the lines of the civilians' faces. Watched him warily, shucked forward and balanced on the edges of their seats. Like they might bolt at any moment. Like they were just biding their time. Waiting for their chance to escape.

And that odd, obvious pattern to the seating arrangements...

Henricksen cast his eyes around, noting that sharp divide again. Civvies sticking to the corners, military claiming everything else.

Strange dynamic, military and civilians housed together. Surprised Kinsey had done that, to be honest, but then, maybe it wasn't his idea.

Only so much space on a station, after all. And the RV-N project allotted just this one section for its personnel.

Henricksen nodded to a stiff-looking young man walking toward him—plate in one hand, glass of some kind of juice in the other. Waistcoat buttoned tight over a banded collar shirt. Shiny leather shoes, coifed hair slicked back on his head.

The engineer—he assumed that's what these civvies were, no other reason to house them here otherwise—blanched and ducked his head, hurrying past Henricksen to the civvie section of the mess hall. Plunked down and started shoveling food in his face, putting his back to Henricksen so he had a plausible reason not to look at him.

"Wimp."

Henricksen moved on, joining the queue at the chow line. Noticed something else while he shuffled his slow way forward, waiting his turn to grab food. Another subtle divide, this one less obvious than that between the civ and military personnel.

Not the collar devices—everyone wore those, enlisted and officers—nor the uniforms, either. All of the military here wore coveralls except Henricksen and Sikuuku. Every last uniformed person dressed in the same black on black on black. But the mechanic's uniforms sported a few extra pockets—storage space for hand tools and spare parts the RV-N crews' flight suits didn't need. And the mechanics sat separate from the others. Didn't mingled with the flight crews at all. In fact...

Henricksen twisted, taking another good look around. "You see that?" He touched at Sikuuku's arm, nodding to a nearby table, another shoved up against the wall.

Sikuuku looked at him, and at the two tables, shrugged his burly shoulders and shuffled another step along the line. "Not unusual for the enlisted and officers to sit separate."

"Not what I meant." He caught Sikuuku's eye, nodded to the room in general. "They're new. They're *all* new."

Sikuuku blinked, frowning. "Can't be. Program's been running for years."

"Maybe." Henricksen frowned himself, trying to explain what he saw.

People sitting in pairs, *sticking* to those pairings rather than surfing the room. *Huddled* together, all but ignoring the crew at the other tables.

"Look at 'em." He waved at the people at the tables. "Military, I mean. Ignore the civvies for now." Hard to read them. Civvies always seemed distant around the military, no matter what the situation. "Do any of them look all that comfortable to you?"

Sikuuku paused, considering. Sizing the room up. "No," he said slowly. "Not really. Chiefs in the corner, maybe." A nod to the personnel in question— anchors on their collars, heads bowed together, deep in conversation.

Ignoring Henricksen and Sikuuku for the most part, after that whole "attention on deck" thing they'd started. The only two people in the room, in fact, that didn't seem all that interested in either of the new arrivals.

"Rest of 'em..." Sikuuku frowned again, head shaking. "Might be right. Don't quite have the vibe of crew that's settled in."

Henricksen quirked an eyebrow, giving him a look. "Odd, wouldn't you say?"

Sikuuku's face darkened. "Fucking ridiculous is more like it. And before you ask, he didn't tell me. I swear. Kinsey said he needed crew, but he didn't—"

"'S'alright," Henricksen told him, raising a hand. "Intel operators always were a bunch of closed mouth assholes." He smiled ruefully. "Why should Kinsey be any different, just because he's your friend?"

"Told you. He's *not* my friend." Sikuuku grabbed a plate and shoved it at the mess cook, snatched it back when he loaded it and moved down the line.

Henricksen pursed his lips, watching him, letting Sikuuku move ahead. Mad—read that in Sikuuku's movements. The stiffness of his back. Angry and embarrassed at having talked Henricksen into this assignment only to arrive here and find things decidedly not as advertised.

Didn't blame him for being angry. Or for the situation either. Gunner wanted Black Ops and he got it. Just didn't take into account that Black Ops was about lies and obfuscation in addition to sneaking around.

So he let Sikuuku move ahead of him, giving him some space. Time to cool down. Grabbed a plate for himself while the gunner chatted up the woman working the dessert section—older lady, handsome, though not quite pretty.

Not that it really mattered. Sikuuku chatted up pretty much anyone who bothered to give him the time of day.

"'Ere ya are, Cap'n." The line cook smiled widely—crooked teeth, a couple of them missing. Talked like a pirate—Henricksen wasn't quite sure what to make of that. Winked at Henricksen as he passed over a plate.

Beef and bell peppers—standard mess hall fare. Noodles of indeterminate nature. Some kind of freeze-dried, overcooked vegetable that almost resembled squash. Not all that bad, all things considered. Nothing fancy, but better than some stations offered. A vast improvement over the reconstituted stuff they'd been fed on the transport.

Henricksen nodded his thanks to the gap-toothed cook as he moved on down the line. Scanned the half-dozen desserts on offer while Sikuuku chattered away with his new girlfriend, selecting a slice of cake that smelled strongly of coconut. "Drinks?" he asked, when Sikuuku paused for breath.

The dessert server smiled, looking him up and down. Pointed to a row of spigots sticking out of the wall. "Water and juices," she said, and leaned forward, pointed her finger toward the bar. "Beer on tap, so long as you're not on duty."

"Pass for now. Water'll do just fine."

"Your funeral." The cook shrugged, turning her smile on Sikuuku—knowing, suggestive, hinting that she'd like to lock him in a room and get to know him better. Winked at the gunner—slow closing of one eyelid, lip caught between her teeth—as she leaned across the chow line and slipped a couple of extra cookies onto his plate. "Don't tell," she said, laying a finger across her lips.

"Never do." Sikuuku returned the smile. The wink for good measure. Gathered up his plate and nabbed a drink—water, just like Henricksen—before turning around and walking over to an empty table. "Still got it," he said, hooking a chair with his toe.

Henricksen claimed the chair across from him. "What is it with you and lunch ladies, anyway?"

"Dunno." Sikuuku shrugged. "But they've got cookies, and they like to give 'em to me." He picked up a cookie and bit it in half, looking quite pleased with himself. "You. Ensign Boy." Sikuuku waved to Fisker, pointed to the seat beside him. "Sit."

Fisker stopped a few steps away, eyes flicking from Henricksen's table to the others around it. Nervous about sitting with them—that came through clearly. Nervous about being an ensign sharing dinner conversation with the senior staff. "Not really all that hungry," he said, setting his plate down on a nearby table. "I'll roust the rest of the crew while you—"

"Sit," Henricksen ordered, kicking the chair out. "Most of the crew's here, from what I can tell. Rest'll trickle in when they get hungry."

"Yes, sir. If—if you say so, sir." Another look around the room, as if hoping one of the other crewmembers would save him, and Fisker retrieved his abandoned food. Walked over to Henricksen's table and slid into the chair beside him.

SEVEN

Fisker devoured his food in silence, each forkful a precisely timed and meticulously executed movement: bite of meat, bite of veg, sip of drink—repeat, and repeat, and repeat again.

Academy training again, that rhythmic consuming. Eating in perfect squares. Some kind of sick game the command cadre had, making the cadets suffer through meals in that manner. Took a while to break them of it. Retrain the shiny new ensigns the Academy pumped out to eat like normal people again.

Stupid tradition. Pointless. A holdover from the old days, like the sharp creases and starched uniforms.

Sikuuku, of course, found it all highly amusing. Sat there chewing his own food with a big, goofy grin on his face.

Nudged at Henricksen's elbow, and started copying the ensign. Exaggerating the movements. Having a bit of fun at his expense.

"Grow up, would ya?" Henricksen forked a piece of beef into his mouth, giving the gunner a sour look. Chewed and swallowed—synth, for sure, though better than the soy crap, likely some lab-grown type of meat—and snatched up another bite, eyes flicking to Fisker now and then, watching him methodically clean his plate.

Dessert sat untouched near his elbow. Academy training again. Couldn't have the cadets spoiling their meal by eating their dessert—that just wouldn't do.

"So, was it Sosholo or Yunshinshin?" Henricksen scooped up his knife and sawed through a piece of beef as Fisker froze, eyes lifting, fork half-raised to his mouth.

"I'm—I'm sorry." Fisker blinked, lowering his fork, folding his hands in his lap. "Was what, sir?"

"You're Academy. I can tell that from your collar." Henricksen pointed his fork's tines at Fisker's crisply pressed uniform, collar points the very picture of starched perfection, the rest of it just so. "Can always pick you Academy boys out 'cause you're uniforms are so goddamned purty." He smiled crookedly, applying fork and knife to an innocent piece of synth meat. The tines speared it, holding it place while the knife slid through the piece of meat, scraping sharply against the plate beneath. "So was it Sosholo or Yunshinshin that spat you out?" Henricksen asked, lifting a bite to his mouth.

"N-Neither, sir," Fisker stammered, flush creeping up his cheeks.

"Neither? Really?" Henricksen chewed and swallowed, eyebrows lifting in surprise. "But you *are* Academy."

Fisker licked his lips, head dipping. "Saint-Cyr, sir. Graduated last spring."

"Saint-Cyr?" Henricksen stared, honestly surprised. "Didn't know that Old Earth Academy was still running."

Long history to that place. The fact that Henricksen—who'd never seen Old Earth, nor particularly cared to—even knew about it spoke volumes about its reputation.

He slid his eyes to Sikuuku, giving the gunner a considering look. "Sounds like you and Ensign Fisker here have something in common."

"You're—you're from Earth, sir?" Fisker looked desperately hopeful.

Not many Earthers out here, so far from that old home world. Hard for them to fit in with others in the Fleet because of it. That, and the stigma most held against them. Stupid thing, really. Result of the ties back to Old Earth loosening over the years. Cradle of humanity it might be—the genesis of the Meridian Alliance and part of it still, but time passed, and Earth... Earth became separate. Different. Ancient and outdated, military minds running centuries behind the far flung ships of the Fleet.

And now here came Fisker—young and naïve, an ensign so eager to please.

"I am," Sikuuku told him—solemn now, the laughter and teasing entirely gone. He snatched up his napkin, wiping at his lips before tossing it back down. "But I'm not a sir. Chief Gunner's Mate." He tapped the stars and anchor on his collar, the winged badge on his chest. "You call me Chief, Fisker, and I call you Ensign. You do that and we'll get along just fine."

"Yes, sir. I mean, aye, sir. I mean, Chief." Fisker blushed even brighter. Started to salute before realizing that wasn't needed and nervously shoving his hand back down.

"There ya go." Sikuuku winked and leaned over, punching Fisker lightly on the shoulder. "Now grab me a beer, Ensign. It was a long, boring trip in and I could severely use a drink."

Fisker pushed back his chair, abandoning his knife and fork and the remains of his meal as he headed for the bar to one side.

"Grab one for the Captain while you're at," Sikuuku called after him.

"And one for yourself," Henricksen added, killing the mess hall conversation for the second time that evening. "What?" he asked, as heads lifted, eyes turning his way. "Can't a guy buy an ensign a beer?"

Silence from the crew around them, everyone frowning and glancing at each other like they had no idea what to do. Silence that stretched on and on forever, blanketing the room.

And then a chief burst out laughing—squared-faced woman tucked up at a table in the corner, brown hair the color of tree bark pulled back in a messy ponytail, blue eyes like a stormy sky—and the entire mood of the room changed.

"Spill some for me while you're at it, Fisker!" she cheered, holding up her mug. "In fact..." A smile and the chief climbed up on her table, lifting her glass high. "Drinks are on me tonight, boys and girls. Everyone gets a round!" She waved grandly, laughing at the jeers and catcalls, bowing at the waist to acknowledge the ironic clapping as she climbed back down.

Not exactly a magnanimous offer, buying the crew drinks. Beer came free on the station, after all. Still, it was the thought that mattered, more than the actual expenditure of funds.

Fisker busied himself at the bar as the conversations around the room resumed, voices filling the mess hall with low, droning buzz. No bartender here, which mean everything was self-service. And Fisker, by default, voted to serve everyone on the chief's behalf.

He filled up mugs, pouring foaming beer from a spigot, lining up a half dozen at a time. Shucked around the bar to deliver that first round to the nearest tables before hurrying back to pour more suds.

Civvies watched it all from their corner, looking increasingly uncomfortable the more drinks Fisker handed out. Finished up their meals in a hurry and quietly retreated, slipping circumspectly through the mess hall's double doors.

Henricksen noted it, and considered saying something to Kinsey. Decided to leave it alone for now. Until he got the lay of the land.

"Ensigns." Sikuuku snorted, smiling to himself as Fisker bustled about. "Adorable."

"Prettier than you. That's for sure."

"I'd say cook over there feels differently." Sikuuku scooped up a cookie and bit into it, chewing slowly, smug smile playing about his lips. "Don't see *you* gettin' any free cookies, old man."

"Nothin's free, Akiwane." Henricksen slid his eyes to the cook at the dessert station, tilted his head, giving Sikuuku a meaningful look. Sat back when Fisker dropped three mugs in front of him and plunked down, scooching his chair close to the table. "Much obliged, Fisker." Henricksen snagged a glass and raised it in salute.

Fisker smiled sheepishly—pleased and embarrassed at the same time. Glanced around and saw everyone drinking—Henricksen and Sikuuku included—and, with the slightest of hesitations, collected the third from the table, pulling it toward his plate.

"Finish your meal first," Henricksen told him. "Young buck like you, drinking beer on a half-empty stomach." He shook his head hard. "Be drunk inside of a minute. Probably dancing on the table, causing all kinds of ruckus."

"No, sir. Never." Fisker looked mortified that he'd even suggest such a thing. He pushed the mug away, sending it sliding across the table on an express trip to the floor.

Henricksen snagged it just as it reached the edge, stopping it dead with his fingers. "Joke, Fisker." He caught the ensign's gaze and held it, pushed the mug of beer back to him, setting it beside Fisker's half-full plate. "Beer's on Chief." A nod to the woman in the corner, drink clasped firmly between both hands. "But you eat first, ya hear?"

"Yes, sir." Fisker eyed the beer mug sweating on the table. Picked up his fork and finished his meal under Henricksen's watchful gaze.

"Atta boy." Henricksen sat back, smiling, sipping at his beer.

Awful stuff they served here. Typical mess hall half-piss, half-water swill. But it was beer, and he was thirsty. Besides, crew was watching. And appearances mattered.

"So, who is she?" he asked, nodding to the table in the corner. The chief who'd bought everyone beer.

Fisker twisted, taking a look. "Shaw. Runs the mech gang on the hangar deck. They do maintenance and adjustments on the RV-Ns."

"Know what she's doing?"

Fisker shrugged, forking a last bite into his mouth to clear his plate. "Kinsey recruited her off of *Cerberus.*"

"*Cerberus.*" Sikuuku whistled appreciatively. "I'd say that's a "yes"."

Henricksen grunted noncommittally, eyeing Shaw in the corner as he took another pull at his beer.

Second sip tasted no better than the first one. Henricksen grimaced, swallowing it down. Caught Shaw's eye when she looked over at him, dipped his head and raised his beer in acknowledgment as she smiled and returned the gesture.

"What about her tablemate?" Henricksen asked, nodding to the dark-haired woman sitting next to Shaw. Slight and slim, skin the color of burnt umber, eyes like amber nuggets. "What can you tell me about her?"

"Chief Kapoor." Fisker frowned, thinking. "Came in last week. She and Shaw were stationed together somewhere." Another frown, Fisker's eyes dropping to the table as he dredged something from his memory banks. "Dreadnought, maybe? I want to say *Gorgon*, but I'm not sure that's right."

"She's flight crew?" Sikuuku turned around, inspecting the chief sitting with Shaw. Examining her in an entirely different light.

"Scan tech," Fisker told him. "You'll like her." Quick smile—lips lifting then dropping again.

"Oh yeah?" Sikuuku folded his arms, giving Fisker a flat-eyed look. "Why's that?"

"Well, she's—" Fisker swallowed hard, coughed and tried again. "It's just that she's—"

"Bossy and blunt and knows how to keep her crew in line? *That* what you're trying to say?"

Fisker nodded, shoulders hunching, clenched fists raised as if he expected a punch.

Not Sikuuku's style, though, abusing ensigns. Liked to make fun of them now and then, but Henricksen had never known him to knock fists with anyone that didn't deserve it.

He sat there a moment—lips pursed, considering the ensign, eyes flicking to Kapoor in the corner. Grunted and started chuckling as he lifted his beer mug to his lips. "You're right, Fisker." He raised the glass, saluting before taking a drink. "Blunt and bossy are pretty much my type."

Fisker relaxed noticeably. Smiled and took a pull at his own drink, looking visibly relieved.

"So what about the rest of them?" Henricksen waved his glass at the uniforms gathered around the mess hall's tables.

"Well, there's Sullivan and Malloy." Fisker nodded to a couple of mechanics a few tables over. "They're under Shaw. Keep the deck gang in line." He paused, thinking, looking at Henricksen across the table. "I don't suppose you're all that interested in the mechanics at the moment, though, are you, sir?"

"Not that I'm not interested," Henricksen told him. "Just more concerned about the flight crews right now."

Fisker nodded, scanning the room, eyes skipping across the tables before settling on two loudmouths shooting pool in the rec room. "Baldini and Petros." He peeled a finger from his beer mug and pointed to a squat, balding spark plug of a man—dark hair shorn to a fuzz in an attempt to hide the thinning—leaning over the pool table, cue stick in hand. Angled that finger to one side and zeroed it in on a barrel-chested Adonis leaning against the wall.

Full head of hair on that one—a short cap of thick, dark curls. Smile on his face—confident, cocky, the kind of smug, self-satisfied grin the very rich and privileged were prone to wear. Handsome devil—Henricksen gave him that—despite the conspicuously blue chalk mark smeared between his eyes.

Lieutenants' bars on the Adonis's collar, and that of his pool shooting friend. Officers, then, and flight crew, apparently. Which made the both of them—

"Pilots?" Henricksen glanced at Fisker for confirmation and saw him nod.

"Came in two weeks ago. Baldini," a nod to the shooter, "came off a Titan. Think Petros," aka, Mr. Curly Hair, Smudgy Temple, "was on an Aurora. Maybe a Dreadnought." Fisker caught his lip between his teeth, thinking a moment. Opened his mouth to say something and then glanced at Henricksen—at the stars on his collar—and seemed to change his mind. "First rate, from what I hear."

Didn't sound like he believed it. The guilty flush that crept up his cheeks. And from the way he looked at Henricksen...didn't like them. Read that clearly in Fisker's face.

Sikuuku saw it, too. Caught Henricksen's eye, eyebrows lifting in interest. "Troublemakers?"

Fisker ducked his head, shrugging uncomfortably. "Classmates. Sosholo," he said, sneaking a look at Henricksen. "Tight. Ever since they got here."

"Ring knockers. Lucky us." Sikuuku swirled his drink, watching the two lieutenants shoot pool.

Baldini lined up his shot, but seemed to change his mind at the last second. Flicked his fingers at Petros, nodding to someone sitting on a couch.

Smiled wickedly as he adjusted the cue stick's angle and cracked off a shot, midnight eight ball flying free of the table, connecting with the back of the unsuspecting crewman's head.

She doubled over, clutching at her head. Leapt off the couch spitting curses as she marched over and slapped the pool stick from Baldini's hand.

An argument ensued, the crewman tech rightly angry, Baldini proclaiming his innocence, insisting the cue stick slipped. Henricksen thought about intervening, and then decided to let it go. Use the opportunity to get a sense of the hierarchy around here.

"Apparently they don't like enlisted any better than ensigns."

Dark look on Sikuuku's face. Dark and disapproving as the argument continued to escalate.

"Or Earthers," Fisker said softly, eyes lifting to the gunner's face.

Sikuuku grunted and sat back, sharing a look with Henricksen sitting across the table. "Couple of first class pricks Kinsey assigned to us."

"Pricks I can deal with," Henricksen told him. "In fact, I'm giving *you* license to deal with them *for* me."

"Now we're talkin'," Sikuuku murmured, chuckling low in his throat.

Fisker looked at him, and at Henricksen, brow wrinkling in confusion.

"Who else?" Henricksen flicked his fingers at the remaining uniforms. "What about those two?" he asked, nodding to a couple of chiefs standing by the bar.

"Schenck and Grunewald." Fisker nodded in approval. "Steady, sir. Reliable."

Schenck had the tall, thin build of a mad scientist. Grunewald looked like an unfinished statue—everything thick and square and hard as stone.

"Better be." Sikuuku tapped the anchors on his collar. "Chief," he said. "Reliable's job one."

Fisker's cheeks colored.

Sikuuku slumped, sighing heavily. "Who?" he asked. "Who's ass do I have to kick?"

Fisker licked his lips, eyes flicking around the room.

"Easier to just spill it now," Henricksen told him. "Sikuuku'll sniff it out anyway."

"Nunez."

"Where?"

Fisker hesitated, twisted searching the other side of the room. "Doesn't appear to be here at the moment." He faced back around, reaching for his beer mug, lifted it, sipping quickly before setting it back down.

Picked it up and took another sip immediately after—nervous gesture, trying to cover something up.

"Who else?" Sikuuku prompted when Fisker raised the mug a third time.

Fisker froze, glass tilted, bit his lip and set it back down. "Mahal," he said grudgingly. "She's—She's..." He flushed brightly, looking apologetic all over again. "She's also not here at the moment, sir."

"Lemme guess." Sikuuku folded his arms, head tilting. "She and Nunez are off having a good time."

Pool and drinking were all well and good, but mealtime offered a rare opportunity at privacy. A chance for two fools to get together and enjoy more pleasurable pursuits than the rec room offered.

Fisker shrugged, flush deepening as he dropped his eyes. Confirmed Sikuuku's suspicions without saying a word. Sat there tracing patterns in the water ring his beer mug left on the table, looking so damned guilty Henricksen just *knew* there was more to this than the ensign let on.

"Officer?" he guessed. "Mahal one of the pilots Kinsey recruited?"

"Yes, sir." Soft voice from Fisker. The barest whisper of breath. Wouldn't look at Henricksen while he said it—too embarrassed, too ashamed. Fisker's face said it all. Betrayed every last thought in his head.

"Chief and a lieutenant." Sikuuku grabbed up his drink, shaking his head. "What a mess."

Fleet didn't strictly forbid fraternization between crewmates—things happened during long deployments, birds and the bees and such. But pairings between officers and enlisted often led to trouble. *Usually* did, in Henricksen's experience.

"Separate them." He locked eyes with Sikuuku across the table. "Run 'em hard in training. Put 'em on different flight crews, with different rotations. Can't watch 'em all the time, can't keep 'em from shackin' up when everyone else is sleepin' but we can whip the piss out of 'em. Tire 'em out so bad the rack-side mambo will be the *last* thing on their minds."

Sikuuku nodded, smiling wickedly. "Hard to be in the mood for luvvin' when you can't even keep your eyes open."

He drained his glass and set it down, throwing thoughtful glances at the mess hall doors. Dug around in a pocket, retrieving a pencil nub and a tiny little notebook, laying the latter open, using the former to scratch out some notes. Record a few names.

EIGHT

People shifted around them—crew finishing meals, collecting fresh beers from the bar before retiring to the rec room to one side. Joining Petros and Baldini at the pool table. Slipping into the sofas and chairs to watch some trash action vid that was short on plot, but chock-'o-block full of explosions, and swearing, and nudity—the trifecta of terrible taste.

Henricksen smiled to himself, enjoying the familiarity of the setting. Each ship had its own unique rhythm; stations and planetary bases the same. But mess halls and rec rooms were identical the Fleet over: bad food and cheap drinks, cut-rate vids and endless hours of pool, and card games, and other mindless activities to fill the empty hours.

Missed that about *Hecate.* Missed a lot of things about the Aurora.

Hecate.

The smile slipped, reminiscence replaced by self-recrimination. A hundredweight of crushing regret.

"Sir?" Fisker eyed him worriedly. "Is something wrong? Did I—Did I do some—?"

"Fine, Fisker. You're fine." Henricksen nodded to the ensign, offering a small, encouraging smile. Let *Hecate* go for now, because this wasn't the time or the place to indulge his melancholy remembrances.

Deal with that later.

When he and Sikuuku had the luxury of getting good and drunk.

"Continue," Henricksen ordered, sipping at his beer, waving at the people in the room.

Fisker licked his lips, looking like he wasn't quite sure he should. Nodded and glanced around, picking out a table of four playing cards. "Abboud and Ahmadi. Scan techs."

Both dark-haired and umber-skinned like Kapoor. One tall and hatchet-faced, the other softer, rounder, with wide-set eyes.

Woman sitting across from them—wavy brown hair, snub-nosed face. Almost pretty, but not quite. Boisterous laugh, smile that showed all her teeth.

Liked that in a woman. Looks came and went but a sense of humor…hold onto a woman like that.

"That's Pritchard." Fisker smiled to himself. "Cheats at cards," he confided. "She and Fontaine." A nod to the sandy-haired, boyish looking crewman sitting next to Pritchard. "They've been fleecing just about everyone the last couple of weeks."

Sikuuku smiled crookedly. "Anyone figure it out yet?"

"Nope." Fisker smiled back.

"'Sides you, of course." Henricksen sipped at his drink, trying not to choke, studying the ensign across the rim. "Notice a lot of things, don't you, Fisker? Got just about everyone here figured out."

"Guess so, sir." Fisker flushed again, shrugging uncomfortably. "My job, sir. Ensign in charge of admin and personnel." He showed his teeth in a rueful smile, raised a hand and flipped a mocking salute. "In addition to being Mr. Kinsey's batman, of course."

Henricksen blinked blankly. "A what-man?"

"Batman, sir. Valet?" he offered when Henricksen shook his head.

Sikuuku leaned over, not-quite-whispering behind his hand. "Small words, Fisker. Captain here don't cotton to those fancy-pants titles and such."

"Shut it, Chief." Henricksen glared at Sikuuku, flicked his eyes to Fisker squirming uncomfortably, taking a sudden and intense interest in the tabletop in front of him. "Speak plain, Fisker. Lose the shiny, obscure words."

Fisker opened his mouth, closed it and just sighed. "Lackey, sir," he said, shoulders slumping. "I'm Mr. Kinsey's lackey."

"Lackey," Henricksen grunted. "Well, now. We'll just see about that."

Sikuuku looked at him, at Fisker's freckled, dispirited face. "That what you trained for, Ensign?" Chief's voice now—a half-angry, half-disapproving bark Sikuuku had mastered over the years. "Academy drill all that spit and polish, 'yes, sir' and 'no, sir' crap into you just so you can go off and play lackey to some senior civ administrator?"

Fisker stiffened, bright spots of color blooming on his cheeks. "No," he said, jaw set, eyes flashing. "Engineering, sir. Engines are my specialization."

"Told you before, Ensign. I'm not your sir." Sikuuku's eyes flashed, too, staring in challenge.

Fisker, for once, didn't back down. "Chief," he corrected, raising his glass, inclining his head. Tilted it and finished it off as well, leaving Henricksen no choice but to follow suit.

Didn't want the rest of it, frankly, but he gulped it to be polite. Slid the empty across the table, snagging Sikuuku's mug as well. "Refill, Fisker." He tapped a finger against the glass in the ensign's hand. "Refills all around."

Fisker smiled, nodding, scooped up their glasses and left without a word. Returned a couple of minutes later with fresh ones foaming over with beer. Doled them out as he sat down, taking small sips of his drink as his eyes scanned the room.

Good habit, that. One Henricksen espoused himself.

"How long have you been here, Fisker?" He leaned back, taking his drink with him, couching it against his stomach as he stared across the table at his oh-so-observant ensign.

Fisker blinked, pointing a finger at his chest. "Me, sir? Three weeks, sir. Give or take." He flashed a smile, shifting in his seat.

"Longer than the others, then." Sikuuku reached for his drink, watching the ensign intently.

"Shaw was already here." Fisker sipped his beer, nodding to the chief in the corner. "And Mr. Kinsey, of course. The rest came in after." He waved vaguely, indicating everyone else in the room.

"Everyone?" Henricksen sat up straight, setting his drink on the table. "Civvies too?"

Fisker nodded.

"Well now, isn't *that* interesting."

"That's one word for it." Sikuuku snorted, frown creasing his face.

Fisker blinked, brow furrowing as he looked from Sikuuku to Henricksen. "Why is that interesting?"

Henricksen tilted his head, eyebrows lifting. "Project's been underway for years, right?"

"Yeah," Fisker said slowly, looking no less confused.

"Military rotate in and out on a fairly regular basis, but swapping *all* of them out at once?" Henricksen touched at the rim of his drink, tracing its circle with a finger. "Bit unusual, wouldn't you say?"

Fisker thought on that a moment. "Yes, sir. I suppose so, sir."

"Civvies now…" Henricksen's eyes shifted to the tables in the front corner—empty now, with the civilian engineers all gone. "Engineers tend to stay put. Might lose one or two along the way, but it's damned stupid changing out an entire engineering team. 'Specially when you're dealing with an experimental starship like the RV-N."

"Yes, sir. If you say so, sir," Fisker murmured uncertainly.

Sikuuku slid a look Henricksen's way, tattooed face troubled. Sipped at this drink, listening intently as Fisker resumed his staff evaluation, rattling off information that Henricksen only half-absorbed.

Knew he should pay attention, but he was already overloaded. Never had been any good with names.

Lucky if I remember half of 'em in the morning, he admitted, but he'd get them eventually. With enough repetition.

Always did, every assignment. Til then he had Fisker, and the records system to shore him up. Match names with faces and specializations. Help him figure out the best pairings of crew for these high-tech, experimental ships.

Figure out the AI, eventually—no idea what mindset they'd used as the basis for these Ravens, nothing at all in system about prior deployments, which made him suspect they were probably new.

But all that would come later. First order of business involved humans. Picking out the RV-N crews.

Four man ops teams in the Ravens: pilot, gunner, scan tech and engineer all working in unison, crewing the ships together. Early designs showed a fifth for comms—pretty much standard for a starship's bridge—but no matter how they arranged the stations, they simply couldn't find enough room. Not without significant modifications, anyway, which just wasn't going to happen this late in the game.

Modifications meant money—funding Kinsey obviously didn't have, considering the hard time he was having just getting billets for crew.

Fisker prattled on for about five minutes before the double doors to the mess hall burst open, cutting him off. In walked a whipcord-thin lieutenant—blond hair buzzed into a square-sided flat top—and an equally thin, ebon-skinned woman, with dark hair clipped tight to her skull, and eyes that sparkled like topaz stars.

Determined looking pair. As purposeful looking as Henricksen had ever run across. They stopped dead as the double doors closed behind them, staring in surprise at Henricksen and Sikuuku for a few of seconds before remembering themselves and bracing up hard. Arms bent, hands angling precisely as they snapped off matching, pitch perfect salutes.

Fisker leaned close, pitching his voice low. "Janssen and Adaeze," he said, nodding to flat-top on the left, the sable-skinned woman to his right.

Lieutenants. Startled at finding a captain in their midst. Probably wondering why no one had bothered to warn them.

"As you were," Henricksen nodded, offering his own, slightly less perfect salute. "Drinks are on Chief." He pointed at his glass, hooked a thumb at Shaw in the corner, smiling to himself as the lieutenants nodded and looked at each other, shrugged in unison and walked over to the bar. "More fraternization?" he asked, sliding a look Fisker's way.

"What? No!" Fisker looked startled. "No, sir. Not them."

"You sure?" Sikuuku stared after Adaeze, admiring the view from behind. "I know if *I* were that boy I'd be tempted to do some fraternizing."

Good looking woman—no doubt about that. Henricksen would've been tempted too, once upon a time. Couldn't look at them that way once you became captain, though. Saw one too many commanding officers kicked out of the military completely for offering dancing lessons to the juniors in their private quarters.

No *way* Henricksen was going out that way. Wasn't a prideful man, but he didn't want *that* kind of reputation following him around.

"Knock it off," he growled, kicking Sikuuku under the table. "Bad enough we got Nunez and Mahal knocking boots in quarters. Last thing I need is you ogling that pilot's ass every time she turns around."

"Fine," Sikuuku huffed, slouching in his chair. "Shame, though. *Really* nice ass. 'Specially in that flight suit. Am I right, Fisker?" He smiled knowingly, nudging the ensign in the side.

Fisker stammered something unintelligible, blushed and buried his face in his drink. But Henricksen caught him glancing up and around every now and then, sneaking glances Adaeze's way. Wistful look on his face while he watched her, like he wished he were just a little bit older. Or bolder. Anything other than a very junior, very inexperienced ensign.

"Been there, kid." Henricksen smiled at the startled look Fisker threw his way. "Pilots, though..." He frowned, thinking, shook his head hard. "You just be careful, Fisker. Pilot like that'll break your heart."

Sikuuku glanced over, face indignant. "I get kicked for admiring her ass, but Junior here gets love lessons?"

"Junior doesn't have to keep this lot in line. You do."

Sikuuku scowled, scooping up his glass. Drained half of it in one gulp and slammed it back down.

"Grumpy old cuss."

"Takes one to know one, Grandpa."

Henricksen laughed, raised a hand and stifled a yawn. Rubbed at his eyes and slouched in his chair, realizing just how weary he was. "Hard to believe after three days of sheer boredom, but I'm wrecked. And this beer is terrible." He swirled his glass, grimaced and put it down. Shoved it to the middle of the table and wiped his hand on his pants leg for good measure. "Your choice if you want to stay and mingle a while, Chief, but I for one, am heading to bed."

Sikuuku looked at him, and at the mug in his hand. Considered the laughing crew playing pool behind him and shrugged his burly shoulders, draining his glass dry. "Think I'll stay a bit. See if I can charm some of your young lieutenants out of their hard-earned pay." He flashed a smile and pushed back his chair, standing up. "What about you, Junior? Wanna learn how to shoot pool?"

"Me?" Fisker blinked, caught entirely off-guard. "I—uh—well I, uh—" He glanced across the table. "Would you—would you mind, sir?"

Henricksen smiled crookedly. "Be my guest. Just don't bet against him," he warned, nodding to Sikuuku across the table. "You'll just be throwing your money away."

"Yes, sir." Fisker shoved his chair back, nearly knocking it over in his haste. "Thank you, sir."

"Fisker," Henricksen called as the ensign turned away. "I don't need a lackey. You understand?"

"Sir?" Fisker frowned, head tilting, clearly *not* understanding at all.

"You're an officer, Fisker. A green-as-grass ensign, granted, but an officer just the same. And despite what he may think, Kinsey doesn't own you. You're done with all the fetch and carry. You're flight crew, starting tomorrow."

"But Mr. Kinsey—"

"I'll deal with Kinsey. Don't you worry about that. Now go." Henricksen flicked his fingers, waving the ensign away. "Have some fun."

"Yes, sir. Thank you, sir." Fisker smiled uncertainly, nodded and took off for the rec room.

Sikuuku started after him, but Henricksen grabbed his arm, holding him still while Fisker moved away. "Watch out for him." He flick his eyes at Fisker, nodding at the ensign's back. "Petros and Baldini... I've seen their type before. Stuck up pricks who think chewing up ensigns and enlisted is some kind of sport. Don't know Fisker—may wash out in the next few weeks—but I at least want him to get a fair chance. Understand me?"

The gunner looked at him, and at Fisker standing by the pool table. "Aye, sir," he said, flashing a smile. Flipped a smart-ass salute—Sikuuku's specialty, reserved for assholes and Henricksen, when it was just the two of them alone— and stuffed his hands in his pockets, whistling tunelessly as he ambled away.

Leaving Henricksen to buss up the table, dumping plates and utensils in a bin by the chow line, dropping beer mugs at the bar. A last look at the rec room— everyone smiling and laughing, Fisker sticking close to Sikuuku, watching his every move—and he wended his way through the tables, nodding to Janssen and Adaeze as he passed.

Halfway to the double doors and he spotted Shaw watching him. Slowed and took a good, long look.

Of them all, Shaw was the only one that seemed settled. She and her drinking partner, Kapoor, though even Kapoor looked around a lot. Sized up every person that entered the room.

Something to that, Henricksen thought, measuring the vibe of the room again. *Everyone new, all the old crew swapped out. Something to that.*

Something *important*, he sensed. Damned if he knew what it was, though. Kinsey's doing, without a doubt. Maybe his fault. Pissed off the Brass and lost his funding at some point. Had to start over, begging and borrowing to fill his tin cup.

Henricksen made a mental note to talk to Kinsey about that. Find out what happened. Figure out what other surprises this Black Ops project had in store for him.

Shaw might know something.

His eyes drifted back to that corner. To Shaw leaning casually, comfortably in her chair. Smiling—it suited her—as she and Kapoor chatted and sipped their beer.

She raised her mug when she caught Henricksen looking. Emptied it in one go and slammed it down, calling for another. Laughing aloud.

Good laugh—that suited her too. Liked Shaw right away. Wouldn't mind getting to know her better.

But first he had to get those birds flying. Get crew trained and ready to test out the RV-Ns.

Henricksen sighed, feeling a weight of weariness pressing at his shoulders. Making his legs feel like two impossible heavy, wooden logs. He shoved the mess hall's double doors open, exiting with the sound of pool ball's *clacking,* Shaw's laughter ringing in his ears. Made his slow way back to his quarters and opened the door, stood there a while, staring at the rooms on the other side.

Suite felt strange, *looked* strange from the hallway. No shelves for knick-knacks and personal possessions like he'd had on *Hecate.* The two Titans he'd commanded before her. No windows looking out on the stars either. In fact, he was hard put to find one single thing about those rooms that even *approached* giving them character.

Ten-meter-square cell—that's what they gave him. A tiny box of a room with a smaller, equally square box attached. A couch and two chairs for comfort. A desk shoved in a corner with a system link-up inside. Wardrobe and chest of drawers in the bedroom. Hard bed for sleeping on if he was tired enough to manage it.

Private bathroom, at least. That was something. Hated sharing a bathroom with others. Officers could be pigs, no matter what their rank.

"Home sweet home," Henricksen muttered, stepping inside, pulling the door closed.

He spun the wheel until it sealed up tight, wandered over to the couch and collapsed onto its unforgiving surface. Sat there and surveyed his captain's quarters. His home on Dragoon for the next few weeks. Or months. Or years. However long this assignment lasted.

Second consideration went better than the first. Now that he was actually *in* the room, he decided he didn't mind it being small. Nothing to put in it anyway.

Besides his own tired self, of course. Wished there was a window—missed that about *Hecate,* best part of being in space was the stars.

Windowless Dragoon, with its plasmetal and cement hallways, its grey-on-grey dreariness reminded him of a dungeon. Some kind of godforsaken hole in the ground where they locked people away. Left them to die.

Henricksen shook himself, putting that lovely image aside. "Need to get that bird flying," he muttered, looking around. "Get back to the stars before I go crazy sitting in this bunker."

Laughter drifted to his ears, coming from somewhere down the hall. Muted conversation with it, cutting off as a hatch screeched open and slammed heavily closed.

Crew, he thought, smiling. *My crew.*

And a ship out there waiting. A new AI, a whole new chassis to figure out.

"Hopefully the goddamn thing doesn't kill me." He winced, regretting the words immediately. Rubbed at his face, pressing his fingertips against his eyelids until he saw stars.

Remembered *Hecate* exploding. Saw her die all over again.

"Damn. God damn." He sighed shakily, pushing to his feet. Wandered through the open doorway into the bedroom and stopped there, blinking as the lights cut on.

Uniform laid out on the bed in front of him: black on black, just like Fisker's. Nametag on the left breast, stars on the collar. More uniforms in the wardrobe when he checked, and some personals in the attached bathroom.

Everything he needed, courtesy of Kinsey.

And Fisker.

Ensign must've done this. Sent someone to retrieve them from the admin section. Damn sure Kinsey wouldn't have bothered. Not when that stiff-assed son-of-a-bitch hadn't wanted Henricksen here in the first place.

He stared at the uniforms laid out on the bed in front of him, hand drifting to *Hecate*'s patch on his shoulder. Picked up the pants and matching jacket and stowed them in the wardrobe with the others. Chucked the boots they'd left him in there as well. Sat down on the bed and stripped off his old uniform—*Hecate*'s uniform, dark blue and silver—the black boots he'd just broken in. Held them in his hands, wondering what to do with them now that *Hecate* was gone.

"Should probably just burn it all."

He'd never wear it again, anyway. Not with *Hecate* dead. But burning it felt like sacrilege. Felt *wrong* after all they'd had been through together. So he folded everything neatly and stowed it away inside the wardrobe, keeping the jacket for now, with its torch and keys patch. The midnight blue trousers, those broken in and oh-so-comfortable boots.

Only thing left of *Hecate* now, that uniform. His and Sikuuku's, those of the hundred and fifty crew that safely made it off her before she blew. Suppose there was a copy of her AI someplace, but a copy wasn't her. Not the *real Hecate.* Not the one he knew.

Copy lacked her memories. The experiences she picked up along the way. Two hundred years of service...no way a copy could emulate that.

A last touch at *Hecate*'s patch, tracing the torch and key with one finger, and Henricksen shut the wardrobe door, closing it up tight. Wandered over to the bed and climbed under the covers, staring at the ceiling as the lights cut off, plunging the room into darkness. A pitch black nothingness that lasted just a few seconds before the night time glow panels lit, providing a soft illumination close by the floor.

Lay there feeling tired as hell, completely wrung out. Wanting to sleep but unable to, partly because he kept unconsciously turning to one side, looking for the window he expected to find there. Searching for the stars he felt, even if he couldn't see them with his eyes.

Mostly because he saw *Hecate* dying. Each and every time he closed his eyes.

"Fuck it," Henricksen growled after an hour of tossing and turning. Climbed out of bed and walked into the front room, sinking down in the chair by the desk. Powered on the system and spent the next few hours poring over personnel records, getting to know his new crew.

NINE

Toss up who looked worse the next morning: Henricksen or Sikuuku. Both of them shadow-eyed and worked over, trying not to look as dragged out as they felt.

Sikuuku definitely had the better time *getting* that way. Didn't return to his quarters until the wee hours of the morning. Stood outside his quarters, mumbling to himself while he messed with the wheel, trying to get the latch to work—three sheets to the wind, from the sound of things, and on the edge of passing out right there in the hallway.

Henricksen sat there, staring at the door to his own quarters until Sikuuku finally got his shit together and figured out the latch-and-wheel combo. Shambled drunkenly inside, leaving the damned thing wide open behind him.

Put himself to bed not long after. Even managed to get a few hours of sleep before the alarm went off and the room lights woke, rousing him from slumber. And now here they both were, standing in the control room looking down on the hangar—two dog-tired men holding back yawns. Doing their best to seem interested as Kinsey droned on, introducing them to a long list of civ engineers and scientists working on the RV-N project.

Missed most of the names—went in one ear and right out the other. Karansky stuck, though—lead engineer for the RV-N project and kinda, sorta, but not really number two to Kinsey himself. Middle aged and showing it. Paunch starting at his middle, nondescript face made remarkable only by the two enormous, wriggling caterpillar eyebrows nesting on his brow.

Carried a strange air of disappointment around him. Like this project was beneath him. Wasn't where he thought he'd end up in life. Serious, though—all of them were, every last one of the civvies Kinsey introduced—and Karansky even more so. Karansky in his starched shirt, and starched white lab coat, shoulder length hair that looked starched as well.

Project leads beneath him were Wallace and Song. Wallace ran the airframe team, in charge of propulsion and chassis modifications—a blond-haired, pink-skinned woman with a bookish, schoolmarm kind of thing going on. Almost cracked a smile when Karansky introduced her. Remarkable really, considering the stony, stoic faces of pretty much everyone else in that room. And Song…Song hovered at the edges, reader cradled in one arm, fingers constantly rattling at its display. Song managed the stealth system team, responsible for the RV-N's electronic camouflage, sensors and cryptologic package, all the other sneaky Pete aspects of the ship.

Karansky, Wallace, and Song. Karansky, Wallace, and Song. Henricksen repeated those three names, committing them to memory. Losing the thread on the others in the process.

Long list of names, a veritable sea of young, earnest faces. But Karansky, Wallace and Song—those were the ones that really mattered. Rest were just underlings. Did whatever those other three told them to.

Henricksen smiled politely at them anyway. Shook their offered hands. Tugged at the sleeves and collar of his flight suit when no one was looking—stiff things and new, not quite comfortable. The fit entirely different than *Hecate*'s jacket and matching pants.

Hecate.

He turned his head, staring forlornly at the empty spot on his shoulder.

Hard to get used to that. Felt naked, almost abandoned without a patch to mark him. A ship to call home.

A last introduction—Fergus or Ferguson, something like that—and Karansky excused himself. Gathered up Wallace and Song, dismissing the gaggle of nameless, faceless junior engineers as he drew his team leads into a huddle on the far side of the room.

Kinsey went with them. Stood there—arms folded, lips pulled downward— listening closely as the engineers started arguing, pointing at something on the panel in front of them.

Henricksen inched a few steps closer, eavesdropping on the conversation.

Apparently, there was a problem with the propulsion system. Something about an incompatibility issue between the jump drive initiators and the stealth system camouflage, of all things.

"Not exactly confidence inspiring, is it?" Sikuuku said, leaning close.

"No. It isn't." Henricksen frowned, listening for a while. "Keep this to yourself for now." He flicked his eyes to Sikuuku, giving him a meaningful look. "No sense worrying the crew."

"If the ship's buggy—"

"It'll stay put," Henricksen told him, throwing a sidelong look at the windows. "Engineers will either fix this incompatibility issue or they won't. Either way, those RV-Ns don't leave the hangar bay until I'm one hundred percent confident they won't blow up or wig out on us." He caught Sikuuku's eyes and held them. "You and I know there's a problem. More importantly, Karansky and his engineers do. Crew doesn't need to know right now. Crew doesn't need that kind of distraction."

Sikuuku frowned, considering the huddle of engineers on one side, and the control room windows on the other. "Aye, sir. If you say so, sir."

Henricksen eyed him a moment, considering this chief of his. "Sir" from Sikuuku meant the gunner didn't agree with his approach. *Two* "sirs" meant he'd humor him, but only for so long. "I know what I'm doing, Akiwane."

"'Course you do, sir."

Three "sirs" now. Henricksen sighed. This was going to be a long day.

"C'mon, you grumpy old bastard." He waved for Sikuuku to follow as he stepped across the room, leaving Kinsey and his engineers in the corner. "Let's take a look at those ships."

Lights on in the hangar bay below them, shining through the control room windows as Henricksen and Sikuuku stepped close. Far side of the hangar bay lay cloaked in darkness, near side bathed in a bright white glow filtering from the ceiling above.

Six sharp-sided shapes sitting in the middle of it, arranged in a circle with their engine ports marking the edge. Most ships rested on the decking when not out there, soaring through space. But the stealth ships…the RV-N's squatted—ugly, sinister looking things, even with the lights on.

Figures moved in the circle of space between them—Shaw and her deck gang busily working away at an RV-N's ass end. Already removed the hull panels around the vent ports, starting to disassemble the machinery beneath. Pieces of RV-N lay everywhere, laid out in a carefully arranged pattern. Supposed that was so they knew what went where when they put the whole thing back together again. Didn't end up with a bunch of spare parts that got chucked in the "just in case" bin.

No robots helping them, which was unusual. Not robots *anywhere* on this base, come to think of it. But then, Dragoon was Black Ops territory, and full to overthrowing with secret squirrel, hush-hush type projects.

Might not want all those electronic eyes scuttling about. Mobile data collectors recording every last thing they saw.

Henricksen's gaze shifted, focusing the lab coats down there with Shaw's crew. Three of Karansky's engineers running diagnostics while the mech gang worked away at the engines—plugging cables into a dozen different places to capture data on the fly, feeding it to the softly glowing readers clutched protectively in the engineers' hands.

From there to the terminals in the control room. Into the systems beneath, and their vastly more capable processing power.

"Definitely not taking *those* out anytime soon, are we?" Sikuuku grunted, watching the mech gang scurry around. "Ya know, Shaw tells me—"

"Had a good time last night, I see?" Kinsey stepped in behind them—arms folded, face reflecting off the windows, lips set in a tight, disapproving line.

"Slept like crap." Henricksen turned around, copying Kinsey's stance. Matching that critical look with one of his own. "Rack's hard as a rock. Room smells like an old trunk."

Sikuuku ducked his head, coughing to cover his smile.

"I offered you better quarters." Kinsey tilted his head, giving Henricksen a flat-eyed stare. "Offer still stands, if you want them."

Henricksen flipped his hand, dismissing the topic entirely. Didn't really want to get into a pissing match with Kinsey right now.

"So, what's the plan?" he asked, nodding to the windows, the stealth ships sitting on the hangar bay's floor. "Birds aren't flying. Guessing they haven't been since the crews started coming in." He quirked an eyebrow, looking a question at Kinsey. Stayed that way—he was nothing if not stubborn—until Kinsey nodded stiffly, moving in beside him.

"Four weeks—that's my timeline for Karansky." A look in Henricksen's direction. "For you and your crew as well."

"From the looks of things, there's quite a bit of work to do." Henricksen pointed a finger at the partially disassembled stealth ship. "You think Karansky'll make it? Have those birds ready to fly?"

Kinsey looked at him—right at him, staring steadily at Henricksen's face. "Not a doubt in my mind."

Gauntlet thrown. Kinsey never even batted an eye.

Henricksen inclined his head, accepting the challenge. "So, what? Simulators for training?"

Kinsey nodded, turning, looking across the room to a locked door with a sign stuck to its hard surface. A red placard with white letters reading "Authorized Personnel Only". "Not as good as the real thing, obviously, but the best we can do for now. Helps them learn the controls and the intricacies of the RV-N's systems." He slid his gaze to Henricksen, lips curving in a condescending smile. "How to work with one another while they're at it."

Henricksen saw the smile and ignored it. With an effort. "You make the assignments?"

Second nod—slow movement of Kinsey's head. "Based on their records and competencies." A pause, dark eyes searching Henricksen's face. "You're welcome to change them, of course."

Considered it—didn't like inheriting decisions he'd had no say in—but Henricksen shrugged his shoulders instead, not yet ready to commit. "We'll see. Like to observe them in the sims awhile. Study the data before I start swapping crew around."

"Alright," Kinsey said slowly. "Sims are that way." He hooked a thumb at the security locked door. The one with the sign, and the glowing red light sitting beside it. Second sign beneath it, reading "Caution. Simulation training in progress when red light is lit".

"Go ahead," Kinsey told them, looking at Henricksen and Sikuuku both. "I've got a briefing at 0800 to explain this mess with the RV-N engines to the Brass." He scowled at the disassembled ship, shaking his head in disgust. Turned around and moved away from the windows, glancing around in surprise when Henricksen called his name, laid a hand on his arm.

Fake arm—the prosthetic, though Henricksen hadn't realized it until he touched it. A high tech piece of equipment with built in micro-sensors and miniature motors, making it look, and move, and act like the real thing.

Didn't *feel* real, though. Cold limb beneath Henricksen's fingers. Cold and hard, unpleasant to touch. A circuit-infused piece of plasmetal and electronics, not a real arm at all.

Kinsey stared at Henricksen's hand until he released him. Tugged at his cuff, checking the fit of his prosthetic arm.

"Engineers are new."

Statement, not a question. Kinsey glanced up sharply, face twitching on one side. Pulling at his lips before finally going still.

"Mechanics are new, too, aren't they?" Henricksen moved in close, felt Sikuuku slip in behind him, listening. "Flight crews...well, I know how long *they've* been here. Only one who *isn't* new is you." He locked eyes with Kinsey, trying to read his face. "What happened, Kinsey? What's going on?"

For a moment he thought Kinsey would answer—give him the truth of the situation without the bullshit for once. And then something changed. Henricksen saw it in his face.

Kinsey's eyes hooded, locking their secrets away. "Not sure what you mean, Captain."

"The hell you don't." Henricksen stepped close, conscious of the engineers around them—eyes and ears eavesdropping on their conversation—and dropped his voice, looking Kinsey right in the face. "Spill it, Kinsey. Tell me what's going on."

Kinsey stared back at him—onyx eyes filled with secrets, lips pressed in a cold, hard line. A tug at his lapels to smooth them and he adjusted his cuffs, the fit of that prosthetic arm again.

Nervous habit, that obsessive checking. Henricksen made a note of it. Filed it away with all the other potentially useful information he'd picked up.

"Let's get one thing straight here, Captain." Kinsey flicked a fluff from his sleeve, eyes lifting to Henricksen's face. "*I* run this project. *You* run those crews." He pointed at the simulator room door without looking. "I suggest you focus on that, and get those crews ready. Let *me* worry about the rest." He stared a moment, making sure Henricksen got the message, nodded to Sikuuku as he turned away.

"And if the rest of it gets them killed?"

Kinsey stiffened, looking back over his shoulder. "They're Fleet, Captain. Every assignment could get them killed. You of all people should know that."

Henricksen winced—cheap shot, dredging up that business with *Hecate*, but it still hurt. Suspected it always would.

"You get those crews ready, Captain." A last, withering look and Kinsey stalked away. Yanked the door to the control room open and let it slam closed behind him as he stepped into the hall.

"That went well." Sikuuku folded his arms, looking Henricksen up and down. "Not real good at making friends, are you?"

"Your friend, not mine." Henricksen stared after Kinsey, turned his eyes to Sikuuku beside him. "Friend like that I don't need."

A last look at Sikuuku and he abandoned the windows, heading for the locked door with the red light on the opposite side of the room. Glanced aside the gunner fell in beside him, matching him stride for stride.

"Kinsey…" Sikuuku trailed off, biting his lip. "He's not that bad."

"He's a prick," Henricksen snapped. "And he's keeping secrets. Two things I don't like." He stopped at the security door and jammed his hand to the scanner, letting it read his palm print before entering his access code at the prompt. The lock flashed and *whirred*, processing his credentials, chimed politely and granted him access. "But he's right about one thing." Henricksen hauled the door open, looking back over his shoulder. "Best thing we can do right now is train these crews. Ships…" He frowned, shaking his head hard. "Goddamn things may never work right. But if this project fails, I won't let it be because of training. I won't do that to them." He stabbed a finger at the darkened room on the opposite side of the doorway, square-sided simulator pods humming away, crew locked up inside. "Now get your ass in there, Chief. Let's see what we've got."

Sikuuku stared a moment, grunted and stepped past Henricksen without a word. Stopped just inside and examined the layout—monitoring room with a glass wall separating it from the sim pods, door set in the middle providing access to the other side. Touched at a display panel, waking the system that ran everything—assigned the simulations, captured data on the test runs, monitored the activities of the crew during training—and took a look at who they had inside.

Henricksen pulled the door to, dropping the room into darkness. Waited there by the door until a muted, red glow appeared. Lights in the corners bathing the monitoring room in blood-red illumination. Reflecting off the glass wall separating the monitoring room from the row of sim pods on the other side.

Cameras set in the cabin of each one. Microphone in the crews' helmets recording every communication, every last thing they said. Training system's software picked simulations at random, recording the crews' reactions, spewing out streams of analytical data the monitoring system consumed.

Six sim pods in total, but just three of them active at the moment. The other three crews due to come on at mid-day.

Five hour shifts to start out, with just a small break in between each run. Debrief after to go over the vids, analyze what they'd done.

Sikuuku's idea, staggering the training. Easier to assess the crews' capabilities with just three on at a time. He pulled up the feeds from the three active sims, watching the simulations play out in real time.

Baldini occupied one pod—loud as ever, swearing like a sailor, yelling at his crew as he piloted his simulated RV-N through a sea of false chaff and fake starships. Schenck in there with him, long body stuffed into the Artillery pod's tight confines. Mateus sitting Scan on one side of Baldini, Pritchard at Engineering on the other.

System identified them. Floated names over stations because in their flights suits, with those visored helmets covering their faces, they all looked the same. One indistinguishable from another, even gender obscured.

All male crew in that particular pod, of course, which sort of made that last point moot. Henricksen wasn't quite sure he liked that set-up—mixed crews performed better in his experience than single gender teams. Male or female, it didn't seem to matter. Include all of one and none of the other...well, things tended to go wrong.

Kinsey, he reminded himself. *Kinsey set these assignments up.*

And obviously didn't share his qualms about single sex crews.

Henricksen frowned, tempted to break up the party. Swap out the male pilot. Maybe one of the other crew.

Frowned harder and decided to leave it alone for now, and see how things played out. Snap decisions tended to be bad ones, and he *had* been known to be wrong. Not often, but it did happen. No one was perfect, after all.

A touch at one of the monitoring station's panels and he toggled the vid, pushing the data from Baldini's pod into a corner, bringing the feed from Adaeze, working the Number Two pod, to the center.

Fontaine in there with her, manning Engineering. Grunewald on the guns, Kapoor at Scan calling out information. Simulation running an asteroid field with DSR ships around it, the stealth ship itself just coming in on approach.

Calm voice from Adaeze as she flew the ship, twitching it side to side. Minimal comms filtering through, which meant minimal noise, unlike loudmouthed Baldini in the next pod over.

Henricksen watched her a while, admiring her skills. Her control over this unfamiliar ship. Adaeze was smooth as silk on the stick, sliding gracefully between the ships surrounding the sim asteroid field, sneaking the cloaked RV-N into the tumbling mass of boulders with the sim DSR none the wiser.

"Cool as a cucumber," Sikuuku grunted, nodding appreciatively. "Unlike our Sosholo lieutenant."

A touch at the panel and he dialed up the comms from the Number One pod, listening to Baldini whoop and shout. A blast of plasma fire and he dodged sideways, hauled the RV-N around and lined it up with a target. Reached around and thumped the Artillery pod behind him, hollering for Schenck to blow it to hell.

"Believe our young lieutenant forgot he's flying a stealth ship, not a combat fighter. Idiot," Sikuuku sneered, cutting the comms off.

The simulation ran another twenty minutes before finally winding down. Baldini pumped his fist as it cut out, yanked off his helmet and whooped aloud.

Started high-fiving his crew, until Henricksen interrupted, keying the mic to open comms to the pod.

"Mind telling me what that was all about, Baldini?"

"That," Baldini said, flashing a cocksure grin at the camera, "was called kicking the enemy's ass. Sir," he added, flipping an offhand salute.

"Kicking the enemy's ass." Henricksen crooked a finger, beckoning Sikuuku over. "Is that the point of this project, Mr. Baldini? Is that what we're supposed to do?"

"Yes, sir. Kick ass and take names. Show the enemy—"

"No. That is *not* what we do."

Baldini stared at the camera, eyes wide with surprise. Snuck a look at the crew around him and sat back, poking sullenly at his station while Henricksen schooled him on the finer points of being a stealth ship pilot.

"Kicking ass and taking names is for yahoos and dumbshits who don't know better, Mr. Baldini. The sooner you wrap your thick head around that, the better off we'll be."

"But, sir—"

"Shut it, Lieutenant," Sikuuku snapped.

Baldini's face darkened. "I do *not* take orders from—"

"You will goddamn well take orders from whoever I tell you to, Mr. Baldini. And that includes Chief Sikuuku."

"But I'm an officer!" Baldini objected.

"And a fucking piss-poor one, Baldini. Fucking piss-poor."

Baldini's eye bulged, mouth sagging open. He sat there, staring at the camera like a landed fish, all but apoplectic at being dressed down in front of his crew.

Not the best way to deal with junior officers, normally, but Baldini had developed some severely bad habits. He and Petros both, based on what Henricksen saw in the mess hall the other night. First order of business was to nip that in the bud. Knock those two down a few notches and get them playing as part of a team. Lot of ways he could do that, but the fastest way—the most effective way, in Henricksen's experience—was to tell them they flat-out sucked.

"What are you flying, Lieutenant?"

Baldini frowned, obviously thinking this some kind of trick. "Sir?"

"What are you flying?" Henricksen repeated, ice creeping into his voice.

"Uhh…simulator? Sir?"

Henricksen sighed and cut the comms, counting to ten so he didn't tear the goddamn lieutenant's head off. "Box of rocks, this one. Box of fucking rocks."

Sikuuku smiled crookedly. "Officer," he said, flicking an imaginary fluff from his chief's anchors. "Most are."

"Quiet you," Henricksen growled, opening the comms back up. "What *kind* of simulator, Mr. Baldini?"

"Stealth ship, sir. Simulates the RV-N."

"Exactly. And that little display of yours? All the fancy moves and shooting? Would you say that was stealthy?"

Baldini blinked, processing the question. "Uh. No. Not really."

"Therein lies your problem, Mr. Baldini." He folded his arms, waiting for the moment of enlightenment, but Baldini just stared at the camera, shaking his head. Henricksen sighed again, cutting the comms. "I stand corrected. Rocks make this guy look brilliant."

Sikuuku barked a laugh as Henricksen stabbed at the panel, trying again.

"Stealth ship means stealth *flying*, Mr. Baldini, and guns as a last resort. Now reset the simulation." He paused, rolling his eyes as Baldini and his crew groaned. "Yeah, yeah. My heart's breaking. Now run it again, and this time do your damn job. Any more of that showboating, hot jock bullshit and I'll run you out of this program. Are we clear, Mr. Baldini?"

"Yes, sir." Baldini shoved his helmet over his head, clearly sulking, muttering about "hardass captains and son-of-a-bitch chiefs". Forgetting, in his peevishness, about the mic inside said helmet, picking up his every word.

Sikuuku listened a while, lips twitching. "He's right, ya know. You *are* a pain in the ass. Sometimes," he amended, at Henricksen's sour look.

A touch at the panel reset the simulator, launched the mission and shot the simulated ship out into simulated space.

Sikuuku watched a while, examining the data, straightened and threw a look Henricksen's way. "Thinking we need to break that crew up. Baldini's," he added, by way of explanation.

"No argument here. In fact, I was thinking exactly the same thing. Change 'em out tomorrow," Henricksen decided, nodding to the Number One pod. "Cycle the crew out every couple of days for the next two weeks. Give everyone a run with Baldini. See what sticks and what doesn't."

"What about Fisker?"

Henricksen grimaced. "Fisker too. Hate to do it to the kid, but it can't look like I'm playing favorites. 'Sides," he added, flashing a smile. "Working for a prick can be educational."

Sikuuku snorted. "Say that again."

"Was I really *that* bad as a junior lieutenant?"

"Not like Baldini." Sikuuku watched the vid from Baldini's pod a moment, shrugged his shoulders, looking over at Henricksen. "Knew better than to order a chief around. Always treated the enlisted fair." He tipped an invisible cap, accepting a nod of acknowledgment in return. Went quiet for a while, watching Baldini's simulation without really seeing it. Thinking about days long gone.

"But?" Henricksen prompted, sensing there was one.

"Big damn chip on your shoulder." Sikuuku looked over, flicked his eyes back to the panel. "Wore your pusher history like a goddamn badge. Bristled up like a puffer fish anytime one of those Academy boys came around."

"Can ya blame me?" Henricksen spread his hands, eyebrows lifting. "Look at Baldini. Would *you* wanna hang around with an asshole like that?"

Sikuuku rolled his eyes. "They're not *all* assholes. Adaeze's alright and she's Academy. Janssen. Fisker."

"Fisker's Earth Academy. That's different."

"Whatever," Sikuuku muttered, shaking his head. "What about Mahal?" he asked, nodding to the Number Three pod. "What's your read on her?"

Honestly wasn't sure.

Henricksen muted Baldini, checked on Adaeze—everything green there, simulation running just fine—before queuing up the feed from the last of the three active pods.

Lot of chatter on comms—Mahal mostly, Scan and the other stations now and then. Too much chatter for Henricksen's liking—not obnoxious blabbering like Baldini, but noisy just the same. Lot of noise on that channel, especially for Black Ops. Pilot's job was to listen, take in the information fed to her by the crew, but Mahal's voice dominated comms, harrying Ahmadi at Scan—he'd replaced Nunez, the one and only change to crew Henricksen had made so far—questioning every bit of information the scan tech brought back.

Missed the first beacon because of it. Got her ship blown to hell and had to restart her run because she was too damned busy questioning her crew to pay attention to her own job.

"Cut it," Henricksen ordered with the simulation just halfway through.

"You sure?" Sikuuku asked him.

"Yeah. Cut it. She's making a hash outta this run."

A touch at the panel and the simulation ended abruptly, leaving the crew confused and complaining. Mahal angry as hell.

"What the fuck, Karansky? Doesn't *any* of this shit equipment work?" Mahal ripped off her helmet, glaring at the camera.

"Shit equipment's working just fine," Henricksen told her. "Now climb out, Mahal. Need to talk to you a moment. Rest of you stay put. We'll reset in five." He cut the comms and waited while Mahal unstrapped from her pilot's seat, exited the simulator and buzzed through the glass door to the control room, tucking her helmet under her arm as she snapped off a salute.

Tiny woman. Pixie cut hair, pixyish face to match. Dark hair, shot through with orange streaks that definitely weren't regulation. Blue-grey eyes—striking, piercing—set in a brown-skinned face.

Not what he'd expected, based on all the swearing. Not your typical pilot either, those tending to run at the tall, spindly end of the human body composition range.

Sikuuku looked at him, eyebrows lifting as Henricksen returned the salute, and Mahal settled into a parade rest stance.

"Sorry, sir," she said, eyes locked onto something just over Henricksen's shoulder. "About the swearing. Bad habit. Trying to break myself of it."

"Good luck with that." Sikuuku folded his arms, leaning against the glass wall. "Better officers than you have tried and failed. My advice—"

"Shut it," Henricksen snapped, making a chopping gesture with his hand. "Look, Mahal." He sighed and stepped close while Mahal kept staring at the corner. "Personally, I don't give two shits about the swearing so long as you keep it clean around the Brass."

Mahal blinked in surprise, eyes snapping away from the corner, focusing on Henricksen's face. "You—you don't?"

"Swearing is swearing," he shrugged. "Happens all over the Fleet. But you need to cut the chatter. You're mouthy as hell, Mahal, which means you're not paying attention to what you're doing. Now I know you're upset about Nunez." He held up a hand to forestall her objections. "But that was my call. You're shackin' up on the side and I won't have your raging hormones distracting you from the mission."

Mahal opened her mouth to object—hand or no hand, she obviously meant to speak her peace—thought better of it at the last moment and went back to staring at the corner. "Yes, sir. Anything else, sir?" she asked tightly.

"Damn fine stick," he told her.

From the look on Mahal's face, the compliment seemed to surprise her even more than his acceptance of her swearing.

"Read your record. Saw that bit on *Sisyphus*. Quick thinking, getting him out. What I saw in there," he nodded to the simulation room, "was spot on when you weren't distracted giving Ahmadi the business. So cut the chatter, Mahal." Henricksen stepped in front of her, setting a hand on Mahal's shoulder, squeezing it until she looked at him. "You're their pilot, not their keeper. Crew's there to help you. You do your job, they do theirs. Got it?"

Mahal thought on that, and nodded. "Yes, sir. Aye, sir."

"Good. Now get back in there." Henricksen nodded to the Number Three pod. "Run it again."

Mahal saluted and spun around, stuffing the helmet over her head. Buzzed through the door and climbed back into the pod, buckling herself in.

"When you're ready," Sikuuku called over the control room comms.

Mahal tugged at her harness, ratcheting the straps down. "Scan."

"Go."

"Artillery."

"Go."

"Engineering."

"Green across the board."

"Ready," Mahal called, and grabbed the stick as the simulator started, pod bucking as simulated engines kicked in.

Mahal's run went better the second time—better, but not flawless. Still plenty of room for improvement. Baldini was quieter his second time through, but just as aggressive. Obviously needed *lots* of work.

Henricksen hoped swapping out crew would help with the situation. Honestly, though, he really wasn't sure. Adaeze on the other…

Adaeze stood head and shoulders above both of them. Needed practice, just like the rest of the pilots, this being a completely new ship, but she picked up on the RV-N's idiosyncrasies much more quickly than the others. Learned from her mistakes and didn't make them again.

Four full simulation runs he put those crews through before swapping them out. Watched dog-tired personnel drag themselves from the simulators and stumble across the monitoring room as two fresh crews arrived to replace them.

"Should probably get in there ourselves," Sikuuku noted as Janssen's crew strapped down in one pod and Petros's in another. "Could use the practice. Well, not *me*, of course," he amended, flashing a smile. "You, on the other hand…"

"You callin' me rusty?"

"Well, it *has* been a few years."

Henricksen grunted, eying the two crewmen in the corner, patiently waiting their turn in the mill.

Rusty wasn't the half of it. Last time he piloted a ship was twelve years ago. Twelve years and four rotations. And that was an Aurora. Nothing at all like the experimental ship recreated in this sim.

Henricksen chewed his lip, watching Janssen launch his first run. "Get a fix on Janssen and Petros first. Then we'll swap in."

Sikuuku nodded, setting the system to capture the data. Watched it with Henricksen—quiet, the two of them, just observing for now.

Predictable results from the first go-round, Petros as much of a train wreck as Baldini, Janssen as solid as Adaeze.

"Satisfied?" Sikuuku scooped two helmets from the shelf, tossing one to Henricksen, keeping the other for himself. Waved to Abboud and Taggert—scan tech and engineer, respectively—as he opened the door on the simulation room and climbed into the Number Four pod. "Let's go, Captain," he called, poking his head out. "I'm sure these junior officers are just *dying* for you to show them how it's done." He winked, smiling mischievously as he ducked back into the pod.

"Pain in the ass," Henricksen muttered, turning his helmet over, studying the scar-faced reflection showing on the visor's glass.

Twelve years. That's a lotta rust.

Hoped he still had it. Hoped he didn't make a fool himself in front of the crew. No way around it, though. And only one way to find out if he still had the right stuff.

"Never shoulda let Sikuuku talk me into this." A last look at the simulator room and Henricksen stuffed the helmet onto his head, pushed through the glass door and climbed into the Number Four pod.

TEN

Simple layout to the RV-N bridge pod—stations set in a diamond pattern placing the Pilot's station front and center, slightly forward of the others, with Scan and Engineering to left and right, Artillery backing it up behind. Gimbaled pod for the gunner—same design used on every last one of the Fleet's warships—it's oversized orb crowding the others stations. Consuming a good half of the available space.

Blood-red lights, just like in the control room, turning the crew into soft-edged shadows, the stations into fortresses in which they hid. Hum of machinery in the air, greeting Henricksen as he stepped into the doorway. Bass *thrum* of engines—simulated, like everything else since the pod had none, nor needed any—an undercurrent to the higher pitched *buzz* of the electronics powering the diamond-patterned stations.

Smell of metal and electronics, cold and plastic filling his nose. Familiar scents. Clinical and antiseptic. The scent of every starship bridge everywhere recreated here. Duplicated to perfection, right down to the hard, uncomfortable seats. The harness that gripped and strangled, wrapping over shoulders, binding securely at the waist and chest.

Real. So very, very real, the layout of that bridge. The sim made to look, and feel, and even smell like an honest-to-goodness warship, not just a machine for training. And the lighting inside it... that glow. That blood-red glow.

Reminded Henricksen of *Hecate*. Of the emergency illumination flooding her bridge as she slid into combat and the stars outside lit up with plasma fire.

Hecate.

Henricksen locked up tight, hand gripping the doorframe, breath quickening as combat instincts kicked in. Memories of smoke and fire setting his pulse to racing as a blinding explosion seared across his brain.

He closed his eyes, caught up in that memory. There and not there—just like when it happened. Watching from afar as *Hecate* floated amongst the stars and shredded ships in those last few moments before she died.

Not real, he told himself. *Not now.*

Didn't want those memories. Didn't want to lose them and forget her either, but he didn't need them right now.

Not the time for that. Definitely not the place. Couldn't afford to get lost in the past when there was crew here that needed him. Training to be done.

A deep breath—in and out, echoing and amplified in the confines of his helmet—and Henricksen shrugged his shoulders, shaking the memories off. Smothered the combat instincts under a mantle of calm, letting the adrenaline work its way through his system. Take the jittering twitch of his fingers with it.

Training run, he reminded himself, taking another deep breath. *Learn the machine. Dust off the skills. That's it.*

No death and destruction. Not here. Not today.

"Captain?" Sikuuku kept his tone carefully neutral—none of the joshing, good natured heckling now. "You comin'?" he asked, the slightest hint of worry coming through.

Sensed something wrong. Knew Henricksen well enough, long enough to know when something wasn't quite right.

Henricksen shook himself, grateful for the helmet hiding his face. Knowing he looked like hell at the moment. "Yeah. Sorry." He scanned the bridge pod, noting how tight it was—one station running into another, seating arrangements requiring an order of operations to how the crew entered—the closeness of the windows, the diamond-shaped arrangement that no warship ever employed.

Different from *Hecate*. Ship's bridge—no doubt about that—but not *Hecate*'s. Not the same.

He pushed away from the doorway, grabbed the sim pod's hatch and pulled it closed. Slid between the tightly packed stations, squeezing through the gap between Artillery and Engineering to get at the Pilot's seat.

Plunked down and buckled the harness, pressure suit adjusting as the straps slid into place. Long time since he'd worn such a thing. No need for a pressure suit on a warship where the movements were slower, the stressors shared out across the ship's larger mass. Forgot how damned uncomfortable the things were, binding everywhere, squeezing at sensitive bits. Materials were better these days—some kind of high-tech, carbon-latex, spun metal weave—but they pinched and flattened just like the old ones, pressing at somewhat…intimate places.

He wriggled in his seat, trying to get more comfortable. Tugged at the pressure suit's seams digging painfully into his flesh.

Sikuuku snickered behind him, obviously enjoying the show. "Something wrong, Captain? Got ants in your pants or somethin'?"

"Damn thing's givin' me a wedgie." Henricksen grabbed the crotch of the pressure suit and yanked hard, giving his nether regions some well-needed relief.

"That's it, Captain. Show that suit who's boss."

"Quiet, you." Henricksen twisted, thumping a fist against the outside of Sikuuku's pod. Faced around and surveyed the Pilot's station, studying the set-up of the sim.

Twin panels in front of him with access to all the ship's systems. Shouldn't need it—that's what the other crew was for—but a pilot survived on a constant flow of information. And in space, just about everything could and did go wrong.

Single control stick he gripped with both hands—wide and flat with curving handles he wrapped his fingers round. Display in front of him where the front windows should be, simulated stars showing while the system waited for the program to start.

Henricksen stared at them a moment, knowing they were fake, comforted by their presence just the same.

Loved the stars. Born to them. Lived the bulk of his life among them. Couldn't imagine being stuck on a station or some dirt ball planet. Spending the last of his days standing still. Looking upward and outward, wishing he was out there again.

A hand landed on Henricksen's shoulder, startling him out of his reverie. "You do remember how to start this pig, don't you?" Sikuuku kept his voice light and teasing, but the worry was back, running just beneath.

"Yes, mother." Henricksen shrugged the gunner's hand from his shoulder, flicked at switches, activating his station.

Checked and rechecked the harness to make sure all the straps were nice and tight—last thing he needed was to be thrown out of the Pilot's seat mid-simulation.

Rusty was one thing, careless was just embarrassing.

Silence all around him as Henricksen settled in. Bridge crew watching and waiting—dark shapes in black-on-black uniforms, glossed helmets like obsidian hiding their faces, obscuring their heads.

Nervous crew—he sensed that about them. Felt the tension crackling in the air. Honestly couldn't blame them since he'd been there himself, once upon a time. Ten years he'd been commander in charge of his own ship—long enough to become comfortable with the responsibility, not so long that he'd forgotten the feeling that came with being a junior officer confined in close quarters with a superior. And a new one at that.

They'd get over it soon enough, though. Once the newness worse off. And if they didn't, he'd swap them out. Shuffle them over to another crew with one of the other pilots.

Nervousness had its benefits—kept the crew sharp and watchful, mindful of their responsibilities—but unconstrained anxiety led to mistakes. Couldn't afford that with a new chassis. Especially one designed for stealth missions.

Henricksen leaned to one side, flicking more switches, running through the entire pre-flight check while Sikuuku tested out the Artillery pod behind him, Navigation and Engineering came to life. Paused, considering, as a prompt appeared asking if he wanted to run the AI.

Sim allowed for it—fake AI, like everything in here—but Henricksen opted against it. Toggled the default setting off. A prompt appeared immediately, asking him if he wanted to connect to one of the Raven AI—real ones this time, snuggled inside those stealth ship bodies in the hangars—presenting a list of ship's registries to choose from.

Henricksen hesitated, considering, knowing some of the other crews went that route. Not a bad idea, actually—gave them a chance to interact with that mindset, figure out just what kind of AI they were dealing with—but right now…not what he wanted. Hard enough adjusting to a new AI after *Hecate*. Didn't want to waste time interacting with an AI that wasn't even real, wasn't quite ready to start over with a mindset he didn't know. Besides, AI tended to be chatterbugs, and overly helpful. Stepped on toes and generally got in the way. Rather learn the RV-N's quirks without it. Mess things up on his own rather than with some AI's help.

He banished the prompt, opting for full manual as he settled into his seat, giving his harness a last good yank. "Scan."

"Go," Abboud answered, helmeted head turning, one side bathed in the light of Scan's multi-colored panel, the other reflecting the bridge pod's blood-red glow.

"Artillery."

"Go," Sikuuku called, adjusted his targeting visor, linking it to the RV-N's main gun.

"Engineering."

"Go." Taggert touched at his panel, cycling the engines, bass *thrum* settling into a deep-throated roar.

Simulated sound to go with the simulated vibrations. Everything cutting edge, state of the art and very, very real.

"Glad to see they didn't cut corners," Henricksen murmured.

"Sir?" Taggert's head pivoted, visored face staring in the semi-dark.

"Nothing, Taggert. Just talking to myself." Henricksen touched at the panel in front of him, reviewing the mission plan for the simulation. A blessedly *simple* mission plan, as it turned out—in and out, snagging some data along the way.

Exactly what a rusty pilot needed for his first run. Luck of the draw the system spitting that one out, considering the simulations were created at random, and this mission just one of a million combinations available. Couldn't help but wonder if the system was somehow looking out for him, though. Throwing him a bone so he wouldn't make a complete fool of himself on this, his very first run with his new crew.

"Looks like we're in luck, boys and girls." Henricksen pushed the mission specs to the other stations. "Skulk run. Nice little op to cut our teeth on."

"Skulk run. Seriously?" Sikuuku sounded offended. But then, Taggert and Abboud didn't seem all that enthused either.

Skulk run meant hours of sheer boredom, especially for a gunner. Ship came equipped with weapons in case something went wrong—something usually did, things hardly ever went to plan—but they were primarily meant for defense. Small caliber, mostly. Plasma cannons and rail guns, which were nothing to sneeze at—powerful enough if they found the right target, but not really meant for a head-to-head contest with a warship. Even the cobbled together, secondhand vessels the DSR used.

Stealth ship meant stealthy, after all. Engineers never designed them for combat missions.

Sikuuku scanned the mission package, closed it with a sound of disgust. "You need me, I'll be back here taking a nap." He folded his arms and kicked up his feet, making himself as comfortable as possible in the cramped Artillery pod.

"Chiefs," Henricksen snorted. "Always lyin' down on the job."

A hand snaked from the Artillery pod, finger extending, pointing upward like a flag.

Henricksen caught himself just short of laughing—wouldn't do to encourage that kind of behavior in front of the others. Get them thinking they could take the same liberties with their new captain. "Appreciate the gesture, Chief, but you can put that back where you found it."

Kept his voice even, just a hint of steel creeping in. Sikuuku—stubborn cuss that he was—let that full bird salute hang out there a moment longer anyway. Tucked it up when he was satisfied and stowed it safely away.

Straightened up a bit while he was at it, giving Henricksen that much. Took a second look at that mission package while Henricksen keyed the simulation, activating the pod.

"Main propulsion."

"Online and ready, sir." Taggert glanced at Henricksen, nodded to the simulated stars outside. "Stealth system's showing nominal. Should be invisible to anything out there. Well except for the engines, of course." He shrugged helplessly. "Can't really hide those."

Still getting smart on the stealth system, but the engineering specs claimed it hid the ship's shape from sensors. No idea how it all worked—lot of mumbo-jumbo and techno-jargon that made absolutely no sense at all. Something about electronic camouflage using a combination of white noise and scan refraction to mask their signature and confuse the sensors.

Supposedly the human eye could still spot a cloaked ship, assuming it came in close enough, of course. Sim recording system would capture everything plain as day—this being training simulation, not a one hundred percent perfect mission recreation—but in real life, in a real ship, not the virtual reality of the sims, there'd be nothing *to* see if the stealth system worked correctly.

Except, as Taggert pointed out, for the engines. Couldn't hide those. Fleet hadn't figured out how to mask that kind of energy signature. Not yet, anyway.

Henricksen thought about that conversation in the control room—Karansky and his engineers arguing about the stealth system and the engines. Thought about telling Taggert to turn it off as a precaution. Mission specs stipulated cloaked entrance, though. So, against his better judgment, Henricksen decided to leave it on.

"Whenever you're ready, sir," Taggert prompted when Henricksen just sat there, staring at the windows.

"Right. Spool up the jump drives, Taggert. We're go in 3, 2, 1, launch!"

The RV-N kicked like a bitch, even in simulation. Rougher ride than *Hecate,* who was smooth as silk outside the chaos of combat. Propulsion pinned Henricksen to his seat and held him there as the RV-N's main engines pushed hard, shoving it toward the stars.

Lost himself for a moment, staring at those pinpricks, feeling the ship shudder around him. Thought he was back there, holding tight to *Hecate's* Command Post as the warship banked and shifted, dodging plasma fire.

Shook himself—angry, annoyed that he'd slipped again. Fingers trembling as he touched at Helm's controls, adjusting their course and speed, getting a feel for how the RV-N maneuvered under propulsion.

"Touchy," he grunted, as the simulated ship slewed sideways, back end kicking out before he muscled it into line.

Sensitive controls. Everything balanced on a knife's edge. Sharp-sided chassis and maneuverable as hell, but twitchy. Instantly reacting to the slightest change.

Almost lost it, he thought, heart hammering. *Right out of the gate.*

Another touch—softer this time, infinitely careful, and the stealth ship lurched and shot forward, veering off-line. He recovered—just barely—bringing it back under control before it spun completely about.

Heard the crew gasp, clutching at their panels. Sikuuku snickering softly in the pod directly behind him.

"Need some lubricant for those rusty reflexes, Captain?" Sikuuku kept his voice low this time, keying his helmet comms to a private channel so Taggert and Abboud wouldn't hear.

"Shut it," Henricksen growled. "Like to see *you* try to fly this slick-as-snot thing." He checked their location and the target specified in the mission package. Relayed the jump coordinates to Taggert and held on tight as the buckle formed ahead of them, sucking the RV-N into the hyperspace trough. "Shit. Holy shit," he swore, ship pitching and yawing, shaking fit to wake the dead as it bumped along the trough. "Is this normal?" he asked, looking over at Taggert.

A shrug of dark shoulders, Taggert shaking his head. "RV-N's far from smooth, but it's not usually this bad."

"Betting the pilot's not usually this bad either," Sikuuku muttered across that private channel to Henricksen's helmet.

"Thought you were taking a nap."

"Who can sleep with all this going on?"

"Monitoring system's showing some kind of feedback." Taggert tapped at his panel, analyzing the data the jump drives sent back. "It's interfering with the hyperspace drive system."

"What kind of feedback?" Henricksen demanded.

"Not sure." Taggert cycled through the data, searching for clues. "Saw something like this earlier. On one of the other runs. Didn't get a good fix on it then, not quite sure what it is now."

"Run a capture. Have the engineers look at it later."

"Aye, sir."

Taggert looped in the monitoring system, setting it to record and process the data the engines put out while Henricksen throttled the controls, making minute adjustments to smooth the ship's run. Calm things down.

Improved their situation a little bit, but the ship still rattled alarmingly. Bumped and kicked the whole way through the trough.

Short trip, thankfully—thirty seconds in hyperspace and they dumped back out again. Real space amazingly smooth. A welcome relief from that bone rattling trip through jump.

Henricksen sighed as they exited, relaxing his death grip on the ship's flight controls. Not the most auspicious of beginnings, but at least they were through. The first part of the simulation successfully passed, the more difficult part yet to come.

As if on cue, Scan lit up, contacts flooding Abboud's display.

"Asteroid field dead ahead," she called—calm, and cool, and dialed in tight.

Henricksen frowned inside his helmet. "Asteroid field. You sure about that?"

Mission plan specified the target location, but it hadn't said anything about that.

"Ugh. This again," Taggert grumbled. "I *hate* this one."

Henricksen glanced at him in surprise. "You've run this simulation before?"

Asteroid field seemed an odd choice for a simulation in the first place. Ships typically steered well clear of those tumbling, spinning rocks.

"Few times," Taggert told him. "System's glitched or something." He flicked at switches, toggling displays. "Supposed to be randomized simulations, but we must've hit this asteroid field a half dozen times in the last two weeks."

Sikuuku leaned out of his pod, tapping Henricksen on the shoulder. "Wasn't Adaeze running an asteroid field simulation?"

"Not sure," he said, glancing over his shoulder. "Coulda been."

Paid more attention to the pilots than the actual simulations, to be honest. But he thought he remembered obstacles. A similar sea of spinning rocks.

"Hardly get through a day's training without hitting the asteroid field simulation," Taggert muttered, still grumbling. "Slipshod software if you ask me. Whole damn thing's a mess."

"Sounds like," Henricksen murmured, studying the screen in front of him. The simulated windows looking out on simulated stars. "I'll talk to Karansky tomorrow. See if—"

"Sir! I've got something!" Abboud bent over Scan's panels as the sensors sent back data, long lines of information crawling across the station's screens.

"What?" Henricksen prompted. "What is it? What's out there?"

"I thought..." Abboud trailed off, shaking her head. "Sorry, sir. I thought I had something, but it's gone now."

"Gone. What do you mean 'gone'?" Henricksen growled. "What the hell was it? What did you *think* you saw?"

"I thought—I'm not..." Abboud's hands curled into fists, pressing hard against the station's panels. "A ship," she said. "A ship's beacon. Maybe more than one."

"Where?"

"There," Abboud said, pointing at the windows. "Inside that asteroid field ahead."

Henricksen tore his eyes from the simulated windows, looking over at Scan. "What kind of ship? One of ours?"

"I don't know," Abboud told him, voice edged with annoyance. "The scans picked up on something and I thought, for a minute..." She spread her hands, staring at Scan's panels in frustration. "Gone, sir. Whatever it was, it's gone now. Or blocked," she added, tone turning thoughtful as she took another looking at Scan. "Rocks keeping moving around. Getting in the way of the scans. Sensors are having fits trying to get a fix on anything in there."

Sensors didn't like obstructions. Scans hit those rocks and bounced right back.

Kinda like our stealth system, Henricksen thought.

Had to wonder if that's how the engineers came up with the idea in the first place. Scientists were good at that. Stealing ideas from nature.

"Run the scans again," Henricksen ordered, bothered by that anomalous signature. That there and not-there blip Abboud caught on Scan. "Broad spectrum spread, overlapping pattern."

Abboud looked at him. "I don't see—"

"Just run 'em, Abboud. It'll make me feel better."

"Aye, sir," she said, confused, uncertain, humoring Henricksen because he was senior officer in charge. "Nothing, sir," she reported a couple of minutes later. "Scans are clean. Nothing but rocks as far as the eye can see."

Which was very far in this case. Those eyes being attached to a RV-N class stealth ship equipped with the latest and greatest reconnaissance package. A view obstructed only by that mass of asteroids out there—a dense sea of tumbling rocks hiding god-only-knew-what inside.

I don't like it, Henricksen thought, staring through the simulated windows. *Got a bad feeling about flying in there blind.*

But that was the mission: work his way into an open space the mission plan showed at the asteroid field's center, gather information on whatever was in there—phantom vessels, for instance—and skedaddle. Get his ship and crew back out.

Simple. So very simple. Except that scan blip still bothered him. Made him wonder what kind of nasty little surprises lurked inside those rocks.

"Screw it," he muttered, gripping the control stick with both hands. "Taggert. Cut the engines. We're going in."

"Aye, sir."

A last rumble and the RV-N's propulsion cut out. Momentum carried them the rest of the way—a long, smooth slide across an expanse of open space. Sensors wide open, drinking in data on everything around them, the Raven's sharp-sided shape closing the gap to the asteroid field quickly, sneakily, hiding behind a cloak of electronic darkness.

"Big one," Sikuuku grunted as the asteroid field hove into view. "Gotta be *thousands* of rocks in that thing."

And every last one with its own orbit. Each one spinning in a wobbling, repeating pattern, the field itself a carefully balanced ecosystem—a stone sea of harmony just a hair's breadth from complete chaos.

One wrong move and we're all dead.

Sobering thought, even in simulation. Henricksen sucked in a few breaths to settle his nerves, feathering the maneuvering jets to aim the ship toward an opening. Eased it through and into the leading edge of the asteroid field, sliding neatly between two lumpen shapes.

Blew the entrance—he realized that immediately—coming in way too hot, carrying way too much speed. Human error—AI would've caught it, used the reverse thrusters to decrease their rate of approach—made by a rusty pilot, too long out of the seat.

"Fuck," Henricksen breathed, coming up against a rock. He yanked hard on the control stick—reflexes kicking in, muscle memory operating on instinct—and slewed the ship to port. Pushed the stick forward to angle the RV-N's nose downward, slipping the ship beneath the next rock because there wasn't any other choice.

Proximity alarms went haywire, warnings lights igniting on nearly every panel across the bridge. Scan worked like crazy, trying to plot the asteroids around them, calculate their orbital points and rates of rotation to find a safe way through to the open space the mission plan promised lay at the asteroid field's middle.

Meanwhile Henricksen kept dodging. Zig-zagging desperately as each new obstacle appeared.

"Um...sir? *Sir?*" Taggert sounded panicked. Crossed his arms and grabbed at his harness, fingers clenched in a death grip at his shoulders. "Are you sure you—"

"Fuck no, Taggert. I've got no *fucking* idea."

He tapped the maneuvering jets, setting them to full reverse to try to slow the ship down. Jogged the ship hard to port as an oversized rock appeared from nowhere, tumbling on a collision course with the RV-N's starboard side, and found himself head on with a trio of asteroids, all of them tumbling in time.

"Shit!" he yelled. "Shit, shit, shit!"

A touch at the panel fired the maneuvering jets again, shoving the ship away. Second touch brought the back end around, the way ahead growing increasingly cluttered the further they moved in.

"Fuck!" He jammed the control stick sideways, spitting curses as the ship scraped a rock. Flipped the RV-N in the opposite direction and found his path obstructed—rocks everywhere, blocking every available path.

The klaxons changed tone, warning of an imminent collision. Something large and potentially deadly heading their way. Henricksen hauled the ship over, banking hard to starboard as they came up on the biggest asteroid yet. Overcorrected to avoid it—knew it right away—and felt the ship wobble and roll over, sending it into an unrecoverable spin.

"Brace! Brace! Brace!" Henricksen yelled, wrestling with the ship, trying to get it back under control.

He almost had it, just about stopped the spinning, but the wing clipped a passing asteroid and they ricocheted away. Slammed into a rock and rebounded, flew straight on into another asteroid and exploded in spectacular fashion.

The simulation cut off, the display at the front of the bridge flashing '*Failure! Failure Failure!*', mocking them with pictures of flowers and sympathy cards sent to their families with the Fleet's condolences.

"Fuck!" Henricksen punched the panel in frustration. Punched it again and sat back seething with anger, rubbing at his sore hand.

His fault, that failure. New ship, so that was part of it, but overcorrecting like that...

"Sloppy," he muttered, angry all over again. "Rusty as hell and sloppy to boot."

Taggert looked at him, shrugged his shoulders and wisely held his tongue.

Sikuuku sighed behind, resetting the Artillery pod. "Well, that went about as expected."

Henricksen yanked off his helmet and twisted, staring murder at the gunner. "Reset," he barked, keying into the system. "We're running it again."

The simulation reinitiated—recon mission this time, Fleet ships around them, not an asteroid in sight. Henricksen grabbed the stick and eased the ship forward, determined not to fuck it up this time.

ELEVEN

Second run went better than the first—didn't kill anyone this time, even managed to bring the ship back in one piece. Helped that there was no asteroid field to contend with this run, just a station with a couple of dozen ships scattered around it—DSR, ostensibly, which meant lots of sneaking about and poking at communications.

Earned themselves a partial pass on that one—ship and crew returned intact, the mission itself incomplete due to a "lack of viable intelligence", which meant supposedly they'd missed something. Encrypted comms package or some such. For her part, Abboud felt differently. Swore up and down that they'd covered everything. Every channel, encrypted or otherwise.

Not that it mattered. No arguing with a simulation. Henricksen logged the partial pass and reset the pod. Gave the crew fifteen minutes to reinitiate systems and run through the usual pre-flight checks before starting over again.

Third launch was ugly from the get-go—doomed to failure, despite Henricksen's best efforts. Crew was tired by then, grumbling and dispirited. The sim picked the asteroid field run again—the same run as the first time, with the exact same mission—and, as an added bonus, threw in a scattering of DSR ships patrolling the asteroid field's outer layer.

Made Abboud feel better, coming across them. Embarrassed as hell after that first run, thinking she'd spooked and started seeing things. Inventing sensor blips that simply weren't there. Made everyone feel better when Henricksen slipped by them without crashing into anything. In fact, they were all feeling pretty damn good about themselves and this ships of theirs until a second smattering ships appeared further in.

Reared up right in front of them, hiding in the shadows of the tumbling rocks. Henricksen grabbed at the controls and twitched the ship over, bobbled the maneuver in his hurry and bounced it off an asteroid. Dented the RV-N so badly the cloaking system shorted out, taking the starboard side sensor array with it. Woke those patrolling ships up—better believe that—so they bailed out in a hurry. Tucked tail and ran—half-blind, asses hanging out in the wind—as plasma fire lit of their backside, chasing them all the way out of the asteroid field and into open space. *Kept* chasing them as Taggert spooled the hyperspace engines and jumped them back to base, system recording a second failure, mocking them with more sympathy cards and flowers.

Henricksen sat there, glowering, as the sympathy cards disappeared, taking the simulated flowers with them. Unbuckled from his seat and followed Sikuuku into the debriefing room—a twenty-by-twenty square attached to the monitoring room, equipped with a lectern at the front and a video system projecting images on the wall.

Rows of those odd little chair desks crammed inside it, facing the front wall. Crew slid in looking exhausted, staring dully at the wall as the first of the vids started.

One for each run—all the runs, for all of the crews. The lot of them critiquing each other, providing analysis and commentary on what went right and what went wrong.

Plenty to work on in that later category. All of them flubbed something, not just Petros and Baldini, those two loudmouthed Sosholo boys. Good crews overall on this project, but young and inexperienced. The RV-N chassis like nothing any of them had ever flown before.

Three hours Henricksen kept them there, staring at the flickering images from the simulation runs. Three hours in that debriefing room before he took pity on them. Noticed Fisker sitting glass-eyed at his desk—half-asleep, but pretending not to be—while Taggert leaned against a wall, unabashedly snoring as the last video played out.

"Get," he ordered, shutting the vid off.

Taggert woke with a snort, blinking blearily as he looked around.

"Grab a meal and hit the rack. No drinking," Henricksen added as crew stood and shuffled toward the door, eliciting a chorus of groans. "Yeah, yeah. Boo-hoo. I need you rested, not hung over and stumbling about in the wee hours of the morning." He caught Mahal's eye as Nunez stepped in behind her. "That means crew in their racks—*alone*. No carousing after hours."

Mahal's face darkened, but she wisely kept her mouth shut.

"Curfew's at 2200."

More bitching at that announcement. A whole *chorus* of put-upon groans.

Crew never did like curfew—universal fact of the military—and normally Henricksen didn't bother. But Kinsey had pretty much given the RV-N crew the run of the place the last two weeks, and from the sim results, it was obvious they needed a little structure.

"It's 2100 now," he said loudly, silencing the last of the complaints. "Which means the chow line's about to shut down. Grab a meal, get a shower. You can relax in the rec room after that. But come 2200 I expect everyone in their racks. We'll start back up again at 0600 tomorrow. Dismissed."

Crew left grumbling—Petros and Baldini the loudest among them, giving Henricksen the stink eye as they walked by. Pissed off at the curfew and kybosh on drinking. Egos wounded by the criticism he'd doled out.

Academy boys—delicate temperaments. Didn't like being called out in the debriefings. Being told they'd fucked up.

Henricksen stared them down—stony-faced and entirely unapologetic. Watched Mahal and Nunez follow Petros and Baldini into the monitoring room, noted the way they bowed their heads together, hands reaching, fingers entwined.

Slid a frowning look toward Sikuuku, called Fisker over and told him to make sure Mahal and Nunez kept it clean and slept in their own bunks for once.

Fisker, typically, didn't seem all that comfortable with the assignment. "Um…" He licked his lips, shifting nervously, touching at the ensign's bars on his collar. "How, sir?"

Sikuuku flashed a smile, eyes twinkling with mischief. "Tell the lovebirds the Captain'll be checkin'." The smile widened, turning distinctly evil. "Finds 'em breakin' curfew he'll roust 'em out in their birthday suits for a little midnight trainin' in the hangar bay."

Fisker's eyes widened, shifting to Henricksen's face. "Naked, sir?"

Henricksen shrugged, face deadpan as ever. "If that's the way I find 'em."

Fisker snickered, coloring, glancing guilty around.

"Get outta here, Ensign." Sikuuku flicked his fingers, waving Fisker away. "Grab some food and a shower, and then get your ass in bed." A glance at Henricksen, giving him a considering look. "Got a feelin' it's gonna be a long day tomorrow. You, the rest of 'em," second nod, this time to the crew crowding around the door, "you're gonna need all the rest you can get."

Fisker sobered up, freckled face turning thoughtful. Glanced to one side, eyeing Janssen and Adaeze huddled up, talking quietly in a corner, replaying a section of Adaeze's run. A nod and he saluted, spun on his heel and chased after Mahal and Nunez.

Janssen and Adaeze finished up soon after, stepped into the hall still discussing Adaeze's vid. Ugly bit of flying in the middle of it—bobble similar to Henricksen's, though the end result hadn't been quite as bad.

He waited until the two pilots left, slid behind the lectern and pulled up the feed from his last run. Set it to play as he sat down in the front row, nodding to Sikuuku as he settled into a seat beside him. "Lucky I didn't kill us again." Henricksen froze the feed, parsing through the associated data.

"Partial pass on that second run," Sikuuku reminded him. "Nothing to crow about under other circumstances, but not all that bad, honestly. For a first day."

"Maybe," Henricksen muttered, watching the video from their third run. He ran it through and rewound it, replaying the bobble that cost him the ship again and again. "Sloppy. God damned sloppy."

"Don't be so hard on yourself." Sikuuku slouched in his seat with his legs stretched in front of him crossing at the ankles, folded his arms, letting them rest on his stomach. "Ten years since you sat in the pilot's seat. And the last one was what? A Titan?"

"Aurora," Henricksen corrected, eyes never leaving the screen. He watched the RV-N blow for the tenth time, swore softly and wound the feedback to the beginning.

Sikuuku tapped him on the shoulder, pointed his chin at the door. "So, whaddya think? About the crew?" he explained at Henricksen's puzzled look.

"Solid, for the most part." Even Petros and Baldini, loudmouthed and obnoxious as they were. "First rate skills, the lot of them, but they need focus. Don't know how to work together as a team yet, much less a squadron." Henricksen sighed, shaking his head. "Kinsey's let them have the run of things too long."

Sikuuku grunted, slouching a little bit lower, watching the sim feed as Henricksen rewound it, playing the entire thing from start to finish this time. "Damned odd," he muttered.

Henricksen glowered in disgust. "Shit, is what it is. Rusty doesn't even *begin* to cover it."

"No. Not that." Sikuuku sat up and leaned forward, twirling a finger in the air. "Start it up from the beginning."

Henricksen looked at him and at the blank wall in front of them, shrugged and queued the video feed, watching Sikuuku out of the corner of his eye as the images started: simulated ship jumping into hyperspace, bumping clumsily through the trough.

"That." Sikuuku pointed a thick finger at the images in front of them as the ship shuddered, violently skipping about. "You're rusty but you're not *that* rusty." A flick of his eyes to Henricksen, eyebrow lifting in question. "Ship pretty much runs on autopilot once it hits the trough, doesn't it?"

Henricksen frowned, nodding, wondering where this was going. "More or less. Once you pass through the buckle..." He shrugged again, shook his head. "Hard to explain, but the trough sort of pulls the ship along. Pilot's almost redundant at that point. Don't really need to make any course corrections. Don't really *want* to make course corrections, honestly. Too many twitches and you'll spin the ship out of the trough entirely."

"And this?" Sikuuku touched the miniature panel built into the half desk connected to his chair, ran the feedback to the start of the trough run and let it play through. "Lot of skipping and drifting." Another look at Henricksen. "Was that you?"

"No." Henricksen's frown deepened, eyes locked onto the feed displayed on the wall. "Like you said, I'm rusty, but I'm not *that* rusty."

"Sim?" Sikuuku asked him, eyebrows lifting.

"Maybe."

Hated to blame the sim because it felt like an excuse. Then again, software had its own problems. Never quite recreated the real thing.

Henricksen chewed his lip, thinking that over, sighed and waved a hand. "Problem for another day," he decided, killing the video, shutting everything down. A check of the clock showed it was going on 2130—late and late after a long and grueling day. "C'mon," he said, crooking a finger. "Let's see if we can find some food before the mess hall closes for the night."

"Leftovers at this point. Chow line must've shut down."

"Better than nothing. 'Sides," he said, flashing a grin. "I'm sure your lady friend set something aside."

Sikuuku brightened noticeably. "She *did* mention something about pie."

"You and your pie." Henricksen rolled his eyes as he stood and stretched, wincing at a twinge in his back.

"Sore?"

"A little."

Sims did that. Hours and hours in a cramped space eventually took their toll. Younger crew likely wouldn't notice until morning. Shrug it off once the blood got flowing. But the abuse added up over the years. Body like Henricksen's took longer to recover.

"Getting old, old man." Sikuuku's smile widened, disappeared as he grunted, wincing himself, rubbing ruefully at his neck.

"We're both getting old," Henricksen said, lips twisting in a wry smile. His stomach rumbled loudly, reminding him it was empty, complaining about the delay. "C'mon, old man." He clapped Sikuuku on the shoulder, led him across the room. "Let's see if we can scrounge up something to eat."

Mess hall was quiet when they arrived, and mostly empty. Civ engineers long gone, a few of the hangar deck crew huddled together at a table—empty plates shoved to one side, data tablets passing between them—Shaw herself ensconced in her favorite corner. Taggert and Abboud sitting with her, a slim woman with a heart-shaped face that Henricksen remembered as Ogawa— Engineering Officer, on Janssen's crew at the moment.

Intense conversation going on in that corner. Passionate discussion centered around a couple of data readers resting on the tabletop, a third making the rounds of the table's occupants.

Taggert doing most of the talking—no surprise there. Abboud interjecting now and then, pointing to one reader and another as Shaw listened and frowned, swapping one device for another, scrolling through the contents of everyone.

Ogawa watching everything, eyes flicking everywhere.

Quiet, that one. Observant. Eyes and ears drinking in everything, analyzing the information on offer before interjecting herself.

Damned smart, from what Henricksen could tell. Most of the quiet ones were.

Ogawa spotted Henricksen and Sikuuku as they stepped through the mess halls doors, nudged at Taggert and leaned close, murmuring in his ear. Pointed, causing the entire table to turn, hands lifting, sketching quick salutes before the lot of them resumed their conversation. The three readers laid out like playing cards between them, the table's occupants huddled around them, arguing this point and that like the world's most ardent group of gamblers.

"Whaddaya suppose is goin' on over there?" Sikuuku asked.

"Probably complaining about the sims."

Shaw's deck gang maintained them, along with the RV-Ns in the hangar bay. Someone—usually Taggert—always seemed to be complaining about *something* related to the sims.

"Taggert was bitching about the randomization routines before we started that first run."

"Hopefully he'll talk to her about the seats in those pods. Hard as rock," Sikuuku grumbled, rubbing his behind. "Ass feels like it went three rounds with an angry buffalo."

Henricksen gave him a look. "I have absolutely no idea what that means. Not sure I want to either," he added, when the gunner started to explain.

He set off across the room, winding through the mess hall's tables, angling for the chow line at the back. As expected, the food was pretty picked over— congealed leftovers gone mostly cold by now, line cooks shuttling warming trays between the chow line and the kitchen, clearing away what little food remained.

"No pie," Sikuuku noted, sounding distinctly disappointed. "Think I'll just skip—"

"Oh, no you don't." Henricksen grabbed a plate and shoved it into the gunner's hands. Filled it before he could refuse and grabbed another for himself.

Nodded to a table by the wall—close to where Shaw held court in the corner—and guided Sikuuku over, dropping into the chair across from him as the gunner plunked down, yawning widely. Scooped up a fork and just sat there, staring at his plate.

Dog-tired, from the look of him. Exhausted as Henricksen himself. Long time since either of them ran sims for hours at a time. Plenty of combat experience—always exhausted after a fight—but sims were different. Live fire maneuvers were all about instinct and adrenaline—high level plans and reacting on the fly, an experience the sims attempted to copy but never quite got right.

Different challenge, working in the sims. Intense levels of concentration required. Anxiety amped up by the fact you knew—just *knew*—there was a way to beat this and claim a win.

Nothing at all like live fire combat. No redo in real life. No restarting the mission and trying again.

And yet, for all that, Henricksen hated them. Despised the sims with a deep and all-encompassing passion. Couldn't wait to finish up basic training and get into the real thing when they sent him to that OCS combat school. Sims there were killer—pounded hell out of the trainees who ran them—but they had nothing on the RV-N sim.

Rough one, that trainer. Required just about everything he had. Daunting, imagining what the real thing would be like after suffering through that virtual ride.

"Eat," Henricksen ordered, taking a bite himself.

Wasn't all that hungry, but the body needed calories. And experience told him skipping meals was a seriously bad idea for crew in training.

Sikuuku blinked and shook himself, dipped his fork into the mound of food in front of him. Scooped up a bit and sniffed at it, grimaced and upended the fork, returning the contents to the pile. "Smells like shit," he said, pushing the plate away.

"Eat. That's an order." Henricksen shoved the plate back, glaring at the gunner until he picked up the fork and scooped some food into his mouth.

"Tastes like shit," he mumbled around a mouthful.

"Curry, supposedly." Henricksen waved at the lump of yellow goo piled in front of him. "'Least, that's what the sign said." He frowned doubtfully, examining the toxic yellow sludge on his plate.

Didn't look like curry. Or any other recognizable form of food, for that matter. And the smell of it…well, curry meant spices, but the odor wafting from the meal in front of him did indeed remind Henricksen of an animal's backside emissions.

Tastes like it, too, he thought, choking a mouthful down.

He grimaced and kept shoveling, chasing mouthfuls of curry with some protein and electrolyte-infused juice until he cleaned his plate. Made sure

Sikuuku did the same, ignoring the grumbling along the way. Skipped the beer he wanted because tired and beer was a seriously bad combination, especially since he'd banned drink for the rest of the crew.

Sat back still sipping at his juice, idly scanning the mess hall while his taste buds puzzled over the taste of his drink, trying to give it a name. Noticed a couple of Raven crew partaking of the bar's offerings—Petros and Baldini, predictably—but decided to leave it alone since they seemed to be taking it easy. Nursing their drinks over a subdued game of cards, skipping the pool and vids tonight.

Muted chatter in the mess hall this evening, now that he stopped to notice. Even the discussion with Shaw in the corner starting to wind down. Tired, the lot of them—he read that in their faces. The snatches of conversation he picked up.

Chatter about the day's training, mostly. General consensus indicating that everyone had had a severely bad day.

Actually made Henricksen feel a tad better, that. Might be old and rusty but even the young bucks were having a rough time with this chassis. Feeling their age, as it were.

"Kinsey's been soft on them." Sikuuku caught his eye, nodded to the crew scattered around the mess hall as he scraped a last mouthful off his plate.

"Just thinkin' that," Henricksen nodded, leaning back in his chair. A sip and he lowered his drink, couching the glass against his stomach. "Hate to tell 'em, but it's gonna get harder from here on out. A *lot* harder."

And that was just the sims. They still had the RV-N to deal with. The *real* spacecraft, not the virtualized environment of the software-based faux chassis.

Sikuuku's head swiveled, eyes considering the bar. A look from Henricksen convinced him to steer clear—that and the fact he might have to interact with Petros and Baldini—so he settled for the purple-red juice instead. "Pomegranate?" he guessed, taking a sip.

"God only knows," Henricksen said, the murmur of conversation in the corner drawing his eyes to Shaw again.

Interesting woman, Shaw. Tough as nails from what he'd seen, the bits and pieces he'd picked up from the flight crews. Not masculine, as so often happened. More the kind of woman who'd pair a ball cap with a ball gown and see nothing at all strange about it.

Liked that kind of woman, as it so happened. Liked that kind of woman a lot.

Enlisted though, which came with its own set of complications. Fleet frowned on officer and enlisted fraternization. And Shaw…not a direct report, but technically she lay somewhere within his chain of command.

"Not many of her mech gang here." Henricksen gestured with his glass at the half-empty room. "Wonder what that's about."

Sikuuku shrugged his shoulders and sipped at his drink, lips twisting at the tart yet sweet taste. Smacked his lips after, like he didn't know if he liked the juice or not. "Engineers aren't here either," he noted, eyes flicking to the corner the civvies typically claimed. "Kinsey wants the RV-Ns running. Got you and me whipping the crews into shape. Expect he's got the civs and the mech crews working overtime getting the chassis ready to fly."

"Maybe." Henricksen tilted his head, thinking. Remembering their introduction to Kinsey. His mention of experimental trials and two burnt out pilots. "Sure is in an all-fired hurry, isn't he?"

Bothered him, that. Rushing tech into service never went well. Usually led to disastrous results. People getting hurt.

Sikuuku tilted his glass, frowning at the contents. Shrugged his shoulders, tracking Petros and Baldini as they walked across the room. "You heard him. Project's behind schedule. Government's threatening to pull the funding." The two pilots exited and he turned his eyes back to Henricksen. "That happens and our billets go, too. We get shipped off to whatever leftover ship has an opening."

Henricksen bowed his head, considering the drink in his hands. "Fleet always needs gunners. You'll land on your feet."

"Needs captains, too," Sikuuku told him.

Henricksen grunted, lips twisting in a bitter smile. Fleet only need as many captains as they had ships. He might get lucky—boot some poor commander off an Aurora, find an opening on a Titan somewhere. More likely he'd end up in some admin position. Languish stationside for a few years before the Fleet quietly processed him out.

He closed his eyes, rubbing wearily at his face. Didn't want that. God he didn't want to end his career that way. "I'll talk to Shaw and Karansky. See where they are with the RV-N."

Sikuuku nodded, raising his glass in thanks.

"I want you to up the flight crews' time in the sims, though. We took it easy on 'em today—"

"Easy. Right," Sikuuku grunted. "Five hours in the sims isn't exactly what I'd call easy."

Henricksen shrugged his shoulders, swirling the juice in his glass. "Real thing's gonna be a whole lot harder." He glanced up, catching Sikuuku's eyes. "Run 'em hard in the sims, give 'em a taste of what they're in for."

Sikuuku was quiet a moment, studying Henricksen across the table. "Push 'em too hard and you'll break some of 'em."

Henricksen nodded slowly. "Rather break 'em than kill 'em." Didn't feel good about saying that, but sometimes the lesser of two evils was the best you could do. "You heard Kinsey—that chassis put two pilots in the hospital. Two that we *know* of. Messed up so bad they had to be medically retired. Can't live with that," he said, shaking his head hard. "I won't put *any* of this crew into the RV-N until their damned good and ready."

"And the ship?" Sikuuku asked quietly. "Train 'em in the sims all you want, but how do you know when the ships are ready?"

Tough question. Difficult to answer since he wasn't an engineer. Henricksen's eyes drifted to Shaw sitting in the corner. Shaw who ran the pit crew, and likely knew the RV-N's design specs back to front.

"Shaw'll know." He flicked his eyes to Sikuuku, nodded to Shaw in the corner. Just she and Ogawa sitting there now, Taggert and Abboud having left a few minutes ago, ostensibly to go back to the barracks. "Karansky's Kinsey's man. Not sure if I can trust what he tells me. But Shaw…"

No-nonsense woman. Ran her deck gang like a factory. Had no qualms at all about ordering Karansky's civ engineers around.

Liked having Shaw in charge of RV-N maintenance. Felt a hell of a lot better about strapping his ass into that pilot mangler they called a stealth ship knowing Shaw and her deck gang had had their hands on it.

Sikuuku yawned widely, eyes drifting to the bar again.

"Go," Henricksen ordered, waving him away. "Keep it to one, though. Need you sharp, tomorrow, ya hear?"

"Always sharp," Sikuuku retorted, lips skinning back in a cocksure grin. "Pilot's a bit rusty but this gunner's got it goin' on."

"Oh, you've got *something* going on, alright," Henricksen said sourly. "Just not sure what it is."

Sikuuku barked a laugh, flipping an off-handed salute. Shoved back his chair and ambled over to the bar and poured himself a beer.

Sipped at it, drinking it slowly while he made the rounds of the crew in the mess hall, stopping now and then to swap a few words.

Henricksen watched him a while, envying him that drink, disgusting as the beer here was. Checked the time and found he had an hour yet before curfew, decided to treat himself to a drink as well.

Half a glass only. To settle the godawful curry. Make sure it stayed down.

TWELVE

Henricksen upped the pace on the flight crews' training the very next morning. Rousted everyone out of bed at 0530, allowing them thirty short minutes to shower, and eat, and scrub the cobwebs from their brains before shoving them into the trainers—all six crews at once this time—and keeping them there the rest of the day.

Eight full hours in the sims, with just a short break at mid-day to grab lunch from the chow hall. The few minutes it took the sim to reset between runs to catch their breath, let the adrenaline bleed out.

Brutal schedule, that day. Hard on the body. Mind as well. Needed to be hard on them, though—nothing at all easy about Black Ops and this experimental ship. A chassis Kinsey freely admitted had already crippled two of his most experienced test pilots. And sneaking around the galaxy trying to act like a ghost...nothing at all easy about that.

'Course, they had the AI to help them. Henricksen still refused to use them—not yet, that time would come—but the other pilots tested them out. He could hear them cutting in during training, shy little voices offering advice when prompted. Encouragement when they thought it needed. Eager, so very eager despite that shyness. Wanting to be part of this whole process, and yet afraid to intrude, which felt...wrong, somehow. That approach, their mannerisms, none of it felt right.

Part of the reason he avoided them. *Hecate* was never shy. Didn't *need* to be eager, because she knew her place. Staked her claim long, long ago.

Crew showed *her* respect, not the other way 'round.

But if the flight crews wanted those shy little AI voices in the sims, he wouldn't begrudge it. Not necessarily a bad idea, familiarizing themselves with the mindset that ran the *Raven* chassis. Supposed *he* should, eventually. When the time was right.

Until then, he focused on training. Running the crews all day with those sprightly little AI voices dipping in and out. Pointed their tired, sore carcasses to the tiny classroom for debriefings afterward. Two full hours of video review with the flight crews critiquing each other while Sikuuku and Henricksen looked on, offering their own thoughts every now and then, but mostly letting the crew do the talking.

Kept a stiff upper lip and took their own lumps when the time came because, the fact was, Henricksen's runs had just as many problems as any of the others. Did better on his second day than the first—just one failed mission this time and no simulated deaths—and the third day's training went even better. A week in the sims and the muscle memory started to return, instincts kicking in, reflexes with them. Training pod felt less and less like simulation, and more and more like the real thing. Its reactions known and expected, if awfully twitchy. His own responses second-nature, adjustments made without even realizing what he'd done.

Hyperspace jumps felt just as bumpy—rough road through jump in these Ravens, but Henricksen was starting to get things down. Finally catching up with the younger pilots—better believe that felt good. Hadn't been a half-bad jump jockey once upon a time—pushers weren't warships, and the Titans and Aurora's he'd piloted were a far cry from this sharp-sided, on-the-edge-of-chaos stealth ship they'd stuck him in, but he held his own. Taught Petros and Baldini a thing or two while he was at it.

Petros. Baldini.

Henricksen shook his head just thinking about the two Sosholo boys. Trouble, the both of them. Reined them in a bit that first week, pushed them hard—pushed everyone hard—to wring the piss and vinegar out of them, clear the egotistical asshole out of their minds. Made some progress, but those two had *years* of practice being assholes—a mountain of baggage to overcome.

Would, though—Henricksen was confident about that. Made it his own personal mission to beat that arrogant Academy crap out of the two pilots. Take some time, though, and likely a whole lot of patience. Maybe more than he had.

Henricksen was good—very good, wouldn't have made captain the old fashioned way if he wasn't—and doggedly persistent. His own kind of asshole when he needed to be. But he wasn't a miracle worker. Couldn't fix stupid overnight.

Luckily, the rest of the crew was solid. Every last one of them. Even Petros and Baldini when they let the attitudes go. Huddled together in the mess hall after training and debrief, swapping stories, congratulating and complaining, pairings starting to develop—pilots and gunners, scan techs and engineering officers—that Henricksen dutifully jotted down.

Always interesting how that happened. Often times it was crew who didn't even particularly like each other that clicked in training. The same characteristics that put them at odds in real life making them complementary in the strapped down virtual reality of the sims.

Three weeks Henricksen worked them, hitting the crews hard. Shoving them in the sim pods early and keeping them there for hours. Debriefs afterward, reviewing the training data in exacting, excruciating detail. Food because the body needed fuel to keep pace with that grueling schedule. Sleep to recharge. Prevent them from completely burning out.

Curfew to make sure crew *got* that sleep. Remove the temptation to skive off and get drunk. Mess around in a neighbor's rack.

Crew bucked it, of course, not liking that restriction. But a week in and they stopped complaining. Too damn tired. Not even particularly interested after a few days of Henricksen's training sessions.

A week in, and 2200 found the mess hall all but deserted, the exhausted flight crews long since gone to their beds. Three weeks in, and the mech gang owned the mess hall from 2000 on.

Three weeks—that's all it took to break them. Three solid weeks of sim training, without a single day off.

"They're starting to feel it." Sikuuku nudged at Henricksen's arm, pointing to Fisker nodding off in a corner—eyes closed, chin resting on his chest, body sprawled in that boneless way only corpses or sleeping people could.

Rest of the crew in the debrief room didn't look all that much better. They yawned and rubbed at their faces, blinking bleary eyes. Fighting sleep like Fisker, and yet too damned stubborn to admit they were tired.

"Think we should call it a night?"

"Might as well. Crew's knackered." Henricksen yawned, stretching in his chair. Winced as abused joints popped and overworked muscles cramped, complaining at the unrelenting abuse. "Could sleep for a week myself," he admitted. "Get 'em outta here." He rubbed at his eyes, waved at the people in the room. "Make sure no one skips chow, though."

Huge mistake, forgetting to fuel the body. Tired body recovered with enough sleep. Tired, hungry body just ate itself. Eventually collapsed under its own weight.

"Alright, boys and girls." Sikuuku walked over to the podium and shut the projector off. "Captain's decided to take it easy on you bunch of lazybones and set you loose early."

A modicum of sleepy cheering greeted that announcement, accompanied by a smattering of lethargic applause.

"Yeah, yeah. I'm just as happy as you." Sikuuku smiled, hooking a thumb toward the door. "Now get outta here, ya slugs. Grab some chow and some rack time. We'll be back at it at 0600 tomorrow."

Crew groaned, immediately complaining. Apparently they'd expected a lie-in in addition to the early dismissal.

Huh-uh. Not happening. Henricksen's charity only went so far.

He stood, joining Sikuuku at the podium, folded his arms and turned a stony stare upon the room. Kept staring until the grumbling quieted, crew slipping from their seats, slouching toward the door.

Weary, every last one of them. Heads bowed, shoulders slumping, looking like it took every last bit of energy left in them just to walk across that room.

Almost felt bad for them—Henricksen knew that feeling himself. Felt half-wasted himself right now, but refused to let on. Refused to admit to himself just how dog-tired exhausted he felt.

Combat trained you to live with it. Treat that feeling as normal and move on.

Keep going.

Fight harder.

"Taggert." He crooked a finger at the engineering officer, pointing to Fisker leaning against the wall. "Take him with you."

"Poor, wee fella. All tuckered out." Taggert walked over and shook Fisker awake, wrapped an arm around his shoulders and led the mumbling, exhausted ensign out of the room.

That left Janssen and Adaeze—the usual suspects. Those two pilots always seemed to linger behind the others—heads bowed together, taking one last look at the video captures, discussing some bit of data on a reader shared between them.

Hard workers, those two. The best pilots of the bunch. Henricksen rated his own skills about even with Janssen's, but Adaeze...honestly still chasing Adaeze. Good reflexes on her. Lot of focus. Cool under pressure, seldom if ever rattled.

Respected that. Respected the *hell* out of that. But even the best needed to rest now and then.

"Janssen. Adaeze."

The two pilots kept talking, ignoring Henricksen. Probably oblivious to the fact he'd even spoken.

Henricksen cleared his throat—loudly—coughing a few times for good measure. Smiled good naturedly when he finally had their attention, and pointed to the reader in Janssen's hand. "Shut it down. That's enough for tonight." Janssen opened his mouth to object, but Henricksen cut him off with a raised hand. Stepped around the podium and yanked the debriefing room door open. "Out," he ordered, pointing to the sim room on the other side. "Now. Food, sleep, get back at it tomorrow."

Janssen shared a look with Adaeze, yawned and nodded—pale face ghostly with exhaustion, dark circles showing under his eyes. He scooped up the reader and twitched his fingers at Adaeze, jerked his head toward the door before heading across the room, Adaeze following a step behind.

"You too, Chief." Henricksen crooked a finger at Sikuuku standing at the podium.

"Thought we might stay a while. Talk about crew assignments." Sikuuku nodded to Janssen and Adaeze—still fixated on that reader and whatever analytical package or test report they'd been going over before Henricksen kicked them out. Waited until they exited before turning his eyes Henricksen's way. "Four weeks, remember?"

"Yeah. I remember."

Kinsey's timeline, not Henricksen's. A bogus, arbitrary number that failed to take into account whether or not the RV-N itself was ready. They'd already burned through three of those weeks in sim training, swapping crew around each day in search of six perfect combinations that probably didn't exist. Honestly could've used three more, but they were up against it now. Just about out of time and definitely testing Kinsey's patience.

"Later," Henricksen promised.

"When?" Sikuuku folded his arms, chin lifting, giving Henricksen his stubborn look. "Crew's getting antsy. They're tired of the constant changes."

"I know." Henricksen sighed, closing his eyes, pinching the bridge of his nose. "Believe me, I am too."

"You're avoiding this," Sikuuku accused.

Some truth to that. More than Henricksen wanted to admit.

"Later, alright? Let's just grab a drink in the mess hall. I'm sick to death of this goddamn room."

Sikuuku pursed his lips, considering, mouth twitching at the corners. "Think I'm that cheap of a date, eh?"

"Know you are." Henricksen smiled. "Out. Now," he said, pointing through the door. "Before I change my mind."

"Aye, sir. Drinks ahoy, sir." Sikuuku tapped two fingers to his temple and slipped past Henricksen into the sim room, waiting for him on the other side.

Shut everything down and locked the room up before taking off. Caught up with Adaeze and Janssen in the control room—the two of them walking and talking with that reader between them, making a slow job of it as a result.

"Enough of that." Henricksen snatched the reader from Janssen's hand, powered it down and passed it to Sikuuku so he couldn't just turn it back on. "And don't think I haven't noticed you two sneaking back into the debriefing room after chow call."

Janssen had the decency to blush. Adaeze just smiled, entirely unapologetic.

"Mess hall," he said, shoving them toward the door. "Drinks are on me."

"Drinks?" Janssen perked up noticeably. "As in more than one?"

"Just so long as you don't get sloppy. Now march," Henricksen ordered, hustling them out the door.

Just a short walk back to the berthing section, but four tired, slow moving crew turned it into an epic slog. Henricksen ended up walking side-by-side with Adaeze, making small talk to pass the time while Sikuuku followed after, admiring the view of the pilot's behind.

Henricksen glanced over his shoulder, giving the gunner a stern look, but Sikuuku kept right on staring—smiling unabashedly as they ambled along. A sigh and Henricksen left him to it. Figured Adaeze would deck him if she got offended—not exactly a shrinking violet, that one.

"Noticed that little maneuver of yours back there," he said, in his most casual, just-two-pilots-talking voice. Strolled along beside with his hands in his pockets, acting like he didn't have a care in the world.

Adaeze saw right through it, smiled innocently back. "Oh yeah? And what maneuver was that?"

"That slingshot business. Using the asteroids' pull and your maneuvering jets to hopscotch around the boulder field."

Adaeze flushed—dark face deepening a shade—and ducked her head, lips twisting. "Noticed that, did you?"

"Neatly done," he told her, tipping an invisible cap. "Been a long time since I saw anyone try something like that."

Pusher technique, what she'd executed. Designed to save fuel. Practical maneuver, considering the pushers lived and died by the bottom line, but risky as all get-out. Especially if you didn't quite know what you were doing.

Mess up your timing, and you'd slam the ship head-on into a rock. Get it wrong, and it'd cost you a whole lot more than you bargained for. Take your ship *and* your life.

"Last I checked, Academy didn't teach their pilots techniques like that." Henricksen stopped at the pressure door and entered his credentials, waiting for Adaeze's answer.

"No," she admitted. "It doesn't." Adaeze folded her arms, head tilting. "Which makes me wonder how *you* know about it, Captain."

"Pusher," he told her, pointing a thumb at his chest. "You?"

"Merchant transport." Adaeze lifted her chin, flashing a proud smile. "Fifth generation star hauler."

Henricksen grunted, surprised. Impressed all over again. "Fifth generation. Lot of investment."

"A bit," she nodded.

"So, why'd you leave?"

Adaeze barked a laugh and grabbed the door, pulling it open. Stepped through and held it as Henricksen followed after. "Four sisters. All of them older. All of them working that ship."

"Ouch." Henricksen winced in commiseration.

"Tell me about it." Adaeze rolled her eyes, throwing a look over her shoulder as Sikuuku and Janssen stepped through, letting the pressure door *clang* closed. "Drea was eldest, which meant she'd be captain once Momma stood down. The others..." She shrugged, eyes flicking to Henricksen walking beside her. "Well, when you're fifth in line, you can't expect to get any of the cherry assignments. Momma said something about putting me in charge of the cargo hold so I skipped out." Adaeze smiled widely. "Applied to the Academy on Greshalon. Got out as soon as I could."

"Bet that didn't make Momma none too happy."

Adaeze laughed again—a good, rich sound. "No. It most certainly didn't."

"This. All this." Henricksen waved at the hallways around them, the pressure door behind, the hangar deck on the other side. "Fleet's not forever. Ever think about going back?"

Adaeze stopped dead, smile slipping, looking back at Janssen again. "Nothing to go back to."

"I'm sure Momma wasn't *that* mad."

"Not Momma."

Adaeze looked at him and Henricksen's heart sank. "Shit. What happened?"

"DSR." Adaeze kept staring—eye to eye, not wavering one bit. "Ship was on a run to Androneer. DSR..." A flicker of something and she ducked her head, toe digging at the decking. "Wasn't much left by the time the DSR were done."

Shit.

Henricksen sighed, hand lifting, rubbing at his face. There'd been something in her record, but he hadn't remembered. Not until now. "I'm sorry, Adaeze. I didn't—"

"Don't be," she told him, raising a hand. "Past is past. Nothing to be—"

"Sir!" The doors to the mess hall banged open, light and noise spilling into the corridor along with a frantically waving Fisker.

Terrible timing, that ensign. Probably the *worst* moment he could have interrupted.

"What is it, Fisker?" Henricksen growled.

"There's a fight." Fisker flinched as the sharp sound of shattering glass washed over him. "Hurry, sir!"

"Aw, hell." Henricksen sprinted down the hallway with Adaeze running as this side.

Sikuuku lumbered after them—moving surprisingly quickly for someone so burly, completely outpacing long-legged Janssen with his graceful, loping strides. The four of them burst through the door in a tight knot, sweeping Fisker along with them. Swarmed into a room turned to bedlam—tables knocked over, plates and glassware lying shattered on the decking, civvies fleeing in a hurry, bumping into Henricksen and the others in their rush to get out.

Military clustered at the mess hall's edges, watching the conflagration from a safe distance, looking slightly put out. And at the center of it all, two uniforms, grappling amidst the devastation. Baldini was one of them—no mistaking that bald-headed sparkplug of a pilot—and the other one of Shaw's bunch. A hulking lump of flesh named Bent, or Brent, or something equally short and descriptive. The two men latched on to one another, throwing punches as they tumbled about the room. Petros following them like some kind of referee, shouting encouragement to egg Baldini on.

"You two." Henricksen flicked his fingers at Sikuuku and Janssen, waving them to one side. "Take Shaw's man. Adaeze and I will handle Baldini."

They split as they left the doorway—Janssen and Sikuuku moving left as ordered, converging on one combatant while Henricksen and Adaeze went after the other.

Always dicey, coming in on an active fight. Sikuuku grabbed Shaw's man by one arm and pulled him around, nearly getting socked in the face for his trouble. Luckily, Bent—Henricksen was pretty sure it was Bent—pulled his punch at the last moment, realizing who'd grabbed him, and lowered his fist to his side. Baldini, though…pilot was far gone. Swinging blindly, too pissed off to even recognize faces anymore. Henricksen ducked, shoving at the pilot, grunted when a blow landed on his shoulder, another on his chest. Finally managed to get a good grip on Baldini and started to pull him away, while those ham-sized fists kept swinging away.

One caught his ear, sparking a flash of pain, raising a ringing that reverberated around his head. Henricksen ducked the next punch, narrowly avoiding another blow. Saw Baldini's other fist come around and yelled a warning, but he was already too late.

The pilot's fist caught Adaeze squarely on the cheek, spinning her around, sending her stumbling away.

"Shut it down! Shut it down!" Henricksen shoved at Baldini, leaning hard against him as he spat curses and threw punches, doing his best to hold the struggling pilot back. "Adaeze!" He turned his head, trying to find her, risking a blow himself to make sure she was alright. "You okay?"

"Son of a bitch." Adaeze winced, hand pressed to her cheek. Rounded on Baldini with her eyes flashing with anger.

Two quick steps brought her right in front of him, perilously close to those windmilling fists of ham. It also brought Baldini close to *her*, but in his blind rage, he never realized the danger. Never even noticed her arm cocking backward. Not until Adaeze's fist mashed into his face.

"Guh!" Baldini stumbled a step, blood dribbling from his lips. Snarled and reached for her only to freeze up in horror when he finally saw her—really saw her and realized just who had hit him. Actually backed up a step when he spied the black and blue mouse rising on Adaeze's cheek. "Shit," he breathed, shoulders slumping, fists dropping to his sides.

"What the *fuck*, Baldini?" Knocked the fight right out of Baldini, that one punch, but from the look of fury on her face, Adaeze was just getting started. "What is your major malfunction, you jackass, crack-whacker?"

"I wasn't—I didn't—"

"The *hell*!" Adaeze lunged at him, fingers curled, ready to latch onto Baldini's neck and strangle the shit out of him.

Henricksen stepped between them with his arms spread wide, struggling to hold the two of them back. "Little help?" he called.

Chairs scraped across the floor, uniforms converging, hands grabbing at the two combatants to pull them apart.

"I didn't—I wasn't—" Baldini shook his head, eyes wide as dinner plates. "I didn't mean—"

"Don't give a *fuck* what you meant." Adaeze lunged again and came up against a wall of uniforms. Feinted left and dodged right, thinking to get around them and take Baldini from the side. Stood on her tiptoes when that didn't work and yelled over their heads, spitting curses like a sailor. "You punched me in the fucking face, you fucking gorilla!"

"It wasn't my fault!" Baldini insisted, pointing accusingly at Shaw's man. "*He's* the jackass—"

"Shut it, Baldini!" Henricksen snapped. "You too, Adaeze. We got enough anger in this room right now, the last thing I need is the two of you getting into a dust-up as well."

Adaeze stiffened, thunderclouds gathering on her face. She spat on the floor and whirled around, stalked across the room and barged her way through the mess hall doors.

"Fisker." Henricksen waved the ensign over. "Fix her a plate. Bring it to her room."

"But that's—that's not—"

"I know it's against regs. Just do it," Henricksen ordered.

"Aye, sir." Fisker skittered across the room, gathering up food from the chow line before following Adaeze out the door.

"Right." Henricksen turned around, staring the two combatants down. "Now I'm gonna ask this once, and I want a straight answer: what the *hell* is this all about?"

Brand—that was Shaw's man, Henricksen could read the nametag now—and Baldini both started pointing fingers, shouting angrily at each other as they traded accusations.

"Alright, alright, alright! Shut it!" Henricksen glared them into silence. "Shaw!" he called, looking to her usual place in the corner. "What are these two idiots so worked up about?"

"Sims. Weebles there," Shaw winked at Baldini, puckered up her lips when he bristled and blew him a kiss, "seems to think Brand's been shirking his duties. Falling behind on patching the sim software or some such."

"Sims?" Henricksen folded his arms, staring at Baldini. "*That's* what this about?"

"Goddamn things keep repeating," Baldini grumbled, glaring at Brand on the opposite side of the room. "I told that monkey wagon the software's shit—"

"You shut that down right now," Sikuuku thundered, but Baldini kept right on going.

"I don't know why we're still *in* the damn sims anyway. We've got the *real* thing—"

"Shut. It. Down," Sikuuku snarled, getting right in Baldini's face.

Baldini started to raise a fist, realized that was a *huge* mistake and settled for glowering instead, squinching up his face to make sure everyone knew he was unhappy.

"This repeating thing." Henricksen waited until Baldini looked at him. "Explain."

"Algorithms." Baldini flicked his fingers. "Supposed to drive randomized scenarios, but the stupid things keep repeating. Spitting out that one section over and over again."

Henricksen went cold all over. He'd noticed, hadn't he? Noticed it more and more in just the last week. "The asteroid field," he said numbly and saw Baldini grimace, nod his bald head.

Remembered Taggert remarking on that same fact when he first got here and wished now that he'd paid more attention.

"Random my ass," Baldini muttered.

"He spoke to you about this?" Henricksen flicked his eyes back to Shaw.

"He did. And I had Brand take a look at it. Twice," Shaw said, showing him two fingers.

"And?"

"Everything patched and perfect. If there's a flaw in the software, it's the engineers' fault, not my guys. *They* build the shit, *we* just install it."

Henricksen chewed his lip, thinking. "I'll talk to Kinsey about it."

Shaw dipped her head, raised her beer in thanks.

"You two." Henricksen pivoted, looking from Baldini to Brand. "Stay away from each other. Don't have to like each other, but the last thing I need is fist fights in the mess hall after eight bloody hours in the sims." He turned his head, looking from one face to the other. "You two apes think you can manage that, or do I need to assign a chaperone to make sure you behave?"

Brand flushed and dropped his eyes, mumbling something unintelligible under his breath. Baldini stiffened, eyes blazing. Spun on his heel and stalked into the rec room, presumably to murder pool balls for an hour or two before curfew.

"Want me to go talk to him?" Sikuuku curled a hand into a fist, smacked it against his open palm.

"No. Don't get me wrong—boy could severely use an ass whoopin' to drive that shit-stick attitude out of him—but there's been enough punches thrown tonight. Let him take out his frustrations on those pool balls. We'll work on the rest another time."

Sikuuku shrugged, clearly disappointed. "If you say so."

"I do," Henricksen nodded, eyes flicking to Baldini as the pool balls in the next room cracked. "How about that drink?" he suggested, nodding to the bar across the room. "Round for the crew, while you're at it."

Hadn't done that since they first arrived. Couldn't buy drinks too often or they'd grow to expect it, but gestures were important. A good way to settle nerves jangled by Baldini's fist fight.

"Done and done." Sikuuku started to smile, stiffened and turned as the mess hall doors opened and a very starched, very stiff and uncomfortable looking petty officer stepped inside. "Company," he said, nodding to their visitor by the door.

"Hollings." Henricksen nodded to Fisker's replacement—Kinsey's new aide-de-camp. "Is it Friday already?"

"Yes, sir. Sorry, sir." Hollings shrugged apologetically. "Mr. Kinsey sent me in case you forgot."

Had, actually, though Henricksen wouldn't admit it. Kinsey invited him to dinner every Friday evening—a social visit cum business meeting in which the administrator peppered Henricksen with questions, grilling him over an opulent dinner in his quarters.

Meant to impress him, those meetings, but mostly they just pissed Henricksen off. Not fair, mixing soft surroundings with hard questions. Inviting someone to dinner only to give them the fifth degree.

"If you'll come with me?" Hollings held the door open, nodded the hallway on the other side.

"Rain check," Henricksen said, glancing at Sikuuku beside him. "Looks like you'll have to have that drink on your own."

"But—but the assignments!" Sikuuku fished a reader from his pocket. "You can't keep avoiding this," he said, holding it up.

"Not avoiding it," Henricksen assured him. He waved at stiff-shirted Hollings, shrugging helplessly as he joined him by the mess hall doors. "Duty calls, Sikuuku. I'll be back later."

"Where are you *going*?" Sikuuku demanded.

Henricksen flashed a smile, glancing back over his shoulder. "To meet with Kinsey. I've got a scintillating evening of rubber chicken and boring conversation ahead of me and I don't want to miss a minute."

Truthfully he wanted to miss *all* of it, but the Friday evening meetings were Kinsey's one requirement. The *only* demand he'd place on Henricksen outside of that four-week timetable.

A timetable now three weeks gone.

Henricksen grimaced, eying the crew scattered across the mess hall, wishing he had just a few more weeks. "I'll be back late," he said, nodding to Sikuuku as he faced around. "Don't wait up."

"And the beer?" Sikuuku called after him.

"Put it on my tab." Henricksen waved without looking, following Hollings out the door.

THIRTEEN

Long, winding path from the RV-N project's section of the station to the berthings for the station's senior staff and high ranking administrators. One musty, grey corridor giving way to another, until Hollings buzzed them through a security door, leading Henricksen into a section of the station that was obviously, entirely different.

The smell of the place was the first clue—no mildew odor in the air, not anywhere in this section—and the look of it, the *feel* of it...

Different. All so very different.

Corridors widened, swapping the gathering thunderheads of blank, grey walls for a soft white of puffy clouds. The buzzing electric lights, which swarmed like angry bees across the rest of the station, quieted here. Became moths gathered around candle flames. Butterflies fluttering in the early morning sun. More than that, more than *anything,* it was quiet here. Not silent—no station ever was—but as close to noiseless as an active station ever got.

Buffers in the walls, he supposed, muting the constant hum of machinery to a whispering, soothing purr. Environmentals chuffing discretely, breathing pine-scented air through the compartments and corridors while simulated sunshine filtered from above.

Soothing, so very soothing, this section of the station. These opulent, well-appointed spaces where the Fleet Brass and senior civilian administrators all lived. And oh how Henricksen hated it. The forced mingling and polite smiles, the endless rounds of saluting as he walked the softly carpeted halls. Environmentals might cover the mildew stench pervading the rest of the station, but this section stank just the same. Reeked of wealth and privilege, leaving a pusher kid turned starship captain like Henricksen feeling decidedly shabby in comparison. A ragged scarecrow in his uniform of black on black.

Hollings stopped in front of a brass and steel door, wood trim banding the edges, and pressed a finger to an old fashioned doorbell set in the wall. Clasped his hands behind him and waited, nodding politely to Henricksen until the intercom buzzed and Kinsey's voice came through.

"Yes?"

Bored tone. Entirely unfriendly.

Hollings smiled and nodded, eye flicking to a spot just above the door where a discretely hidden camera lurked. "Evening, sir. Captain Henricksen's arrived."

A pause—nearly five seconds—before Kinsey answered. "Send him in."

The intercom clicked, abruptly cutting off. A soft *whir* and a light appeared—red and glowing—just beside the door. Hollings waited, rocking heel to toe, heel to toe, until the red light turned green, door lock chiming politely as it clicked over and invited them in.

"There you are, sir." Hollings grabbed the latch and pushed the door open— *held* it open, standing just to one side.

Henricksen looked at him, and at the open doorway, wanting nothing more than to turn around and head back. "Don't suppose I could get you to join us?"

"Sorry, sir. Afraid it's just you, sir. Mr. Kinsey's orders." Hollings shrugged apologetically, nodded to Kinsey's rooms inside.

A last glance down the corridor, staring longingly at the security door that brought them here, and Henricksen stepped inside, letting Hollings pull the door to, lock clicking as it closed.

Henricksen shivered, hating that sound. Lavish as these spaces were, they always put him in mind of a prison—a place that, once entered, never let you out.

He thought about leaving again—no one there to meet him in the front entryway, no sign of his dinner host in the enormous room beyond. Went so far as to turn around and grab the latch protruding from the door before Kinsey's voice intruded, bringing him up short.

"Good evening, Captain." Kinsey appeared like magic, immaculate as always in his pinstriped suit and shiny leather shoes. "You're late."

Right to it. Not pulling any punches tonight.

Never did when it came to his schedule. Kinsey despised tardiness—still figuring him out, but Henricksen picked up on *that* pretty quick—and 1830 for dinner meant arrive five minutes before, not nearly an hour late.

Not off to a good start this evening. Then again, maybe if he showed up late often enough, he'd piss Kinsey off so badly he'd stop inviting him back for these uncomfortable little chats.

"Sorry," Henricksen said, not really meaning it. "Training," he explained, with a distinctly vague wave.

Kinsey stared in silence, watching, judging from the center of the bright, white room attached to that entryway. Long fingers reaching, tugging at the cuffs of a crisp, white shirt. "Dinner's ready. I hope you like fish."

He didn't, actually. Aquaculture on the stations, fish fed a steady diet of waste food and garbage—cook them however you wanted, fish always tasted like trash. But Henricksen nodded politely anyway, keeping that little newsflash to himself. Followed Kinsey's beckoning finger across the entryway to the front room where he waited—an oversized square filled with white carpet and white furniture, a glitzy, glass and chrome chandelier pending from the ceiling, hanging halfway to the floor.

Swanky, if not exactly Henricksen's style. Everything in that room fresh, and clean, and modern. White, and chrome, and glass.

Monochrome pallet, not a spot of real color anywhere. A showroom, not real quarters. Nothing here of Kinsey himself. Kept that all locked away, hidden behind the closed doors set in that front room's four walls.

Kinsey's quarters and his right to jealously guard his spaces. Kinsey's choice to confine his visitors to the snow-white front room with its glitzy, enormous chandelier. The wood-paneled dining room off to one side.

Henricksen crossed the soft carpets, following his host's stiff-backed form. Tilted his head, studying him, noting an odd, hitching movement to his gait.

Clipped steps, the barest hint of a limp as he rotated his left hip.

Prosthetic, he reminded himself.

Forgot about that, sometimes. Remembered the arm each time he clasped it, but Henricksen often forgot about Kinsey's prosthetic leg.

Advances in artificial limb technology allowed for unimpeded movement, even a limited amount of tactile sensation, but the joins with flesh remained imperfect. Machine parts subbing in nicely, but still learning the fine points of natural human motor movement. Not yet the master of the dance.

The carpet stopped at an arched doorway, downy white flooring giving way to fern green tile and wood paneled walls the color of cinnamon. The stark white modernity of the front room evaporated, replaced by the warmly lit confines of a formal dining area: table at the center, taking up most of the space, sideboard against one wall, door leading to a kitchen in which sumptuous meals were made.

Just two place settings on that table when Henricksen entered. Seating for twelve, but with just the two of them eating, only two sets of china and glassware, knives and forks and other utensils laid out. Serving dishes filled the table's center, lined up just so, lids securely in place, ensuring the food inside stayed warm. Soft music filtered from hidden speakers—some sort of stringed instrument composition, the kind that went out of style a quarter of a millennia ago. The kind no one but Kinsey seemed to listen to anymore.

Huge aquarium to Henricksen's right as he entered, filling the entirety of the wall. Brightly colored fish gliding serenely through the water, a suspicious set of eyeballs watching them, buried deep in the sand below. Playground of castles and coral reefs in miniature to entertain them, waving fronds of some slimy green weedy thing, a diver in miniature—belled helmet bubbling, creating tiny spots of chaos in that small sea of otherwise calm—with a tiny, spotted octopus wrapped around it, slowly strangling it to death.

Colorful. Bright and cheery, especially after that monotone horror show of a front room. Henricksen paused in the doorway, eyes drawn it. To the streams of bubbles roiling the fish tank's surface. The schools of fish swimming to and fro.

Always meant to ask about the tank's occupants, but Kinsey never gave him the opportunity. Poured the wine and jumped right into the interrogation, avoiding or outright ignoring any subject that didn't involve the RV-N project and the training in the sims.

Focused son-of-a-bitch—Henricksen had to give him that.

"Have a seat, Captain." Kinsey pointed to the chair closest to the doorway, stepped across the room and claimed a seat at the opposite end of the table.

Defensive position. Put Kinsey's back to the wall, leaving Henricksen's exposed to the open doorway. The bright, white room on the other side.

Henricksen glanced at the doorway—couldn't help it, old habits died hard—as he pulled out a chair. Snatched a napkin from the table and fluffed it, laying it across his lap as he sat down.

Helped himself to the food on the table without asking—Kinsey gave him a big, old frowny face for that, but he honestly didn't care. Grabbed a wine glass and filled it with a crisp, white vintage that smelled of fruit and flowers, snagged a second glass and topped it off with water for good measure.

Doubtful he'd get drunk on wine, but alcohol in any form tended to loosen the tongue. Encourage an honesty that wasn't always in Henricksen's best interests.

Didn't necessarily like Kinsey, but he watched his mouth around him. This man of secrets who guarded knowledge like a dragon sitting atop a golden hoard. Ate with him, because it was Friday and that was expected. Answered Kinsey's questions as best he could, but he kept his personal opinions to himself because he didn't quite trust him. Hadn't known him long enough for that.

Silence in the dining room, Kinsey watching as Henricksen filled his plate, carefully avoiding his eyes. First serving dish held green beans and carrot coins, stalks of stinking asparagus that lay like tiny tree branches on Henricksen's plate. He dished up a double portion to use up real estate and leave less room for the dreaded fish. Added a pile of roasted potatoes speckled liberally with some vaguely green dried herb. Swapped the serving dish for a platter loaded down with fish fillets, hesitating when he caught sight of their dinner's cousins watching from the tank.

"These yours?" Henricksen nodded to the cooked fish on the platter, waved at the live ones swimming nearby.

Kinsey flicked his eyes to the tank and laughed softly, shaking his head. "No. Not mine." He picked up his fork and knife and started carving, sectioning his piece of fish into perfectly sized bites. "Those are only for show, Captain. Not particularly tasty. These, on the other hand," he paused in his carving, flicking his knife at the platter in Henricksen's hand, "are considered a delicacy. Patagonian Toothfish. Old Earth species," he explained, at Henricksen's blank look. "Seeded them in the oceans on Sandogene. They've done quite well from what I hear. High productivity rates in the southern waters along the continental shelf." Kinsey smiled at him across the table—cold thing, a brief lifting of bloodless lips—and nipped a bite of fish from the tines of his fork, chewed and swallowed, watching Henricksen all the while. "So. Training." The eyes blinked slowly— onyx pools that had no end. "Have you made crew assignments yet?"

Right to it this evening, no messing about.

His fault, for showing up late. Threatening Kinsey's plans with the admirals. No time for the usual softball questions and polite banter. Kinsey's schedule said drinks at 2000 and he obviously meant to be there.

Henricksen considered the question a moment, selected the smallest piece of fish the serving tray had on offer and dropped it onto his plate. "Just so happens Sikuuku and I were just discussing that. That's why I was late."

Partial truth, though not quite an answer. He speared a green bean and nibbled at its end, hoping Kinsey would leave it at that.

"Were you now?" Kinsey murmured, knife dangling from one hand, fork from the other. "And?" he prompted as Henricksen skewered another bean.

Henricksen chewed and swallowed, taking his time about it, refusing to be rushed. "Still deciding," he said, popping a carrot into his mouth.

Kinsey stared, eyes hooding. "What's the holdup?" he asked, carefully setting the fork and knife down.

"No hold up. Just need some more time."

"Four weeks. That was our agreement."

"Don't remember *agreeing* to anything. *Do* remember being told." Henricksen grabbed his wine glass and drained half of it in one gulp.

Kinsey stared along the length of the table, face cold as a corpse. "I see you like the wine."

Cheap shot, suggesting he was a drunk. Henricksen pointedly ignored it. Took another sip before setting it aside. "Better than that piss beer they serve in the mess hall."

Kinsey stiffened, eyes widening with indignation. Relaxed with a visible effort and offered a very fake sounding laugh. "My offer still stands." He gestured at the room around him, retrieved his fork and speared a piece of fish. "I've got rooms set aside, just waiting for you to move in. Soft bed, stocked bar, fish tank if you want it."

Leave the barracks, move into the lofty, over-decorated quarters Kinsey assigned him in the first place.

Annoyed Henricksen to no end that Kinsey kept asking. Three weeks of these meetings and each and every time Kinsey tried to get him to move up here. Give up his closet in the RV-N section for a chance to sleep in these shiny, expensive quarters with the other senior officers.

Kinsey pressured—repeatedly—and each and every time Henricksen refused. Politely, of course—kept it to "no" and "thank you" rather than "kiss my ass, you insufferable prick"—but Kinsey kept asking. Kept badgering him to move.

Didn't understand it, honestly. Easier to agree and make him happy, but Henricksen always was an insufferable cuss. Never could do anything the easy way. Didn't *want* to kiss Kinsey's ass and share cocktails with the Brass. Whole point of bringing him here was to get the RV-N crews ready. That meant, eating, sleeping and training with them, day after day after day. Bugging out each night to sleep in swanky quarters like Kinsey's just wasn't his style. Sent an entirely wrong message to the crew under his command.

"No. Thank you." Wooden answer, Henricksen carefully controlling his answer, trying hard to keep it from showing on his face.

He speared another carrot coin and shoved it in his mouth, grinding it to dust.

Kinsey watched him, fingers drumming on the table, dark eyes inscrutable as always. "Your choice, of course." His lips lifted, curling at the corners. "But the offer still stands. If you change your mind."

Henricksen twitched his shoulders, hand wrapping tight around his utensils. Mashed at the fish with his fork to carve a piece off. Shoved it in his mouth and almost spat it back out again, because—delicacy or not—Patagonian Toothfish still tasted like trash.

"I spoke with Karansky." Casual tone this time. Kinsey sipped at his water glass, picked up his fork and turned it sideways, using the tines to cut a potato in half. "He says the engine modifications are just about complete. They're running a few test scenarios while Shaw bolts everything back together, but the RV-Ns should be ready to fly by the end of the week."

Henricksen tensed, knowing what was coming. "They're not ready. Adaeze's the best pilot of the bunch and even *she's* struggling with speed wobbles in the trough. They need more *time*, Kinsey. You can't—"

"Don't!" Kinsey snapped, smacking the table so hard he nearly tipped his glass over. "Don't tell me what I can and can't do." He glared across the table, eyes flashing with challenge. Turned his head away—a sharp, dismissive gesture—and carefully set the fork he held down. Tugged at the cuffs of his finely pressed shirt, smoothed the lapels of that perfectly tailored jacket. "Three weeks in the sims, Captain." The head turned, eyes cold now, face a mask of bland dispassion. "Three weeks of twelve-hour days—don't think I haven't noticed." A hint of anger returned—a carefully controlled amount that disappeared as Kinsey folded his hands together, resting his elbows on the table. "I've seen the results from those sim sessions and they're impressive. Scores are way up since you arrived."

Henricksen nodded stiffly, accepting the compliment. Waiting for the other shoe to drop.

"Any particular reason you separated Mahal and Nunez?"

The lovebirds—not the shoe Henricksen expected.

"Noticed that, did you?" He scooped up his water glass, lips twisting in a rueful smile.

Kinsey copied it, adding a touch of cold, a hundredweight of condescension. "I notice a lot of things, Captain. That's my job, after all." The hands unfolded, one dropping to Kinsey's lap while the other reached for the wine glass, lifted it to deposit a measured amount on his tongue. "I need those crew assignments, Captain." Kinsey raised a hand to forestall Henricksen's objections, treated himself to another sip of the wine before setting the glass down. "You want more time—I know. I heard you. But here's the truth: You can keep them in the sims another three weeks. Or four. Or a hundred. Swap the crew around for days on end, but you'll stop seeing results eventually. Sims are good, Captain, but they're not the real thing. Not by a long shot."

Henricksen bristled, threw his fork down. "You think I don't know? I've seen just as much combat as you. More to the point, I've run those sims— hundreds of hours before they let me crew Helm—and I know their limitations." He scooped up his wine and drained the glass, slammed it back down. "No substitution for combat. *None.* Nothing at all like the real thing."

Kinsey blinked slowly, studying Henricksen from the opposite end of the table. "Glad to see we finally agree on something." He raised his glass in salute, drained it and refilled it, offering the bottle to Henricksen after.

Henricksen considered it before accepting, tipping the neck over his glass.

Probably shouldn't, but anger and drinking were sort of a thing with him. Tended to even each other out.

"Pick your crews, Captain." Kinsey pointed his glass across the table as Henricksen set the bottle down. "Get them in those birds. You find out you made bad choices, you swap them out after the fact."

Orders now. From Kinsey of all people.

Henricksen leaned back, smiling bitterly. "That easy, eh?"

"Not really. But dragging your feet isn't going to help."

"I'll announce the crew assignments when I'm ready."

"Tomorrow."

"No."

"Why not?" Kinsey demanded, staring in challenge.

Henricksen shrugged his shoulders, staring right back. Didn't really have a good answer. Truth was he'd mapped out half the crews in his head already. Just needed Sikuuku's input to finalize the rest.

Been dragging my feet, he admitted. *And now I'm outta time.*

He sipped at his glass, watching a fish swim by. Cobalt body striped with sunshine, fanlike fins waving sedately, rippling with each movement.

"You make your assignments tomorrow." Kinsey took a drink, lowered the glass and just held it casually in his hand. "How much longer will they need in the sims?"

Henricksen popped a potato into his mouth, chewed and swallowed, stalling for more time.

Impossible to answer that question until he ran through a few test scenarios. Figured out if all the crew combinations they came up with actually worked. But a week should be plenty. More than enough time, unless he got it totally wrong.

Back to the drawing board if I do. Reset the clock and start all over again.

He snuck a look at Kinsey's face, realized he'd never allowed it. Crew wouldn't like it either. Truth was crew were sick to death of the sims. Asking about the RV-N as often as Kinsey because that's why they were here: to fly the real thing.

"Not really sure." Henricksen plucked another potato from his plate, savoring the look of disgust on Kinsey's face as he bit it in half, holding one side with his fingers while he chewed and swallowed before shoving the rest into his mouth. "What's the hurry, anyway?"

Kinsey stared a moment, face unreadable. "This project cost billions." A pause, considering, and Kinsey sat back, taking the wine glass with him. "The admirals are impatient."

"Admirals are always impatient."

Kinsey inclined his head, raising the glass. "Nevertheless, the Brass want results. I told them four weeks and in four weeks they expect the RV-Ns to be flying. Completing missions, not gathering dust in the hangar bay."

Casual tone, now. Relaxed demeanor. Just two military vets having a little chat over dinner.

Never mind that the schedule was shit. What Kinsey asked completely ridiculous.

"What's the goddamn hurry?" Henricksen demanded.

Kinsey's face changed, turning hard as stone. "They're threatening to cancel the project."

Henricksen lowered his glass, resting on the table. *That's not it,* he thought, studying Kinsey's face intently, seeing something in his eyes. *Not by a long shot.*

"What aren't you telling me?"

Kinsey sipped at his drink, refusing to answer. Tongue locked up tight.

Well, two could play at that game. Henricksen copied him—drink for drink and look for look—until Kinsey sighed in annoyance and set his drink down.

"I've given you three weeks, and I'll give you one more."

Said that like it was a gift. Like he'd somehow given Henricksen more time.

Kinsey traded the glass for his knife and fork, applying both to an unsuspecting potato. "*One* week, Captain." He pointed the knife across the table. "But that's it. One week, not a day more."

"Week might be good for the crew, but that chassis—"

"The chassis will be ready. Karansky's promised me that and I mean to hold him to it. Whatever it takes." Kinsey looked up, catching Henricksen's eyes, dropped his gaze back to the food on his plate. "Sims are all well and good but I need live tests, Captain. Ships with crew on board capturing data. Running the systems under load."

Henricksen was quiet a moment, watching him dissect that potato. Thinking about the sims and that untried RV-N chassis. "The asteroid field scenario."

Kinsey froze, knife embedded in the potato's skin. Raised his head and stared at Henricksen across the length of the table. "What about it?" he asked stiffly.

"The sims repeat. Keep choosing that one scenario over and over again."

"So?" The knife moved, sawing through the potato, scraping loudly on the plate beneath. Kinsey set it down, stabbed a chunk of potato with his fork and lifted it to his mouth.

"So either your sims are shit or you're repeating that scenario on purpose."

Kinsey's eyebrows lifted. "And why do you think I'd do that?"

All but an admission, despite the casual tone. Not crap software then. Not that at all.

"What's in there?" Henricksen asked quietly.

Kinsey dipped his fork, selecting a piece of fish from the bites on offer. "That's the question isn't it?" Smile on his face now—mocking, enigmatic. The face around it cold as ever, inscrutable as a statue frozen in time.

"DSR?" Henricksen asked him, going very still.

They'd seen ships in the sim—in the asteroid field, around it, even detected something at the center, but they could never get a good fix. Never quite see what it was.

"Maybe," Kinsey told him, lifting the fork to his mouth. "Most likely," he admitted, sliding another bite into his mouth. A grimace and set he set the fork down. Knife with it. Pushed the entire plate away for good measure. "We've noted some recent vessel traffic around that asteroid field—ships moving in and out, that kind of thing."

"Could be they're civ ships, not DSR at all."

"Could be," Kinsey nodded. "No beacons, though, so it's hard to tell." Long look at Henricksen. Long *meaningful* look after that.

"Rocks, maybe? Blocking the signal?" Henricksen chewed his lip doubtfully. Asteroid fields wreaked havoc on sensor systems. Ships squawked oceans of electronic chatter, though. Usually *some* of it slipped through.

"Maybe." Kinsey picked up his glass, swirling the contents as he studied the fish tank to one side. "Or it could be they're turned off."

Henricksen went very still, fingers clenching his glass. "Against the law, running a ship in space without an active beacon."

Spoke of hiding and secrets—two things the DSR was all about.

"Indeed," Kinsey nodded, lips curling in a secretive smile.

"Could be they're civvies," Henricksen argued. "Unregistered. Up to no good."

It happened—all too often, in fact. Pirates everywhere, not just the DSR you had to look out for these days.

"Civvies," Kinsey grunted, giving him a look. "Not a pilot myself, but I've heard it's quite a feat, navigating an asteroid field without turning yourself into space dust. Civ ships tend to steer clear of asteroid fields."

"Unless they're mining."

"They're not." Flat out—no room for argument in that answer. "No civ ships are authorized to be in that area. And the surveys show nothing of interest. Nothing *worth* mining even if they were out there for that."

Henricksen thought a moment, fiddling with his glass. Picked it up and set it back down, spinning it on the tabletop with his fingers. "How many ships are we talking about?"

"Another good question." Kinsey swirled the wine in his glass, took a sip and set it down. "We don't know for sure." He touched the glass, stroking the stem with his finger. "Probes go in, but they don't come out. Sensors can't get a good set of scans with all those asteroids in the way."

Henricksen tilted his head, brow furrowing. "So why not send a few ships in? If they're DSR—if you even *think* they're DSR—why all this skulking about?"

Kinsey smiled again—condescending as always, slightly amused. "Send in an armed force—that what you're thinking? Roust the ships out, blow anything that resists to hell?"

"That such a bad idea?" Henricksen leaned back, arms folded tight to his chest.

"Actually, yes."

"Why?"

Kinsey started to answer, paused and tilted his head. "Because we know those ships are there, but not why, or what they're up to. We send in a force and my guess is they'll run. Jump away and take whatever their hiding with them."

"Hiding?" Henricksen's eyebrows lifted. "So now they're *hiding* something?"

Kinsey shrugged again—he was full of shrugs tonight—face blank, eyes swirling with secrets.

Henricksen pursed his lips, studying the man across from him. "So, what've you got? What makes you think there's anything besides ships inside that asteroid field?"

The smile came back, twisting Kinsey's lips, never quite making it to his eyes. "Oh, they're hiding something alright. Secrets are my business, Captain. I can smell 'em." He lifted a finger, tapped the end against his nose. "And the secret to secrets is stealing them without anyone knowing. That's where the RV-N comes in."

"And the sims keep repeating—"

"Because I want those crews to know that rock field like the backs of their hands. I want them in and out—scans and video, every last piece of information they can gather recorded in the RV-Ns' systems—and then I want them to go back, and do it all over again. And again. And again." Kinsey pounded his fist against the table, rattling the dishes, keeping time with his words. "Until we know what they have, and how to take it ourselves." He was quiet a moment, dark eyes blinking slowly, fingers curling around the forgotten wine glass. "Do you understand now, Captain? Do you see why I need those stealth ships flying?"

He did, but he still didn't understand the hurry. Why this four-week timeline was so important.

Henricksen stared a moment, trying to read him, turned his head and considered the fish tank, searching for answers amongst its brightly colored occupants. Wondering what the DSR could be hiding inside that asteroid field. Why he himself was so loathe to make those crew assignments so they could find out.

"A week, you said, and that chassis'll be ready?"

"I'll make sure of it. I'll run Karansky's crew all night if I have to. Question is: will your crews be ready as well?"

Not sure, he thought, *but they'll mutiny if I keep them in the sims much longer.*

Henricksen sighed, setting his drink down. Pushed his chair back and climbed to his feet. "They'll have to be, won't they?" A nod to Kinsey and he turned around, retracing his steps across that pristine, white-on-white room as he showed himself out.

FOURTEEN

Hollings guided Henricksen back to the RV-N project's section of the station. Never knew where he came from—wasn't outside Kinsey's quarters when Henricksen left them—but the petty officer appeared out of nowhere before he reached the administrative section's security door, nodding politely as he caught up with Henricksen, keyed him through and set off for home.

"Thanks," Henricksen said, stopping with Hollings outside the pressure door leading into the RV-N projects' berthings. "Appreciate the help. Think I can take it from here." He clapped the petty officer on the shoulder, lips twisting in a self-deprecating smile. Gave his hand a good, firm shake before releasing it and stepping back.

"Anytime, sir. Station's a maze. No doubt about that." Hollings braced up and saluted, spun on his heel and marched away, leaving Henricksen staring after him—watching Hollings round a corner and disappear from view.

Turned around as Hollings's footsteps faded, putting his back to the berthing area as he headed for the airlock providing access to the hangar bay—the one place in this section he hadn't yet visited. Not once in the weeks since he and Sikuuku arrived.

Hadn't really given the RV-Ns more than a passing glance from the control room, to be honest, because they weren't really ships yet. Not until they were ready to fly. Well, that day was coming—like it or not—and it was high time he gave the RV-Ns a once over. At least have the decency to set foot inside one.

A stop at the airlock to enter his credentials and Henricksen punched a button, cycling it open. Checked the hallway to make sure no one was looking— nothing to stop him from going out into the hangar, no rules forbidding crew from entering, he just wanted some time to himself—as he stepped inside the airlock, letting the door seal up.

Enviro suits hung on the side walls—helmet and pressure suit in three generic sizes that really fit no one at all. Crew got better for flight ops, but he'd have to go all the way back to his quarters to fetch it, risking a thousand questions and unwanted intrusions along the way.

First time in the RV-N. Didn't really want company. Not even Sikuuku this time. He just wanted to look the ship over—touch it, feel it, get a sense for the AI he'd so far avoided.

Little things. Little things that mattered.

Henricksen grabbed a suit at random, picking one from the "tallish" section in the middle, since that just about summed him up. Tugged it over his uniform, cursing the suit as it bunched up in places, hung loosely in others. Managed to wrestle it into place eventually and plunked a helmet on his head after, bulbous shape connecting to the suit via a gasket that clicked into place, sealing up tight.

Checked his reflection in the glass after and realized the end result was terrible, the entire thing a horrible fit. Yards of brownish material pooched at the stomach, puddling in loose folds by his feet. Sleeves bunched up to allow room for gloves. A helmet that smelled like rancid butter for some reason, forcing him to breathe through his mouth or risk vomiting in his suit.

Didn't need it all that long, though. Most of the hangar was vacuum—far too big of a space for the station to light and heat twenty-four seven—but, with Shaw's crew working the RV-Ns, they'd thrown up a shimmer shield, creating a bubble of heat and atmosphere around the six stealth ships lurking beneath the control room's windows.

Long walk from the airlock, unfortunately. Entry point into the hangar bay being somewhere near that echoing space's middle, the ships he wanted lying far to the left. Long walk, but practical from a safety standpoint. Didn't want engines and welders,and all sorts of spark- and fire-creating equipment running right next to the station access point, after all.

Henricksen checked the seals on his enviro suit, punched the button next to the airlock's hangar-side door and waited, feeling the thrum of machinery through the soles of his boots. Watched the numbers on the display ticked down to zero as the locked pumped the air out, flashed green and opened up.

Vast space on the other side. Vast and dark, the only light a dim glow filtering from the control room far to the left of the lock, windows looking down on the hangar bay floor.

Henricksen touched the side of his helmet, turning a headlamp on. Swung it around, getting his bearings before setting off.

Left turn out of the airlock, straight shot from there to where the stealth ships waited. Yellow lines provided a path laced with intermittent arrows—a trail of breadcrumbs leading all the way to the sharp-edged ships. Shimmer shield bounced his headlamp back at him when he reached it, blinding Henricksen for a moment, waking dazzling stars that lingered long after he stepped through into atmosphere, removing the helmet with a grateful sigh. Shucked the bulky, ill-fitting enviro suit from his body and let it puddle on the floor.

"Fire the guy who designed that godawful thing." He kicked the suit and helmet into a pile, turned in a circle and surveyed the sleeping ships around him. Noticed the back hatch of one was open, light showing inside. "What the hell?"

Habit made him reach for a pistol—stupid instinct drilled into him years ago, back when officers used to carry one everywhere. Nothing on his hip right now, though. No one but the shift guards carried weapons on station, and those high velocity pulse rifles, not something so simple as a pistol.

Henricksen dropped his hand, cursing himself for being an idiot. Spied a rolling tool case parked next to one of the RV-Ns and rifled through its drawers until he found a satisfyingly large, satisfyingly heavy wrench inside.

"That's better." He hefted the wrench, walking soft-footed over to the lighted stealth ship, wincing at every echoing sound.

Dark lumps surrounded the ship's backside, tool chests and spare parts scattered around it, hull panels removed to make it easier for the mech gang to get at the engines beneath. From the looks of things, they had most of it put back together now—an encouraging sign, one that hopefully meant Kinsey was right, and Karansky's engineers just about had the engines issues solved.

Henricksen skirted a stack of hull panels, slipping between two tool chests as he crept to the edge of the open hatch. Slowed and approached on tiptoe, sneaking a look inside.

Not all that much to see, really. The outer hatch led to an inner airlock, with a cargo area beyond. A lock that showed green—heat and atmosphere on the other side—and open, not security locked like it should be.

Odd that, finding the ship's inner door unsecured. Then again, that outer hatch shouldn't be open either. And the lights he spied in the cargo bay most definitely shouldn't be on.

Somebody in there.

One of Shaw's crew, most likely. Pulling a late shift, finishing some odd job up.

Henricksen lowered the wrench, feeling incredibly foolish. Thought about dropping it in one of the tool chests, but decided to keep it in the end. Took it with him as he stepped into the airlock and pushed at the inner hatch door.

Illumination on the other side—a double row of buzzing light bars throwing back the darkness, shining down from the ceiling onto a rectangle of composite metal decking. On plasmetal walls set with reinforced glass panels. A door to Henricksen's right providing access to the stealth ship's single, central corridor.

Simple layout to the RV-N, one he'd memorized while studying the stealth ship's design specs during that three-day trek to Dragoon. Just three levels to the ship, unlike *Hecate*'s eight, a Valkyrie's ten, with a single corridor running the length of each. Bottom tier was cargo and provisions, munitions storage, spare parts and the like. Middle tier held common spaces—kitchen and dining area on one side, rec room on the other—and provided forward access to the bridge. Top tier was crew berthings—four snug cubby-holes equipped with bunks and little else, sufficient for racking out during long deployments.

Shared spaces, not assigned. Black Ops was a waiting game—couldn't assume you'd be back in time for a dinner and a solid eight hours in a stationside bunk—and the ships a conveyance. A tool for the job, not a home.

Not like *Hecate*. Not like other warships in the Fleet.

Henricksen considered the ship's innards, scanning the empty cargo hold from the doorway. Stepped inside when he found no one around.

The hazy glow in the cargo bay brightened immediately, sensors picking up movement, waking the sleeping lights along the walls. A click and a voice issued from speakers in the ceiling, echoing tinnily off the walls.

"Good evening, Captain," the ship greeted him, tones carefully neutral, scaring the crap out of him just the same.

He froze up tight, wrench lifting, fingers clenched in a death grip around its handle.

"What brings you here tonight?" A pause, camera in the corner swiveling, lens adjusting as it zoomed in. "And what's with the wrench?"

"Oh, you know." Henricksen lowered the wrench, forcing himself to relax, willing his voice to calm. "Trouble sleeping. Thought I'd go for a little walk."

"A walk?" The AI sounded puzzled. "Why would—"

"Walk my ass," a new voice interrupted. "I know snooping when I see it."

"Shaw?"

Sounded like the mech gang chief. Definitely female, anyway.

"You know, if you wanted a tour you could've asked me."

Henricksen shrugged, looking up at the camera, assuming Shaw was watching remotely. "Impromptu decision. 2200. Figured knocking on your door and asking for a guided tour would be considered rude."

Shaw laughed aloud—a deep, throaty sound filled with genuine amusement. "Well, you showed yourself in, so I assume you can find your way around. I'm on the bridge tweaking systems. Wanna come up and give me a hand?"

Henricksen shrugged again and headed across the cargo hold.

"By the way, why *are* you carrying that wrench around?"

"What? Oh." Henricksen tucked the wrench behind him. "Found it. Lying on the decking." He waved vaguely at the open hatchway behind him, indicating the hangar outside.

"Uh-huh." Shaw sounded suspicious.

A quick look around showed no tool chests anywhere. Henricksen thought about tossing the wrench in the corner—he felt increasingly silly carrying the damned thing around—but with Shaw watching, decided to keep it for now.

A touch at the security panel on the wall and he buzzed through the inner door to the stealth ship's central corridor—everything simple and durable here, composite metal and ultra-durable plastics, triple-thick reinforced glass. Climbed the aft ladderway to the second tier and walked the length of that nearly identical hallway to the bridge at the stealth ship's bow.

Door there was closed, but it opened at his touch. Space inside looked nearly identical to the sim pod, except with brighter lighting. The blood-red, low light combat illumination swapped out for a soft yellow glow.

Didn't see Shaw at first. Just heard her curses drifting from the front of the bridge pod, somewhere close to the floor. A few steps in and Henricksen spied a pair of legs sticking from under a panel between the Artillery pod and the Pilot's station, the rest of Shaw's body invisible, crammed inside an open access panel as she worked away at the electronics.

"That you, Captain?"

"Were you expecting someone else?"

"Not really. Can you hand me that diagnosticator?" A hand appeared, finger pointing to an open toolkit.

Henricksen walked over and squatted down, sorting tools out of the way to get at a couple of electronic devices.

Didn't recognize either of them. Had no idea what a diagnosticator was in the first place. Maintenance crew saw to the systems on the warships. Captains just flew them around, made sure they didn't run into things.

He picked one at random, held it out. "You mean this?"

"Other one," Shaw told him, waving the device off. "The electro-magno-differential-whatsis machine."

Henricksen swapped the one electronic device for the other, placing it on Shaw's open palm.

"You still got that wrench?" Shaw asked him, hand disappearing into the panel.

"Uh. Yeah. You need it?"

"Not really. Wrench that big isn't all that much use when it comes to electronics." Laughter in Shaw's voice. Having a good time at Henricksen's expense. "Drop it in the tool kit." The pointing finger made a brief appearance before Shaw's hand tucked under the panel again. "I'll put it back where it belongs."

Henricksen slid the wrench in with the other tools in Shaw's kit. Plucked a pair of pliers from the Pilot's seat while he was at it. A coil of wire from the floor.

"There." Shaw wriggled from under the Pilot's station, diagnosticator in hand, smear of grease on the end of her nose.

"You've got a little something." Henricksen pointed at Shaw's face, tapped a finger to his nose.

"Oh. Thanks." Shaw turned her hands over, studying the grease on her palms. Swiped at her face with a sleeve instead, adding more grease to the spot on her nose. "Better?"

"Perfect." Henricksen flashed a thumbs up. "So what were you working on?"

"Navigation linkage." Shaw dropped the diagnosticator in the toolkit, dusted her hands before wiping them on her already greasy coveralls. "Had to disconnect everything while the engineers messed with the propulsion system. Idiots." She grabbed the access panel and fitted it into place, tightened the bolts with a wrench pulled from a pocket. "Supposed to be a bunch of egghead brainiacs but they don't know the first thing about ships outside design diagrams and systems specs." She twisted, looking up at Henricksen, wrench in hand. "Spend all that time overhauling the systems and the first thing they do is try to fire up the engines without bringing the AI online. Can you believe that?"

Shaw's wrench swung wildly, narrowly missing Helm's panel, just about clipping Henricksen's knee.

"Civvies," Henricksen snorted, moving a step backward. "What're ya gonna do?"

"Fire 'em all and start over." Shaw torqued on the panel's bolts, making sure everything was tight.

"Heard that's what they did the last time."

Shaw froze, arm outstretched, reaching for the toolkit. "Heard that, did ya?" She opened her fingers, letting the tool drop. "They also tell you they fired my whole damn mech gang? Three damn years they'd been working on that chassis and then one day I come in to find they're all gone." Shaw flopped down in the Pilot's seat, grabbed a rag and scrubbed angrily at her hands.

"Hadn't heard that. Not directly, anyway." Henricksen settled into the station next to her, feeling odd and out of place sitting at Engineering. "Noticed, though. Couldn't *help* but notice that first day I stepped into the mess hall."

Shaw grimaced, spat on her palm and rubbed vigorously at a stain. "That obvious, huh?"

"Not to someone who hasn't crewed a ship, maybe. But a few assignments and you get pretty good at picking the ones who know what they're doing and the ones just pretending and hoping the others don't figure it out."

Shaw grunted, nodding. "Moved the whole damn operation. Bet you didn't know *that*."

Henricksen blinked, processing this newest piece of information. "No, I didn't. Assumed the RV-N project was always here."

"Not originally. Started out on Kepler. Hush-hush base the Meridian Alliance had on the planet. Something happened, though." Shaw frowned, shaking her head. "Not sure what—Kinsey never told me. Never told anyone, as far as I know. Just packed everything up and shipped it off. Never even heard of Dragoon until they brought us here. Whole damn thing'd been mothballed. Took an age to get the smell out of the berthings and common areas."

"It's still there," Henricksen told her.

"Really? Huh. Guess I've gotten used to it." Shaw ducked her head, smiling ruefully. Looked up at Henricksen, considering a moment. "So. Back to our original subject: what brings you here at this late hour, Captain?" A last swipe at a still dirty finger and Shaw gave up, tossed the rag into the toolkit. "Not that I mind the company but I've never seen you so much as set foot in the hangar before now."

Henricksen grunted. "Spend a lot of late nights in here, do you?"

"Deadlines." Shaw shrugged her shoulders, lips twisting in a lopsided smile. "Can't have your star jockeys waiting on my girl here. Ain't that right, sweetie?" She patted a panel, looking up at a camera.

"Let me at 'em, Chief," the AI quipped.

"That's my girl." Shaw smiled fondly, stroking Helm's panel.

"She?" Henricksen quirked an eyebrow. "What's makes you think it—she's a she?"

Generic voice to his ear. Nothing particularly male *or* female about it that he could tell.

Shaw winked, tapping a finger to her nose. "Mechanic's intuition."

"Okay," Henricksen said slowly. "So, does *she* have a name?"

"RV-N-26."

"That's not much of a name."

Shaw flipped a hand. "She'll pick a better one eventually. Two-Six is good enough for now." She smile widely, looking surprisingly proud. "She's one of the originals. The best of that first batch they churned out." The smile slipped, Shaw's face turning thoughtful, a touch sad. "The only one that's left now, as far as I know."

Henricksen shook his head, giving her a blank look. "Meaning?"

"First manufacturing run cranked out thirty RV-N chassis." Shaw sat back, folding her hands over her stomach, kicked up her feet, resting them on Helm's panel. "You mind?" she asked belatedly.

"Not so long as you clean up after yourself."

"Aye, sir." Shaw smiled crookedly, tossing off a saucy salute. "Half of them failed outright—got chopped up and used for parts in the others." She waved vaguely at the bridge door, indicating the stealth ships in the hangar outside. "Rest of them…" Shaw sighed, dropping her eyes, fingers lacing together as she twirled her thumbs. "Test pilots thrashed them mercilessly. Ran them to failure. Blew most of them up. But Two-Six here," she touched the panel beside her, proud momma smile reappearing, "nothing could take her down. Been working overtime to get her ready. Make sure she's upgraded and dialed in. Everything just right."

"Let me at 'em, Chief!" the RV-N repeated, genderless voice filled with exuberance.

"Not exactly a talker, is she?"

Not like *Hecate*. The gender confusion was part of it—easier to identify with an AI when it emulated more clear-cut traits—but there was a distance to the AI he wasn't used to. A feeling of sitting back and watching, interacting when prompted, but otherwise just standing on the edges.

Noticed that in the sims, too, when the other pilots ran them. AI observing, but not participating. Not really engaging unless asked to, or absolutely necessary.

Could be problematic in combat.

His first consideration, each and every time. Combat required quick decisions and seamless interactions. Better no AI than one that hesitated. Wasn't sure when to step in and when to butt out.

"Specs say the AI's eleventh generation. Dreadnought's cousin or some such."

Shaw considered, head bobbing side to side. "More or less. Engineers started with the Dreadnought specs and then tweaked them to give the stealth ships more…personality, I guess you'd call it."

"Really?" Henricksen eyed the watching camera skeptically.

"Really. Oh, she's shy right now, but wait'll you get to know her." Shaw patted Helm's panel again. "Takes a while for an AI to mature, you know. Develop a personality. New ones…they're almost like kids, ya know? Still learning." She tilted her head, considering Henricksen a moment. "Your last ship—*Hecate,* right? Aurora?"

Henricksen nodded tightly, swallowing around a lump in his throat.

"Sixth generation. Solid mindsight. Heard they used it as the basis for the Valkyrie's design."

Henricksen shrugged and nodded, wondering where she was going with this.

"Sixth generation that makes her, what? Close to two hundred years old?"

"One hundred and ninety-eight. *Hecate* had just passed the anniversary of her commissioning date when she—" He broke off, ducking his head, lips pressed tightly together to stop them from trembling.

"*Hecate* was legend." Soft voice from the AI—a touch of the female tones Shaw hinted at coloring her speech this time. "Twenty crews and twenty Captains. Two hundred and fifty-two battles in her time amongst the stars."

"She was a badass, alright." Henricksen swiped at his face, blinking back tears. "Fought her way across the length and breadth of the galaxy—and that was *before* I landed a place in her chair."

"You miss her." Two-Six sounded surprised. But then, she'd never had a captain. Didn't understand the bond that developed between an AI and the ship's commanding officer.

"I do," Henricksen told her. "I miss her every day."

He could hear it now, more and more clearly. The tones and inflections, the higher pitched qualities that came with a female voice as the AI opened up. Crept warily from her shell.

Shaw ducked her head, hiding a smile.

"What?" he asked self-consciously.

"Told you you'd like her." She winked, smile turning mischievous. But it faded, Shaw's face turning thoughtful after a while. "Two-Six doesn't have *Hecate*'s years." She barked a laugh. "Hell, she doesn't even have a proper name yet because she's only been *around* a couple of years."

"Three years," the AI corrected prissily. "The engineers woke me three years ago, Chief."

"Alright. *Three* years." Shaw dipped her head in apology, eyes flicking to the camera. "But that still proves my point."

"Which is?" Henricksen asked, baffled about where all this was going.

"That you can't just bust an AI out of a box and expect it to be all puppies and rainbows and a perfect fit for its captain. Takes time for it to find itself. Develop its own personality."

"Won't really matter if the chassis isn't ready, now will it?"

"Oh, it'll be ready," Shaw assured him. "I'll make sure of that. Even if it means I have to pump my crew full of stims and run 'em twenty-four seven for a week."

"It means that much to you?" Surprised him. Never worked with a mech gang boss who cared that much. Then again, a lot of things surprised him about Shaw. Her knowledge of AI, for instance. Her obvious familiarity with his record. "*Why* does it mean that much to you?"

Shaw's shoulders lifted. "Mechanic's got her pride."

Truth, but not the whole truth—Henricksen read that in her eyes. In the lines of her face. "These engine modifications your crew's been working on. Tell me about them."

"What do you want to know?"

"Well, for starters, are the damn things gonna work?"

Shaw shrugged again and leaned forward, dropping her feet to the decking. Braced her elbows against her knees, clasping her hands in front of her. "Data looks good. Ran every diagnostic I can think of and they all came back nominal. No substitute for live testing, though."

Henricksen grunted, lips curling in a bitter smile. "Funny. Kinsey said something similar at dinner tonight."

"Man's not an idiot. Kinsey's a lot of things—including a son-of-a-bitch, sometimes—but he's not that."

"Unlike Karansky and his engineers."

Shaw barked a laugh. "All I'm saying is the man's got a point. Simulation's all well and good, but sometimes ya just gotta strap in and punch it. See what happens."

Henricksen was quiet a moment, staring at her. "That what those test pilots did? Strap in and punch it?"

Shaw sobered instantly. "Made a lot of improvements since then." Her eyes drifted to the camera, turned back to Henricksen's face. "Dialed back the engines, for one thing. Tweaked the stealth system to reduce the vibrations and noise. Chassis' a helluva lot more stable. Learned a ton from all the RV-Ns we lost."

"Guess I'll have to trust you on that."

"Yeah. You will." Shaw folded her arms, staring in challenge. "I run the mech gang and they service these ships. I wouldn't vouch for Two-Six and the others if I didn't think they were ready." She paused, studying him, searching his face. "You think I want to send crew out there to be killed?"

"Never said that," he told her, shaking his head.

"Then what—*oh*." Shaw sat up straight, leaned back and folded her arms. "I see."

"See what?" he asked, eyes narrowing.

"It's not the ship."

Henricksen scowled. "What are you getting on about? Of *course* it's the ship."

"No. It isn't," Shaw said quietly. "At least, not the chassis. It's the AI. It's *Hecate*."

"This is *not* about—"

"I know you miss her. Hell, I was crew on *Sardinia* when she went down five goddamn years ago and I *still* miss the old girl." Shaw flicked her fingers at the darkened hangar outside. "Worked my way into a station assignment just so I wouldn't have to crew a ship again. Not afraid," she told him, catching his eye. "Not afraid of dying. I just didn't want it. Didn't want to lose an AI, much less friends like that again."

Henricksen nodded. Different for her—crew never bonded with a ship's AI the way a warship captain did—but the connection was there. The sense of family, of belonging that most ship's crew formed.

Auroras, anyway. Titans too, from his experience. Couldn't speak to the Valkyries and Dreadnoughts. And from what he'd seen, the Bastion crew mostly lived in fear of their AI.

"So why this?" he asked, waving at the stealth ship's bridge. "Why sign up for the RV-N project if you were afraid of getting attached to an AI again?"

Shaw flushed, looking embarrassed of all things. "Got tricked," she admitted.

"Lemme guess: Kinsey recruited you, just like he recruited me and Sikuuku."

"And he wasn't exactly forthcoming with the details." Shaw smiled ruefully. "Tells me Black Ops is all hush-hush and secretive so he can't fill me in on the details of the assignment until I sign on the dotted line and get my personals moved in. Shoulda known why he wanted me, though. Warships are kind of my specialty," she explained at Henricksen's raised eyebrow look. "And these babies," she touched at Helm's panel, nodded to the camera watching from a corner, "they're a challenge. Something different." The smile widened. "How many mech chiefs get a chance to work on an entirely new chassis?"

"Not many," Henricksen guessed, studying her. Noting the fondness in Shaw's voice. The way she touched at the ship's systems, smiled at the camera. Talked to Two-Six and about her, hardly mentioning the RV-N itself. "This ship." Henricksen waved vaguely. "Why do you care so much?"

Shaw opened her mouth and closed it, tilted her head, looking up at the RV-N's camera. "Because she's *my* girl." Her fingers moved, hand caressing Helm's panel. "Crew works all the ships but Two-Six is special." She smiled at Henricksen, rapped her knuckles against Helm's panel. "She's gonna be yours, ya know."

Henricksen smiled indulgently. "Oh yeah? What tells you that?"

Shaw winked. "Mechanic's intuition."

"That again." Henricksen rolled his eyes.

"Hasn't been wrong yet." Shaw flashed a smile, showing every last one of her teeth. "But she's gotta get flying first. Which means *you* gotta let Two-Six and her buddies out. Nothing sadder than a caged bird, Captain. Nothing at all."

"Haven't even made crew assignments yet."

Shaw's head tilted. "What's the holdup?"

"Funny," Henricksen grunted. "Kinsey asked the same thing."

"Well, it *is* the question of the moment. That and when we'll have the Ravens put back together. So what *is* the holdup?" she asked him, wiping a greasy thumb on her coveralls.

"Training." Henricksen shrugged his shoulders. "Crew...crew just wasn't ready."

"And now?" she asked, eyebrows lifting.

He grimaced. "Still not sure they're ready."

But he was out of time. Kinsey wanted butts in seats. Crew assignments made so he could get his birds out of the hangar bar and into live trials.

Shaw turned her head, staring through the bridge's windows, finger tracing patterns on Helm's panel. "You sure it's *them* that's not ready?"

Henricksen bristled, face flushing. "Are you suggesting I can't cut it, Chief?"

"Nope." Shaw's head moved from one side to the other. She turned away from the windows and just sat there, studying him a moment. Thinking her words over before offering them up. "But I think your mind's still on *Hecate*. I think—"

"I don't give a good goddamn what you think."

The words came out far more harshly than he'd intended. Harsh enough to hurt, but Shaw just nodded, completely nonplussed.

Henricksen sighed, rubbing at his face. "It's late, Chief." Not quite an apology, but the best he could offer right now.

"It is," she agreed, watching him, studying his face. "You should probably get going." A nod to the bridge's door. "Get those crew assignments made before Kinsey does it for you."

"Yeah. Right," Henricksen grunted, pushing to his feet. He threaded his way between the bridge pod's stations, reached for the latch and opened the door.

"She'll be ready, Captain," Shaw called after him. "She'll be ready when you are. I promise you that."

Henricksen turned his head, looking back over his shoulder. "Thank you, Chief," he said softly.

Shaw raised a hand and snapped off a salute. "Aye, sir. Night, sir."

"Good night, Chief."

He stepped through, pulling the door closed behind him, fleeing Shaw and the ship. Paused long enough to stuff himself into the abandoned pressure suit before exiting the hangar bay and making for the safety of the RV-N crews' berthings. For his rack and the reader, and those assignments he still hadn't made.

FIFTEEN

Nearly 2300 by the time Henricksen returned to his quarters, putting him in violation of his own curfew. No one around to call him on it, of course—unlikely anyway *would* call him on it even if they had been around, him being captain and all. In charge of this squadron and allowed to bend the rules.

Rank, as they say, had its privileges. Not Henricksen's style to take advantage of it—kept the curfew until now to set a good example, eat his own dog food and all that—and, honestly, he was so damned tired most nights that he didn't even want to think about staying up late. Carousing with the young bucks.

Would've, once upon a time. Back when he was a wet-behind-the-ears junior officer burning the candle at both ends. Got away with it for a while, but a few stints in combat wiped that right out of him. A few days without sleep, watching friends and shipmates die made you understand the value of being properly rested. How luxurious sleep was. What a precious commodity it came to be when the shit hit the fan, and everything went tits up.

Unfortunately, that precious commodity pretty much eluded Henricksen that night. He slipped into his quarters and shed his uniform before climbing into bed. Lay there staring at the ceiling for a while, tossing and turning, obsessively checking the clock's time until it flipped over to 0300 and he finally gave up.

Climbed out of bed cursing. Showered, and shaved, and dressed in a crisp, clean uniform—another luxury, clothing changes being as hard to come by in combat as showers and sleeping—and sat himself down at his cramped little desk.

Set his reader down on top of it and just stared at it a while, hands resting on either side of it, fingers drumming against the desktop. Keyed it on with a sigh and started paging through personnel files—official records and his own notes—playing with combinations of crew.

Spent a few hours that way, without coming to any firm decisions. Ticked off a couple of names and set them beside others, but mostly just swapped people around.

Shut the reader down when 0530 came around. Shoved it in a pocket as he grabbed breakfast in the mess hall—powdered eggs and synth bacon, some kind of yellow fruit that tasted faintly of bananas and smelled strongly of protein supplements—and wandered down to the sims.

First two runs were shit—too much on Henricksen's mind and not enough sleep, leaving him distracted. Making rookie mistakes that left the crew wondering, throwing worried looks his way.

"Captain." Sikuuku leaned out of his pod as the second run ended, tapping the side of his helmet as he switched to a private channel.

No *real* privacy in a sim pod—tight quarters, everyone in everyone else's way—but the helmets muffled voices. Private channels allowed for whispered words to be passed in confidence.

"What's going on?"

Couldn't see Sikuuku's face—not with that helmet obscuring it—but the worry came through clearly in his voice.

"Sorry. Distracted." Henricksen shrugged his shoulders, adjusting the seat straps as he toggled the system, setting up for another run. "Didn't sleep well."

"Something I should know?"

"Kinsey." Henricksen shrugged again, flipped a hand without looking around. "Gave me hell about assignments last night."

"Could be he's right." Sikuuku settled back in his pod as Henricksen initiated the start-up routine. "Crew's getting awful tired of this sim hokey-pokey."

"Don't start," Henricksen growled. "Last thing I need is *two* of you riding my ass." He cut the private channel, switching to internal comms. "Pre-flight. Run starts in thirty seconds."

A flurry of activity as crew checked systems—Sikuuku's gimbaled pod pivoting, Hanu running diagnostics, checking status with Ahmadi at Scan. Routine by now, the checks and rechecks, and boring as hell, but they ran it every time. Every damn time.

Routine kept crews alive. Turned actions into instinct, taking the guesswork out of things when the chips were down.

"Scan," Henricksen called, voice calm, steady, cold as ice.

"Go," Ahmadi told him.

"Engineering."

"Go," Hanu answered.

"Artillery."

"You know I'm go," Sikuuku said, smile in his voice.

Henricksen reached for the panel, and the button to launch the next simulation. "Three. Two. One. Launch." A touch of his finger, and the pod kicked hard, pinning the crew in their seats.

\#

Third run started out a beauty—best of the day, one of Henricksen's best ever. Asteroid field again, which distracted him for a moment. Had him thinking about dinner with Kinsey, that cryptic comment about the DSR keeping secrets. Shaw's mention of Kepler, and Kinsey pulling chocks from the planet, moving the entire RV-N project here to Dragoon.

"What the hell is in there?" he muttered.

"Rock," Ahmadi called. "Three o'clock."

"Got it." Henricksen feathered the jets, sliding around the asteroid field, threading his way through the tumbling jumble of oddly shaped stones. Stalking the ships hidden at the center. That massive, mystery object the sensors couldn't quite identify. "Anything, Ahmadi?"

"Not yet." He fiddled with Scan's settings, alternating the patterns of the sensors. "Bits and pieces but the rocks keep getting in the way so I can't get a solid lock."

"Right. I'll take us in closer." Henricksen drew a deep breath, risked another burst of the jets. "Sensors?"

"Nothing yet, sir."

Good sign. Meant those ships out there hadn't spotted them. Nice to know this fancy-schmancy stealth tech might actually be worth its salt.

Sims, after all. Software, theory, not the real thing.

Third burst and a warning appeared, red light flashing on Ahmadi's panel. "Active scan. We've got eyes on us, sir."

"Shit. Where?"

Ahmadi leaned forward, fingers flying across the panel. "Dead ahead. Hold her steady while I—"

"Henricksen."

Shaw's voice, sounding muted, far away. Scratchy channel, piped directly to his helmet's comms, machinery filling the background with noise.

Flight deck, his mind translated, based on that noise.

Odd, that she'd contact him directly, especially from there. Didn't remember Shaw *ever* listening in on their sim sessions much less cutting in to offer commentary, and he honestly didn't need the distraction. Not on this just-about-perfect run.

"Little busy, Shaw. Not really the time."

"It's important," she said, voice insistent.

"I'm sure it is," he told her, hands gripping the control stick as a tumbling rock all but scraped their hull. "But it'll have to wait—"

"No. It can't. Kinsey's got Adaeze in the RV-N."

"What?!"

"Rock, rock, rock!" Ahmadi yelled.

"Shit." Henricksen fired the port-side thrusters, banking hard. Scan lit up like a Christmas tree, warnings popping off everywhere as the simulated ships bathed them in sensors, weapons systems coming alive as they targeted the RV-N's cloaked form. "Shit. Shit, shit, shit."

"Weapons fire!" Ahmadi warned.

Henricksen hauled the ship over, bringing it right into the path of a rock. Skimmed to one side and clipped it—almost made it, but the RV-N's wingtip caught a spike-shaped protrusion, spinning it away from him, sending it crashing into another just like it. "Fuck," he breathed, slamming his hand against the panel. "Fuck me."

Weapons fire behind them, tracking the RV-N's shape, shredding the asteroids to either side. Chunks of rock flew everywhere, setting off a chain reaction that knocked asteroids off their axis, sending them spinning randomly in every direction.

"Fuck, fuck, fuck, fuck, fuck."

Scan signatures showed chaos—asteroids colliding everywhere, bouncing off one another and careening out of control. Henricksen dodged desperately, hands wrapped in a death grip around the control stick as he zig-zagged through an increasingly cluttered landscape, searching for a way out. "C'mon, c'mon, c'mon," he muttered, yanking hard on the control stick, firing the thrusters in a long burst.

A rock rose up in front of him—huge, towering, nearly twice the size of any other in the asteroid field. No time to go around it so Henricksen pulled the stick back, hands trembling, arms shaking with the effort as he tried to fly the ship up and over.

Not gonna make it. We're not quite gonna make it.

"Hold on!" he yelled, thinking he could salvage it. That he could still get the ship and crew home.

And he just about did—might have gotten them out clean, if the rock hadn't continued to tumble, showing them a towering, nub-like projection that hit the stealth ship head-on, bringing it to a sudden and inevitable halt.

Error messages appeared, the pod reporting failure—target destroyed, ship destroyed, the entire run an unqualified mess.

Henricksen sat back, staring at the blinking panel, reached forward and shut the simulation down. "What's this about Adaeze?"

"Kinsey ordered her crew into one of the RV-Ns." Shaw sounded panicked—not like her at all. "He launched them, Henricksen. He launched them on a live exercise."

"Can't be." He reached for the monitoring system, checking on the other pods, convinced Shaw was wrong.

Simulations running in all of them, except for Number Five. Five, which was Adaeze's, and empty. Pilot and crew—Grunewald, Abboud, Fisker, all of them gone.

Fisker. Oh God, Fisker.

He'd missed them shutting the sim down somehow. Got so damned tied up in his own simulation that he hadn't even noticed Adaeze's crew getting called out.

"Son-of-a-bitch," Henricksen muttered. "Son-of-a-*bitch!*" He punched the panel hard, pissed at Kinsey, angry at himself. Tore his seat's restraining straps loose, ignoring the flight crew's questions, Sikuuku's reaching hands as he lunged for the pod's door, ripped it open and climbed out into the monitoring room on the other side. "How long?" he demanded, speaking through the helmet's comms.

"Ten minutes," Shaw told him, voice worried, apologetic. "Would've warned you sooner but Kinsey had the comms blocked. Took me a while to jump a channel to your suit."

"Dammit. God dammit," Henricksen swore, tearing the helmet from his head.

"What's going on?" Sikuuku asked, appearing at his shoulder.

"Kinsey. Your fucking friend Kinsey screwed me over." Henricksen threw the helmet across the room, grabbed Sikuuku's arm and pulled him close. "Did you know about this? Did you know what Kinsey was up to?"

"What? No. *No*," the gunner insisted, angry now, shaking Henricksen's arm off. "Hardly said two words to me since we got here."

Henricksen studied his face, nodded and turned around.

"Garrett." Sikuuku's hand landed on Henricksen's shoulder. "What's happening? What's going on?"

"Told you. He screwed me." Henricksen turned his head, studying his friend with one eye. Grabbed the door and pulled it open, storming across the control room, yelling at the top of his lungs. "Thought we had an agreement, Kinsey." Pinstriped suit by the windows, standing with two lab-coated engineers. Dark face turning toward Henricksen as he strode angrily across the room. "*Your* project, *my* crew. So, explain to me what the *hell* they're doing out there." He stabbed a finger at the windows. At the hangar bay's open doorway and the stars showing outside.

Kinsey straightened, turning, hands clasped behind his back. The lab coats—Song and Wallace, Karansky lurking in one corner—glanced around, blanched when they saw him and took a sudden and intense interest in their stations.

"I needed a live test," Kinsey said in his clipped, no-nonsense tone. "You've been dragging your feet so I took things into my own hands."

"They weren't ready! I told you last night—"

"And *I* told *you* that you needed to makes some decisions." Kinsey stared coldly, face a complete blank. "This project needs to move forward, Captain, and I mean to do that with or without you. Whichever you prefer."

"Move the project forward?" Henricksen barked a bitter laugh, throwing his hands in the arm. "The chassis' not ready." He slid in close, finger stabbing at Kinsey's chest. "You'll *kill* them, you self-righteous—"

"Back. Off," Kinsey warned, slapping his hand away.

Henricksen shoved him hard, sending Kinsey stumbling backward, artificial leg catching on a monitoring station, sending him sprawling to the floor. Hadn't meant to knock him over—didn't think about that artificial leg and Kinsey's chancy balance when he shoved him—but Henricksen was too pissed to apologize. *Way* too angry to back down. "This is *my* Command, Kinsey. *I*—"

"Easy, Captain, easy." Sikuuku stepped in front of him, making placating gestures with his hands. "He sent them out there," a nod to the windows at the front of the control room, "nothing to be done about it now."

Henricksen looked at him, and at Kinsey picking himself up off the floor. "Call them back," he ordered, rounding on the two engineers. "Call the RV-N back to the hangar. Tell Adaeze—"

"Belay that," Kinsey snapped, fiddling with the joint of his artificial leg, adjusting the drape of his suit's trousers as he stood. "Mission is go. No turning back."

"Mission?" Henricksen swung around, staring in angry disbelief. "So it's a *mission* now?"

"Shakedown run," Song interjected, shoulders hunched, clipboard clasped tight to her chest. She flicked her eyes to Kinsey, nodding an apology, reached behind her to tap at a station, throwing a live video feed onto the windows looking out on the hangar.

"The chassis' ready," Kinsey told him. "But the Brass ordered a shakedown run before they'll approve a real launch."

"Why didn't you tell me?" Henricksen moved a step closer to Kinsey, came up against Sikuuku as he re-inserted his burly body between them. "Last night, at dinner—"

"Last night it wasn't ready." Kinsey brushed at his sleeve, tugged at his lapels. "This morning it was. You have Shaw to thank for that." A nod to the windows and Shaw's mech gang in the hangar below.

"She *tell* you it was ready?"

Kinsey twitched his shoulders, waved vaguely at the air. "Shaw wants tests before she'll sign off on anything. Adaeze was available—"

"You had *no* right pulling Adaeze. Her *or* her crew."

"I had every right, Captain." Kinsey advanced on him, coming right up behind Sikuuku, dark eyes staring over his shoulder. "She's your best pilot. She has the best feel for the chassis."

"Control, this is One-Eight-Three." Adaeze's voice sounded impossibly calm as it filtered through the room's speakers. "We are through Checkpoint Alpha, one hundred thousand kilometers out from the first beacon."

Kinsey tilted his head, eyebrow lifting, leaned to one side and activated the comms. "Acknowledged, One-Eight-Three. Proceed on course."

"Roger."

Kinsey lifted his finger, cutting the comms. "I need data on the RV-N's engines and cloaking system." A nod to the video feed showing the RV-N and darkness, the pinpricks of stars. "To get that data, I need live tests." He folded his arms and crossed his legs, leaning against the station. "I run this project, Captain. Which means you, and Adaeze, and every last one of these crew report to me, understand?"

Henricksen's face darkened. "We had a deal—"

"No. We didn't. We had an agreement. One I changed because it no longer suited my needs."

Henricksen glared, hating him. Tempted to deck the smug fucker and knock him right down again.

"Control. Control this is One-Eight-Three." Adaeze again, a hint of annoyance penetrating the calm. "We've reached the first marker. What are your orders?"

"It's too late." Sikuuku's hand landed on his shoulder, squeezing hard to get Henricksen's attention. "It's too late—they're already out there. And we *need* the data. We do," he insisted when Henricksen started to object. "Done as much as we can in the sims, Captain." A flick of his eyes over Henricksen's shoulder as a door opened, releasing a mass of confused RV-N crew into the monitoring room. "They're launched. They're out there. Best we can do is let Adaeze finish this run, and bring that bird back in."

"What's going on?" Baldini demanded, staring at the video showing on the windows. "That a live feed? Who's out there? Who'd you—"

"Control. Control, are you reading me?" Adaeze called.

"Hold position," Kinsey told her, touching a panel, opening a channel to the ship. "Await further orders."

"Adaeze?" Baldini looked indignant. "You sneak crew out of the sims to launch that bird and you put Adaeze—"

"Lock it down!" Sikuuku yelled. "You. All of you," the gunner pointed at Baldini, swept his eyes across the group of crew, "you get back in the sims—"

"No." Henricksen caught Sikuuku's eyes, brushed his hands away. "Let them watch. You're right, we need the data." He flicked his gaze to Kinsey. "Next time you tell me. Your project, my crew. That's the only way this works."

Kinsey lifted his chin, looking arrogant as ever. Considered a moment and nodded tightly—grudging acquiescence, but acquiescence nonetheless. "May I?" he sneered, waving at the video feed behind him.

"Run it," Henricksen nodded. "You get your data and you get that crew back here. Nothing fancy, no extras—engines and cloaking system. You get what you need and you cut it. Bring that bird back to the hangar." He stared at Kinsey until he nodded—stiff and angry, just like before. Turned aside and folded his arms, studying the video feed flickering on the windows' glass.

SIXTEEN

"Proceed," Kinsey said, opening a channel to the stealth ship. "Stay on course to the next beacon. Propulsion engines only for now. We'll monitor from here."

"Acknowledged," Adaeze answered, and dropped the channel into silence.

"You sure about this?" Sikuuku murmured, nodding to Baldini and the others watching from the back of the room. "You say the word and I'll hustle them back into the sims."

"Leave it," Henricksen told him, shaking his head. "Afternoon's shot anyway." Not quite—they still had a couple of hours before dinner—but at best they'd get one more run in. "Doubtful we'll get anything useful out of the crews today. Not with this going on." He waved at the windows, indicating the stealth ship, and Kinsey, the lab coats busily gathering data nearby.

"Control, we're approaching the second beacon." Adaeze again, as calm and collected as ever. Like taking the stealth ship out for a test spin was no big deal. "How's the data look?"

Kinsey looked a question at Wallace, saw her nod seriously, flash a thumbs up. "Nominal on our end, One-Eight-Three." He paused, frowning as Song waved her arms, mouthing a question. "Engineers are asking if you can test out the stealth system before you head into jump."

"On it. Activating the cloak in three, two, one."

A ripple on the video feed and the RV-N disappeared. "Son-of-a-bitch," Henricksen breathed, staring in disbelief. "What do the sensors show?"

Song looked around, shunted a data window to the glass showing the feeds from the Number Two beacon's sensors.

Energy signature there, the stealth ship's engines showing clearly despite the cloak wrapped around the ship. A whispered request from the engineer and even that disappeared as Adaeze cut the ship's propulsion, drifting on momentum.

"Whoa," Adaeze breathed.

"What's wrong?" Henricksen demanded, hearing the tremble in her voice. "What's going on?"

Kinsey twisted, frowning in disapproval, finger raised in warning. "Something wrong, Adaeze?" he asked, casually as always, showing not the least bit of concern.

"Harmonics," she told him, sucking in a shaking breath. "Vibration in the cabin. Must be the stealth system. Sims..." Another breath, voice steadying, returning to normal. "Sims don't really prepare you for that."

"How bad?" Kinsey asked her, brow creasing as he reached for a panel, scrolling through a data window's information.

"Tolerable." Deep breath, long exhalation. "Rattles your bones, though."

"Cabin needs baffling." Shaw slid in at Henricksen's elbow, coveralls splashed with grease. Shaw who ran the mech gang and knew just about every engineering detail about the RV-N chassis. The ins and outs of its stealth system and jump drives, weapons, environmentals, you name it. Who also knew a thing or two to say about those pulverized pilots the Fleet medicaled out.

She nodded to Henricksen and folded her arms, frowning like a thunderhead at Kinsey's pinstriped suit. The lab coated engineers hovering around the monitoring stations, poring over every piece of data the ship and the beacons sent back. "Keep tellin' 'em that." A nod to Song, and Wallace beside her. "Raven's a rough ride on a good day. Beats hell out of the pilots. Command pod needs cushioning to keep them from turning into jelly."

"What's Karansky say?" he asked, eyes flicking to the chief engineer watching from the corner.

"Karansky?" Shaw snorted in derision. "Karansky won't listen to anyone other than his two lackeys over there. Just a deck monkey, after all." She flicked her collar devices, gestured at her grease-stained coveralls. "Big man won't stoop low enough to speak to a wrencher like me."

"So take it up with Kinsey," Sikuuku suggested.

Shaw turned her head, giving the gunner a flat-eyed stare. "Kinsey's in too damn much of a hurry to worry about little things like the crew's comfort." She studied the engineers a moment, slid a look Henricksen's way. "Not my idea, by the way." A wave to the video feed showing on the windows. "Buttoned up the engines and stealth system last night, but I was hoping to have a couple of days to run diagnostics before..." Shaw trailed off, shrugging. "Kinsey," she said, as if that explained everything. "Man's in an all-fired hurry for some reason."

"Yeah," Henricksen murmured. "Yeah, he is."

Sikuuku whistled appreciatively, drawing their eyes back to the windows. To the video feed of the RV-N. "Would you look at that? Ship's damn near invisible!"

Henricksen grunted, eyes shifting from the empty piece of space where the RV-N should be, to the data window layered over it, ship's information streaming endlessly. "Be nice if they could figure out how to mask the engines."

"Yeah, but...damn." Sikuuku blinked, shaking his head in admiration.

"We've reached the second beacon," Adaeze announced. "Want me to take her into jump?"

"Let me at 'em. Let me at 'em," a genderless voice quipped in the background.

Sikuuku frowned, head tilting. "That the AI?"

"That'd be my guess," Henricksen smiled.

"Sounds funny."

"Shaw says they're still 'finding themselves' or some such." Henricksen shrugged his shoulders. "Not much personality yet."

Sikuuku grunted, thinking that over.

"Hold on jump, One-Eight-Three." Song reached to one side, tapping at a panel. "I'd like to collect some more data on the stealth system first."

"Got it. We'll just circle here until you tell us to cut it out."

Song smiled, nodding, leaned over her station and worked at the panel in earnest.

Curious, Henricksen wandered over, checking out what she was doing.

"Direct data feed." Song looked up, pointed at the station in front of her, the video feed on the glass. "RV-N's monitoring system keeps tabs on everything. Since we can't monitor the stealth system remotely, the ship's systems capture it locally and feed it back here." She tapped the panel, highlighting a data window, lines and lines of information scrolling endlessly across its face. "Excuse me," she said, turning back to the station, opening a channel to the ship. "Alright. That should do it. You can shut the cloaking system down." Song turned her head, watching the ship shimmer into existence, nodded to Kinsey as she turned the station over to Wallace.

A look from Kinsey and Henricksen retreated, watching the video feed from the center of the room.

Sikuuku slid in beside him, smile on his face. "Crowded over there, I take it."

"Apparently," Henricksen grunted.

"Alright, Lieutenant." Kinsey keyed the comms, calling to the stealth ship. "Spool up the jump drives."

"Aye, sir. Hyperdrive system is live. Engines are spooling. We're go for jump in three minutes."

"Acknowledged. We'll set the clock." Kinsey nodded to Wallace who set a timer on the front windows, numbers ticking rhythmically as the RV-N glided through space.

Sikuuku nudged Henricksen's arm, nodded to Taggert behind them, sidling surreptitiously toward one of the monitoring stations, eyes flicking around the room as he rattled at the keys, casually logging in. Snuck another look around while the system processed his credentials, tipped a wink at Henricksen and Sikuuku when he caught them looking and raised a finger to his lips.

"What do you suppose he's up to?" Sikuuku asked, pitching his voice low.

"God only knows," Henricksen muttered, pointedly looking away. "Boy's always sticking his nose where it doesn't belong."

Sikuuku looked at him, and at Taggert behind them. "You want me to..."

Henricksen glanced around, considering, saw Taggert raise a hand, waving furiously at Ogawa until she crept over to join him. "Leave it," he said, as the two engineering officers bowed their heads together, huddled over the monitoring station. "My guess is he's snooping through the beacons' data. Kinsey and crew find out and don't like it, they can take it up with Taggert themselves."

"Thirty seconds to jump," Fisker announced.

"This is it." Henricksen leaned forward as the hyperspace buckle solidified—a glimmering hole of endless darkness floating serenely in space.

The clock hit ten seconds, Fisker's voice returning, counting the rest of the way down. "Ten. Nine. Eight..."

Henricksen spread his legs wide, muscles tensing, anticipating the buck and kick that came with jump. Blushed when he realized what he was doing, laughed and nudged Sikuuku in the side when he caught the gunner doing the same.

"Jump!" Fisker called, and the RV-N surged forward, buckle wrapping around it, pulling it into the trough.

The ship's beacon disappeared, jump distortion blocking its signal, but the video kept rolling, tracking RV-N-183 in real time, as it slid along the hyperspace trough.

"Weird, isn't?" Sikuuku nodded to the video feed. "Seeing everything. Watching but not actually *feeling* anything."

"Not quite real, is it?" Henricksen grunted. He tensed again as the stealth ship shuddered—nothing unusual, just the normal hyperspace displacement—relaxed as it settled out, gliding smoothly for a few seconds before dropping out of the trough.

Lot of stressors in hyperspace. Body grew used to the push and pull of conflicting forces that came with faster than light travel. Brain reacted instinctively, not knowing what was real and what wasn't.

Used to hate that feeling, when the ship first entered jump. But over time, Henricksen grew to love it. Crave it, every bit as much as the stars.

Too long. He twitched his shoulders, dispelling a sudden surge of jealousy as RV-N-183's beacon reappeared. *Far too long since I was out there, gliding amongst those stars.*

Sikuuku looked at him, brow creased with worry. "You alright?"

"Yeah. Fine. Just…" He waved at the windows, the RV-N's video feed. "Just miss it is all."

"Don't we all?" Sikuuku grunted, lips twisting in a bitter smile.

"Jump complete," Fisker announced. "We're holding steady at Beacon 3."

Hint of victory in the young ensign's voice. A note of smug satisfaction at successfully completing the RV-N's first ever hyperspace jump.

Henricksen frowned, shaking his head. "Don't get cocky, Fisker. Don't jinx this."

"Engines are running hot." Worry in Fisker's voice now, the smugness completely gone.

"Told you," Henricksen muttered, arms unfolding, unconsciously moving closer to the windows.

"Stand by." Wallace frantically worked at her station, poring through data, cycling through one monitoring system after another. "Sir?" She threw a worried look at Kinsey but it was Karansky who stepped in, inserting himself for the first time.

"They're within tolerances," he said, nodding to Kinsey. "Nothing to worry about."

Kinsey frowned at the chief engineer, looking less than pleased.

Odd dynamic there. Kinsey ran the project, but as the RV-N's designer, Karansky should really be leading this test.

"Engines are within tolerances," Kinsey repeated, speaking directly to the stealth ship crew this time. "Proceed on mission."

Took a moment for Fisker to answer, and when he did, he sounded nowhere near as confident as Kinsey. "Roger, control. Setting up for another run."

Karansky looked at Kinsey, inclining his head. Stepped back, turning the reins back over as he resumed his place in the shadows.

Sikuuku elbowed Henricksen in the side, pointing with his chin, eyes flicking from Karansky to Kinsey. "That seem right to you?"

"Nothing about this seems right," Henricksen muttered, and then shushed the gunner as Fisker's voice issued from comms.

"Jump course plotted. Two-hop to Beacon Four. Straight shot from there back to the first beacon."

"Acknowledged." Wallace cut the channel, frowning as Song leaned close. Whispering something, pointing at her station and the video feed. She turned her head, looking a question at Kinsey—interesting that he ran everything, leaving Karansky watching from the fringes—keyed comms open when he shrugged and nodded, calling back to the ship. "Slight change of plans, One-Eight-Three. Two-hop is go, but we'd like you to activate the stealth system on your way back."

A pause, and Adaeze's voice came through, sounding puzzled and annoyed. "You told us you had the stealth system data."

"Just one last test," Wallace promised. "We want to see how it operates under load."

Another pause, longer this time. "Roger," Adaeze answered. "Jump in thirty seconds."

Comms clicked closed and the control room went quiet, everyone watching the video feed, the data streaming back from the sensors. Thirty seconds and the stealth ship jumped away, reappeared briefly before disappearing again.

Short stop at Beacon Four to relay the ship's status. Fisker still seemed worried about the engines and asked Wallace to run diagnostics and a full spectrum analysis before spooling the jump drives up again.

"Smart ensign you've got there," Shaw grunted, tapping into a station, checking the data herself. "Jump drive system on the RV-N's state-of-the-art—bit overpowered for a ship that size, if you ask me, but super-efficient." She peered at the data, frowning as she straightened. "He's right, though. Engines *are* running a bit hot."

"How hot?" Henricksen asked her. "I've seen ships burn out their jump drives in hyperspace. The results aren't pretty."

"What? Oh! No! Nothing like that," Shaw assured him. "Wallace is right." A nod to the lab-coated engineer across the room. "It's all within tolerances. I'd just like to tweak the settings, is all. See if I can't improve the venting. Cool the damn things down."

Henricksen frowned, sharing a look with Sikuuku, liking this entire situation less and less. "You sure? This is a shake-out run, right? Maybe we should just bring them back in on their propulsion engines."

"Yeah, right." Shaw snorted. "And wait a week for them to get here." She slid her eyes toward Henricksen. "Engines are fine, Captain. Promise. They'll bring your crew back here." She winked, nodding to the windows as RV-N-183 moved forward, slipping into the hyperspace buckle. "Last hop," she said, smiling confidently. "Almost home."

That's when everything went wrong.

The monitoring system caught it first, registering an unexpected energy spike five seconds into the RV-N's last jump. A spike that *kept* spiking, oscillating badly, causing the ship to wobble and start slewing around.

Not a good situation, especially when transiting the hyperspace trough.

"Control!" Adaeze sounded panicked, not her usual calm, cool self. "Control we've got a situation. The ship—the ship—"

Kinsey touched at the comms panel, leaned close to the mic. "Talk to me, Lieutenant. What's going on?"

"Can't—can't," she panted. "The ship—"

"I'm sorry," the AI cut in, genderless voice filled with mourning. "I'm so sorry, Shaw."

A flare of light blotted out the video feed, monitoring system throwing up warnings, data windows blanking as the comms channel crackled and went dead.

"What just happened?" Henricksen stared at the blanked out video feed, turned toward the engineers and saw them glance at each other—eyes wide, brows wrinkled in confusion—shaking their heads. "*What the hell just happened?*"

"Some—some kind of error," Song told him, voice shaking, arms wrapped tight around her middle. "I'm—I'm not sure—" She licked her lips, throwing desperate glances at Kinsey, blinked and stared at the windows as a video feed appeared.

"Is that the ship?" Sikuuku squinted, moving closer to the windows. "*Is that the ship?*" he repeated when Song just stood there, shaking her head.

"It's the beacon." Wallace pushed Song aside, bent over a station and started working away. "Sensors on Beacon One are picking up something. Looks like..." She froze, head lifting, looking Kinsey's way. "It's an energy signature."

"What *kind* of energy signature?" Kinsey asked, voice carefully controlled, back ramrod straight.

Wallace swallowed hard, face paling. "Hyperspace displacement," she said, voice the barest whisper. "It's a jump signature, sir." She pointed a trembling finger at the video feed on the windows as the dark void of a hyperspace buckle appeared, flashed brightly and spat the pulverized remains of RV-N-183 out.

SEVENTEEN

Fleet investigators descended on Dragoon within a day of the accident—a dozen of them in total, dressed in starched shirts and crisp suits because somehow that was meant to be more comforting. More *inviting* than a bunch of smartly pressed uniforms decked out with racks upon racks of ribbons.

Problem was, they still *looked* military. Suit and tie couldn't change that.

Square-sided haircuts on the male investigators, overly severe buns on their female counterparts. Everything spit and polish—backs straight, eyes sharp as broken glass—entirely spoiling their attempt at obfuscation. Putting everyone even *more* on edge than if they'd just been honest and worn their uniforms. Admitted what they were.

Nothing Henricksen could do about it but try to keep his crews calm. Stand at the edges and watch the investigators comb through the station, interviewing anyone and everyone who had anything to do with the RV-N project. Including the crew. Sikuuku and himself.

"Relax," Henricksen told them when the first of the summons came. "Tell them what you know and *only* what you know. Don't guess. Don't assume. Don't make accusations. Don't lie to them either." That for Baldini, who could be severely stupid when the notion took him. "Just answer their questions the best you can."

"Say 'sir' a lot," Sikuuku added. "Investigators like that."

That earned a few smiles. A nervous laugh from Taggert. Most of the crew just nodded, though. Angry, the lot of them. Hurting from their losses. Anxious about those investigators showing up here, poking into everyone's business.

"Just tell them truth." Quiet voice from Henricksen, looking each and every one of them in the face. "Simple answers. Don't embellish, don't hold back. This is an investigation, not a witch hunt. You tell them what you know and everything'll be alright."

Hoped that was true. Hard to know for sure since every investigation was different. Some *were* witch hunts—he'd seen it a time or two in his years with the Fleet—but this one...even if this *did* go that route, the crew had nothing to fear.

Witch hunts went after Command. After senior officers in charge. Sometimes civilians—rare, but it did happen. And this project—run by civilians, with an entire troop of civilian engineers...

No one was safe. Not Kinsey. Not Karansky. Not Henricksen himself. He knew it. Sikuuku knew it. And from the looks on their faces, the crew knew it as well. That's why Henricksen volunteered to go first. Suffering through hours of the investigators' endless questions. Enduring three interrogation sessions in total over the course of that week. Going over everything—every last detail. Offering the same mostly useless information again, and again, and again because that's all he had: answers that amounted to pretty much nothing. That's all *anyone* had, because no one, not even Kinsey, seemed to know what happened to RV-N-183 and her crew.

A week passed, crew inching numbly through their work day, operating mostly on remote. Running missions in the sims because that's what Henricksen ordered, and they honestly didn't know what else to do. Sat in silence in the mess hall after, staring at the walls, the ceiling, the blank spaces where Fisker and Adaeze, Grunewald and Abboud used to fit.

That was the worst part. Four crew gone in the blink of an eye, and yet traces of them remained. Reminders scattered about the berthing areas, the common rooms where crew gathered. Quarters still contained all their personals—Kinsey's orders, wanting nothing removed until the investigation wrapped up. Sim room lockers still held their flight suits, helmets sitting on a shelf above. No one touched them. Crew tried not to even *look* at them. Did their best to pretend those left behind items didn't even exist, because denial was easier than remembering. Than coming to terms with four senseless, meaningless deaths.

Hard week, that one. Hard on everyone, dealing with all that loss. And the investigators' interrogations made it all the more difficult. Didn't mean to, but there it was. Crew died and the Brass wanted to why. How. Brought those investigators into question everyone they could get their hands on. Pour through the data Karansky and his engineers collected, trying to figure out where, and when, and why things went wrong.

What to blame. Who was at fault.

Fleet was good at that. Laying blame. Finding fault. The truth was never simple, though. Complex problems had complex causes and a lost crew, a destroyed AI...take more than a week's worth of interviews and interrogations to sort all that out.

Brass didn't want to hear it, though. Brass wanted this unpleasantness put to bed. Everything wrapped up nice and neat and decorated with a little bow so they could move on. Get the project back on track.

To their credit, the investigators tried—bet your life they did, with the Brass riding their collective asses. But three rounds of interviews later, Henricksen started tiring of their repeated questions. Crew grew frustrated giving them the same useless answers.

Played the game, though, the lot of them. Answered the Fleet investigators' questions, suffered through the apologies and wooden commiserations marking each session's beginning and end.

Stressed the crew out, dealing with it day after day. Led to short tempers and snappish communications. But Henricksen...Henricksen just felt numb. Utterly, completely numb having to lock up the pain and anger, push it deep, deep down so he could do his job. Look the crew in their faces. Deal with the investigators and that insufferable prick Kinsey without exploding. Raging like some kind of goddamn lunatic.

Fourth and final interview with the investigators ended like all the others. A few blandly polite words thanking him for his cooperation, and the Fleet investigators released him. Detailed a petty officer—not Hollings this time, some stiff, young woman with a shave-sided haircut—to escort Henricksen back to the RV-N project's section of the station.

Didn't think to ask her name. Not until he entered his security code at the pressure door. Didn't think to thank her either, until she turned around and walked away.

Thought about calling her back to make amends, but a flash of blue and Petty Officer Whatever-Her-Name-Was disappeared around a corner, returning to whatever section of the station she belonged to.

Awkward, calling her back now. Making her retrace her steps for a half-hearted, decidedly too late show of gratitude he wasn't even sure he could convincingly muster. Good at it most days—bad at names at the best of times, but Henricksen prided himself on acknowledging people and giving them their due. But after all those hours answering questions, the week he'd been through...

"Damn," Henricksen sighed, scrubbing fingers through his short, dark hair. "God damn."

He punched the panel, forcing the door open. Stepped through and found Shaw waiting for him in the hallway separating the hangar deck from the RV-N crew's berthing area. Shaw and Sikuuku, Taggert and Ogawa—all of them acting casual, like they just *happened* to be there at the exact moment Henricksen showed up.

Didn't believe it for a second. Recognized an ambush when he saw one.

"Problem?" he asked, folding his arms, bracing his legs wide.

Everyone looked at each other, and at Shaw at their center, electing her to be their spokesperson. "Something to show you." She flicked her eyes to a camera in the corner, nodded to the hangar deck to one side. "Something I think you'll want to see."

Henricksen frowned, considering her, the crew standing with her. Trusted Sikuuku—knew he wouldn't be here unless this was important—but the secrecy worried him. Made him wonder what they were up to.

He half-turned, considering that watching camera. "Alright," he said, facing around. "I'll bite." He nodded to the airlock behind her, just down the hall. Followed Shaw and the others to it and stepped inside, letting the door cycle closed. "So, what's this—"

Shaw grabbed his arm, cutting him off with a sharp shake of her head. "Not here," she said, pitching her voice low. A nod to the comms panel in the airlock—camera there, cameras everywhere, watching everything on this station—and she grabbed an enviro suit from the rack, stuffed herself inside it and slid a helmet over her head.

Taggert and Ogawa dressed in silence, throwing nervous glances Henricksen's way. Sikuuku snagged a suit and shoved it at him, seemed about to say something, but just shrugged apologetically as he cursed and grunted, wrestling his own suit into place.

Henricksen watched him a moment, worried all over again. Wondering what all this was about. Stepped into his own suit and sealed it up tight. Grabbed a helmet from the rack and slipped it into place, holding his breath as the suit hissed and puffed out, excess material ballooning comically around his lean frame.

Shaw checked each of them, consulting the monitoring panel glowing on the breast of each suit, nodded and flashed a thumbs up as she cycled the airlock door on the hangar side and stepped into the vast darkness beyond. A touch at her helmet and a light appeared, glowing silver-white at the front of her head. Henricksen copied her, expanding the circle of brightness surrounding Shaw—an island of illumination that swelled, spreading outward as, one by one, Sikuuku, Taggert and Ogawa added the light from their helmet lamps to that bright spot in the vast darkness.

Cold light, issuing from their helmets. Colder still the empty, echoing hangar deck around them. The entire thing a vacuum—no gravity, no heat or atmosphere, just dark and cold, the sharp-sided shapes of the stealth ships lurking around the vast room's edges. No stars here—not with the hangar deck doors closed—which made the darkness all the more sinister. An inky, cloying black that surrounded them. Threatening to gobble them all up.

Henricksen shivered, feeling a sudden trepidation. Glanced around and saw the lot of them twitch and jitter, bunching up close, all of them feeling it now. That undercurrent of instinctive, almost primal fear as the darkness hemmed them close about.

Comms clicked open, Shaw's voice coming through. "This way," she said, helmet lamp turning, hand lifting, pointing to the stealth ships ahead and to the left.

Second click as the channel closed. Shaw turned her head, looking at them. Nodded and set off, checking once to make sure Henricksen and the others followed.

Long way across that hangar deck, with that looming darkness on every side. Henricksen strode along, shambling and awkward in that oversized, ill-fitting enviro suit. Each step a heavy, leaden movement. Magnetized boot soles sucking at the metal decking to keep him from floating away. The suit's circulation system hissing in his ears, pumping dry as death environmentals around his body, filling his nose with that rancid butter and vomit stink he'd come to associate with this hangar bay on Dragoon.

Hated that suit, but he'd be dead without it. Dead as a doornail within seconds of stepping through the airlock's door. One step and another brought him across the hangar bay—no lights at all in here now, excepting those Henricksen and the others brought with them—never even noticing the shimmer shield until their tiny group was right on top of it, helmet lights reflecting off the surface.

A ripple and it wrapped around them. Second ripple and they passed through, stepping into a pocket of heat and atmosphere, with the stealth ships ringing it round.

Just five of them here now, with One-Eight-Three gone. Five ships arranged in a wide circle, noses pointed at the hangar's walls, back ends bordering the edge of that circle with two dozen others just like them sitting in the shadows of the hangar's fringes.

Lined up in neat rows, patiently awaiting their turn at the big dance.

No crew for them yet. No funding for the billets *needed* to crew them with the RV-N project stalled. And the five here, sitting in a circle around them…Felt bad for those ships, being trapped here, grounded and waiting because humans couldn't quite get them to work.

Henricksen scanned that circle as he stepped away from the shimmer shield, pulling the helmet from his head. Dropped it to the decking when he reached the center of the shimmer shield's pocket and peeled himself out of the enviro suit.

Glanced down as Shaw appeared beside him, hands pressed to either side of her helmet, twisting to remove it before setting it by her feet. "Mech gang's been crawling through their systems all week, trying to figure out what happened to One-Eight-Three." She picked at her suit, working her way through the dozen or so fasteners. "Engineers have all sorts of theories, but so far nothing's panned out." She tugged hard at a last fastener, sighing in relief as the heavy suit collapsed around her. Stepped out of it and kicked it to one side, watching Sikuuku and the others strip, adding their own suits to the pile. "Buncha idiots, if you ask me. The engineers," she explained, at Henricksen's quizzical look.

"Yeah, well. I'm sure Kinsey's all over their asses because of that accident."

That look again—that sharp look of warning from Shaw. "Kinsey's not the problem."

Henricksen looked at her, eyebrow lifting in question, but Shaw just shook her head. Flicked her fingers as she headed for nearest stealth ship, gesturing for Henricksen to follow.

Sikuuku nudged him in the ribs, nodded after Shaw. "C'mon."

Henricksen grabbed his arm, holding him still. "What's this about?" he demanded. "What's going on? What aren't you—"

"Not here," Sikuuku told him, dropping his voice. "Too many ears." He waved at the hangar bay around them, nodded to the ship to one side. Shaw standing at the airlock, palming the door open.

Henricksen nodded tightly, letting Sikuuku go. Walked along at his shoulder, following the gunner and Shaw into the cargo bay of one of the stealth ships, lights coming on as they entered, outer door sealing as Taggert and Ogawa stepped through behind them.

"Good evening," Two-Six greeted them, camera swiveling, pointing Henricksen's way. "It's good to see you again, Captain."

Soft voice from the AI this time. A distinctly female voice, not genderless like before.

Henricksen tilted his head, looking a question Shaw's way.

Shaw shrugged her shoulders. "Been spending a lot of time together."

As if that explained anything.

Henricksen frowned at her, waiting for a better answer, but Shaw just shrugged again and set off across the cargo bay, gesturing impatiently for him to follow.

Cameras tracked them as they exited the cargo bay—Shaw and Henricksen, Sikuuku just a step behind. Taggert and Ogawa bringing up the rear, stolidly maintaining their silence.

Lights came on as they stepped into the hallway, illuminating the path ahead. They climbed the ladderway to the second level and headed for the bridge, but Henricksen slowed halfway there, glancing mistrustfully at the cameras. "Kinsey finds out we're in here—"

"He won't." Shaw tipped a wink at the nearest camera. "Two-Six has got us covered. Dontcha, sweetheart?"

"Communications are contained," Two-Six told her. "It's just us girls here," she added, surprising a laugh out of Shaw.

"Just how much time *have* you two been spending together?" Henricksen asked her.

Shaw winked again, tapped a finger to her nose. Walked the length of the hallway, looking back at Henricksen when she reached the bridge's door. "You mentioned Kinsey." She paused, chewing her lip, thoughtful look on her face. "He never blamed me for the accident. Or Adaeze. Or even Karansky for that matter."

"Really." Henricksen grunted, honestly surprised. Kinsey seemed the blaming type, and those three the easiest targets. "And just how do you happen to know all this?"

"Chief." Shaw smiled crookedly, tapping the insignia on her collar. "Got all sorts of connections."

"I bet." Henricksen matched her smile, lips giving it a bitter twist. "'Spose he's blaming me then. Couldn't possibly blame himself after all."

"Oh, c'mon." Sikuuku rolled his eyes. "He's not *that* bad."

"Jury's still out on that," Henricksen growled.

"Kinsey hasn't blamed anyone as far as I know." Shaw folded her arms, leaning against the door.

"*Told* you he wasn't all bad," Sikuuku muttered, giving Henricksen a look.

"So what's he telling the investigators?"

Shaw shrugged and turned around, opening the door. "Putting it all down to an "unfortunate accident", from what I hear." She stepped onto the bridge, squeezing between stations to get at Scan. "'Course he's promising the Brass he'll fix everything. Get the project back on track and all that."

"Of course," Henricksen snorted. "Gotta get these babies flying after all." He followed Shaw onto the bridge, claiming the Pilot's seat as his own. Saw Sikuuku settle his bulk at Engineering, leaving Ogawa and Taggert standing by the door.

Not a word out of either of them, not in all this time. Suspicious, that. Especially in Taggert's case. Bit of a motor mouth, that one. Holding his tongue wasn't really one of his strong points.

"Might explain what Karansky was up to." Shaw looked at him, and at the windows, leaned over Scan and worked away at the panel.

"What do you mean?" Henricksen grabbed Shaw's arm, pulling her around. "What's going on?"

Shaw blinked at him, glanced down at the hand gripping her arm. "Bastard's always been squirrely, but since the accident..." She trailed off, shaking her head. Rubbed at her bicep when Henricksen finally let go. A tap at the panel brought a video feed onto Scan's panel, second tap pushed it to the front windows of the bridge.

Hangar deck footage. Nothing of note showing at first—just the shimmer shield area with its toolkits and equipment, the back ends of ship showing at the edges. But a few seconds in, and a creeping figure appeared, lumbering along in a bulky enviro suit. A figure that stopped by one of the RV-Ns and started messing around with its engines.

Henricksen frowned, studying those images, watching the figure a while. "Could be anyone in that suit. What makes you think that's Karansky?"

A few strokes of the keys and Shaw added a data window next to the video feed. Highlighted the security credentials entered to gain access to the RV-N's propulsion system.

Karansky's credentials. The Chief Engineer's name captured in the system's data stream.

"Son of a bitch."

"That he is." Shaw nodded. "Been all over my ass since the accident. Caught him messing with Nine-Eight a couple of nights ago after hours." A second enviro-suited figure appeared on the video, gesticulating at the tinkerer.

Henricksen's frown deepened. Engineers stayed in the control room, mostly. Stuck to the science and theory, leaving the grunt work to Shaw and her mech gang. "What was he doing down here?"

"God only knows." Shaw flipped a hand, glowering in disgust. "Screwing things up—that's for sure. Had to run his ass out of the hangar bay."

The two figures on the video feed squared off, arms waving wildly. No audio track to go with the feed, but from the looks of things, Shaw gave Karansky quite the tongue-lashing. Ran him out of there with his ass on fire, tail tucked firmly between his legs.

Shaw touched the panel, killing the feed. "Took me half a day to undo all his changes and set everything back to rights." She swiveled, facing him, shaking her head. "Goddamn pain in the ass."

Henricksen chewed his lip, studying her face. "That why I'm here? You want me to talk to Kinsey? Get him to keep Karansky out of your shorts?"

Shaw dropped her eyes, staring at her hands. "No. Not that."

"Then what?" he asked, baffled. "You said you had something to show me—"

"We," Taggert interrupted, stepping away from the door. He glanced back, waving insistently at Ogawa until she joined him, standing stiffly at his side. "*We*," he said, indicating himself and Ogawa, Shaw further in. "*We* have something to show you."

Henricksen quirked an eyebrow, looking from Shaw on one side to Ogawa on the other.

Shaw shrugged and nodded, one hand resting on Scan's panel. Ogawa met his eyes and quickly looked away. Flipped her ponytail over her shoulder and tugged anxiously at its end.

He slid a look toward Sikuuku, but the gunner stared stonily back. "Alright. Show me," he said, leaning back in his seat, folding his arms. "I'm *dying* to know what all this secrecy is about."

EIGHTEEN

Taggert stuffed a hand inside his jacket, pulled out a reader and plugged a trailing cable into Scan. "We were going over some of the sim data with Shaw— 'scuse, Shaw," he said, smiling apologetically as he leaned between her and the station, plugging the cable into a data port.

"Sim data." Henricksen frowned, eyes flicking from Taggert to Shaw. "Sims are software. Why not talk to the engineers?"

Taggert snorted in derision as he worked at the keyboard, loading a video feed onto the RV-N's front windows. "Engineers don't know spit. Sir," he added, turning his head, nodding an apology to Henricksen. "Ogawa and I keep feeding them data from the sim runs but they don't want to listen."

"What kind of data?" Henricksen asked him.

Taggert shrugged. "Engines, mostly." He nodded to the windows as the video feed started, sim capture showing a RV-N entering jump, slewing about in the hyperspace trough. "Rough as hell," he confided. "Run hotter than anything I've ever seen."

Henricksen frowned, looking from Taggert to the video on the windows. "Fisker mentioned something similar, didn't he? Right before One-Eight-Three ran into trouble."

"They were running within tolerances," Shaw told him, chin lifting, stubborn look on her face. "Engines always run hot. That's *not* what caused the accident."

"And that's not the important part." Taggert waited until Henricksen looked at him. *Kept* waiting—offering no more explanation—until Henricksen finally asked.

"Then what is?" Henricksen snapped, quickly losing patience.

"Shielding." Taggert folded his arms, looking quite smug.

"Shielding?" Henricksen shared a look with Sikuuku, but the gunner just sat there like a boulder, giving nothing away. "What about the shielding?"

"Watch." Taggert waggled a finger at the video feed as the sim ship dropped out of hyperspace, sharp-sided shape shimmering as the cloaking system came on-line. "There," he said, stabbing a finger at the data window. "You see that? You see that spike?" A look at Henricksen and he stepped to the front of the bridge pod, stretching on his tiptoes to touch a finger to the reinforced glass. "Engine temperature increases whenever the stealth shield comes online."

"It's *still* within tolerances," Shaw insisted as Henricksen opened his mouth. "But I asked the engineers to look into it when Taggert brought this to me."

"And?" Henricksen asked her.

"Claimed they couldn't recreate it. Kept telling me it was a software problem in the sim."

"Took them at their word at first." Taggert cupped his chin, studying the data scrolling across the windows. "Sim software always was buggy. But this..." A look at Henricksen behind him and he shook his head hard. "This is different."

"How?" Henricksen asked quietly.

Taggert twisted, waving at Shaw. "Can you run that back? Just the trough part," he said, moving back to Scan.

Shaw nodded, running the feedback to the point where the RV-N slid through the buckle, hit the hyperspace trough and started shifting about.

"Again," Taggert told her, tapping at Scan's panel, shunting a series of data feeds onto the windows, synchronizing them with the video playing out before their eyes. "Freeze it," he called, holding a hand up.

Shaw touched a button, bringing the images to a halt.

"See that?"

Henricksen scanned the data, shaking his head. "Looks like a bunch of gobble-dee-gook to me." He looked a question at Sikuuku, received a shrug in response.

"Gunner. Engines aren't really my specialty."

"We're not sure it *is* the engines," Ogawa chimed in, speaking up for the first time.

"Then what is it?" Henricksen asked her.

Ogawa tugged hard at her ponytail, throwing desperate glances at Shaw.

"Two-Six?" Shaw tilted her head, looking up at a camera. "You wanna help us out?"

"Yes, Shaw. I'm happy to," she said politely.

A slight pause and Scan went into overdrive, cycling through dozens of data windows, chewing through reams of information. Two-Six slid the sim video to the right side of the windows and layered the engine data on top of it. Brought up a second feed and let it run, adding six different data widows beside it.

"More sim data?" Henricksen guessed.

"No," Two-Six said softly. "This is One-Eight-Three."

Henricksen threw a sharp look at the camera. "You watched it? You saw the accident happen?"

"Nine-Six tapped into the video feeds from the beacons and shared it. I served as the conduit for One-Eight-Three."

"Conduit," Henricksen repeated, frowning at the camera. "For the data One-Eight-Three streamed to the control room?"

"Affirmative, Captain."

"Why, Two-Six," Henricksen smiled. "Have you been snooping on Kinsey?"

"Snooping?" Two-Six hesitated for the barest of moments. "Ah, investigating. Yes. I accessed his data. Was that wrong?" she asked worriedly.

"Normally I'd say yes." He flicked his eyes to Shaw, turned his gaze to the images on the bridge pod's windows. "But in this case I'll give you a pass." He studied the data there a moment before looking back to the camera. "Does Kinsey know you have this?" he asked, nodding to the feeds showing on the glass.

"No," Two-Six told him, AI voice serene, placid as a still pond. "The data feed to the control room was blocked. But One-Eight-Three spliced the channel, giving me access to her information."

"So you were in cahoots together." Henricksen chuckled. "Sneaky. Very sneaky. Even for an AI."

Two-Six was quiet a moment, AI brain processing madly, trying to translate that bit of slang. "One-Eight-Three's data tells the real story," she said cryptically, drawing Henricksen's eyes back to the camera.

"Real story?" Henricksen frowned, not understanding. "What does *that* mean?"

"All of it, Captain. Not just the parts you and Shaw were allowed to see."

"What the hell is she getting on about?" he asked, abandoning the camera, looking over at Shaw.

"This." Shaw touched the panel, setting One-Eight-Three's video feed in motion. A second touch and she cleared away four of the data windows, stacking the two that remained above and below each other, setting them beside the video feed. "Engines. Stealth system," she said, pointing to the topmost data window, the one just below it. "Keep your eyes on this bottom window," she told him, letting the feed run.

A buckle appeared and One-Eight-Three slid into hyperspace, skimming along the hyperspace trough.

"See that?" Shaw froze the video, highlighting a section of data in the bottom window. "That's what I'm talking about."

Henricksen stared at the data window, trying to figure out what all that information meant. "Still don't get it," he told her, shaking his head.

"Honestly? We didn't either." Taggert shared a shame-faced look with Ogawa. "Not with just the sim data. It took One-Eight-Three's feed and Two-Six's processing power before we figured it out."

"Figured *what* out?" Henricksen growled, increasingly impatient. "I realize playing Stump the Chump with your captain is fun and all, Taggert, but I'm really getting tired of all this cloak and dagger bullshit."

"Stump the Chump?" Taggert blinked in confusion. "What's—"

"Just—" Henricksen stopped himself on the edge of shouting, clenched his hands and drew a deep breath. "Just get to the point, Taggert."

Taggert licked his lips, sharing a look with Ogawa. "Here." He pointed to the topmost data window, the one right beneath it, highlighting corresponding pieces of data in each. "*Now* do you see it?"

"No, Taggert. I don't." Henricksen sighed heavily, rubbing at his face.

"But—but it's right there!"

"Let me," Ogawa offered, touching at Taggert's arm. "The ship, sir." A nod to Henricksen, to the frozen image showing on the glass. "It drifted offline, yeah?"

"Several times. So what?" He shrugged his shoulders, folding his arms. "Drift happens, especially in the trough."

"True. But that one," Ogawa pointed to the ship's image, "was worse than the others. And when you look at the data..." The pointing finger moved, indicating the data window for the engines, the one for the stealth system. Ogawa pointed again, making sure Henricksen saw it, twisted, looking to Shaw at Scan. "Run the feedback ten seconds, then forward at half speed. Slow the data displays down as well so they synch up."

"Got it."

"Good," Ogawa said, once Shaw queued the feed up. "Let it play through." A flick of her eyes to Henricksen. "All the way to the end."

The feed started over, buckle forming, sucking One-Eight-Three into the hyperspace trough.

"See those spikes?" Ogawa pointed to the data windows, looked a question Henricksen's way.

"Something there," he agreed. "Just not sure what."

"Energy fluctuations. Engines and stealth system at the same time. And layer that over the video…" Ogawa nodded to the camera, watching as Two-Six brought the video and data windows together, layering one over the other, creating a complex, confusing mess in the process.

Henricksen frowned, trying to decipher it all. "I still don't—"

A shimmer as the RV-N's stealth system kicked it, slewing it catastrophically off-line. The ship vanished, video feed cutting out, but the data capture kept running, recording the last, tragic moments of the AI and its human crew.

Henricksen stared, heart pounding, remembering that moment. Feeling it— all of it, all over again. "The stealth system." He turned his eyes to Ogawa, looked from her to Taggert and Shaw. "It shifted her, didn't it? Knocked the ship off course."

Ogawa nodded, flicking her fingers at the windows. "Engines max out in hyperspace—every ship does that. Cloak caused an energy spike that the guidance system couldn't handle. Not in jump. It confused the nav, sent One-Eight-Three drifting off course."

In the close confines of the trough, where the tolerances were already tight.

"Why didn't we catch this?" Henricksen asked quietly, voice shaking. "Why didn't we see this behavior in the sims?"

Ogawa flushed, ducking her head. "Not sure, sir. Software must've covered it. Simulation…" She shrugged helplessly, looked up and back down. "Not the same as the real thing."

"And Karansky? The engineers? They designed this damn ship. You telling me *they* missed this?"

"Energy spikes only seem to happen during hyperspace transit," Taggert told him. "Not sure anyone even tested using the cloaking system during jump."

"Stupid idea anyway," Sikuuku muttered, angry now, disgusted. "Why the hell would you cloak in hyperspace? Burst of energy as the ship exits. Like a big old Roman candle or something, lighting up the night. *Nobody* could miss that."

Henricksen nodded, staring at the windows, thinking hard. "Karansky and his crew know about this?"

Shaw looked at Ogawa, from there to Taggert, all three of them shaking their heads.

"Didn't figure this out until yesterday," Taggert admitted. "Ran it by Sikuuku, brought it to you."

"And now you want *me* to figure out what to do with it." Henricksen sighed again, shaking his head. "Stolen data—"

"I didn't *steal,* Captain," Two-Six objected. "One-Eight-Three shared her information freely."

"I stand corrected," he said, inclining his head. "Doesn't change the fact we've got data we're not supposed to. And a high-tech stealth ship with incompatibility issues. Engines in conflict with its cloaking." He chewed on that a moment, barked a bitter laugh and leaned back in his chair. "What a mess. What a goddamn mess."

Shaw leaned forward, elbows on her knees, hands clasped together. "That 'incompatibility' killed people, Henricksen—"

"You think I don't know that?" He turned toward her, giving Shaw a flat-eyed stare. "Four crew, Shaw. *My* crew," he said, pressing a fist to his chest. "*My* responsibility—"

"And mine," she cut in, eyes filled with anger, voice shaking with pain. "Four crew and an AI, and the ship they were in *my* responsibility. So don't you *dare* think I'm not hurting. Don't you *dare* act like I don't care *every* bit as much as you."

Shaw glared angrily and Henricksen glared right back—neither of them giving an inch. Refusing to back down.

Silence descended on the bridge pod, Taggert, Ogawa and Sikuuku watching the standoff from the edges, Two-Six's camera monitoring everything from above. And then the AI's voice intruded—soft, gentle, instantly diffusing the anger in the room.

"One-Eight-Three flew," she said, voice wistful. "She flew, and it was beautiful. *She* was beautiful."

Henricksen glanced at the camera, wondering at the longing in that voice. The sorrow lurking beneath it. "Can you fix this?" he asked, looking a question at Shaw. "With the data available to you, can you adjust the engines, or the cloaking system, or whatever to fix the incompatibility issue that destroyed One-Eight-Three?"

Shaw sighed, slouching in her chair. "Maybe. With some help. For now, I can set a failsafe." She nodded to Two-Six's camera. "Configure the systems with the AIs' help so the jump drives and cloaking system can't be activated at the same time."

"Rather the damn things just worked correctly," Henricksen growled.

"Me too," Shaw grunted. "Believe me."

"But?" Henricksen asked, eyebrows lifting.

Shaw bowed her head and folded her hands, thumbs tapping together. "You're not gonna like this." Another sigh and Shaw straightened, looking Henricksen right in the face. "I'll need some of Karansky's crew."

A panel lit in front of her, data windows filling its screen. Other panels lit all over the bridge, displaying diagrams and system specifications, all of them marked up, reconfigured with recommended modifications.

"Or not," Shaw amended, as another data window opened, scrolling through lines of configuration changes and setting adjustments, flickering rapid-fire through an entire overhaul package before starting over again. "Got it all figured out, don't cha sweetheart?" She raised her head, smiling at Two-Six's camera. "Hardly need us at all."

"No. You're wrong," Two-Six answered in her calm, serene voice. "I can troubleshoot and design, but I can't build, Shaw. I will always need you for that."

Shaw ducked her head, blushing, looking surprising pleased. "Well aren't you just the sweetest thing?" she murmured, smile curving her lips.

"So you can do it?" Henricksen asked, looking from Shaw to the camera. "You can adjust the systems in the chassis? Make the same updates to the sims?"

"Think so." Shaw nodded. "With a little time. But..." She trailed off, staring out the windows, bottom lip caught between her teeth.

"But?" Henricksen prompted as the silence stretched out.

"I don't know." Shaw sighed heavily, shaking her head.

"Not good enough," he told her. "Not damn good enough by far, Shaw."

"Well, I'm goddamn sorry," she snapped, giving him an irritated look. "I can make some changes, but that's not going to prove anything."

"Why the hell not?" he demanded, angry himself.

"Sims are software." Ogawa blushed, shrugging uncomfortably as everyone looked her way. "The only way to prove out Shaw's fixes is with another data capture. Which means another live test."

"Live data," Sikuuku repeated, arms folded tight to his chest. "As in, non-sim data? As in, climb into one of those RV-Ns and take it for a spin?"

Ogawa glanced at Taggert, and the two of them nodded together.

"Lovely." Henricksen closed his eyes, rubbing at his face. Remembering the feel of the RV-N sim in hyperspace, the shuddering and shaking as he muscled it back into line.

The sense of loss that washed over him when One-Eight-Three disappeared, shredded remains dumping from hyperspace near the Number One beacon.

"No. There has to be another way."

"There isn't," Taggert told him. "Look, the ships are ready. The only way—"

"Did you see that, Taggert?" Henricksen lurched to his feet, stabbing a finger at the windows. "Did you see the way One-Eight-Three and her crew died? Kinsey thought *that* chassis was ready and look what happened. No, Taggert. No way," he said, shaking his head hard. "You're crew, not guinea pigs. And I'm damned sure not sending any of you out in one of those things until I'm comfortable flying it myself."

Taggert tucked up his arms, jaw set, clearly pissed off. "So we're not flying them. Ever. That what you're saying?"

"Not until—"

"I'll test the changes," Two-Six cut in. "Shaw can put my chassis in drone mode. We can test the new configuration—"

"No. Not happening," Henricksen said flatly.

"I'm not crew, Captain," Two-Six reminded him.

"But you *are* sentient." He raised his head, staring hard at the camera. "I've seen too many AIs die already. I don't need another one on my conscience."

"Captain—"

"No," he repeated. "I won't have it, Two-Six." A last look at the camera and he spun around, stalked across the bridge.

"Where are you going?" Sikuuku stood and started to follow but Henricksen stopped him with a raised hand.

"To see Kinsey." Henricksen grabbed the door and yanked it open "I want to know what's so goddamn important that he rushed that chassis into live trials." He stepped into the hall, paused and looked back over his shoulder. "I said no, Shaw, and I meant it. No drones, no crew until I say so. Got it?"

Shaw was quiet a moment, blue eyes glittering in the bridge pod's light. "Aye, sir," she said, tapping two fingers to her temple.

"Good. Now get those ships fixed." He nodded to Shaw, to Sikuuku and the others. "Taggert." He snapped his fingers, pointed to the reader plugged into Scan. "You got a back-up of that data?"

"Yeah," Taggert said slowly, brows drawing downward. "Couple, actually. Backed everything up to Two-Six just before—"

"Give it to me." Henricksen flicked his fingers, snagging the reader from Taggert when he brought it over.

"What are you—?"

"Kinsey may need convincing." Henricksen shoved the reader inside his jacket. "Bastard's certainly not gonna take *my* word on anything, is he?"

Taggert shrugged, looking confused as ever as Henricksen abandoned the ship for the hangar bay, using the comms system built into his enviro suit to summon Hollings to come get him because he *still* couldn't find his way to Kinsey's quarters without a tour guide.

NINETEEN

Kinsey answered the door with a frown on his face. "You're late, Captain. Again," he noted, pointing to an old fashioned wristwatch circling his wrist.

Not the greeting Henricksen expected—honestly wasn't sure Kinsey would answer the door for an uninvited guest—but then he remembered it was Friday, and long past 1830. Going on 2000, in fact, which explained the watch and lapel pin. The other discrete yet obviously expensive accessories Kinsey wore about his person.

Friday evening—drinks with the Brass. Henricksen's lips twisted, sneering in disgust. Crew dead, ship and AI wrecked, an investigation on-going that had the entire project on edge and all Kinsey could think about was schmoozing the bigwigs. Getting some facetime with the senior administrators so he could feather his nest.

Prick.

"We need to talk," Henricksen snarled, shoving at the door.

Kinsey shoved back, refusing to move, blocking the entrance to his quarters with his body. "I'm afraid I have plans, Captain. You can come back tomor—"

"Fuck your plans," Henricksen snapped. "And fuck you while you're at. You've got a bird down, Kinsey, and all you can think about—"

"You want to think about your next words very carefully, Captain." Kinsey stepped in close, eyes flashing with anger, voice cold as an arctic wind. "You want to think very, *very* carefully before you start throwing accusations my way." He flicked his eyes over Henricksen's shoulder, eyeing Hollings standing discretely to one side, the sparse foot traffic moving up and down the hall. "You want to talk privately? Fine. Hollings will be happy to make an appointment."

"No," Henricksen said flatly. "No appointment. *Now.*"

"I told you, I have plans—"

"And *I* said, fuck your plans."

Kinsey bristled, lips pressed in a flat, angry line. "Leave us." He flicked his fingers, dismissing Hollings, eyes never leaving Henricksen's face. "What do you want, Captain?" he asked, once the petty officer moved way. "Why are you here?"

Henricksen pulled Taggert's reader from his jacket, holding it up. "You're going to want to see this."

Kinsey folded his arms, scowling now. Completely out of patience. "And just what *is* this, Captain?"

"Data."

"Data." Kinsey's lips lifted, face twisting in a sneer. "You're wasting my time, Captain." He stepped back, grabbing the door's edge, preparing to swing it closed.

Henricksen stepped forward, forcing his body into the gap. "From the sims," he said, holding the reader out. "From the accident last week."

A pause, Kinsey studying him from the entryway to his apartments, that heavy door standing halfway closed between them. "And?"

Henricksen dropped his voice, hand pressing against the door. "I know what caused it."

Kinsey squinted suspiciously. "Karansky—"

"Is part of the problem."

The scowl reappeared, worry showing at the edges.

"He can't figure it out, can he?" Henricksen guessed.

"No." Grudging admission. Kinsey stared at Henricksen standing in the hallway, dark eyes cold as ice, face a mask of stone. "Who?" he asked, nodding to the reader in Henricksen's hand.

"Shaw. With some help." Kinsey's eyebrows lifted, face filled with questions but Henricksen just shook his head. "You need to see this," he repeated, holding the reader out.

Kinsey considered the device a moment, turned around, leaving the door half open—an invitation, albeit half-hearted and unwilling, for Henricksen to enter. "Ten minutes," he said, turning his back on Henricksen as he walked away. "You have ten minutes to show me this data of yours before I go meet with the Brass."

#

Kinsey watched the video play out, studying the data screens running alongside it—impatient at first, and then increasingly attentive. Very quiet, very still.

Watching. Absorbing. Studying the graphs on those data screens as they spiked and maxed out.

Ran the video back and watched it again at quarter speed, looking deeply disturbed now. "Where did you get this?" he demanded, flicking his fingers at the reader, the images flowing across the wall.

Projection system somewhere in that white and chrome front room, though damned if Henricksen could find it. Reader plugged into a data port on a metal and glass table between two overstuffed, white leather chairs, images appearing on the white-on-white wall like magic.

Henricksen shrugged his shoulders. "It's legit, if that's what you're asking."

Kinsey squinted, giving him a close look. "How do I know? How can I be sure it wasn't tampered with?"

"It's legit. You have my word. I wouldn't *be* here if I thought any of this had been contaminated or otherwise adjusted."

Kinsey considered him a moment, thoughts swirling in his eyes. Turned his gaze back to the video feed's images and watched in silence for a while. "Where?" he pressed. "Who? I want a name."

Henricksen shrugged again, leaning back in his chair.

White chair, like everything else in the room. Overstuffed leather that wrapped around his lean body, trying to eat him alive.

"Taggert," Kinsey guessed.

Third shrug. Shrugs were easy. Didn't cost him a cent.

Kinsey glared, thoroughly annoyed. Froze the video feed, capturing the moment RV-N-183 died, and just sat there, staring. Face unreadable. Backed the images up and let them run through again, looking grim as death.

"Ten minutes", he'd told Henricksen, but nearly twenty had passed. Twenty minutes of reviewing the sim and live test feeds, poring over the data from both.

Couldn't explain it all as eloquently as Shaw and Taggert. Piece it all together as confidently as Ogawa. But a little prompting and Kinsey saw it—recognized the pattern in the data right away.

Smart bastard, Kinsey. Bastard still, but smart. Henricksen had to give him that.

"You said Shaw came up with this, not Karansky?" Kinsey turned his head, looking a question at Henricksen sitting across from him, low-slung, glass and chrome table sitting between them, acres of pure white carpet stretching in every direction.

"Shaw, with Ogawa's help. And Taggert's," Henricksen admitted, ignoring Kinsey's smug, knowing look. "Two-Six—"

"Two-Six." Kinsey frowned darkly, leaning back in his chair. "So you bypassed my chief engineer and dragged one of the AI into this?"

Henricksen shrugged, entirely unapologetic. "AI brain's more powerful than Karansky's. Shaw knew she had something but she wasn't sure what." A nod to the frozen video feed, the data windows layered beside it. "Two-Six did all the number crunching. Layered all the data together to find that correlation between the engines and the shielding."

Kinsey looked at him, and at the images projected on the white-on-white. "This is good work." A nod to Henricksen, fingers flicking at the wall. He turned his wrist over, checking the time, pushed to his feet, adjusting the drape of his trousers over that artificial leg. "I'll get Karansky's crew on it in the morning. The Brass will be very happy about this. A few adjustments and the project should be—"

"Why?" Henricksen asked quietly, bringing Kinsey up short. "Why did you rush the RV-N chassis into live tests?"

Kinsey swiped at his pants leg, scowling in disapproval. "I didn't *rush* anything, Captain. Shaw said the chassis was ready—"

"No. She didn't." Henricksen stared across the table at Kinsey, matching him glare for glare. "Shaw wanted to run analytics, but *you* pushed the RV-N into live tests. Why?" he repeated, stabbing a finger at the images on the wall. "What's so goddamn important about this project that you were willing to risk that ship and its crew?"

Kinsey's scowl deepened, lips pressing together into a thin, hard line. He balked at first, refusing to answer, and then sighed and flipped a hand, stance relaxing, his entire demeanor changing in an instant. "I suppose it's time we got down to that."

Henricksen blinked, frowning in confusion as Kinsey turned away, walking across the room to a bar on the far side—a glass and chrome construction as cold and modern as the rest of the furnishings in that whitely antiseptic space.

Mirrored shelves behind it filled with bottles of pale liquor, racks of cut glass drinking vessels.

Kinsey slipped behind it, artificial leg hitching awkwardly as he twisted and reached up, snagging two square-sided tumblers from a shelf. Shuffled around and pulled a bottle from beneath the bar top, considering the contents and Henricksen sitting across the room with a look on his face like he wasn't quite sure he wanted to crack it open and share.

Started to put it back and then grunted and sliced the wax around the mouth with a fingernail. Pulled the top off and poured a dollop of red-brown liquor into each glass.

Snagged one and emptied it, drinking the contents down. Filled the glass back up from the bottle, studying Henricksen from behind the bar all the while. "We've got a leak," Kinsey said, setting the bottle back down. "We've had one for a while."

Henricksen twitched his shoulders, feeling cold of a sudden. Numb all over. "That's why you left Kepler."

"And moved the project here to Dragoon." Kinsey scooped the two glasses from the bar, carrying them across the room.

Handed one to Henricksen, keeping the other for himself. Stood there, swirling the contents, staring into the bottom while Henricksen lifted his, sniffing at the liquor inside.

"Brandy?"

"Cognac." Kinsey raised his glass in salute, balancing on his good leg as he sank down into a chair. "I was saving this. Meant to share it with the staff once the RV-N passed qualification testing."

"Champagne."

"Hmm?" Kinsey glanced up, brow wrinkled in confusion.

"Champagne's for celebrations. Scotch, whiskey, cognac." Henricksen held up his glass. "Hard stuff's for when the shit hits the fan." He smiled crookedly as Kinsey barked a bitter laugh.

"I suppose you're right," Kinsey murmured, staring at the images on the wall. He raised his glass and then lowered it, leaned forward and clinked it against Henricksen's before sitting back and taking a pull.

"Kepler?" Henricksen prompted, wriggling forward, resting his elbows on his thighs. "What happened?"

"Leak," Kinsey shrugged. "Like I told you. DSR..." He sighed again, shaking his head. "The DSR managed to plant someone on the inside. Not sure how, not even sure when, but station security picked up some access violations— unauthorized data transfers, that kind of thing. Nothing serious at first, you understand. Spook snoops told us to play it cool. Let them conduct their forensics, see if they could find the mole. And then..." Kinsey grimaced and turned his head, staring across the room.

"What?" Henricksen leaned forward, staring at Kinsey's face, untouched drink clasped between his hands.

"Things started disappearing." Kinsey lifted his glass, gulping at the contents. "Prototypes, design specs—hard and soft assets from a dozen Black Ops projects wiped from the database. Stolen from secure storage."

"Stolen," Henricksen repeated, blinking in disbelief. "As in…"

"Unrecoverable." Kinsey bowed his head, swirling his drink. "No backups left behind. No trace they ever existed. Years of research, trillions in funding gone—just like that." He snapped his fingers—brittle sound, impossibly loud in that whitely carpeted space.

"Holy shit," Henricksen breathed.

"Indeed." Kinsey raised his glass in salute, took another sip. "Never did find out who did it. Brought in a whole ream of analysts to work on it, but…" He trailed off, grunted and shook his head. "They're still working on it as far as I know. Major infiltration," he confided. "Tons of data to pick through. As for me," he leaned back, legs folded, glass resting on his knee, "I decided I couldn't wait on them any longer. Couldn't risk someone stealing data on the RV-N project."

"So you packed it up and left."

Kinsey nodded slowly. "Dismissed all the personnel, packed up the ships, the servers, moved everything here." He waved at the room around him, lifted his glass to his lips and lowered it again without drinking. Just sat there, staring at it, hands clasped loosely around the glass.

"Not all of them," Henricksen said quietly.

Kinsey's head lifted, brow wrinkling in confusion.

"Karansky."

"No," he said. Immediate response, without the slightest hesitation.

"He's the only one you kept," Henricksen argued. "The only one who's—"

"No. Not him." Kinsey shook his head hard, having none of it. "Karansky designed the RV-N chassis. He's been with the project since the beginning."

"And you didn't find it strange that he completely missed such a major design flaw?" Henricksen stared at Kinsey, waiting for an answer. Pulled the reader to him when Kinsey just sat there and toggled the display, queuing up another video. "Maybe this will convince you." He fed the video into the projection system built into the coffee table, letting it replace the RV-N's run.

"What is this?" Kinsey asked, frowning. "The hangar bay?"

Henricksen nodded slowly, gestured at the images on the wall. "Shaw caught him down there a couple of nights ago."

"So?"

"He was messing with one of the RV-Ns. Making changes you never approved." Henricksen ran the video forward, let it play through to where Shaw kicked Karansky out.

"This doesn't prove anything." Kinsey waved his glass at the video as Karansky beat a hasty retreat.

"No. It doesn't," Henricksen admitted. "But it sure doesn't look good."

Kinsey chewed on that a while, looking pissed off as all get-out. Lurched to his feet and walked into a side room—office from the look of it, based on the brief glimpse Henricksen got before Kinsey mostly closed the door—and spoke with someone via the station's internal comms.

Security, he assumed, from the snatches of conversation that drifted to Henricksen's ears.

A last few words and the office door opened. Henricksen snatched up the reader and sat back with it, pretending to be engrossed in its contents, not eavesdropping on his host in the other room.

Kinsey didn't buy it. "How much did you hear?" he asked, walking across the room, that distinctive, hitching, rolling gate reminding Henricksen of an old time sailor.

"Not much," he shrugged, setting the reader aside. "Station security?" He quirked an eyebrow, waving at the office, the now-closed door.

Kinsey nodded tightly, bending at the knees as he lowered his butt, perching on the front of his chair. "Karansky won't be coming back to the project. Precautionary measure," he explained at Henricksen's look of surprise. "Not saying you're right, but..." He grimaced and scooped up his glass, draining the last of the cognac inside.

Henricksen watched him a moment, his own drink still untouched. Hadn't expected Kinsey to move on Karansky so quickly and with so little information. Made him wonder about other things. Like what had been stolen from Kepler...

He set his glass down on the table, leaned forward—elbows braced against his thighs, hands folded in front of him. "You know, you never explained why you rushed the RV-N into live tests."

"We had a leak—"

"Uh-huh. And that's part of it." Henricksen tilted his head, thinking hard. "What did they take?"

Kinsey's eyebrows lifted. "They? What makes you think there was more than one person involved?"

"Had to be. No way a single person could steal locked down, super-secret information from a Black Ops facility."

Kinsey grunted noncommittally, reaching for his glass. Brushed it with his fingers and grunted again, leaving it on the table when he realized it was empty.

"So what exactly did Karansky and his accomplices steal from Kepler?"

Kinsey blanked on him, growing cold and distant again. "That's classified."

Standard response. A polite way of telling Henricksen to mind his own business.

Something terrible, then. Or else...

"You don't know, do you?" Henricksen asked. And, on a hunch, "Does the *government* even know?"

Kinsey didn't say anything. Didn't *have* to say anything. His face told it all.

"Son of a bitch." Henricksen stared across the low-slung table, shaking his head in disbelief. "Some DSR snoop hacks into the supposedly ultra-secure systems on a secret squirrel base and you don't even know what they *took*?"

Kinsey flicked at his cuffs, picked at a piece of lint. "Some of it. A few things."

"How is that even *possible*?"

"Black Ops has thousands of mothballed projects, Captain. Most of them never make it out of prototyping."

"You're telling me you don't keep records? You have no way of doing an inventory or something?"

Kinsey grimaced, folded his hands and dropped his eyes.

"Oh God. The backups. They took the backups, too? The hard assets *and* the design specs?"

Kinsey shrugged—stiff, angry movement. Everything about him stiff and angry now. "We're hoping to get it all back." His eyes lifted, head following suit. "That's what the RV-N project's about."

Henricksen straightened, hands resting on his knees, remembering his last conversation with Kinsey in these quarters. Thinking of the sim asteroid field scenario that kept repeating. That massive, unknown something lurking at its center. "That's it," he breathed, eyes widening. "The asteroid field. That's what's in there. Whatever they stole, the DSR are hiding it somewhere in that minefield of oversized rocks."

"That's the theory." Kinsey nodded. "Unfortunately, we haven't been able to get close enough to confirm it. Lot of activity in there over the last few months, though. A lot *more* since we relocated from Kepler."

Henricksen was quiet a moment, watching him, trying to read Kinsey's face. "What they took. Is it that bad?"

Kinsey tilted his head, looking simultaneously angry and amused. "Bad," he grunted. "That's what you assume."

"Black Ops." Henricksen shrugged. "What else am I supposed to believe?"

"I'm insulted, Captain. On behalf the RV-Ns." Kinsey stared at him, dark eyes glittering, face a mask of stone. "Believe it or not, Black Ops isn't all about destruction."

"Meaning?"

Kinsey twitched his shoulders, adjusting the drape of his expensive pants. "Some of the things they took have medical applications. Advanced cybernetics. Cutting edge tissue regeneration research."

"Tissue…" Henricksen frowned, shaking his head.

"Organ regeneration. Regrown limbs." Kinsey touched at his arm—the false one, hidden beneath his pinstriped jacket.

"Soldier repair." Henricksen's lip lifted in a sneer. "Fix 'em up, replace the missing parts, send 'em back out on the battlefield. That the idea?"

"Combat often spurs advances in medical treatment."

Henricksen stared at him, overwhelmed with disgust. "And the rest of it? What else did they get?"

"I told you, I don't—"

"You told me they stole medical research, but that's not all the DSR took was it?" Henricksen leaned forward, eyes locked onto Kinsey's face. "You might not have a full accounting of what's missing—I actually believe that part—but you know something. What is it?"

Kinsey stared silently back, lips pressed in a hard line.

"So it *is* that bad," Henricksen said as the silence stretched out.

A slight pause, mouth opening and closing. "Yes," Kinsey admitted in a soft, dangerous voice. "What the DSR took is very, very bad, Captain."

"How bad?" Henricksen asked just as softly.

Kinsey considered a moment, eyes sparkling with secrets, brow wrinkled in thought. "I'll show you." A nod to Henricksen and he pushed to his feet, retracing his steps to the office. Disappeared inside and returned with a reader—a twin to the one Henricksen brought with him—plugged it into the room's audio-visual system and sat down in his chair.

Crossed his legs, adjusting the drape of his very expensive trousers as the first images appeared: a ship in space, several of them, actually, clustered together in a tight knot.

Colony ships, from the look of them. And at their center, a very large, very familiar-looking silver sphere.

"The Cepheid." Henricksen blinked in surprise. "This video. Where did it come from?"

He knew the answer already. Saw it in the way Kinsey tilted his head, eyebrow lifting. Recognized the perspective, the angle from which the video was shot. But he wanted to hear it. Needed Kinsey to tell him himself.

"*Hecate*," he said quietly, voice a hushed whisper.

"Hell." Henricksen sank down into his chair, reaching for the glass of cognac he'd abandoned. Scooped it from the table and drained it as the video came to life, recorded images playing out the last few moments of *Hecate*'s life.

TWENTY

"Why?" Henricksen rasped, as the first of the flickering images appeared.

Didn't want to see this—he'd watched *Hecate* die once, still carried all that raw pain and seething anger inside him—but he couldn't quite make himself look away.

"Why are you showing me this?"

Instead of answering, Kinsey nodded to the video projecting on the wall, freezing the feed—mercifully—right before *Hecate* received that crippling blow. "That," he said simply, pointing to a silver cloud of stardust spilling from the Cepheid's middle.

Henricksen leaned forward, squinting at the image, but he came no closer to understanding what he was seeing this time than when that cloud was right in front of him, all those weeks ago. "And what, exactly, *is* that?"

Kinsey pursed his lips, running the feed forward, skipping past the collision between *Hecate* and that droned ship, running it right up to the moment that *Gogmagog* entered the combat space before freezing it again. Toggled it to zoom in on one particular section of the video, getting as tight in as the system would allow.

Still not all that much to see, truthfully, but under magnification, tiny objects appeared. Metal, or so it seemed, just as Henricksen initially thought. Beautiful, really.

Like starlight, Henricksen thought. *Starlight and diamond dust. Something twinkling and reflective.*

Something, but still nameless. Shapeless. Impossible to pinpoint with any accuracy because the feed lacked details. Made it impossible for him to tell what he was truly looking at.

"Still don't see it." He sat back—angry now, tired of guessing at secrets.

Kinsey looked at him, and at that frozen image projected on the wall. "No," he murmured. "I suppose you wouldn't. Not unless you knew what you were looking *for.*"

Henricksen glowered at Kinsey across the table. "What the hell is that supposed to mean?"

"Patience, Captain." Kinsey leaned forward, reaching for the reader, digging through folders in search of yet another image file he threw up onto the wall.

Robot this time. Insect-shaped, like all the robots the Meridian Alliance employed. Multi-legged form resembling that of a spider, but flatter, wider, closer to a tick.

"This," he said, pointing at the image, "was collected from that site." A tap at the reader swapped the robotic tick for the ring of silver diamond dust, looping length dividing as *Gogmagog* approached. Second tap and the image changed, zooming out to show the robot in context—a tiny, multi-legged figure barely the size of a ladybug, squatting in the center of a Petri dish.

Henricksen stared, honestly puzzled. "What—?"

"Nannite." Kinsey folded his hands, sitting back in his chair.

"Nannite? Those itsy-bitsy fixer bots?"

"One and the same."

"Thought the Fleet abandoned those years ago."

"Not just abandoned." Kinsey toggled the reader back to the image of *Hecate*'s last battle. "Mothballed," he said, pointing to the shimmering ring of silver surrounding the Cepheid. "Installed them on a few Auroras a decade or so back—supposed to speed up repairs, perform in-combat maintenance to minimize time in the shipyards." A flick of his fingers at the images on the wall. "All very cutting edge and high-tech. Sounded great to the Brass, but they never did quite get them to work. Not the way they were supposed to, anyway. Retired them after a few trials and went back to the TIGs and TSDs. Kept the designs, though. Placed a few production samples in storage on Kepler."

"Retired." Henricksen leaned forward, bracing his elbows against his thighs, rubbing wearily at his face. "That's what they took. Forget all that crap about medical research—"

"It's not crap, Captain." Kinsey touched at his false arm again. "Believe me, it's not. As for the rest of it," a nod to the images from *Hecate* showing that ring of approaching nannites, "this isn't our first run-in with those things."

"So?" Henricksen frowned, puzzled. Sensing a weight of hidden meaning in Kinsey's words. "I don't get it," he said, shaking his head. "What's so terrible about a bunch of nannites? Thought they were built to *fix* things."

"They were," Kinsey said quietly.

Just that, and another of those meaningful looks.

Henricksen sat back, scowling, eyes flicking from Kinsey to the images from *Hecate* projected on the wall. Something clicked then—several moments later, after nearly a minute of silence between them—and Henricksen's scowl faded, replaced by a thoughtful look. "They changed them, didn't they?"

"Weaponized them." Kinsey folded his hands, blinking slowly. "Altered their programming. Modified the design specs to destroy ships, not repair them." He caught Henricksen's gaze and held it. "I've seen it, Captain. I've seen these things strip a starship down to its girders in a matter of *minutes*. Had to destroy the ship entirely to get rid of them. And even then..." Kinsey trailed off, grimacing.

"What?" Henricksen asked, voice hushed.

"They self-replicate." A nod to the single nannite squatting in its Petri dish prison. "Our design, not theirs. Hyper-functional, capable of self-replication, with a direct correlation to an AI bond."

"AI?" Henricksen frowned in confusion. "Thought nannites were *pre*-AI."

Kinsey pursed his lips, considering the question. "More like...quasi-AI," he corrected. "Intelligent machines, but with limited independence. And unlike your *Hecate,* no sense of self-awareness."

"But they breed."

"Replicate, yes. Using whatever scrap parts they can find."

"And the AI bonding?"

"That," Kinsey sighed, lips twisting. "That's the part we couldn't figure out. Our nannites—the ones the Fleet created—would do exactly what you *told* them to do, but they couldn't really think outside the box."

"Which doesn't really help when the shit hits the fan and an AI needs them to fix things on the fly."

"No. It doesn't. That's why they failed field trials. Ended up mothballing the entire project, shoving everything into storage on Kepler." Kinsey was quiet a moment, thinking. "Impressive, really. Never imagined the DSR would crack that AI linkage problem."

"So, what? The DSR's engineers are better than ours?"

Kinsey gave him a flat-eyed look. "I wouldn't go *that* far."

"But they did solve your problem for you," Henricksen pressed. "And since you've got a sample, can't you—"

"Had," Kinsey interrupted. "We *had* a sample."

"Meaning?"

"We don't anymore."Kinsey blinked slowly, face an unreadable mask. "Like I said, we've seen these nannites before. Collected samples thinking to reverse engineer the technology to figure out how to make the AI link work."

"Build your *own* weaponized nannites." Henricksen matched his blank-faced stare.

"But the samples we collected kept self-destructing," Kinsey continued, ignoring the accusation.

"Suicide?" Henricksen barked a disbelieving laugh.

"Maybe." Kinsey climbed to his feet, retrieving the bottle of cognac from the bar. Refilled his glass, did the same for Henricksen's after the slightest of hesitations. "Or a failsafe. Built-in kill switch, something like that. Tied to the AI bond somehow—that much we figured out."

"Do tell." Henricksen sat back, glass in hand, eyebrows lifting in interest.

"That ship I mentioned earlier? The one the nannites stripped to its bones? We nuked the AI they were linked to and the nannites just imploded. Caught a few *without* killing the AI and the same thing happened. Just—*poof!* And they're gone."

Henricksen turned his head, staring at the images on the wall. "Do you think she knew?" he asked quietly.

Kinsey shrugged again. "Maybe. Probably. The nannite project was classified, but the idea's been around for decades." He studied Henricksen from the opposite side of the table, hands clasped loosely around the glass resting in his lap. "*Hecate* knew that ring of objects was a threat. Or at least suspected it."

Henricksen looked at him.

"That's why she ejected her bridge pod." Kinsey gestured with his glass at a diminutive silver shape retreating into the distance. "Moved you and the rest of the crew as far away from danger as possible."

That was *Hecate*, always thinking of the crew. Often even before herself.

Henricksen bowed his head, missing her all the more keenly. Mind drifting for a while before returning to *Hecate* and those nannites. Realized as he stared at her, and them, that a couple of things didn't quite add up. "So, these nannites," he said sometime later. "What do they have to do with that asteroid field and the RV-Ns?"

Kinsey grunted, lifting his drink to his lips. "Surprised you haven't figured it out already." Henricksen sat up straight, face flushing, but Kinsey just raised a hand, holding it palm out in a gesture of peace. "I meant no offense, Captain." A sip of his drink and he set it down. Moved forward, perching on the edge of his chair again, as he bowed his head and spread his feet wide, resting his elbows on his thighs. "In the sims, did you…notice anything near the center of that asteroid field?"

"Yeah," Henricksen said slowly. "Something." He shrugged his shoulders. "Not quite sure what. Sim scenario always dumps out before we can get a good look at it."

Kinsey's head lifted. "Never did get a clean image of it, but from the intelligence we've gathered, it appears to be some kind of…science station. Research unit, something like that."

"Research," Henricksen repeated, frowning. "What *kind* of research?"

Kinsey pointed at the image of the nannite. The ring of them in front of *Hecate*.

"Shit," Henricksen breathed. "Oh shit." He sat back, staring at that image for a while. "Why not just nuke it? Why all this cloak and dagger crap?"

"Nuking the site would destroy everything," Kinsey told him, voice carefully modulated, face purposefully blank. "*Everything,* you understand?"

"And that's a *bad* thing? From what you told me, these nannites are pretty damn brutal. Why would—" He broke off, realizing he was an idiot. That he'd missed the whole point. "You son of a bitch. You lost the tech and now you want it *back*?"

"Not me, Captain." Kinsey shook his head slowly, eyes locked onto Henricksen sitting across from him. "Brass call the shots on this one."

Of course they did. Something like this…Kinsey was high up, but the loss of carefully guarded secrets would go much higher. Several layers over his head.

"The government spent trillions, *tens* of trillions on the projects the DSR stole. They're not particularly interested in investing trillions more. Not when there's an alternative available." Kinsey was quiet a moment, blinking slowly. "We can't risk losing this, Captain. Not again."

"Lose? What do you mean 'lose'? Lose what?" Henricksen demanded.

"The station." Kinsey pointed to the image of the asteroid field. "We found it once before. By accident, actually," he admitted with a rueful shake of his head.

"The station? You *lost* a station. How the hell does *that* happen?"

"DSR jumped it, just as our ships closed in."

"Jumped it," Henricksen repeated. "And just what kind of station is capable of hyperspace travel?"

Mass should make it impossible. Couldn't imagine the size of the engine system needed to move something as big as Dragoon.

Kinsey frowned, waving the question away. "They moved it, Captain. That's all that matters. That's all you need to know."

Henricksen opened his mouth to object and then closed it again, letting it go. "And this science station. It's in that asteroid field? You're *sure* of it?"

Kinsey dipped his head, nodding slowly. "Took us months to track it down."

"But you decided not to tell anyone." Henricksen grunted, lips twisting bitterly. "Kept its location hush-hush this time."

"We had a leak once before. Couldn't take that chance again."

"And the Ravens?" Henricksen asked him. "What's our part in all this?"

"Black Ops is about intelligence, Captain." Kinsey stared across the table, dark eyes hooded, face an icy cold mask. "The RV-N project was on the cusp of being canceled before this debacle came along. The government wants their secrets back and I intend to give them to them. That's what *I* care about. This project—"

"The ships, you mean, not the project. Not the people—that's for damn sure." He stared murder across the table, hating Kinsey all over again. "No wonder you rushed the trials. After all, what's a ship and a few lives worth, am I right? Impressing the Brass—that's what matters. Keeping the project on track—"

"It's *my* project," Kinsey thundered. "And I won't see it fail." He sat there glaring at Henricksen, hands curled white-knuckled around the arms of his chair. Peeled them loose with an effort and shrugged his shoulders, adjusted his cuffs while he calmed himself down. "The loss of crew is unfortunate, Captain. The loss of those *secrets* is unfortunate, but the Ravens..." He turned his head, considering the image on the wall. "Counter-intelligence, *true* counterintelligence...it could end this, Captain. Bring the DSR to its knees. The nannites—"

"They're *already* on their knees, Kinsey. They've *been* on their knees for years now and they just keep right on fighting."

"Guerilla warfare." Kinsey flicked his fingers, voice filled with disdain. "Sabotage. Terrorism. Nothing approaching *real* combat." He touched his arm, flexed his artificial fingers. "Those days are gone, Captain. Dead and buried with the DSR army the day it made its last stand."

"Maybe." Henricksen leveled a flat-eyed stare across the table. "Or maybe they're just playing 'possum. Maybe the DSR's been holding back all this time. Waiting for just the right time to unleash those nasty little critters they stole from Kepler."

Kinsey cocked his head, lips twisting in a smug, self-satisfied smile. "All the more reason to get those Ravens flying, don't you think?"

Henricksen opened his mouth and closed it—angry, embarrassed, realizing he'd been manipulated. Worse still, he hadn't even seen it coming. He leaned back, laughing bitterly, shaking his head. "Walked right into that one, didn't I?"

Kinsey smiled, shrugging. "I had a feeling you'd see things my way. Eventually," he added with a nod. The smile slipped, Kinsey's face turning serious—not cold now, not closed up and vacant, just...serious. Sharp and business-like. A touch concerned. "We need those Ravens flying, Captain. We need to get in that asteroid field and take the Meridian Alliance's secrets back."

"That easy, eh?"

"Nothing's that easy," Kinsey admitted. "But a stealth ship with an advanced recon package...You get those ships in there, Captain." He leaned forward, face intent. "Get us a good set of images, some scans of that station so we know what we're dealing with. Locate the payload—"

"Payload?" Henricksen raised a hand, cutting Kinsey off. "What payload? No one mentioned anything about a payload."

Kinsey blanked again, eyes swirling with secrets. "Container."

"A container of what?"

Kinsey stared silently, giving nothing away.

"Look," Henricksen said, sighing in frustration. "You're gonna have to—"

"No. I don't," he said coldly. "Stealth is your job, Captain. I read you into this, *showed* you how serious this is and now I need you to do your job. Unless you want more ships to go the way of *Hecate*." He pointed at the wall without looking, staring hard at Henricksen's face.

"Why?" Henricksen asked, earning himself an irritated look. "Why not just do what they did? Plant a spook inside the DSR and see if they can work their way into whatever super-secret project they have going."

Kinsey pursed his lips, eyebrows lifting.

"You already did. Figures," Henricksen grunted. "How deep?"

"Deep," Kinsey told him. "Access to the central systems."

"Great! Then have him copy that shit and ship it over!"

"She," Kinsey corrected, dark eyes blinking slowly. "And like I said, nothing's ever that easy." He leaned back, crossing his legs, staring at Henricksen's face. "Took us months to get a contact in there. Most of our agents..." Kinsey bowed his head, flicking at a fluff on his trousers. "Let's just say the DSR's good at sussing them out." His eyes lifted, head tilting as he considered Henricksen across the table. "We can't risk losing her. Can't afford to take her out either. Not when so many others have failed."

"What are you saying?" Henricksen frowned. "You want *us* to get on that station and somehow meet up with her?"

Kinsey smiled crookedly. "No, Captain. I'm just asking you to retrieve something when the time is right."

"This payload of yours. A box full of secrets from your spook."

"Just so," Kinsey nodded.

"And what makes you think it'll be there?"

"Trust me. It will be," Kinsey said coolly. "I have complete faith in our agent. We're just waiting on a communication—"

"From your contact inside."

Kinsey frowned, annoyed at the interruption. Touched at his collar, checking the creases of his stiffly pressed shirt. "She'll send us coordinates for the pickup once the information is packaged and ready."

"Coordinates? *Inside* the asteroid field?"

Kinsey nodded again, eyes never leaving Henricksen's face.

"How the hell are we supposed to—"

"Patience, Captain." Kinsey raised a hand, cutting him off. "One thing at a time. You get those birds flying. Figure out how to get into the asteroid field without the DSR noticing. We'll work on the rest after that."

Not the way he liked to run things. Not even close. Henricksen bowed his head, thinking a moment. "Shaw says she can stabilize the engine and cloaking system interactions, get those birds cleared for operations, but it could take a while."

"How long?"

"Days, weeks." Henricksen shrugged his shoulders. "Hell, I don't know. I'm a pilot, not an engineer."

"We can't wait weeks, Captain. We've already waited too long as it is."

Henricksen barked a bitter laugh. "Well, you're shit out of luck, buddy, because those birds ain't flyin'."

"One-Eight-Three flew. Flew just fine until Fisker fired up the cloaking system in hyperspace."

Henricksen lurched to his feet, stabbing a finger at Kinsey's face. "*Fisker* didn't cause that accident. I showed you the data." He waved at the reader on the table. "You saw what happened. You can't ask me—"

"I can and I am," Kinsey said crisply, face an emotionless mask. "I'm not saying I like it—"

"The ship is *unstable!*" Henricksen shouted. "You fire up that stealth system in hyperspace and it turns into a fucking *bomb*."

"Then don't," Kinsey said quietly. "You said it yourself: there's no good reason to be cloaked in hyperspace. Not with that energy signature to announce your arrival." He leaned forward, staring intently at Henricksen. "Cloak's for sneaking, Captain. Nothing at all sneaky about a hyperspace jump."

"So don't use it. That what you're saying? Just stay off the cloak in hyperspace and everything'll be fine?"

"I'm saying there's a simple enough workaround until Shaw and Karansky's engineer's work out the engine and cloaking system incompatibility. And I'm saying we are *severely* out of time, Captain."

Henricksen chewed on that, thinking of the failsafe Shaw mentioned. How she could configure the AIs themselves to keep the crew from doing something stupid. "How long?" he asked, reluctantly relenting. "How long since that communication from your spook?"

"Two weeks." Soft voice from Kinsey, utterly devoid of any emotion. "Two weeks, and not a word since."

"Long time. You think they're on to her?"

"No," Kinsey said, without hesitation. "I think she's being smart. And careful. She'll come through with those coordinates, Captain. And when she does, you need to be ready to launch. Immediately, you understand me?"

Because objects in space drifted. And if they waited too long, those coordinates wouldn't mean spit.

Henricksen closed his eyes, rubbing at his face. "Yeah. Yeah, I get you." But God, he didn't want to do this...

"Good. Now I need crew in those ships." Kinsey scooped up his glass, spun it between his palms. "I need those Ravens flying, Captain, so they're ready when—"

"Yeah. Yeah. I get it," Henricksen sighed, waving a hand. "Months of waiting and now everything's a big fucking hurry."

Kinsey laughed—actually laughed!—surprising the hell out of Henricksen. "Isn't that always the way?" he said, lips curving in their first real smile.

"Didn't use to be," Henricksen muttered. "There was a time..." He trailed off, thinking of those early days with *Hecate*. His first command on *Harbinger* and how different that was. "Hell," he said, flopping down in his chair. Leaned forward, elbows braced against his knees, head cradled in his hands. Stayed there for a long time, thinking things over, considering the options laid out before him, finding every last one of them sucked. "Fuck," he breathed. "Fuck me."

"Captain?"

A deep breath and Henricksen straightened, staring bleakly across the table. "You'll have crew assignments in the morning, Kinsey."

"Thank you, Captain."

Surprised him, those softly spoken words. Hadn't expected gratitude. Not from Kinsey, who was short on compliments and kind words.

Henricksen stared at him a moment, caught completely off guard. Pushed to his feet and stood there, looking down on Kinsey's seated form. "You can thank me if we actually get those birds flying without blowing up."

"Fair enough." Kinsey dipped his head in acknowledgment, flicked his fingers, dismissing Henricksen from his quarters. "Good night, Captain."

"Night." Henricksen turned to leave, moved a few steps away and stopped again, looking back over his shoulder. "Do you think you could—"

"Hollings should already be waiting," Kinsey told him, lips curling in an amused smile.

"Thanks," Henricksen muttered, blushing. Turned away and hurried across the room, yanked the door open and stepped into the hall.

TWENTY-ONE

Late by the time Henricksen returned to his quarters. Late beyond late, and well past curfew. No crew moving about at this hour, no voices drifting from the locked rooms on either side of the branching hallways, no one in the mess hall when he poked his head in to take a look.

Wasn't always that way. Crew kept the curfew, for the most part, but curfew didn't extend to Shaw's gang or the civ engineers. Most nights there was *someone* hanging around after hours—watching vids, playing pool in the rec room, that kind of thing. Not tonight, though. Not since the accident. Something changed after the RV-N disaster. Four crew died, leaving the rest in mourning. Leaving *everyone* in mourning. Stealing the life from the RV-N project.

Henricksen backed out of the mess hall, letting the double doors swing closed. Retraced his steps to his quarters, swapping Taggert's reader for his own, checking to make sure all the personnel files were loaded before stepping across the hall and banging on Sikuuku's door.

"Go 'way," the gunner called, voice muffled by the heavy metal portal.

"Open up, Akiwane." Henricksen pounded on the door again—harder, louder this time. "We need to talk."

Grumbling from inside, followed by the sound of heavy footsteps slogging across the floor. Sikuuku opened the door—mostly naked, completely disheveled, entirely pissed off. "What's so goddamn important that it can't wait until morning?"

Henricksen almost smiled. No 'sirs' from Sikuuku, not when it was just the two of them. Known each other too long for that. "Crew assignments," he said, holding the reader up.

"What? *Now?*" Sikuuku blinked blearily, rubbing at his eyes. "What time is it?"

"Late. Close to midnight, if I had to guess."

"You've been dodging crew assignments for weeks now." Sikuuku leaned against the doorframe, giving him a look. "What's the rush?"

"No time like the present," Henricksen said, flashing a crooked smile.

"Seriously?" Sikuuku sighed heavily, scrubbing at his face. "Can't it wait? You woke me from a dream about Tahitian beauties."

"I doubt they're going anywhere." Henricksen pushed past him, forcing his way into Sikuuku's quarters. Rousted a desk from the corner because there was no other table available and dragged it to the center of the room.

Sikuuku turned around, watching him, arms folded tight to his chest. Naked except for his underwear, ass end facing the wide open door. "What about Kinsey?"

"Yeah. About that." Henricksen dropped the reader on the desktop, bowed his head and rubbed wearily at his eyes. "We're gonna need something to drink."

"Against regs having liquor in quarters, Captain." Sikuuku reached behind him, discretely shutting the door. "Offended you'd even *think* I'd do such a thing."

"Cut the crap, Akiwane. I know you better than that." Henricksen hooked a chair with his toe and pulled it over to the desk. Snagged another just like it from the corner and set it on the opposite side of the makeshift table. "Bet you've got half a dozen bottles squirreled away in here."

"Don't know what you're talking about," Sikuuku insisted, playing the innocent still.

"Oh, for the luvva—I'll replace it, alright?"

Sikuuku folded his arms, chin lifting. "You said that last time."

"And?"

"And I'm short a bottle of tequila."

Henricksen rolled his eyes in exasperation. "That wasn't good tequila. It didn't even have a real worm!"

"Still short," the gunner told him, shrugging his burly shoulders.

"Fine," Henricksen growled, quickly losing patience. "I'll replace the tequila *and* whatever you've got lying around."

"With interest," Sikuuku told him. "Compounded." He considered a moment, lips moving as he did arithmetic in his head. "Case of whiskey should do it."

"A *case?* That's highway robbery!"

Another shrug, Sikuuku's lips parting in a toothy grin. "Teach you to steal from my stash and not replace it."

"Fine," Henricksen sighed, flopping down in a chair. "No idea where I'm gonna find an entire case of whiskey on this station, but I'll pay your ransom, you thief."

Sikuuku's smile widened. "Might be I know someone."

Of course he did. Sikuuku always knew someone.

"Just grab a bottle, Akiwane, and let's get down to business."

"Aye-aye, sir, your majesty, sir." Sikuuku snapped off a saucy salute and stepped through an open doorway, started rooting around in a wardrobe inside his closet-sized bedroom. Returned with a bottle and a couple of mismatched drinking glasses, a pair of uniform pants thrown over one shoulder, depositing the breakables on the desk before tugging on his trousers. "So. Kinsey." He cracked the seal on the bottle and spun off the cap, pouring them each a dram. "Spill it," he said, settling into the chair across from Henricksen. "Tell me everything."

#

"That," Sikuuku said, "is a hell of a story." He grabbed up the bottle and refilled his glass, tipped it over Henricksen's and topped his drink off as well.

Amber liquid, this time, not red-brown like Kinsey's cognac. A sniff of the glass's contents revealed hints of citrus esters. Something that reminded Henricksen of woodlands. Old Earth cedar or pine.

Scotch, and not a bad vintage from the smell of it, the taste of it as it slipped across Henricksen's tongue. Damnably expensive tipple, especially out here. Especially for the good stuff.

"Do I want to know where this came from?"

Sikuuku shrugged his burly shoulders. "Probably not. Oh, and just so we're clear, if I get busted for having it, I'm gonna claim you gave it to me."

"Of course," Henricksen snorted. "I'd expect nothing less." He picked up his glass and held it out, smiling crookedly as Sikuuku *clacked* his own drink against it.

"So." Sikuuku sat back, slouching in his chair, glass of Scotch resting on his stomach. "We really doing this?" His eyes flicked to the reader sitting on the desk between them, returned to Henricksen's face. "Did you really agree to take a handful of glitch-ass stealth ships into an asteroid field stuffed full of DSR ships and god only knows what other nastiness?"

"Sounds crazy when you put it that way." Henricksen set his glass down, finger resting lightly on the rim. "But I had my reasons."

"Oh yeah?" Sikuuku tilted his head, eyebrows lifting. "Gonna share?"

"Back's against the wall, Akiwane," Henricksen said quietly. He raised a hand, pinching the bridge of his nose, bowed his head and stared into the depths of his drink for a long, long time. "Karansky, whoever he was working with, they stole some bad shit from Kepler."

"What kind of shit?"

"The kind that killed *Hecate*." Henricksen raised his head, catching Sikuuku's eyes. "Nannites, Akiwane. *Weaponized* nannites. The kind that eat ships."

"Shit. Holy shit," Sikuuku breathed, tattooed face turning pale.

"Brass wants its secrets back. Nominated us to go get them." Henricksen reached for his glass, hesitated and snatched up the reader instead, sliding it between them. "Crew assignments, Chief. Time we got down to it."

"Yeah," he said softly, shoulders twitching with a shiver. He raised his hands, scrubbing thick fingers through his hair. "Yeah, you're right." A deep breath to steady himself and Sikuuku hitched his chair around, moving closer to Henricksen. Leaned forward, resting his forearms against the desktop as Henricksen keyed into the reader, accessing the personnel records stored in its memory.

Twenty-four records in total, one for each RV-N crewmember. Twenty-four digital tiles—photo showing, personnel details available beneath—arranged in four neat rows.

Sikuuku turned the reader a bit so he could get a better look. Grimaced when he spotted Adaeze's tile mixed in with all the others. Fisker's sitting next to it. Grunewald's and Abboud's side by side in the bottom row.

He snagged Adaeze's tile without asking, dragging it with his fingertip to the display's bottom corner. Placed the tiles for the three other fallen crew beside it, rearranging the remaining tiles to cover up the holes.

Henricksen watched in silence, fingers wrapped loosely around his glass. Stared numbly at those four tiles clustered in the reader's corner. At Fisker's smiling, freckled face looking so, so young.

Fisker.

He closed his eyes, remembering Fisker in the mess hall that first day on Dragoon. Stiff, and nervous, and oh-so-eager to please.

Dead. He's dead now. They all are.

And the AI—One-Eight-Three lost as well. All because Kinsey was in a hurry. Sent a ship out that wasn't quite ready. A crew that had no idea about that chassis' fatal glitch. And now here they were, making decisions on assignments. About to send five *more* crews out in that exact same ship.

How did we get here? How did it come to this?

"Garrett? *Garrett.*" Sikuuku grabbed his arm, shook it hard. "You with me?"

"Yeah," Henricksen said softly. "Sorry." He opened his eyes and found Fisker staring back at him. Fisker with his shy smile and trusting face.

Hell.

Henricksen grabbed up the glass and emptied it, refilled it from Sikuuku's bottle, topping off the gunner's while he was at it.

"Not your fault," Sikuuku told him, touching a finger to Fisker's tile.

"Somebody's fault." Henricksen gulped at his drink, grimacing as the Scotch burned his throat, slithered its way down to his stomach. "Might as well be mine."

Sikuuku opened his mouth and then closed it, brow wrinkled with worry. "Kid just about worshiped you, you know." He reached for Fisker's tile and opened the record, scrolled through the information. "Busted his ass for weeks trying to get you to notice."

"I noticed," Henricksen said softly. "Damn fine engineering officer."

Sikuuku looked at him, thoughts swirling in his eyes. "Wanted on our crew. Figured he was a shoo-in since—"

"No," Henricksen rasped, closing the record. "Too green. Adaeze." He nodded to the pilot's record. "Always knew he'd do better with her."

"So you made that decision without me?" Sikuuku sat back, arms folded, looking none-too-pleased. "Thought *we* were making crew assignments."

Henricksen shrugged his shoulders. "Made sense. Her skills and his raw talent. Seemed like a good fit. Figured you'd agree."

Sikuuku pursed his lips, thinking a moment. "Not sure I would've. Kid was green, yeah. Green as grass, never even came close to combat, but—"

"I've done green," Henricksen said quietly. "And I don't need it." A sip at his drink and he set it down, twirling the glass on the desktop. "I'm not exactly the best teacher, either. Think we'll both agree on that."

Sikuuku laughed softly, raising his glass in salute. "To Fisker. Best ensign I ever knew."

Henricksen clinked his glass against the gunner's, drained it and filled them both back up. "So where do you want to start?" he asked, waving to the reader on the desk.

"Oh, I don't know. Our crew, maybe?" He scanned the rows of tiles, plucked two from the pack and moved them to the top of the screen.

His own tile, Henricksen's sitting beside it.

Sikuuku sipped at his drink, studying Henricksen over the rim. "You already ruled out Fisker for Engineering. Even before..." He grimaced and trailed off, face filled with apology. "Who *did* you have in mind for Engineering?"

Henricksen pressed a finger to the reader's surface, moving a tile up beside his. "Ogawa," he said, letting it drop.

"Ogawa," Sikuuku grunted. "Really?"

"Problem?"

"Nope." Sikuuku sipped at his drink, set it back down. "Respect the hell out of Ogawa. Best engineering officer I've run across in a long time. Just figured you'd go for Taggert."

Taggert with his snub nose and boyish face. Taggert who wasn't as young as Fisker, nor as inexperienced, but looked it. Acted like it sometimes.

"Close second," Henricksen admitted. "For the same reason I assigned him to Baldini."

"Baldini," Sikuuku snorted. "So that's *another* decision you made without me."

"Recommendation," Henricksen corrected. "I'm open to options."

Sikuuku grunted and sat back, thinking a moment. "Taggert's a bit of a pistol, isn't he?"

"Stubborn and opinionated," Henricksen nodded. "Gives back as good as he gets."

"You sure putting him with Baldini's a good idea?"

"Nope. Baldini's an arrogant little prick, and Taggert's mouthy as all get-out. But he's got a few more years under his belt than Baldini. Won't be afraid to stand up to him. And honestly, Baldini needs that."

"Someone to argue with him?"

"That," Henricksen nodded. "And someone with a backbone and common sense."

"Think we could all use that," Sikuuku smiled. "'Cept you, of course," he amended, scooping his glass from the desktop, raising it in an ironic salute. "The Right Good Captain Henricksen's got everything figured out. Got backbone *and* common sense. Don't need no one else."

Henricksen barked a laugh. "Not so sure about all that, but I got you. That's argument enough."

"Flatterer," Sikuuku snorted.

Henricksen flashed his teeth. "Not the smartest officer to come through the Fleet's Academies, but I do pick things up. Learned to listen to others a long time ago." The smile slipped a bit, Henricksen's face turning serious. "Lucky enough to have a crusty old chief take me under his wing early on. Teach a poor pusher kid-turned-ensign a few lessons. Make sure he understood that the best pilots *listen* before shooting off their mouths."

Sikuuku chuckled softly. "Chiefs are good for that."

Henricksen raised his glass, inclining his head. "Taggert's a know-it-all and a pain-in-the-ass. He and Baldini were made for each other. Should do just fine."

"And you want Ogawa."

Henricksen shrugged and nodded.

"Don't have a say in this one either, do I?" Sikuuku's smile took on an edge. "Seems like you've got all the assignments figured out. Maybe," he said, shoving back his chair, climbing to his feet, "I should just go back to bed."

"Sit down, ya big baby." Henricksen pointed at the empty chair, giving Sikuuku a stern look. Stared at him, refusing to look away until the gunner harrumphed loudly and flopped down. "Scan," he said, waving at the reader's display. "*You* pick."

"Hanu." Sikuuku folded his arms, staring in challenge.

Surprised the hell out of Henricksen with that one. Hanu was quiet like Ogawa, a taller, slimmer version of the dark-haired, golden-skinned engineering officer. Shared those tilted, amber eyes but kept her hair clipped in a short fringe.

Pretty, that one. Slim build, oval face. *Very* pretty, as it just so happened.

"Hanu," Henricksen repeated, giving the gunner a suspicious look. "Because she's a looker, or because she has a nice ass?"

"Both." Sikuuku smiled and then sobered. Leaned forward, resting his elbows on his knees, glass clasped between his hands. "She's also damned good."

Henricksen nodded slowly. "Heck of a scan tech—I'll give you that."

"But?" Sikuuku prompted when Henricksen went quiet.

"But she's missing something. She's aces in the sims—don't get me wrong." Never saw someone take to the sims as quickly as Hanu. Buckled into her seat, instantly at home. Absorbed everything—all the inputs and outputs, the constant calculations—like some kind of machine. Suspected that's why Sikuuku liked her—gunners wanted constant feedback, vectors and ranges, contingencies for different scenarios, anything and everything the sensors picked up. "She lacks confidence," Henricksen told him. "Sims are all well and good, but they're not the real world."

"So you don't think she can do the job." Edge to Sikuuku's voice now. Two assignments made without his input—three if you counted poor, dead Fisker— and now Henricksen questioned this one.

Henricksen opened his mouth and closed it, pulled the reader to him and just stared at it, thinking hard.

Hanu had the capability—never second-guessed that—but he didn't want Sikuuku distracted. Didn't want the gunner distracting *her* with unwanted attention.

"Just the opposite," he said, nodding to Hanu's tile. "Hanu and Ogawa...they work well together. Best scan tech-engineering officer combination I've ever run across, hands down." Damned if he was passing that up just because Sikuuku thought one of them was pretty. "You keep it clean, ya hear?" He leveled a stern look the gunner's way. "Cockpit's no place for romance. Don't," he said when Sikuuku started to deny it. "You've got your eye on her, I can tell. But she don't want you, Akiwane."

Sikuuku sat up straight, looking offended. "Oh yeah? How would *you* know?"

"Because I've been watching her." Henricksen tapped a finger next to his eye. "And *she's* been watching that wee lass on Shaw's team."

"Who?"

"What's her name." Henricksen waved vaguely. "The one with the big wrench and the bigger mouth."

Sikuuku's jaw sagged, eyes bulging. "*Urquhart?*"

Henricksen snapped his fingers. "That's the one. So you just stick to ogling lunch ladies, Akiwane. Last thing I need is you lavishing Hanu with unwanted attention and pissing her off. Or Urquhart for that matter," he added, thinking of that wrench.

"Urquhart," Sikuuku muttered, shaking his head. "Never would've guessed that."

"You listenin' to me, Akiwane?"

"Yeah, yeah. No hitting on the hot chick. Now what about the rest of them?"

"No hitting on *anyone* in the RV-N project," Henricksen said sternly.

Sikuuku rolled his eyes. "That's not what I meant." He turned the reader toward him and started swapping around tiles, moving Hanu's next to Ogawa's, transferring their cluster of four to the top right hand corner before collapsing the rest of the tiles into three rows.

"Don't forget Taggert." Henricksen pointed to the tile in question. "Goes with Baldini."

Sikuuku separated the two tiles, setting them side-by-side beneath Henricksen's crew. "Baldini." He pursed his lips, staring at the pilot's tile, grunted and sat back. "Now *there's* a tough nut to crack."

"Petros and Baldini, both." Henricksen nodded.

Drill schedule beat most of the piss out them. Tired them out enough that they stopped giving the civs and enlisted hell during their off hours. But the sims seemed to bring out the worst in the two pilots. The pressure to perform making them obnoxious and demanding. Blaming every wobble and bobble, every poor result or flat-out failure on one of the other crew because god forbid they admit they weren't absolutely perfect.

"None of the crew want to work with them," Sikuuku warned. "Taggert included. That boy is *not* going to be happy about his assignment."

"Tough," Henricksen grunted. "Obnoxious as they are, they're not half-bad pilots. Better than not half-bad," he amended, because that was the truth. "Somebody has to crew with them. That's just the way it works."

Sikuuku folded his arms, eyes flicking across the remaining tiles. "Schenck would probably do alright at Artillery. Guy's about as lively as a moss-covered boulder, but he seems to get along with everyone."

"Sold." Henricksen moved Schenck's tile before Sikuuku could change his mind. "Ahmadi for Scan?"

"Good as any," Sikuuku shrugged. "Seems to be able to tune the blabbering out, which helps."

"Ahmadi it is." Henricksen placed the scan tech's tile next to Schenck's, completing Baldini's crew. "Petros?" he asked, eyebrow lifting.

"Petros." Sikuuku sighed heavily, thinking on that a while. "How about what's-his-face?" He pointed to a tile in the lower left corner. "Mr. Potato Face there. Surosa—Surosis—Suria—"

"Surosovic?"

"That's him. Built like a sack of suet. Personality of a sponge."

Harsh as it sounded, Sikuuku pretty much nailed it. God—if there truly *was* a god, singular or plural—gifted Surosovic with a sharp mind and some *severely* unfortunate genetics. Not his fault, but there it was.

"Never says a word in the debriefings," Sikuuku grumbled. "Just sits there, typing away on his reader, making notes on his runs." He paused, head tilting, slid a look Henricksen's way. "Does he even *talk* to anyone outside of the sims?"

"Not that I've seen," Henricksen shrugged. "Keeps to himself for the most part." Odd, but nothing really wrong with it. Hadn't heard the other crew say anything bad about Surosovic, anyway. "You thinking he goes with Petros?"

"Considering it. Might not be the most sociable person, but on the plus side his lack of people skills means he probably doesn't give two shits who he works with." Sikuuku flashed a smile as he reached forward, moving Surosovic's and Petros' tiles together, creating a new line below Baldini's crew. Slid Nunez's tile up with them while he was at it and then sat back, waiting for the expected objection.

"You sure that's a good idea?"

Sikuuku shrugged, obviously not caring. "He's gonna bitch no matter where we put him unless it's under Mahal." He scanned the tiles a moment, pointed to one near the bottom. "Put Kapoor with him. Shaw's give-'em-hell friend should provide some entertainment." Sikuuku's smile turned wicked. "Listening to Kapoor and Petros go at it should distract Nunez from his misery for a while."

Henricksen wasn't quite sure about the soundness of that decision-making process, but he moved Kapoor's tile anyway, finishing Petros' team out.

The rest of the assignments fell out easily once they settled on Petros' and Baldini's crews. Janssen took Fontaine and Travers, Mateus for Scan. Felt good about that match-up. Much better than the other two, anyway. Rock-solid combination, those four. Ran that crew together a few days ago and they clicked instantly, acted like they'd been training together for years.

Mahal took the leftovers—Pritchard, Karras for Artillery, a brash, young scan tech named Salazar who kept fiddling with the sim's systems during her off-hours.

Not bad, honestly. Except that scan tech. Henricksen honestly wasn't so sure about her.

"That one's trouble." Sikuuku pointed a finger at Salazar's tile, echoing Henricksen's thoughts. "Rousted her out of the sim room a little before midnight. Claimed she was just 'fixing a few things'. Yeah right," Sikuuku snorted. "Fixing things, my ass. Other scan techs are complaining about her. Says she keeps changing the default config of their systems. Toggling settings and then applying them across the board. Annoys the hell out of Mateus."

Henricksen grunted. "Tweaks all have their preferences." Liked to set their stations up just so, and severely hated anyone changing anything. "Sounds like Mateus caught on to Salazar's "improvements", anyway." He looked a question at Sikuuku. "Noticed he's been showing up early for sim training. Assume that's so he can switch everything back to the default settings?"

Sikuuku nodded. "They're all doing that now. Spend twenty minutes wiping out Salazar's settings, another half hour starting over from scratch. 'Spose it doesn't matter anymore, though. Sim days are just about over." He chewed his lip, thinking hard, snorted and flashed a smile. "Mahal seems to find all the scan tech in-fighting highly amusing. She'll get on well with Salazar." He rapped his knuckles on the desktop, sealing the deal with a decisive nod. "Think you made a good choice there, Captain."

"In that case…" Henricksen moved the last few tiles together, locked the five groupings and saved them to the personnel files. "We're done." He scooped up his glass and drained it, reached for the bottle of Scotch.

"Assuming they don't crash and burn, of course."

Henricksen froze, bottle tilted, just about touching the rim of his glass. "Not funny, Akiwane." He filled his glass, set the bottle back down. "Not funny at all."

"Sorry." Sikuuku ducked his head, flushing. "Wasn't thinking."

"S'alright," Henricksen said quietly. But it wasn't alright. Wasn't even close to alright. Not so soon after that accident. Not with one crew so recently in their graves. "Hell," he rasped, gulping at his Scotch. Half the bottle gone now, and with Kinsey's cognac already stewing in his belly, Henricksen was feeling decidedly tipsy. "What time is it anyway?" he asked, looking around.

"Late."

"Well, that's helpful."

Sikuuku shrugged his shoulders, reached for the reader and toggled the display. "0145." He tossed back his drink, slammed the glass down on the desk. "Captain. I regret to inform you I am in violation of curfew and *entirely* unfit for duty. But," he added, splashing more Scotch into his glass, "I am well on my way to being drunk."

"Cheers," Henricksen said, smiling as he clinked his glass against the gunner's. They drank together and sat in silence after, both of them thinking their own thoughts. "Guess I should be going." He pushed to his feet, grabbing up the reader. "Figure out the best way to break the news on these assignments and then get some sleep."

"Or, we could finish this bottle." Sikuuku pointed to the bottle in question, measuring the remaining contents with his fingers. "Two of us drinking so this won't get us falling down drunk, but I'll settle for sloppy-happy. Been a while since I got sloppy-happy drunk." He flashed a smile, holding the bottle up. "Whaddaya say, Captain? Shall we see this soldier off?"

He shouldn't, but it was tempting. Especially after Kinsey's news. "Why not?" Henricksen decided, sinking down in his chair.

"Excellent! Now grab your glass and let's go." Sikuuku shoved his chair back and wandered into his bedroom, digging something out of the closet.

"Go where?" Henricksen called after him.

"Well, we're not gonna drink *here*. That's just pathetic. Ah! There it is." Sikuuku came back fully clothed, stuffing something inside his uniform jacket. Scooped up the bottle of Scotch and headed for the door. "You coming?" he asked, when Henricksen just sat there, frowning at his back.

"What are you up to, Akiwane?"

Sikuuku shrugged, smiling as he reached inside his jacket and pulled a reader out.

"What's that?" Henricksen asked suspiciously.

"Bad idea for how we can have a little fun." A wink and Sikuuku keyed the device on, turned it around and held it out.

Henricksen considered the reader a moment, stood and retrieved it, studying the display. "Language programs? This having something to do with those Tahitian beauties you were dreaming about?"

"Hardly," Sikuuku snorted, folding his arms, leaning against the door. "Look, I'm not going out there with some bone-stock AI. Chassis' chancy. Can't be flying it with some dumbed down drone with no personality."

"So, what? You wanna give them vocabulary lessons? A pusher kid and a former fisherman's brat?"

"Who better?" Sikuuku smiled.

"Oh, I don't know...someone with a formal education and training in linguistics?"

"Pfft. Education's overrated. You and me got character. *That's* what our little AI friends need."

Henricksen considered him, and the reader in his hands. "This isn't just a bad idea, it's a *terrible* idea."

"The best ones always are." Sikuuku flashed a winning smile and pushed the door open, waited until Henricksen joined him before setting off down the hall.

TWENTY-TWO

A few hours later, in the wee, wee hours of the morning, Henricksen wound his way back to his quarters—dog-tired and on the downside of drunk, wanting nothing more than to fall down and get some shut eye, knowing full well that was not going to happen. Just under an hour before reveille—enough time to shower and pull on a fresh uniform, not even close to enough time for sleeping. So he ditched the uniform that stank of Scotch, and sweat, and the inside of the hangar bay's enviro suit, and laid out a clean one. Pinned on the silver nametag and the stars for his collar before jumping into the shower to drown his muddled brain in soap and water.

Set the tap on cold and left it there, shivering miserably because no sleep and give or take a half a bottle of Scotch was not a good combination. And he really, truly did *not* want to confront the crew with assignments smelling like a distillery. Looking shadow-eyed and unsteady on his feet.

For a good ten minutes Henricksen froze himself, letting the shock of that cold water scrub the lingering effects of the alcohol from his system. Reset his brain from fuzzy stupor to something approaching intelligent thought. Cranked up the heat when he absolutely couldn't take it anymore. When his toes started complaining and his manhood went all scared turtle, doing its best to suck itself up inside his guts. The shivers continued for a while after, spasms that set his elbows to twitching, making his hands shake so badly he kept dropping the soap. But the trembling eased as the steam billowed around him, filling his quarter's tiny bathroom with a thick layer of fog. He scrubbed and scrubbed inside that warm, wet blanket, pale skin turning pink, the now scorching water making that jagged, bone-white scar on his temple show all the more clearly. A stark reminder of what he'd left behind him.

A ship and crew, a past far from buried.

Hecate's legacy, that scar. A constant reminder of that now-dead ship. He touched at it unconsciously, tracing the zig-zagging line with his finger as the soapy water swirled around his feet, disappearing down the cross-hatched, metal drain in the shower's floor.

"*Hecate,*" he breathed, staring blindly, steam wrapping him close about.

In his mind's eye he could still see her: disc-shaped form limned in starlight, the Cepheid's silver orb rising in front of her like a bright metallic moon. That diamond dust cloud of nannites racing hungrily toward her crippled ship's body, ready to eat her from the outside in.

He shivered despite the heat, mind flashing through a dozen scenarios—a hundred horrible things that might have happened to *Hecate* if those nannites had reached her before *Gogmagog* destroyed them, and the Cepheid that set them free. Wasn't quite sure AI felt pain, but *Hecate*, in her sentience, understood fear. And anger. The horror that came with a slow death. The agony of being eaten alive.

A twitch of his shoulders, as Henricksen lowered his hand, fingers clenching in a fist that trembled at his side. He closed his eyes and leaned forward, bracing his forearm against the plas-metal wall. Turned up the heat just that little bit more and let the scalding water cascade across his neck and shoulders. Bowed his head and rested his brow against his arm.

In his memory, *Hecate* drifted, helpless and alone. But a flash of fire—cobalt blue, bright and blinding—and she ended. Everything that *Hecate* was and ever would be, snuffed out in an instant—mind and body, the totality of her consciousness destroyed with the Cepheid. Obliterated by *Gogmagog*'s withering fire.

"Damn." Henricksen sucked in a shaking breath, scrubbing at his face. "God damn."

He pushed away from the wall, willing those images away. Doused his short hair in shampoo and rubbed it around, hating the antiseptic smell of it. The artificial pine scent the military insisted on including in its standard issue toiletries.

Woke him up, though. Chased away those last, lingering memories of *Hecate*. Killed the tremors shuddering through his body. Settled his hands enough that he managed to shave without cutting himself. He stepped from the shower feeling fairly close to human, looking fresh enough to pass for someone who'd actually gotten something approaching a good night's sleep. Toweled off and dressed in the fresh, crisp uniform lying on his bed. Taking his time about it, checking the folds and creases, the position of his nametag, the set of his collar devices, wanting everything just so.

Crew assignments today, after all—a task long overdue. Not the best idea, staying up all night drinking, messing around with an AI's language processing systems, but, damn, he'd needed that. Hadn't let loose and done something completely irresponsible in a long, long time.

'Course, he couldn't exactly let the crew know what he'd been up to. Didn't set a good example, carousing at all hours, tampering with Fleet equipment. So he spent an extra few minutes checking the fit of his uniform, tugging and straightening until everything line up perfectly, exactly matched Fleet regs. Slapped his cheeks to get some color back into them. Scrubbed hard at the dark circles lurking under his eyes.

Didn't completely work, but the Henricksen that walked out of that bedroom looked nothing like the shambling wreck that had wandered back to his quarters just an hour earlier. Combat experience helped with that. Taught you to fake it. Large-scale battles meant days with little or no sleep, food when you remembered and could grab it, showers to clear the mind and clean off the blood. So you learned after a while—out of necessity if nothing else. Figured out how to trick the mind and body into thinking they weren't tired. Convince your comrades you were rested, and ready, and firing on all cylinders when in truth you were just barely holding it together. Balanced on a knife's edge and just about to drop.

A last tug, straightening the jacket, reaching for holster that wasn't there—old habit, reaching for that pistol, and hard to break after so many years of going just about everywhere armed—and Henricksen vacated his quarters, reader gripped firmly in hand. Navigated the corridors to the mess hall, pausing outside to draw a deep, steadying breath before pushing the double doors open, and wending his way through the gauntlet of crew-crowded tables on the other side.

Sikuuku spotted him as soon as he entered, signaling to Henricksen from a table in the corner—plate piled high with food sitting in front of him, Shaw in a surprisingly clean pair of coveralls occupying the chair to his right. Shaw, who was casual as always—foot drawn up and resting on the seat of her chair, arm wrapped around her shin, hand clasping a battered metal mug.

"Good morning, Captain." Sikuuku waved Henricksen over, pointing to an empty chair. "Starting to wonder where you'd gotten to." A flick of his eyes to Shaw beside him, lips lifting in a smile. "Thought you might've chickened out and changed your mind."

"Just stopped to freshen up a bit." Henricksen tilted his head, looking Sikuuku up and down. "See you didn't bother."

"Changed my uniform." Sikuuku winked, smoothing a crease in his jacket. Clean jacket, pants as well—rumpled, the both of them, so likely dug out of the back of a drawer, but clean, nonetheless. Damp hair, so he'd at least showered, but Sikuuku still had that slightly muzzy, slightly too happy look of a man who'd been up on an all-night bender.

"Grab some coffee. You need it," Henricksen insisted when Sikuuku started to object. "Grab me some while you're at. And some food. No eggs, though." Couldn't stomach the synth protein concoction this station called eggs—a scrambled concoction that tasted of rubber and foam. "Take whatever else they've got, but not that."

A nod and Sikuuku pushed back his chair, turned and headed for the chow line at the back of the hall.

"You two boys have fun last night?" Shaw smiled secretively, sipping the coffee in her mug.

Henricksen grunted, nodding at Sikuuku's back. "He certainly did."

Shaw pursed her lips, eyes flicking to the gunner, back to Henricksen's face. "You treat my girl right, you hear me?"

"I'm not sure what you—"

"You know what I mean." Shaw set her mug down, wrapped both arms around her shin. "Word's come down from Kinsey," she said, dropping her voice, eyes flicking around the room. "You and the others, you'll be taking the RV-Ns out *tout de suite.*"

Henricksen frowned. "What the hell does *that* mean? I thought they weren't—"

"They aren't," Shaw interrupted, eyes snapping back to his face. "We haven't had time to make the modifications we spoke about. But the AIs know about the problem."

"This failsafe of yours." Henricksen shook his head, not liking it. Not liking it at all.

Shaw leaned forward, staring earnestly. "Two-Six and the others, they won't let your crew fire up the stealth system while the jump drives are active. Not even if they want to." She paused, searching his face. "They'll look after your crew,

Captain. But I need *you* to look after *them*. Can you do that for me? Will you look after Two-Six and the other Ravens?"

"You know I will," Henricksen said softly.

Surprised she'd even ask that. Shaw knew about *Hecate*. Knew what her death meant to him.

Shaw held his gaze a moment longer, nodded and sat back. Scooped her coffee mug from the table and sat there, swirling its contents. "So what's that?" she asked, nodding to the reader in his hand.

"Crew assignments." He held the reader up, nodding to Sikuuku as the gunner slid an overflowing plate of food in front of him, dropped a steaming mug of coffee beside it. "Time to make a few love connections," he said, forcing a smile onto his face. He excused himself and walked to the center of the room, stood there, waiting patiently, until everyone quieted. "Alright. Listen up," he called, turning in a circle, picking the Raven crew out of the crowd. "You've all been asking, and you all know I've been delaying."

Crew looked at each other, frowning uncertainly as Henricksen held the reader up, making sure everyone saw it. Set it down on an empty table and moved a step away. Spread his feet wide and clasped his hands behind his back.

Staring at them. Taking a long look around.

"Crew assignments. Who's interested?"

A collective gasp of indrawn breath—surprised faces everywhere, everyone staring at Henricksen like they weren't quite sure if he was joking—and crew abandoned their tables, pushing, shoving, almost knocking each other down in their rush to get to that reader first.

Taggert ended up winning. Snatched the reader from the table and clutched it to his chest like a baby as he scooted between the mess hall's tables and into the rec room, connected the reader to the AV system and projected the crew assignments onto the far wall.

The rest of the crew piled in after him, loudly complaining about the engineering officer's thievery. But they settled quickly, perching on couches, the pool table, the room's few chairs to study the five crew rosters in offer. Good natured squabbling giving way to intense discussion—a low murmur of conversation punctuated by brief explosions that drifted clear across the mess hall. Right to Henricksen's ears.

He smiled, listening to them. Enjoying the banter and bitching—familiar sound, and universal to Fleet crew everywhere. Thought about joining them, being a part of it, but ultimately decided to leave it alone. Retreated to the corner table and breakfast, instead. To a plate all but overflowing with food: the hated eggs he'd *specifically* told Sikuuku not to bring him, a stack of pancakes, and half a dozen strips of something approximating bacon.

"Got the boys ready." Sikuuku flexed his arms as he raised both fists, kissing the knuckles each. "Ya know, in case there's a fight." He winked, smiling, swapping fists for a fork and knife. Set about cleaning his plate, shoveling huge wads of those disgusting, not-quite-eggs into his mouth.

"Thanks," Henricksen said, carving a pancake into small bites. "Hoping it won't come to that, though."

Sikuuku grunted, washing a mouthful of eggs down. Turned his head and slowly set his coffee mug down. "Garrett."

He tapped the table, catching Henricksen's eyes, nodding to the rec room doorway as a lone figure emerged.

Mahal, glancing backward. Waiting for Salazar to catch up. Janssen and Fontaine right behind her. The rest of the crew emerging in ones and twos. Finding places at tables, retrieving abandoned utensils. Breakfasts laid out on plates. Everyone shuffling around and making room as flight crews—newly assigned and still in mourning over their fallen members—sat down together and started talking.

About RV-Ns and flying—*really* flying, their sim days just about done. About One-Eight-Three and that accident—heard that all over the mess hall, it still being fresh in everyone's minds. About the stars and vectors. Jump points, and way stations, and all the usual things crews talked about.

Engrossed in those conversations. Completely ignoring Henricksen and Sikuuku sitting in the corner.

Not quite the reaction Henricksen expected. Figured at least *one* of them would ambush their table, demand to know what the *hell* the two of them were thinking when they came up with those crew assignments.

He glanced at Sikuuku and saw the gunner's eyes narrow, fork tines tapping contemplatively at his plate.

"Well, now," he murmured, scanning the room. "*That* went better than expected."

"You sound disappointed." Henricksen chopped another pancake, forking it into his mouth one bite at a time.

"No." Sikuuku scooped up some eggs, chewed and swallowed, taking his time. "Not disappointed, exactly. Just…surprised, is all. Figured at least Taggert would have a beef." He quirked an eyebrow, pointing his fork at the untouched yellow mound on Henricksen's plate. "You gonna eat those?"

"Hell no." Henricksen shoveled the unwanted eggs onto the gunner's plate, glad to be rid of them.

"I'm sure there'll be some horse trading later." Shaw nodded to the crew sitting around the tables. "Twenty crew. Bound to disappoint somebody. No way around that."

"Disappointment I can deal with." Henricksen snagged a pancake from Sikuuku's plate—payment for the recently donated eggs. "Pissed off could be more trouble."

"Thought that's why you had *him*." Shaw smiled crookedly, waving her mug at Sikuuku.

Henricksen grunted, nodding, finished his pancakes and cast a thoughtful eye across the people in the room. Conscious of Shaw watching him, sipping at her mug.

"Anyone need a refill?" She held up her empty cup, collecting the others from the table when Sikuuku and Henricksen both nodded. Abandoned her chair and headed back to the chow line and the huge cauldron of coffee that never seemed to run out.

"You think anyone will?" Sikuuku waved his fork, gesturing vaguely.

"What? Ask to be reassigned? Expect so. Be surprised if they didn't." Henricksen shrugged his shoulder and snatched up a piece of bacon, sniffed at it and nibbled at a one end.

Smelled real, tasted real, but he was pretty sure it wasn't. Meat, possibly. Some kind of protein, that much was sure, but bacon meant pig, and pigs—*real* pigs, not the lab grown synth meat most of the stations served—were damn hard to come by. Expensive as that Scotch Sikuuku denied having. Twice as difficult to secure.

He finished the strip and started in on another before the bacon-but-not-quite-bacon flavor started to turn his stomach. Tossed the remains down and drained the dregs of his coffee, nodding to Sikuuku as he pushed back his chair. "Crew gives you any trouble, you let me know."

"Wait? What?" Sikuuku glanced up, looking slightly alarmed. "What about—what are you—where the hell are you going?"

"Things to do," Henricksen said vaguely, turning away.

Sikuuku grabbed his arm, pulling him back around. "Really? That's all I get?"

Henricksen grimaced, looking away. "Quarters," he said. "I need to…" He sighed, rubbing at his temple, feeling a headache coming on. "It's past time we removed the crew's personals from the barracks, don't you think?"

Fisker and Adaeze. Grunewald and Abboud. Hadn't been allowed to touch their belongings before now. Kinsey wanted everything kept as is until the investigation finished up.

Sikuuku winced, snatching his hand back. "Need some help?"

Apology in his voice now. Written across his tattooed face.

"My job," Henricksen told him. "My responsibility. My *crew*, and now—"

"Garrett." Sikuuku caught his eye, gave a sharp shake of his head. "Don't go down there. You don't want to start down that road."

Henricksen dropped his eyes, holding onto it anyway. Wrapping the pain and anger around him like armor. Realized that was stupid—no use at all for martyrs in an operation like this—and sighed heavily, letting it go. "Yeah. Yeah, you're right." He sucked in a breath, blew it back out. Glanced up and around, giving the mess hall another look. "Stay here," he said, nodding to Sikuuku across from him, Shaw to one side. "Cover for me in case—" He grimaced, ducking his head again. "In case anyone asks."

"Yeah," Sikuuku said softly. "No problem."

Shaw nodded, face thoughtful, slightly confused. "Open bar'll help." She pointed a finger to the bar on the far side of the mess hall. "Bad news always goes down better with strong drink."

"And we ain't even got that," Sikuuku snorted. "Best we got is beer. And the beer in here's about as bad as the food."

"Still beer," Shaw told him. "And it's still free." She leaned back, tucking one leg under the other, giving him a raised eyebrow look. "If there's one thing I've learned in the military, it's that free drinks make just about everyone happy."

"Beer, though? At six-thirty in the morning?" Sikuuku shuddered, disgusted. "That's cruel, Shaw."

Shaw picked up her fork, dragging it through the leftover food on her plate. "No worse than this fakin' bacon and powdered egg mash they're eating."

"Bad food is one thing. Bad beer?" Sikuuku shook his head. "Beer for breakfast with sim practice after is a sure-fire recipe for disaster. Last thing we need is a bunch of pissed off flight crew cleaning puke out of a sim pod."

"No," Henricksen agreed, taking another look at the crew. "No sims today. Or tomorrow," he added on a whim. "It's the real thing from here on out." He flicked his eyes to Sikuuku, nodded to Shaw beside him. "Open bar, just as she said."

Sikuuku frowned uncertainly, shrugged and tapped two fingers to his temple. "Aye, Cap'n. Whatever you say."

A nod to the two of them and Henricksen abandoned their table, and the mess hall for the empty, echoing hallway outside.

Always quiet this time of the morning. Barely 0630 now, which meant most of the RV-N project's personnel were still in the mess hall, scarfing down breakfast before their shifts started at 0700. Henricksen passed a few people—late arrivals hurrying to get to the mess hall before the chow line shut down—but mostly he had the corridors to himself.

Enjoyed that after the hustle and bustle, the hurry and worry of the last few weeks. Took his time, savoring it, that unusual feeling of being alone in these moldy old spaces. Ambled his way down that main corridor, taking the first right hand turning. Walked all the way to the end—head down, hands in his pocket—stopping at the last door on the right.

Adaeze's room. Fisker's across the hall on the left. Ironic that their rooms were here, in close proximity to one another. Almost as if Kinsey had known they'd end up crewing together when he passed out crew assignments to quarters.

Dead now, Henricksen thought, eyes drifting to Fisker's door. *Both of them dead. Nothing left but a few odds and ends and spare uniforms.*

And soon even that would be gone.

A step brought him to Fisker's door, hand reaching, fingers resting lightly on the oversized wheel jutting from the middle.

Soldiers, he reminded himself. *Soldiers serve knowing they could die.*

But not in training. No one should ever die in such a senseless manner. Soldiers deserved dignity, and dying during a training run…

"Where's the honor in that?" Henricksen rasped, voice filled with bitterness, heart heavy with pain. "Where's the purpose?" He wrapped his fingers around the wheel, gripping it hard, spun it and hit the latch, shoving Fisker's door wide.

Stepped into a suite as tiny his own quarters. Same layout—front room, bedroom and bathroom off to one side—with the same drab, uncomfortable furnishings because, apparently, whoever designed this particular section of the station didn't seem to think there was any need to have more than one suite configuration available.

"Probably a good thing," Henricksen muttered, looking around. "One less thing for people to bitch about."

Never mind that the enlisted personnel slept in barracks. Half a dozen men and women sharing quarters while the officers enjoyed a private, if somewhat small, suite of rooms.

He stepped inside, leaving the door to Fisker's quarters open behind him, and turned in circle, looking around.

Not really much to this particular suite of rooms. Nothing on the walls. No trinkets or decorations. Just a hard couch and two straight-backed chairs, the usual desk in the corner with a stack of flight manuals piled atop it.

Nothing at all that screamed Fisker. At a glance, these quarters could've been anyone's. Any officer anywhere, on any ship or station.

Except those binders piled atop the desk. Flight manuals—a whole stack of them, squared off, one laid neatly atop the other.

Henricksen considered them from across the tiny, closet-like room. Walked over and grabbed a binder off the top of the stack, holding it one hand while he paged through it with the other.

Strange, seeing paper. Most people used electronic files, preferring the condensed portability of a reader to a heavy stack of printed out manuals. Suppose that said something about Fisker, though Henricksen wasn't quite sure what. Files might've come with the room, for all he knew. Standard issue along with the hard, uncomfortable furnishings. The grey-on-grey-on-grey walls.

Then again, maybe Fisker brought these with him. Saint-Cyr was Old Earth Academy, after all. With Old Earth ways.

Henricksen paged through the manual, snapping it shut when he reached the end. Set it back atop the pile of others and moved them all to the center of the desk. Rifled the drawers and found another book—this one an old fashioned text on sea creatures, pressed flower bookmark stuck between the pages—and a tiny vial filled with grains of sand, but not all that much else. Stacked those few belongings with the flight manuals on the desktop, leaving them while he searched the bedroom to one side. Pulling down uniforms and plucking up boots, snagging spare nametags and collar devices from the wardrobe, digging through drawers of socks and underwear and other spare items Fisker had squirreled away.

Found a holocube tucked in there, all the way at the back. Powered it on and stared at the flickering pictures of friends and family, a smiling line of uniforms with Fisker at the center, arms wrapped around the shoulders of a man and woman standing to either side.

Powered it off, thinking to add it to the stack of personals on the desktop, hesitated—staring at the cube in his hand—and tucked it inside his uniform jacket, feeling slightly guilty at the theft.

Not right, keeping it—not his, after all. The cube itself wasn't anything special, just a run-of-the-mill data storage device, the kind you could pick up cheap from any of a thousand stationside electronics dealers. But the images inside it...the pictures of a dead son.

Fisker's parents would want those. Brothers, sisters, whatever family Fisker left behind.

"I'll make a copy," Henricksen promised. "Send them along with the rest of his stuff."

Which wasn't all that much. Toiletries and spare uniform items, that book and vial, the flight manuals from the front room. A shiny new medal the Fleet awarded posthumously.

Combat medal, for courage under fire. Fisker, Adaeze, Grunewald, Abboud—they all got one. According to official records, they all died in battle, not on some messed up Black Ops training mission.

Henricksen fished the medal from his pocket, opened the case—leather and gold leaf, a pretty little thing—and stared at the lump of brass inside. Traced the embossed pattern of crossed swords and oak leaves with his finger. The clustered stars of the Fleet's insignia. The square-edged letters of the Meridian Alliance stamp.

A shiny thing, that medal, and entirely a lie. Better for Fisker's family, though, thinking his death had meant something. Better for *all* the crew's families than having to live with the senselessness of the truth.

Better for the Fleet—that first and foremost, because the Fleet wasn't about charity. The lie of that medal was far easier for the military than owning up to its mistake.

Henricksen stared at it, hating it. Closed the case up and dropped it in a footlocker with the rest of Fisker's belongings.

A last pass of the room to make sure he hadn't missed anything and Henricksen sealed the footlocker up, and set it outside the door. Crossed the hall to Adaeze's quarters to repeat the process.

TWENTY-THREE

Henricksen climbed into Two-Six's pilot seat feeling surprisingly nervous. Hadn't felt that way in a long, long time.

Not since he was an ensign piloting his first ship.

"You okay?" Sikuuku pitched his voice low, sensing Henricksen's discomfort. Using the private channel—helmet to helmet comms—as he squeezed into the Artillery pod behind the Pilot's station.

"Yeah. Fine," Henricksen lied, wincing as the pressure suit adjusted. Holding tight to the flight controls as it sucked against his stomach, squeezing like vice grips around the rest of his body. "Just...weird, ya know? After the sims."

And yet, strangely *like* the sim pod. Same close quarters. Same blood-red emergency lighting. Same darkly uniformed crew arranged around him, faces hidden behind full head helmets, mirrored visors covering their eyes.

Hanu and Ogawa, Sikuuku on the guns. Crew—*his* crew, his *ship*—and those stars outside. The dream of stars he'd been waiting for. A dream of space long denied.

"You ask me, it's a relief," Sikuuku said, buckling the straps of the Artillery pod's seat. "Sims smell like the inside of a goddamn sweat sock."

Henricksen barked a laugh.

Couldn't argue with that. Sims had years on them—tens of thousands of flight hours, software swapped out, configurations updated for each new airframe—and yet the base components remained the same. The guts of it used over and over again.

This Raven, though...clean cockpit. Everything brand new. No sweat stink, no recycled air. No musty station odor creeping in from the RV-N project's spaces. Clean, just...clean. Unspoiled. Theirs and only theirs, not some hot-racked sim shared between a couple of hundred different people.

Felt good, being the first to fly her. Special in a way that made Henricksen all the more nervous. Afraid he'd fuck it up despite all the training. The hours upon hours spent in the sim.

A deep breath to calm himself and settle the butterflies in his stomach, and Henricksen started his pre-flight checks. Flicking switches, confirming configurations and settings, scrolling through endless lists of diagnostics and quality assurance checks.

"'Sides," Sikuuku said, fiddling with his helmet, setting the comms to the default channel. "Training's boring. 'Bout time we got down to the real thing."

"Amen to that," Ogawa muttered. "Been looking forward to taking this bad boy out for weeks now—"

"'*Scuse me*?!" Two-Six's voice cut across the channel, sounding distinctly upset. "I ain't no 'bad boy', sister. I'm an eleventh generation AI badass stealth ship and I'll thank you to remember that."

A click as Sikuuku toggled his comms, switching to the private channel again. "Did she just say 'badass'?"

"And 'ain't'." Henricksen twisted, throwing a look at the gunner behind him. "You didn't *really* upload that lexicon we built, did you?"

Sikuuku shrugged, working his way through the Artillery pod's start-up routines. "Seemed like a good idea at the time. Maybe no one will notice?" he asked hopefully.

"Maybe." Henricksen faced around, glancing at Hanu to one side, Ogawa on the other.

If they'd noticed Two-Six's enhancements, they didn't show it. They just worked away at their stations—heads down, finishing up their pre-flight routines, murmuring back and forth to each other, querying the AI now and then. Everything on the up and up, nothing at all out of the ordinary. Until...

"Are you *kidding* me?"

Henricksen flicked a last few switches, throwing a sidelong look at Scan. "What's the problem, Hanu?"

"Salazer, that's what. Bitch's been messing with my systems."

"*Me-ow,*" Sikuuku said, earning himself a nasty look.

"Not the time," Henricksen warned, thumping a fist against the gunner's pod. And to Hanu, "What do you mean? What systems?"

"Language processors. AI's speaking gibberish. Can't half understand her. Bad enough Salazar kept resetting the defaults on the Scan system in the sims, *now* she's messing with AI language processors?" Hanu shook her head, disgusted. "Huh-uh. That's bullshit. I'll kill her," she said, punching angrily at a button. "I'll skin that skinny bitch alive if I catch her messing around with my ship again."

"Salazer. Right." Henricksen snuck another look at Sikuuku. "I'll, um, I'll have a talk with her later. Make sure she—"

"Cut the chit-chat, Captain." Kinsey, listening in as usual. Sounding slightly annoyed, entirely impatient at the delay. "Finish your pre-flight checks and get that bird out of the hangar."

"Roger, Control." Henricksen pressed at the Pilot station's buttons, running through the launch routine. "Status of the hangar bay?"

"Locked down. All personnel accounted for."

Lights appeared in the hangar bay's ceiling—a blood-red line running the circumference of that empty space. They pulsed once as the outer doors opened—massive, triple-thick panel splitting down the middle, the twin sections trundling to either side.

Stars appeared—silver-white and shining, calling to Henricksen from the depths of space.

"Hangar bay is clear," Kinsey's voice said. "You may launch when ready, Captain."

Henricksen shook himself, pulling his eyes from the stars. "Acknowledged." He locked in the settings on his Pilot's station, checked the progress of the crew around him. "Primary systems checks complete. We are go in ten."

"Ten minutes. Launch clock is set."

A timer appeared in the upper left hand corner of Henricksen's panel, glowing orange numbers steadily counting down.

"Got it. Stand by for launch." Henricksen closed the channel, blocking Kinsey out. Toggled comms to an internal setting for privacy—crew only, no nosy station administrators allowed. "You hear that, Two-Six? You ready to party?"

"*Scythe*," she answered. Just that, and nothing else.

Henricksen glanced at a camera, blinking in confusion. "Uh, excuse me?"

"It's *Scythe* now," she told him. "Not Two-Six. Two-Six was a prototype. *Scythe lives.*"

"Okay..." Henricksen was quiet a moment, trying to puzzle that one out. "So, you...named yourself?"

"*Duh.* Numbers are cute and all, but you can't expect me to go by Two-Six forever."

"No," Henricksen murmured. "I suppose not. And you chose *Scythe* because..."

"We're Ravens. Harbingers. Companions to death."

"And...?"

"A scythe cuts. It's deadly." *Scythe* sounded slightly miffed.

"But you're a stealth ship," Henricksen noted.

"Yeah, well. I liked it. And it sounded tough." Miffed. Definitely miffed.

"Tough. Right," Henricksen grunted, smiling inside his helmet. "So, have you—"

"Systems are updated. Beacon, registry, everything shows my proper name now."

"Well, aren't you efficient?"

"AI," *Scythe* said proudly. "Efficient comes with the territory."

Henricksen laughed aloud.

"*You!*" Ogawa twisted, pointing a finger at Henricksen. "It was *you*."

"Me? What about me?" Henricksen asked, flipping casually at switches, cringing at the defensiveness in his voice.

"*You* did this," Ogawa accused.

"No." Henricksen flicked more switches, checking and rechecking settings he'd already rechecked twice. "Not even sure what you're talking about."

"Yeah, you do. The language processors. *You* messed with them. It wasn't Salazar at all!"

Henricksen shrugged, maintaining his innocence. Winced as *Scythe*'s voice cut in.

"Course it wasn't Salazar," she sniffed. "Ain't no way I'm letting anyone who isn't *my* crew touch *my* systems. *Especially* a second-rate scan tech like Salazar."

"Ain't?" Ogawa folded her arms, helmeted head tilting. "She said 'ain't', Captain. Only you and Sikuuku—" She broke off, visored face turning toward the gunner sitting in the Artillery pod. "*You*," she breathed, voice dripping with accusation. "The *two* of you did this. *Together.*"

"*Me?*" Sikuuku leaned out of his pod, pointing a finger at his chest. "Why would I—"

"Oh, yeah. You were in on it alright." Ogawa harrumphed loudly, turning her back on the gunner as she finished her station prep. "Messed up our AI's language centers," she muttered. "Talks like a pirate now. What kind of ship does that?"

"Oh, stop grousing," Sikuuku told her. "At least she has personality."

"Damn straight," *Scythe* chimed in.

"See?"

"*Your* personality," Ogawa shot back. "You *ruined* her—"

"Ruined?! What are you talkin' about? She's perfect! Couldn't be—"

"Lock it down! The both of you!" Henricksen snapped. "We've got five minutes to launch and the *last* thing I need is my crew arguing about our AI's new language routines."

"Thank you, Henricksen," *Scythe* said primly, AI voice filling the silence that followed. "I quite like the new me," she added, sounding supremely smug.

Ogawa glanced up, clearly sulking, stabbing at the panels in front of her. "I'm making some changes when we get back," she warned the crew in general. "Fix some of the bad habits those two taught her." A waggle of one finger, including Henricksen and Sikuuku, both.

"Fine. Whatever," Henricksen said to appease her. "Just finish those start-up routines."

Ogawa muttered something under her breath, fingers tapping angrily at Engineering's panels. Powered main propulsion into an active state and examined the data before giving Henricksen the all-clear. "Engines are ready, Captain. Jump drives on standby."

"Roger. Hanu?"

"Scan is go."

"Sikuuku?"

"Artillery systems on-line."

"Roger." Henricksen toggled the comms, opening a channel to the station. "Control, this is Two—this is *Scythe*." A nod to the AI's camera. "Systems are on-line and green across the board. We are ready for launch on your mark."

"Acknowledged." Lights appeared on the hangar bay floor—a double line of yellow bars this time, stacking end-to-end, leading away from the ship to the gaping mouth of the hangar bay doors. "Perimeter defenses have been notified of the launch."

Precautionary measure, this being a military base, with military defenses. Any unauthorized intrusion doomed to be shot down.

"You are go in two minutes, thirty seconds," Kinsey told them.

"Roger. Synching the launch clock." Henricksen set a counter in the ship's system, matching it to the one from Control. Pushed the timer to the corner of the bridge's front windows as he checked the straps on his Pilot's chair, making sure everything was snugged down tight.

Tugged again at the seams of his pressure suit—damned uncomfortable, nothing to be done about that—checked the seal of his helmet, twisted it to reset it before checking it again. "God I hate this thing," he muttered, shrugging his shoulders, stretching his neck.

"Amen to that," Sikuuku said, fidgeting himself.

"Everybody ready?" Henricksen called, glancing to either side.

"And waiting," Ogawa murmured.

Hanu—typically—just nodded, eyes locked on the panels in front of her.

Sikuuku leaned forward, pounding a fist on Henricksen's shoulder.

"Minute thirty," Henricksen told them, silence descending upon the bridge pod as he wrapped his fingers around the Pilot's controls.

Heads lifted, staring across the hangar bay to the doorway and the stars outside. Bodies fidgeted, fingers rattling nervously against panels as the launch clock ticked down, and everyone found that one last thing that needed doing before they completely ran out of time.

"Disengaging mag locks," Henricksen warned, pulling up a ship's schematic, tapping at the symbols on her nose and tail, belly and wings.

The ship shivered with an ominous, metallic *clunk*—the sound of the hangar's docking mechanisms releasing, retracting into the floor. *Scythe* stayed put for a second or two, and then lifted, suddenly weightless, drifting free in the gravityless environs of the hanger bay.

"Ogawa. Stabilizers."

"On it." A tap at Engineering's panel woke the engines in *Scythe*'s belly, filling the bridge with a thrumming hum.

Henricksen called up the feeds from the hull cameras, cycling through them until he found a rearward face view showing a soft blue glow—stabilizers, compensating for the absence of gravity. Holding *Scythe* steady in the hangar bay's cavernous space.

"By the way," Sikuuku drawled. "Taggert's got a bone to pick with you."

"Oh yeah? About what?"

"Baldini. Made it *quite* clear he wanted onto our crew. Thinks he's been blacklisted or something. Wants to know why *he* drew the short straw and got assigned to Mr. Attitude instead of one of the others."

"And you told him...?"

"Suck it up, buttercup."

Henricksen grunted, smiling inside his helmet. "Guessing he didn't like that."

"No, he did not."

The clock hit zero and Henricksen opened up Comms. "Control. This is *Scythe*. We are go for launch. Repeat, we are go for launch."

"Roger, *Scythe*. Perimeter is clear. Proceed in your own time."

"Acknowledged. We're taking her out." Henricksen left the channel open, letting Kinsey monitor their comms. Listened with half an ear to the low mutter of voices coming back to him—Taggert and the others watching the test run from the control room, huddled up around the monitoring stations, parsing through the data in real time. "Here we go," he murmured, touching at his station's panel.

Maneuvering jets fired, pulsing in waves. The stabilizers eased as *Scythe* lifted, putting some distance between herself and the hangar bay's gridded floor panels. More pulsing—harder this time, *Scythe*'s body shivering in time—and the ship slid forward, rotated, turning forty-five degrees as *Scythe* lined herself up with the hangar bay doors.

Henricksen sucked in a breath, blew it back out. "Alright. Here we go, boys and girls."

A touch at the panel in front of him fired the maneuvering jets in a long, hard burst. *Scythe* accelerated, escaping the hangar bay for the stars.

"Hanu. Status," Henricksen called as they cleared the station.

"Board shows green—all systems operating at nominal."

"Perimeter defenses?"

"Tracking us, but maintaining weapons hold." Hanu tilted her head, listening to a communication. "Station Control's compliments, Captain. Says we look pretty badass out here."

"Damn straight." *Scythe* waggled her wings, showing off a bit for the cameras. Fired her thrusters in a flaring, cobalt burst.

"Alright. That's enough." *Scythe* harrumphed in disappointment, making Henricksen smile. He glanced at a camera, tapping a finger to the side of his helmet as he cut the comms over to a private channel. "Later. Promise," he told her. "Once we're finished with Kinsey's tests."

"Holding you to that," *Scythe* warned.

"Noted." Henricksen switched the channel, toggling his voice back to the common address system. "Ogawa. What's our engine status?"

"Main propulsion is on-line. Jump drives—"

"Won't be needing that just yet." Nervous about taking the ship into hyperspace. Kept seeing that scattered cloud of metal bits that used to be One-Eight-Three and her four crew. "Let's keep it to maneuvering thrusters until we clear the station's perimeter."

Ogawa's head turned, visored face staring a moment. "Aye, sir," she said softly, turning back to her panels. She primed the main engines, monitoring the distance from station, bringing them on-line when they reached five kilometers out. "On your mark, Captain."

Henricksen nodded, flexing his fingers around the ship's control levers as he breathed in and out, heart thumping inside his chest. "Firing main propulsion in three. Two. One. Go!"

He touched a button and *Scythe*'s engines kicked in—a brutal burst of energy that pulverized Henricksen's body, pinning him to the Pilot's chair. A second kick, harder this time, and *Scythe* rocketed forward, leaving Henricksen holding on for dear life. Gasping for air as the violence of that acceleration bruised his flesh, twisted his bones.

Three seconds of suffering—three long, endless seconds—and the pressure suit finally adjusted, squeezing tightly to compensate for the stressors around him. Easing up once they found the magic middle—*Scythe* doing her own part by adjusting the atmosphere in the cabin, the gravity holding everything inside it in place.

Ten seconds and everything started to settle and come into alignment. Working together like it should. The pain melted away soon after, taking that twisting, rending feeling with it. That sense of slowly but surely being mashed to a pulp. Henricksen sucked in a shaking breath when he could manage it, feeling the heavy hand of engine-induced pressure lift away from his chest. Shrugged his shoulders, sitting up straighter as suit and cabin compensated, working in unison to strip the engine's abuse away.

"Everyone alright?" *Scythe*'s camera pivoted, AI voice drifting through Henricksen's helmet. "Hello? *Helloooo*?"

"Fine. We're fine, *Scythe*." Henricksen touched a shaking finger to the panel in front of him, adjusting the ship's course.

Crew moved around him, tugging at seat straps and pressure suit seams, breathing deep, laughing nervously as they looked around.

"Engines have one helluva kick." Sikuuku shrugged his shoulders, flicking at switches inside his pod. "'Bout wet myself before the damn suit eased off."

Fast though—god that ship was quick. And so far they'd only used the main engines on their lowest setting. Hadn't touched the auxiliary propulsion systems, never mind the hyperspace drives.

Henricksen touched at the panel, risking a bit more speed. Held on tight as *Scythe* shot forward, streaking past the first beacon, reaching the second less than a minute later. Yanked hard on the controls to slingshot her around it and felt the pressure suit kick in again as the stealth ship turned on a dime, slowing not the least bit as she retraced her path, rocketing along her outward bound track.

Quick, so very quick. Sims couldn't quite recreate that. Couldn't give you the *sense* of speed that came with a sharp-sided ship like this.

"Shit," Henricksen breathed, feathering the engines to slow the Raven down a bit. "Holy shit, *Scythe*. What happens if we open *all* the impulse engines up?"

"Dunno," she told him, smile in her voice. "Shall we find out?"

"Hell yeah." Henricksen scooched down in his chair, fingers wrapping around the flight sticks' handles. "Control, this is *Scythe*. Running an alpha test of the propulsion system. Ogawa. Bring everything online."

Ogawa looked around. "You sure, sir?"

"Oh yeah," he purred, smiling. "Time to have some fun."

Sikuuku snickered, yanking hard on his restraining straps to snug them down just that little bit more.

Hanu glanced around, visored face staring at Henricksen as she hunkered down, hands gripping the edge of her chair.

"Mains and auxiliaries at full, Captain," Ogawa said, bringing everything but the jump drives online.

"Right. Engines firing in three. Two. One. *Now!*"

Scythe screamed like a banshee as the impulse engines opened wide, a sound of purest, most ebullient joy erupting from her speakers as she raced past Dragoon station, banked and wheeled, chasing after the stars.

TWENTY-FOUR

Henricksen monitored the status of the four RV-Ns from the control room, scanning the video feeds projected on the room's huge windows, fingers reaching for the panels, the data streams on display.

Hard just sitting here, watching those birds fly. Wanted nothing more than to be out there with them, but *Scythe* was grounded at the moment. Shaw and a couple of her mech monkeys elbow deep in the RV-N's electronics, making a tweaks to her stealth system—the first of many, she warned—based on the data capture from her first run.

Likely take several sessions to implement and test all the changes. To their credit, Shaw's crew developed a schedule to space them all out and avoid too much down time—a maintenance rotation that kept four of the five ships flying at all times. Just so happened *Scythe*, being first out of the gate, was also the first one in the maintenance hopper. Oh, she'd be out there flying tomorrow—her first round of maintenance complete, all her piece-parts back where they belonged— but until then, Henricksen was stuck here. Watching from afar.

"God I hate this," he muttered, glowering at the ships outside, listening to Baldini prep for jump.

"It's *one* day." Sikuuku plunked down in a chair, lifted his feet and rested them on a panel. "We'll be back out there tomorrow and it'll be prick boy there sitting up here, watching the rest of us have fun." He flashed a smile and tipped a wink, neither of which did anything to improve Henricksen's mood.

He stabbed at the panel, opening comms. "Two-hop to Beacon Four, Baldini. And stay off the—"

"Yeah, yeah, yeah," a razzing voice cut in. AI voice, if you could believe it, impertinent as it was. "Stay off the stealth system. We all get it, Captain man. So relax, kick back, and let me and my man Baldini here cut loose and have a little fun."

Henricksen glowered at the video feed, the stealth ship outside. Lot of attitude in the Ravens these days. Lot of mouth and showing off. "Beacon Four," he said tightly. "We'll run data capture on our end."

"Roger-dodger!" A waggle of wings and the AI cut comms. Thrusters fired, lining the stealth ship up with the buckle, sharp-sided shape disappearing as it slipped into the hyperspace trough.

"What's that one calling itself now?" Sikuuku nodded to the feed on the control room's windows as the ship in question wobbled unsteadily through hyperspace, dumping out near the marker on the other side.

"*Sever*, I think."

"*Sever*. That's right." Sikuuku grunted, lips curving at the corners. "Guess that drunken lexicon wasn't the only thing *Scythe* shared around."

"Meaning?" Henricksen asked, sliding a distracted look the gunner's way.

"You didn't notice?" Sikuuku caught his eye, nodded to the video feed again. "*Scythe* down there in the hangar bay. Baldini's flying rocket jockey in *Sever*..." He trailed off, eyebrows lifting, letting Henricksen puzzle the rest out for himself.

Took him a while—didn't see the pattern at first, to be honest. Never *had* been much good at things like that. *Scythe* and *Sever*—two decidedly uncuddly names—and Petros flying *Shriek*. Mahal paired with *Sharp*. Janssen piloting *Snicker-snack*. "They've got a thing for blades, don't they? And the letter S," he added, frowning.

"Apparently," Sikuuku grunted, watching the images a while. "You suppose they got the idea from the Valkyries?"

"Maybe," Henricksen said doubtfully.

Valkyries chose their names based on Old Earth islands and deserts, not sibilant terms pertaining to knives and violence. But the thought was the same. A pattern of commonality in naming specific to a class of ship.

"They're growing up," Sikuuku murmured.

Henricksen glanced at him, surprised by the fondness in the gunner's voice. Turned his eyes back to the windows as *Shriek* made a run of the beacons—Petros showing off by short-hopping it from one to another. "Watch it, Petros," he warned, keying comms. "You burn out those engines you're not getting replacements for a while."

"Back off, buzzkill," *Shriek* chimed in. "These are *my* engines, and I'm pretty sure I'd know if—*ow-wow-wow!* Hot-hot-hot-hot-hot!"

Shriek slowed precipitously, propulsion system monitors red-lined and throwing all sorts of alerts. He cleared them and ran a round of diagnostics, cruising on impulse until his engines cooled down, and the propulsion system data returned to normal.

"Mouthy little bugger, ain't he?" Sikuuku nodded to *Shriek*'s overheated shape, pursed his lips, turning his eyes Henricksen's way. "You think we might've overdone it?"

"Maybe. Probably," Henricksen admitted. "They've got attitude, that's for sure."

Sikuuku nodded, face thoughtful, studying the video feeds of the ships outside. Head tilted as he listened to the banter passing back and forth across the comms channel. "Not sure all of that's us," he said sometime later. "Language update might make 'em colorful, but not *this* colorful. This..." He waved at the video images flickering across the glass separating the control room from the hangar deck beyond. "This is like a personality overhaul. No *way* our language lessons did that." He folded his arms, tucking his hands up tight. "We mighta been drunk but we weren't *that* drunk."

Henricksen shrugged again and moved closer to the windows—close enough that he could look down and see *Scythe* sitting in the hangar bay below. "Shaw says they've been listening in on the sim sessions."

"Oh god." Sikuuku sat up straight, eyes widening. "So Petros—"

"And Baldini." Henricksen turned around, leaned against a monitoring station's panels. "And Taggert."

Sikuuku whistled appreciatively. "That's a lotta attitude."

"Tell me about it."

"'Course, there's Hanu," the gunner said, after a moment's thought. "And Ogawa."

"Adaeze." Henricksen winced. "Fisker."

"Solid crew," Sikuuku told him. "Hopefully some of their common sense snuck in too."

"Hopefully," Henricksen murmured, thinking of *Hecate*. Missing her all over again. No time for cobwebs and melancholy memories, though, so he shook them off, offering a wry smile to counter Sikuuku's worried frown. "Whatever they are now, it's better than they were. Rather have a little attitude than some out-of-the-box intelligence. Can't quite trust an AI who doesn't have a little flare."

"Flare." Sikuuku chuckled. "Is *that* what you call it?"

"Something like that." Henricksen pushed away from the panel, watching *Shriek* turn in a circle, looping round and round.

Three days they'd been at it, working the RV-Ns amongst the stars. Three days running test patterns while Kinsey and his engineers captured data on the engines and the stealth system, the airframe interactions with both. Oceans of data collected en masse over the course of endless test sessions. Downloaded from the ships to the station's systems for processing and analytics.

Lived and died by that data—a precious commodity leveraged by Kinsey and his engineers. Shaw, to a certain extent. Pilots, though...pilots honestly weren't all that interested. More to flying than just data. More to a *ship* than the information it pumped out. Facts and figures were one thing, but what pilots wanted was the *feel* of the ship. The tactile experience the sims approximated—g-loads and pressure changes, atmosphere, everything that came with crewing a vessel in space—but never quite got right.

Sims weren't real, after all, no matter how advanced the software and hardware the Fleet used. But the ship...when he sat in her cockpit, Henricksen finally knew what was *really* going on with *Scythe*. Made that connection that linked pilot and AI: hands on controls, feet pressed to the shivering deck plates, breastplate rattling with the bass hum of the engines as propulsion systems kicked in, hammering at his bones.

Tactile experiences—*that* was a ship in transit, not Kinsey's facts and figures. The sim's software recreating flight. Approximating the stars the stars that were everywhere. Blanketing the galaxy around them.

Missed that feeling, piloting a ship on the move, surrounded by stars. Nervy, jumping *Scythe* into hyperspace that first time. Nervier still, bringing the cloaking system online. Scary as hell feeling that stealth shield wrap her, the sense of cold and electricity that came with it lifting the hair on the back of his neck. And below it, in that not-quite-audible range of hearing, a whining *thrum*. A sound felt more than heard. A noise that set his eyeballs to jittering, waking a roiling in his belly that almost made him want to throw up.

Creepy, Sikuuku called it. Prickling and weird.

Henricksen wasn't quite sure how to describe the sensation himself, but he did know he didn't need Hanu to tell him when that stealth shield slid into place. Never felt anything like that cloaking system. Remembered Shaw mentioning something about baffling around the bridge pod and thought that was a very, *very* fine idea.

Baffling would have to wait, though. Get in line behind the engine incompatibility work. Crew's comfort was one thing. Preventing the crew from blowing up by accident? *Tiny* bit more important.

Failsafe, he reminded himself, watching *Snicker-snack* shimmer, cloak coming on-line. *AIs won't let us do that. Got strict orders not to let us grunt pilots run the jump drives and the cloaking system at the same time.*

But AIs were fallible, and these AIs still young. Unknown and untried. Nothing at all like battered, battle-scarred *Hecate* who'd spent two hundred years flying. Machines glitched—not often, but it did happen. Even sentient, super-powered artificial intelligences sometimes had a bad day. Better to just fix the chassis and remove the issue entirely.

Failsafe was still a workaround. A temporary fix, not a solution to a problem.

Henricksen watched the ships a while, thinking that over. Touched at the panel to open comms. "Petros. One last run and then I want you back in the hangar."

"Aww, man!" *Shriek* objected. "We just got *out* here."

"Yeah, yeah. Quit your bitchin' and finish up. You're next in the maintenance rotation, bucko, and Shaw—"

"Shaw's a butcher," *Shriek* grumped. "I don't *wanna* come back inside."

"Really." Henricksen shared a smile with Sikuuku. "So you *don't* want those upgrades Shaw's—"

"Upgrades? No one mentioned upgrades." A panel came to life, data windows opening and closing, information scrolling lightning quick as *Shriek* read through Shaw's reports, digesting the design specs and maintenance plan, all the fancy, whizz-bang new features on offer. "Three percent efficiency upgrade!" *Shriek* whistled appreciatively, dipped his wings and circled around. "On my way, Captain, sir!" Comms crackled, channel opening in the hangar deck below. "All hands. Clear the deck. I'm coming in!"

"Flare," Sikuuku grunted, shaking his head. "God save us all."

#

Henricksen woke to the ominous sound of thudding. Not rattling. Not tapping. *Thudding.* A thunderous banging, coming from the front room of his quarters. A sound his muzzy, sleep-deprived brain eventually translated as someone pounding incessantly on his door.

"Not now," he moaned, pulling the blankets over his head.

No idea what time it was, but it had to be early. Felt like he'd just laid down, barely closed his eyes. Alarm hadn't gone off, anyway—thing shrieked bloody murder to wake him, no way he would have slept through that—and since he'd rolled into bed after curfew, there shouldn't be anyone awake and moving around, much less banging on his door at this hour.

Drunk crewman, he thought. *Got turned around, thinks this is a barracks. Probably looking for a booty call.*

"Go 'way," Henricksen mumbled, pulling the pillow over his head.

Two days since *Scythe* cycled out of maintenance. Two long, hard days of training, trying to get as much flight time in as possible before Kinsey pulled the plug. Called in his marker and sent them out to that asteroid field for a recon mission.

That put sleep at a premium. The last thing he needed was some drunk crewman interrupting his beauty sleep because he was looking for some action.

"Go 'way," Henricksen repeated when the fist kept pounding. Rolled over, wincing at the pain of sore ribs and aching muscles, joints turned stiff and balky, on the edge of locking up.

Desperately abused body—thank the pressure suit for that. Kept the crew from getting jellified by the g-loads the Raven's flight path put on them, but they bruised the body something fierce. Made him feel like he'd gone ten rounds with a deranged elephant by the time he stripped it off.

And the training itself...

Hours in the cockpit, piloting that brutally fast stealth ship. Hours of processing reams upon reams of information, focused in the entire time. Mind dialed down and locked on tight.

Brain suffered for it. Felt like someone'd carved off the top of his skull and shoved a load of cotton batting inside his head. But the instincts came. The reflexes. That almost preternatural anticipation a pilot felt when they finally connected with a ship.

Missed that feeling. Long time since Henricksen felt anything like that. Not the same as with *Hecate*—not even close—but *Scythe...Scythe* was something special. Different from any other ship he'd flown.

Not Hecate, *though. Never that.*

He drifted, thinking of her. Dreaming of standing on *Hecate*'s bridge. But the pounding pulled his mind back to the here and now.

"Hell." He rolled onto his back, hand flailing for the button that activated the clock set in the bedside table.

The projection system woke, casting cool, blue numbers on the wall.

0450—later than he'd thought. Early, but not *that* early. Well past drunken booty call time, which meant that pounding on his door was serious. A problem Henricksen, as captain of this stealth ship squadron and senior officer assigned to the RV-N project, probably shouldn't ignore.

"Fuck."

He threw off the covers, wide awake now and all but jittering with worry. Rolled over, wincing as overused muscles protested, and climbed out of bed. Stalked across the bedroom naked but for his underwear, hand lifting to shade his eyes as the motion sensors kicked in, drowning the room in harsh, white light.

Bang-bang! Bang-bang-bang!

"I'm coming! I'm coming!"

He shambled across the from room, moving as quickly as his tired, sore body would allow. Grabbed the heavy wheel set in the outer door's center, and spun it. Hit the latch and pulled it wide.

"What?" he snapped. "What's so goddamn—?"

"It's about time, Captain."

Angry voice, disapproving—Henricksen's sleep-starved brain registered that. He blinked a few times, gritty eyes trying to understand the face on the other side of that door hat went with it. The stiffly starched shirt and perfectly pleated trousers, jacket tailored to hang just so.

Only one person he knew of that could look that pressed and perfect at this indecently early hour of the morning.

"Kinsey." Henricksen folded his arms, leaning against the doorframe. "Slumming it, I see."

Kinsey frowned, tugging at his jacket's cuffs. "Can I come in, Captain?"

"What are you doing here?" Henricksen demanded, standing his ground. Blocking the doorway with his body. "And what the hell is so important you came all the way down here to wake me up in the middle of the goddamn night?"

"We've had a communication." Kinsey pursed his lips, head tilting. "We need to talk."

Henricksen went very still, skin prickling with goosebumps as a sudden and intense feeling of cold washed over him, settling deep inside his bones. "Damn. God damn," he breathed, rubbing at his face, wishing he'd had the presence of mind to at least grab a pair of pants before answering the door. "Muzzy as hell, Kinsey. Can it wait an hour or—?"

"No," he said flatly, dark eyes blinking slowly as he stared at Henricksen on the opposite side of the door. "Time is of the essence, Captain. We need to talk now."

"Hell." Henricksen straightened up, shoving past Kinsey as he stalked across the hall.

"Where are you—?"

"It's four fucking early in the morning. If I'm up, he's up." Henricksen hooked a thumb at Sikuuku's door, throwing a look at Kinsey over his shoulder. "And I'm too damned tired to repeat everything you're gonna tell me just so Sleeping Beauty in there can finish his dreams of Tahitian beauties." He raised a clenched fist, hammering on Sikuuku's door. "Up!" he shouted. "Up, you lazy bastard!"

Took him damn near as long to rouse Sikuuku as it took Kinsey to get Henricksen out of his own bed. The grumbling came first—muffled by the triple-thick layers of that composite metal door—followed by cursing and a chaotic banging that sounded suspiciously like many heavy things being picked up and tossed around.

Henricksen glanced at Kinsey behind him, flashing as a thumbs up. Faced around as the door whipped open, revealing a bleary-eyed Sikuuku standing naked as a jaybird on the other side.

"What?" he snapped, yawning widely. "What's so goddamn—shit." The gunner rubbed at his face, staring murder at Kinsey across the hall. "This can't be good."

"Quarters." Henricksen nodded to the open door behind him. "Now."

"Why do I—?"

"Misery loves company, Akiwane." Henricksen slid a look at Kinsey standing outside his door. "And I think you're gonna wanna hear this."

"They're *all* going to want to hear this." Kinsey moved a step forward. "Wake your crew, Captain. It'll go easier if they all hear what I have to say at the same time."

"*All* of them?" Henricksen turned around, brow knitting in confusion, synapses firing sluggishly in his sleep-fogged mind. "You're launching us," he breathed, finally making the connection. He reached for Kinsey, fingers wrapping around his arm. "Now? You're launching us *now*?"

"I told you, Captain. Time is of the essence." Kinsey shook his hand off, brushing wrinkles from his oh-so-fine jacket. Touched at his wrist, consulting that ancient watch he wore. "It's coming up on 0500 now. I'll expect your crews in the debriefing room at 0600." A nod and Kinsey stepped past him, moving down the hall. "One hour, Captain," he said, looking back over his shoulder. "Use the time wisely."

"Wait," Henricksen called. "What about—"

"One hour," Kinsey repeated, marching down the hallway with that distinctive hitching, rolling gate. "And for god's sake take a shower, would you? Grab a clean uniform. At least *try* to look professional before you brief our crews on this mission."

"Prick," Henricksen muttered after him, watching Kinsey disappear around a corner. He slid his eyes to Sikuuku standing buck naked in the doorway. "How the hell did you ever get to be friends with him?"

"Acquaintances," Sikuuku corrected, yawning widely, scrubbing fingers through his short-clipped hair. "Told you, we met a few years ago. Ran into each other every now and then." A pause as he leaned out of the doorway, searching the empty hall. "Not sure anyone's really *friends* with Kinsey. Knows a lot of people, but I haven't met anyone who referred to him as a friend."

Henricksen grunted, shivering as the cold of the hallway soaked through his skin. An icy chill that infected the entirety of the station. Pervasive as the mildewed stench blanketing its spaces. "Wake Shaw," he said, nodding to the end of the hall. "Tell her she needs to get *Snicker-snack* sorted." They'd taken him down for maintenance, planned to keep him out of the flight rotation until tomorrow. "Wake the crew after that. Make sure they grab breakfast."

Long day ahead of them. They'd need all the calories they could get.

Sikuuku pursed his lips, eyebrows lifting. "Early wake up. Crew's not gonna like that."

"Tough," Henricksen told him. "You heard the man: flight briefing at 0600. You make sure the flight crews get their asses down to the debriefing room on time."

Sikuuku screwed up his face, on the edge of refusing. Changed his mind when Henricksen gave him a good glare. "Fine," he huffed, stepping into the hall.

"Whoa there, partner." Henricksen stopped him dead with a hand to his chest. Glanced meaningfully at the free-swinging manhood dangling between the gunner's legs. "Grab some pants first, *then* go wake everyone up."

"Prude." Sikuuku managed a tired smile. Retreated to his bedroom as ordered, drawers and doors banging as he dug around searching for something moderately clean to wear.

Henricksen left him to it. Turned around and headed across the hall to his own quarters, shivers growing worse with each step.

Shower seemed like a good idea all of a sudden. A very fine idea, in fact.

TWENTY-FIVE

The shower helped immensely. Woke Henricksen up a bit. Leeched the station's pervasive cold from his weary bones. He stepped into the hallway dressed in a fresh uniform—midnight dark pants and jacket, those silver captain's stars winking brightly on his collar—ducked into the mess hall to grab some breakfast, forcing a couple of pastries on a protesting stomach, chasing them down with a hastily gulped cup of coffee before slipping back out again.

Passed a few yawning crew along the way—shadow eyed and half asleep, rubbing at weary faces and bleary eyes—but he didn't see Sikuuku. Figured he was still banging on doors, trying to round everyone up. Thought about checking his quarters, but the last thing Henricksen needed this morning was another peep show. One sneak peek of the gunner's genitals was quite enough, thank you very much.

A check of the time showed it was just going on 0530, so Henricksen strolled down the hallway to the pressure door protecting the entrance to the RV-N crew's berthings, buzzed through with his security code and walked the length of the corridor on the other side. Climbed the stairs at the end and stepped into the darkened control room, lights coming on at the edges as he shut the door and ambled over to the floor-to-ceiling windows.

Stopped there and looked down on the hangar bay. On Shaw and her mech gang—a dozen or so deck crew clustered near the back end of *Snicker-snack*'s sharp-sided shape—dodging around each another as they buttoned up the hull panels protecting the stealth ship's engines. Wrenches turning a mile a minute as they raced to finish up their maintenance on the stealth ship's propulsion system and return the RV-N to service.

The rest of the squadron squatted nearby, huddled up in a tight circle near the hangar bay's center. *Scythe* among them, though damned if Henricksen could pick her out. Stealth ships all looked the same in the hangar bay's gloom.

Scythe and *Shriek*, *Sharp* and *Sever*, all of them waiting on *Snicker-Snack* to get his act together so they could head out into the stars. Henricksen stared at them, studying them. The way they blended into the darkness. Wrapped the shadows around them to hide in plain sight. Touched at a panel and opened a channel to the hangar bay—private communication, pinpointing one of the ships below.

"*Scythe*," he called softly, eyes flicking across the clustered ships, wondering which shape was hers.

"Good morning, Captain," she greeted him. "I hear we're in for an adventure."

Laughter in *Scythe*'s voice. Excitement and anticipation.

He envied her for that. Remembered those feelings, even shared them once upon a time. Back when he was a boot ensign fresh out of combat school. These days, though...six ships and a couple of decades in the military changed things.

Gave him a different view on combat. Made him appreciate the quiet times in between. Nothing but he and *Hecate,* the crew and the stars.

"Garrett?"

Shadowed shape near the control room's doorway, footsteps approaching, hand settling on Henricksen's shoulder. Sikuuku stepped in behind him, worried face reflecting off the control room's reinforced glass. Cords of thick muscle bulging beneath a short-sleeved, black t-shirt. Scar tissue twisting in ragged patterns on the gunner's forearms, burn marks twining amongst the blue-black tattoos he'd worn for years and years.

Henricksen stared at them, remembering *Hecate* dying. The sound of Sikuuku's screams.

"Garrett?"

The hand slipped to Henricksen's bicep, fingers wrapping around it, squeezing hard. Pulled him around, bringing him face to face with that tattooed visage. Friendly face. Worried now. Creases showing around the eyes.

"Everything alright?"

"Yeah." Henricksen touched at his face with trembling fingers, tracing the long line of that jagged scar he wore. "Yeah. Just tired." He mustered a bit of humor, offering a sickly smile. "Too goddamn early for this shit."

"Tell me about," Sikuuku snorted, head turning as the door to the behind him opened.

Janssen stepped in with half dozen crew hot on his heels. Nodded to Sikuuku and Henricksen as he crossed the control room, motioning for the other crew to follow. Glanced back as he opened the door to the sim area, giving Henricksen a curious look before slipping in, heading for the debriefing room on the other side.

"We should probably get in there." Sikuuku nodded after them, checking the clock. "Kinsey said 0600. Look awful bad if the big boss himself was late."

Henricksen smiled crookedly. "Since when do you worry how I look?"

"Always. You know that, Garrett."

Serious tone now. Deadly serious look on Sikuuku's.

Henricksen's smile slipped, sliding slowly from his face. "Yeah," he said softly. "Yeah, I do." He wrapped a hand around the gunner's forearm, squeezing it hard. Glanced behind him at the windows, thinking of Shaw and her crew, wishing they'd hurry it up and get *Snicker-snack* back together because, dammit, they were out of time. Kinsey in an all-fired hurry to launch.

"Garrett."

Sikuuku again. Nagging. Impatient. Worried still.

"Yeah." Henricksen faced around, clapped the gunner on the shoulder. "Let's go."

Crew were just settling into their seats in the debriefing room when Henricksen and Sikuuku arrived. Kinsey glanced up from his place at the podium, dark eyes following them as they moved to the back of the room—standing, not sitting like the rest of the crew. Watching Kinsey from that vantage point as stared down a last few stragglers, waiting until they found their seats before addressing the room. Laying it all out.

Well, not quite *everything*. Mostly he skimmed across the surface, skipping most of the details along the way. That ugly business on Kepler. The stolen secrets and forced relocation.

The nannites, and *Hecate*—those details most of all. *Important* details that Kinsey glossed over. Offering just a few, terse statements to sum everything up.

"Information gathering mission," he told them. "You locate a can, retrieve it and come home. Simple as that."

"Simple," Sikuuku grunted. "Not fucking likely." He frowned, listening, as Kinsey kept talking, keyed into the projection system, bringing a star chart up. "He's not gonna tell them, is he?" he said, pitching his voice low.

"Doesn't look like it."

"Think we should?"

"Oh, I plan to." Henricksen turned his head, sliding a look the gunner's way. "Crew deserves to know—"

"Drop coordinates," Kinsey said loudly, drawing Henricksen's eyes back to the front of the room. He stared a moment, dark eyes blinking slowly, reached inside his jacket and pulled a reader out. Plugged it into the lectern, replacing the images on the wall with the data from that handheld device.

Long strings of data. Half a dozen sets of multi-partite numbers that Henricksen recognized as coordinates—markers that meant precisely jack without a star chart for reference.

"What the hell is this?" Henricksen demanded, nodding to the numbers on the wall.

Kinsey held up a finger, toggling the projection system's settings to bring the star chart back. "The drop coordinates are here," he explained, zooming in on one planet in particular. A lonely, red orb that was way, *way* out.

Henricksen squinted, reading the data tag beneath it. "Terinassis. That's a Class II, right?"

Kinsey nodded slowly. "Surveys completed a decade ago. Samples collected, but that's about it."

Which meant it hadn't been terraformed. Might *never* be terraformed if the data tagged to that star chart was correct.

Young planet, from the look of it. Big sucker, though. Core analysis showed a blast furnace center—heavy metals laced with uranium and thorium deposits—surrounded by a bubbling, fire-encrusted surface. Lava erupting in geysers, magma flowing in crisscrossing rivers, painting the planet in a red-orange glow.

Moons orbiting around it—many and large, pulling at the molten surface, making the crust swell and break like tides. Atmosphere, of a sort—a toxic stew surrounding the planet—but no water. Not a drop of liquid anywhere.

"Nice place." Taggert twisted, searching for Henricksen standing near the back wall. "How the hell are we supposed to retrieve anything from there?"

"Not there." Kinsey stared at the back of Taggert's head, waiting until he faced back around. Touched at the reader's screen to reorient the star chart, moving Terinassis to the center, highlighting a section of space nearby. "Here," he said, pointing to the corresponding image projecting on the wall.

"Great. Another asteroid field." Taggert sat back, shaking his head in disgust.

Ogawa leaned forward, reaching for Taggert's arm. Grabbed it and shook it, wanting his attention. "Tag. It's the same one." She glanced at him, flicked a finger at the image on the wall. "That's the same asteroid field the engineers programmed into the sims."

"The very same." Kinsey nodded.

"And the drop coordinates this spook of yours sent?" Janssen asked, speaking up.

"Inside." Kinsey touched at the reader again, toggling the screen back to the long lines of coordinates, layering them onto the star chart next to a tiny red dot. "That asteroid field is twenty kilometers long and almost as wide, half again as deep."

Which meant rocks, and lots of them. An ocean of tumbling obstacles with no fixed position, and no steady orbit.

"*Inside*," Janssen repeated, eyes flicking to Henricksen at the back. "You want us to go *in* there to pick up this canister of yours."

"Have to," Taggert said, picking at his lip. "No way for the canister to clear all that debris without some kind of propulsion. And you add propulsion, the DSR will pick it up." He grunted, thinking, shaking his head. "Must've stuck it an airlock. Garbage shoot or something. Explosive decompression would shoot it out pretty far—"

"But not far enough to clear the asteroid field," Kinsey cut in. "May I continue, Mr. Taggert, or would you like to take over?" He stepped from behind the podium, inviting the engineer to slide in, but Taggert just scowled. Slouched in his chair and tucked up his arms, staring fixedly at the wall.

Sikuuku nudged at Henricksen's side, nodding to Kinsey and Taggert. Moved a step forward when he shrugged and pointed at the star chart projected on the wall. "Don't suppose that can has a beacon? Some kind of signal we can track?"

"Can't risk it," Kinsey told him. "A signal, any kind of electronic noise— anything *we* can pick up, the DSR can pick up."

"Great. Just fucking great." Taggert barked a bitter laugh, throwing his hands in the air. "Goddamn needle in a haystack trying to find a metal can with no beacon and all those rocks wandering about."

Kinsey flicked his fingers. "RV-Ns are small and maneuverable." He reached over, toggling the display again, splitting the screen to lay two data windows side-by-side: star chart on the left, RV-N design specs on the right. "You've run that asteroid field dozens of times in simulation—"

"Sims aren't real," Henricksen growled. "I keep telling you that."

Kinsey grimaced, tugging at his cuffs, smoothing the lapels of his pinstriped jacket. A perfectly *pressed* jacket, because that was Kinsey: buttoned up and strapped down, starched within an inch of his life. "What do you want from me, Captain?"

Cold voice now. Face a mask of stone.

Henricksen pushed away from the wall, chin lifting as he stared Kinsey down. "Recon mission. In and out. Get the scans you want. Figure out the lay of the land—"

"No," Kinsey told him, shaking his head.

"Why the hell not?" Henricksen demanded, anger building inside him.

"No *time,* Captain."

"No time." Henricksen rubbed at his face, patience running short. "What the *fuck* does that mean, no time? You've waited *months*—"

"It means this." Kinsey wiped the reader's display, banishing the star chart, replacing it with an image of stars and ships.

An image that moved—one picture becoming many as a video feed started up.

Henricksen watched it a while, only half paying attention. He'd seen this before—twice, in fact, once with his own eyes, a second time in Kinsey's quarters. Ships and stars, images shot from *Hecate's* perspective. Captured in those last moments before she died.

But the crew hadn't seen it. None of them but Sikuuku, who was there when *Hecate* went down.

"What is this?" Taggert leaned forward, staring intently from his seat in the front row.

"Just watch," Kinsey said quietly, eyes flicking to Henricksen standing at the back of the room. "The video explains itself."

Taggert twisted, brow wrinkling in question. Glanced at Ogawa when she touched his arm, whispered something in his ear. Shrugged his shoulders and faced around, slouching down in his chair. Watching in silence with the others as the images advanced, showing a cluster of ships in the distance, stars glowing softly around them.

Closer in and the Cepheid appeared—that oversized, silver orb in all its deadly glory.

"Almost looks peaceful," Sikuuku murmured, stepping to Henricksen's side. "Hard to believe it all went so wrong."

Henricksen nodded without looking, focusing on a muted comms track in the background—*Hecate's* voice and *Seychelles. Gogmagog's* grinding, groaning drawl.

Flashes of light as the first of the droned ships skipped away, camera slewing when one of them speared *Hecate* in the side. He closed his eyes, not wanting to see the rest of it. Fingers curling around the back of the chair in front of him as his mind replayed it anyway. Every last minute of that encounter. Right up to the moment when *Hecate* disappeared—body shredded, AI mind snuffed out in an instant.

"What was that?" Ogawa asked when the video finally ended. "That silver cloud that came out of the round ship—"

"Cepheid," Taggert interrupted. "That was a Cepheid, right?"

Kinsey nodded slowly. Quirked an eyebrow, redirecting Ogawa's question to Henricksen at the back of the room.

Heads turned, eyes staring, everyone waiting for Henricksen to answer.

"Nannites," he said, hating the word. How cold it sounded. How numb he felt inside.

"Modified nannites," Kinsey corrected. "Ship killers, in this case."

Henricksen grimaced, looking away. "Run it back," he said, flicking his fingers. Forcing himself to watch this time. Everything. Every last moment. Right up to when *Hecate* died.

"What ship is this?" Ogawa asked partway through. "The angle...whose cameras recorded this?"

Sikuuku looked at him, waiting for him to answer, but Henricksen just stood there, feeling cold all over. Tremor waking in his hands.

"What does it matter?" he heard Kinsey say, and that was it. The cold retreated, burned away by a sudden and overwhelming feeling of anger.

"*Hecate*," Henricksen rasped, voice shaking, chest tight with pain. "Her name is *Hecate*."

Was, his traitorous mind corrected. Hecate*'s dead now. Nothing left but her ghost.*

"And it damn well matters," he said, glaring at Kinsey across the room.

Kinsey stared blandly back, dark eyes blinking slowly. Touched at a panel set in the lectern and swapped *Hecate*'s feed for another—more stars, more nannites, more ships dying—and that one for another, and another, cycling through half a dozen different video feeds in all. "These ships mattered too, Captain." He froze the last feed on an image of destruction. "Do you know who *they* are?"

"When did this happen?" Henricksen whispered, voice hushed.

"Two days ago." Soft voice from Kinsey this time. Surprisingly soft for such a cold, stiff man.

"Two days. Hell," he breathed, covering his eyes. "How many? How many other ships have these nannites killed?"

"Dozens," Kinsey told him, letting that single word hang in the air. "Ten in this encounter alone, before *Gogmagog* managed to neutralize the threat."

"Neutralize?" Henricksen dropped his hands, head lifting. "How?"

"Drowned them in broad spectrum lasers. Ordered a tactical nuclear strike when that didn't work."

"Drowned them," Sikuuku repeated, staring in horror. "You mean the ships? He destroyed his own ships?"

"And took the nannites out with them."

"*Why*?" Sikuuku demanded, face livid. "There *had* to be another way!"

"No. There wasn't," Kinsey said, turning a flat-eyed stare the gunner's way. "You're not getting this. These things are a plague. An *infection*." He twisted, stabbing a finger at the wall. "They need to be stopped. At *any* cost."

"And grabbing this canister of yours." Taggert nodded to the images in front of him. "That's somehow gonna do that?"

Kinsey stared, sneering, tugging at his cuffs again. "Knowledge is power, Mr. Taggert. And there's more in that canister than information on nannites."

A touch at his prosthetic arm, eyes flicking to Henricksen's face.

"What if it's not there?" Taggert asked, turning around, lobbing his question at Henricksen standing in the back. "What if we can't find it? I mean, the damned thing's got no beacon, right? We could search that asteroid field a dozen times over and still miss it. Hell, if that can's small enough, we could run it right over and never even—"

"Enough!" Henricksen roared, cutting Taggert off.

He stared a moment—surprised, upset—glanced at Ogawa beside him and slumped down, sulking. Mumbling something about "red herrings" and "wild goose chases" under his breath.

Henricksen sighed, hand lifting, shaking his head in apology. Sucked in a breath as the anger faded, feeling weary—just weary, now. Aching in his soul. "Enough, Taggert. Just…" A glance at Kinsey. "Just let the man speak."

A nod from Kinsey—acknowledgment, perhaps gratitude—and he stepped from behind the podium, scanning his eyes across the room. "The truth is there are a thousand ways this could go wrong. And just one way it can go right."

"Find your thing-a-ma-jigger." Sikuuku waved vaguely. "This canister of yours."

"Can't guarantee it's a canister," Kinsey told him. "But, yes. The payload our contact put out there."

"Wait a minute." Taggert sat up straight, face indignant. "If it's not a canister, how are we supposed to—"

"It will be *some* kind of composite metal object, Mr. Taggert." Kinsey frowned in annoyance. "I just can't guarantee it will be a *canister,* per se."

Taggert sat back, sulking again. He was just full of sulky looks today. "Just saying it would be *nice* if we knew what the damn thing was so we knew what to look for."

"Kid's got a point," Sikuuku muttered, sliding his eyes Henricksen's way. "You believe him?" A nod to Kinsey at the front of the room. "You think that canister or whatever it is really has all the information we need to make that happen? Save the universe from the nannite scourge?"

"No idea," Henricksen told him. "Could be his spook left us a buncha recipes. Whole goddamn thing might be a complete waste of time."

"She's not *my* spook, Captain."

Good ears on Kinsey. Hadn't expected him to hear that.

"And I assure you there are no recipes—"

"Joke, Kinsey. Lighten up."

Kinsey's face darkened, voice turning cold. "I'll lighten up once those birds are flying, Captain. Now prep your ships and get them loaded. I want your squadron launched within the hour." He flicked his eyes around the room, looking every last person in the face. Spun on his heel and stalked stiff-backed across the room, hauled the door open and slammed it shut behind him.

The room went very still after Kinsey exited, everyone looking at each other, sneaking glances at Henricksen standing in the back.

Waiting for orders. Wondering what he'd say. Afraid to be the first one to ask what came next.

"Captain," Sikuuku prompted, sticking an elbow in his side.

"Yeah. I know." Henricksen chewed his lip, thinking, staring at that last frozen image projected on the wall. Straightened and walked to the front of the room to address the crew in their chairs. "You heard the man." He hooked a thumb to the door, indicating Kinsey on the other side. "Grab your flight suits and head down to the hangar bay. We've got ships to prep and, apparently, a mission involving a can."

TWENTY-SIX

Scythe dropped out of jump a good five-hundred-thousand kilometers from the Terinassis asteroid field—light years from anything but that uninhabited planet, the rock field nearby. No ship's signals pinging on the monitoring grid. No sensor sweeps or listening devices. Nothing at *all,* based on the scan results, except that asteroid field, and that molten death ball of a planet.

Henricksen studied them both as Hanu ran another set of scans. Asteroid field was problematic—all that tumbling junk wreaked havoc on the sensors, no way to tell what lurked inside. Then again, that problem worked both ways, since anything inside the asteroid field—scavengers, DSR, some as-yet-undiscovered lifeform, whatever—couldn't get a fix on them either.

Still…

Henricksen frowned, distinctly uneasy. Didn't like missing intel. Bad juju heading out on a mission with only sketchy information on hand. "Kill the engines."

"Aye." Ogawa touched at her panel, shutting *Scythe*'s propulsion system down. "Jump drives are offline. Main propulsion is primed and ready. You just give the word."

"Hold for now," he told her, studying the stars outside. "Scan."

"Nothing, sir." Hanu looked up and around. "Just us. And them, of course." A nod to the asteroid field way, way off.

Henricksen grunted, tapping at his panel, surveying the sensors' scans himself. Shut it all down after a cursory look—nothing but stars out there and vacuum, a molten planet and acres upon acres of tumbling rocks—and opened a secure channel, sending an encrypted message back to Kinsey on Dragoon to let him know they'd arrived.

Acknowledged Kinsey's confirmation when it came back, the order that came with it, telling them to proceed into the asteroid field—a daunting, decidedly nervy consideration, now that they were actually here.

Lot of rocks out there. So many places for things to go wrong. But orders were orders—no turning back now. No giving up and going home.

A deep breath and Henricksen reached for the control stick, hesitated and moved his hand past it to Helm's panel. Brought up the data from Scan's sensors, making one last check—no change, just *Scythe*'s shape, limned in darkness and a sea of stars—before bringing up the asteroid field's schematic. A crude, hastily created thing that was mostly guesswork, offering more questions than answers because no one had bothered to actually conduct a proper survey of the damned thing.

Not really important—star charts warned ships away from asteroid fields, mostly. Might never have been important if the DSR hadn't moved themselves in.

"Useless piece of shit," he muttered, setting his flight controls.

"Sir?" Hanu twisted, looking around.

"Nothing," he sighed, pushing the mostly useless map to the front windows, looking from it to the actual asteroid field outside. "Alright, Hanu." He gripped the control stick with one hand, tugging at the seat's straps with the other. "Fire up that stealth system. Let's see if *Scythe*'s fancy-schmancy cloak works as advertised."

"Aye—"

"Stealth system online," *Scythe* interrupted, beating her to the punch.

Hanu's head lifted, visored face staring at the camera. "I was getting to it. I just—"

"Yeah, yeah. Next time, toots." *Scythe* activated her sensors—Hanu's job, scan tech was *not* happy about losing out on that task as well—scanning the area around them. "Wasteland," she reported. "Oh, wait. Scratch that. Stand by for company."

Perimeter alarms sounded, sensors reporting jump displacements behind them and to either side.

"What the hell?" Henricksen reached for the ship's controls, muscles tensing, adrenaline kicking in. "Hanu! What—"

"Friendlies." Hanu consulted her panel, head lifting as the hyperspace buckles resolved, spitting four sharp-sided shapes out. "Looks like our little buddies got antsy."

"Goddammit, *Shriek*." Henricksen stabbed at Comms, opening a secure channel to the other stealth ships. "I told you to *wait,* Petros. That means hang back until—"

"Waiting's for chumps," *Shriek* grumbled. "No way I'm sitting back there while you guys have all the fun."

Henricksen glared at the camera feed as *Shriek* approached, moving up on *Scythe's* starboard side. "Shut down your engines," he ordered. "No telling what's out here, and there's no sense broadcasting our presence to the entire galaxy."

Scans still came up empty, nothing but *Scythe* and those other four Ravens in the vicinity, but you could never be too careful. Never quite knew what eyes and ears lurked about.

"Spin up your cloaks while you're at it," Henricksen added. "We're supposed to be sneaking, remember?"

"Roger-dodger, Cap'n." *Shriek's* engines snuffed out, sharp-sided shape shimmering as his stealth system came online.

Turned him invisible in an instant—nothing at all showing to the naked eye, not a blip appearing on Scan.

"*Scythe*?" Henricksen glanced up at a camera. "You got that magic decoder ring ready?"

"You betcha!" She toggled her sensors, bringing a brand new array online.

Purpose-built equipment, specially designed for the Ravens. Tuned to the stealth system's frequency and the garbled, white noise energy signature it put out. Picked it out from the rest of the background noise of space around it, showing the cloaked ship as a ghostly, flickering image, wavering in and out on Scan.

Scythe fired up the new array and pointed it in *Shriek*'s direction, fiddling with the settings until his signature appeared.

Shriek giggled as the sensors swept across his body. "Ooh. That tickles!"

"Shut it down, *Shriek*," Henricksen growled. "I could do without all the chatter."

"Roger. Shuttin' it down, boss." *Shriek* went quiet, but the channel stayed open. "Sneak-sneak-sneak," he snickered. "Sneaky-sneak-sneak-sneak-sneak."

"*Shriek!*"

"Sorry, sorry, sorry." The line clicked as *Shriek* shut the channel down.

"Blabbermouth," Henricksen muttered.

"Your fault," Ogawa reminded him, sparing a look for the gunner inside his pod. "You and Trigger there did this to them with that drunk-icon you built."

"Trigger?" Sikuuku leaned out of his pod. "Trigger was a *horse*."

Ogawa shrugged. "Takes one to know one. Especially the hind end."

"Oh, so now I'm the *ass* end of a—"

"Shut it down! Both of you! *All* of you," Henricksen ordered, so Hanu wouldn't feel left out. He glanced around, looking at each of them, waggling a finger at Sikuuku until he tucked back inside his pod.

Lot of nerves in that cockpit—felt it, sensed it, even if he couldn't see the crew's faces. Lot of fear and uncertainty underneath the joking, nonsensical banter. Understood it on some level, even commiserated a bit. But Henricksen didn't have time for handholding and messing about. Not with that asteroid field staring him in the face. This wasn't sim training anymore or even live tests. This was a *mission*. This was the *real thing*. He needed crew on task. Focused in and locked down tight, not bickering like school children.

"Concentrate, people." Another look around the bridge pod, comms carrying his voice to the four other Ravens. "You can piss on each other all you want once this mission is over and we're back on station. Right now I need you focused on one thing and one thing only: getting into that asteroid field." He pointed a finger at the floating mass of distant rocks. "We do that without messing up too badly, we move onto step two: finding Kinsey's canister and getting the hell back out. Everyone got that?"

Crew on *Scythe* looked at each other, at Henricksen and the camera watching from above. Nodded and bowed their heads over their panels, busying themselves at their stations. *Shriek* and the others sent their acknowledgments— clipped communications before the comms channel cut out. And afterward came silence. Heavy, foreboding, feeding the tension inside the bridge pod again.

"'M not a horse," Sikuuku muttered. "*She's* a horse."

"No one's a horse," Henricksen growled, stabbing at the Pilot station's controls. "Just drop it, Akiwane. Ya hear me?" He threw a look over his shoulder, waiting for the the gunner's nod. Faced around and looked up at the camera right in front him, looking down on the tight confines of the bridge. "Can you give me that star chart, *Scythe*?"

A map appeared before he finished his sentence—a star chart in miniature laid alongside the asteroid field schematic.

Henricksen studied it a moment, looking the data tags over. "Tight focus on the asteroid field. Layer in the drop coordinates and that schematic Kinsey gave us so we can focus our search."

"Done."

Scythe added the requested information, coordinates covering a broad area—nearly two-thirds of the oblong blob of randomness the star charts tagged as an asteroid field. Layered in that all-but-useless schematic Kinsey gave them, bringing it all together to create quite the mess. A maelstrom of data that said almost nothing at all. Oh, *Scythe*'s scans captured the *size* of the field, gave an approximation of the relative density of the rocks inside, and the star charts gave it context, but that schematic...modeling and guesswork. None of it *real* information, just a rough idea of the asteroid field's layout and contents. A prediction based on pieced together, incomplete data Kinsey's intel spook somehow managed to cobble together.

"Fuck me," Henricksen sighed, pushing the layered map to the corner of the window. "That's not all that helpful, is it?"

"Better than nothing," *Scythe* told him.

"Maybe." He chewed his lip, eyeing the asteroid field data doubtfully. "Lotta rocks out there. Lotta places for a tiny metal canister to hide."

"Sensors might help, once we're actually in. And there's the four of us," Sikuuku pointed out, waving at the crew on the bridge. "Four *more* of us on each of the other stealth ships." He counted on his fingers, shrugged and spread his hands. "That's a lotta eyes."

Henricksen grunted, consulting the star chart, checking their position relative to the asteroid field. Layered in the mission plan they'd developed earlier, splitting the asteroid field into five sections, layering in search patterns for each ship. Kept the focus of that search on the open space the crap schematic showed at the asteroid field's center—the same place Kinsey's intel claimed that DSR science station hid.

Supposed to get scans of it, bring that information back with them, along with whatever Kinsey's spook stuffed inside this mysterious can. Canister itself shouldn't be all that far from the station, in theory, so the search plan he laid out started at the middle, and worked its way out from there.

"Grid pattern." Henricksen reopened the comms line, speaking to all the ships now. "We split up and search for that canister. One ship per sector, just like we planned."

"What about that thing in the middle?" Baldini asked. "That science station or whatever they're calling it? Should we—"

"You just focus on your sector, Baldini. Let me worry about the station."

"Aye, sir." Clipped communication from Baldini, voice just this side of surly.

A click in Henricksen's ear and Sikuuku's voice came through—private channel, direct line to his helmet. "*Someone's* not happy."

"Tough." Henricksen stabbed at the panel in front of him, synching the Pilot's station to the coordinates on the front display. "Got a job to do. Not my problem if Baldini doesn't like it."

A hand landed on his shoulder, fingers squeezing until Henricksen looked up.

Shadowed shape, reflecting off the front windows, Sikuuku's voice filling Henricksen's helmet as the gunner leaned out of the Artillery pod. "Not quite sure he's cut out for this, Garrett. Boy wants to be a hero and blow shit up, not sneak around searching for some intel spook's can."

Henricksen turned his head, considering the gunner behind him, wishing he could see his face. "Kinsey's choice, not mine. You ask me—" He broke off, letting the sentence hang. Sighed and flipped a hand as he turned back to his station. "Doesn't matter. We're here now. Let's just get this done."

"Aye, sir." Sikuuku squeezed his shoulder, hand lifting as he tucked back into his pod. Machinery *whirring* as he flicked at switches, pod pivoting as the targeting system came on-line.

Henricksen glanced at the windows, studying the reflection of that pod behind him. Hopefully they wouldn't need those guns. Best possible outcome of this operation would be a clean sweep and smooth pick-up. DSR none the wiser, oblivious to the fact they were ever there.

"Yeah, right," he muttered, eyeing the map of the asteroid field. The constantly shifting sea of tumbling rocks. "What are the odds of that?"

"Sir?" Hanu turned, visored face looking his way.

"Nothing, Hanu. Just talking to myself." He reached for the panel in front of him, parsing up the asteroid field, passing out assignments to the other RV-Ns. Assigned *Sharp* and Mahal to one of the near-side sectors, Janssen and *Snicker-snack* to the other. *Sever* and Baldini went to the far side of the asteroid field—all the way across the empty space that supposedly lay at its center—with *Shriek* and Petros assigned to an adjoining sector.

Kept the cherry for himself and *Scythe*, a search pattern focused exclusively on the asteroid field's center. Canister probably wouldn't be there, but that science station should. Assuming, of course, that it actually existed.

Better be there, he thought, eyeing the asteroid field in the distance. *Better not be some goddamn wild goose chase total waste of out time.*

"Needle in a haystack," Ogawa grumbled, looking from the schematic on the front windows to the data on her panel. "How are we supposed to find anything in there with all those rocks in the way?"

"We'll find it," Henricksen told her. "Just you wait and see."

Wasn't quite so sure of that, to be honest, but command was about leading, and sometimes that meant faking it and acting more confident than you actually felt.

"Hanu. Give me a sweep of the asteroid field."

Hanu was quiet a moment, head bowed over her panel. "Not much to see, sir." A few strokes of the keys ran a series of overlapping sensors scans, parsers sorting through the results that came back. "Rocks, and rocks, and more rocks," she reported. "That's pretty much all I'm getting from here."

"Well, crap." Henricksen chewed his lip, knowing what he needed to do, dreading it just the same. "Ogawa. Main propulsion." He looked at her, studying her helmeted head in profile as she called up the propulsion system's controls. "What do the calcs say?"

"Hang on."

She pulled up the calculations and checked them over—no need to, *Scythe* had already verified the data, but Ogawa was meticulous when it came to her math. Double checked their current velocity, consulting the star chart and that schematic to figure out where, and when, and how fast to approach the asteroid field. Figure out how much speed they could carry and still safely enter it and maneuver about.

"Five-second burn," she determined, checking everything a second time. "That's the optimal set-up for approach."

Henricksen glanced at the camera, looking to *Scythe* for confirmation. Nodded his thanks when a tiny red light flashed discretely. "Five seconds it is. Bring the mains on-line on my mark. Launch us toward that asteroid field and then you cut 'em, you hear me? All the way down. Nothing but maneuvering jets from there on in."

Stealth system should hide their shape if anyone was looking—live tests proved that system out. But there was no technology he knew of that could mask a ship's energy trail.

Couldn't risk the DSR picking up that tell-tale signature. Rocks messed with the sensors—you bet they did—but the closer they got in, the more likely something would slip through.

"We'll thread our way through to the middle." Henricksen pointed to the open space showing at the center of the asteroid field map. "Split up from there and start searching from the inside out. Canister's probably drifted a bit, but explosive decompression will only throw it so far before it runs into something. And from the looks of things," another glance at the windows, "there's a *lotta* somethings to run into out there."

"Think she reinforced it?" Sikuuku asked. "Composite metal can running up against a few tons of solid rock..." A grunt from inside the Artillery pod, the entire contraption turning to give the gunner a better view of the windows. "Squash that thing flat as a pancake. Probably destroy everything inside."

"I'm sure she considered that," Henricksen said sourly. "Don't know Kinsey's spook, but I assume if she was smart enough to fake her way into that DSR installation, she's smart enough to use a reinforced container to deliver her package."

"What if she didn't?" Hanu asked worriedly, hands hovering above her panel.

Henricksen sighed in annoyance, wishing Sikuuku had just kept his mouth shut. "We'll find it," he repeated. "Now, eyes front, the both of you," he said, looking from Hanu on one side to Ogawa on the other. "Got enough to worry about with all those rocks out there, *last* thing I need is the two of you worrying about whether the goddamn can's flat or not."

"Aye, sir," Ogawa murmured, but Hanu just sat there, hands poised above Scan's panel, visored face staring at the windows.

"Hanu? You with me?"

She shook herself, hands settling on the panel, palms pressed flat. "Aye, sir. Sorry, sir."

"Don't want your apologies, Hanu. Just want you focused on the job at hand."

"Yes, sir." She looked at him, dark shoulders shrugging in the dim confines of the bridge. "Sor—Aye, sir," she repeated, more confidently this time. "Good to go."

"You sure?"

Hanu hesitated, nodded confidently a second or two later.

"Alright then." Henricksen wrapped his fingers around the RV-N's control stick, touching at a panel to open a channel to the ships around them. "I want minimal comms from here on out. You got that, *Shriek*?"

"Me?" *Shriek* sounded indignant. "What'd *I* do? Why are you singling *me* out?"

"'Cause you got a big yap. And your pilot's not much better."

"Hey!" Baldini objected.

"Shut it. Both of you," Henricksen ordered, setting his controls. "And *keep* it shut unless it's important."

"How am I—?"

"*Really* important," he said, cutting *Shriek* off. "Now lock in on the entry point. We're go for burn in three. Two. One. Launch."

Ogawa hit the engines, main propulsion running wide open, pinning the crew to their seats. Sensors picked up the energy signatures from *Shriek* and the other Ravens following behind her, clustered together in an arrow-shaped wedge.

Not a configuration they'd agreed upon—not necessarily a bad idea, but a curious deviation from plan.

Henricksen made a mental note to ask about that later. When he had enough air in his lungs to actually formulate a question. For now, he just focused on breathing, g-load pressing against him like an anvil, pressure suit an overstuffed sausage casing squeezing at his flesh.

Vibration shook the bridge pod, harmonic tremors from the cloaking system increasing in proportion to the ship's speed. Doubled and redoubled, worse than anything Henricksen remembered from the sims or the live tests. The entire *ship* rattling, vibrating with that organ-shaking, eyeball jangling hum.

"What the *fuck*?" Sikuuku gasped, voice strangled, choking from his mouth.

Henricksen tried to answer, but he couldn't quite find the breath. Tried to move his head, his hand, *anything,* an impossibility with that g-load working against. Fighting him. Pinning him down.

Five seconds—just five seconds, those engines burned wide open. But those five seconds felt like an eternity. A lifetime as the crew sat there and suffered. Left Henricksen sweating and shaking, vision wavering as Ogawa reached for the panel, hand straining, arm trembling, gloved fingers stabbing blindly for the engine controls.

Stabbed and missed, again and again. Gave up on the controls after the third try and searched for the engine's kill switch as the burn clock rolled past five seconds and came up on six.

Too long, Henricksen's abused brain had time to think. *We're coming in too fast.*

Six seconds on the burn clock and *Scythe* intervened. Shut down main propulsion and toggled the engine controls, throwing everything into reverse.

Second, brutal shove at the crews' bodies, Henricksen grunting as he slammed against the restraining straps—muscles bruised, bones aching, lungs deflating as every last puff of air rushed out in a gust. G-load returned, making his eyeballs bulge and shake. The world turned grey at the edges, every bone in his body creaking, threatening to break under the strain. And then *Scythe* mercifully cut the engines, shutting everything back down.

Drifted on momentum while Henricksen sat there, wheezing desperately, sucking at the atmospherics his flight suit fed into his helmet, trying to convince his lungs to fill back up.

A flash of light and *Shriek* shot by, engines glowing for a fraction of a second before winking out. Henricksen threw his hand forward, slapping at Helm's panel to bring up the sensor data from Scan. Blinked blearily until the ghostly shapes of the other three Ravens came into focus, strung out in a ragged line behind *Scythe*.

"Shit," he breathed, pressure easing, suit backing off. "What the hell was that?"

"Sorry," Ogawa panted, shaking her head. "Couldn't see. Couldn't find the controls." She bent over, clutching at her stomach, craned her neck, looking up at the camera. "AI got it. Sorry." Another shake of her head. "My mistake. Sorry about that, sir."

Sikuuku groaned loudly, loosening his seat's straps. Doubled over, cradling his helmeted head in his hands. "Think I'm gonna be sick."

Henricksen didn't feel all that great himself, to be honest. Stomach kept flipping over, doing cartwheels inside his gut. Rest of his body felt pummeled—bruised and battered, like he'd been in a bar fight with some iron fisted giant wearing knuckledusters and steel-toed boots.

He winced, rubbing at creaking ribs. Swallowed hard, willing his breakfast to stay put as he straightened up, lifting his eyes to *Scythe*'s camera. "How bad?" he asked her, because they'd blown it. Completely missed that five second mark. He just didn't know by how much. "How far off did we end up?"

"We...overshot the target," *Scythe* said carefully, camera twitching toward Ogawa, jerking back to Henricksen in the Pilot's seat. "I had to throw it into reverse to bleed off some speed and slow us down."

Better than coming up on that asteroid field too fast and splattering against a rock, he supposed, but still...

"Damn near pulverized us," Henricksen growled, shrugging abused shoulders, rubbing at a sore, soon-to-be-stiff neck.

"Fucked it up, sir. Overburned by nearly a second. If it wasn't for *Scythe*..." Ogawa trailed off, shaking her head. Checked their position in relation to the asteroid field, the velocity of their approach. "Too fast. We're still coming in way too fast." She punched the panel in front of her, clearly upset.

"Easy, Ogawa. Not blamin' you."

"Yeah, well, *I* am. Carrying a lot more speed than we planned for, sir. *Scythe* cut our velocity with that back burn, but we *still* need to bleed some more off." Ogawa punched the panel again, sat back in disgust. "We're fucked, sir. Completely fucked."

"So how do we get *un*fucked?" Henricksen asked quietly.

"How the hell would I know?" she cried, throwing her hands in the air. "*I'm* the one who fucked it all up in the first place, remember?"

Henricksen gritted his teeth, forcing himself to stay calm. "*Scythe?* What do your calcs say?"

"We'll need to execute a .50 second full reverse burn before we hit the edge of the asteroid field," she said, panel lighting, calculations running in front of him.

"Full reverse. As in…"

"Main propulsion. Wide open."

Henricksen rubbed at sore ribs, already dreading it. "You couldn't just run that last back burn a little bit longer?"

"I could have. But you'd be unconscious right now. Probably have some broken bones. Internal bleeding—"

"Alright. I get," he said, waving her off. "How long until we reach the edge of the asteroid field?"

"Three minutes, twelve seconds." *Scythe* set a clock on the front window, cool blue numbers counting down.

"Three minutes." Henricksen chewed his lip, thinking a moment. "And our friends out there?" He pointed his chin at the asteroid field in the distance, the DSR station hidden inside. "Five ships running with their engines wide open. That's an awful lotta energy lighting up the night."

Scythe didn't answer right away—that got his attention. And when she did, it sounded rushed. Suspiciously nonchalant. "We should be fine," she said confidently. *Too* confidently for his taste.

"*Should* be," he repeated.

"Uh-huh."

"Hanu?"

"Scans show clean." Hanu looked at him, at *Scythe's* camera watching over them both. "Nothing out there as far as I can tell. And anything *inside* the asteroid field…" She shrugged her shoulders, turning toward the front windows. "Shouldn't be able to scan us with all those rocks in the way. Especially…" She hesitated, throwing another look at the camera. "Especially if we wait until the last moment."

"Wait. What?" Henricksen glanced sharply at Scan.

"The asteroids block signals, right? So we shunt ourselves around with the maneuvering jets—small burn, nothing long range sensors should pick up—and line up with one of those big rocks." Hanu pointed at the windows, the asteroid field that was much, much closer. "Should shield us, right? Once we get in close enough?"

Henricksen looked a question at the camera.

"It should," *Scythe* agreed. "In theory."

"How close?" he asked her. "How close do we have to get?"

Scythe ran the calculations. "Ten thousand kilometers should do it."

"Yikes." Frightfully close at the stealth ship's current speed. "Options?" Henricksen asked, looking around the bridge pod.

"Go back?" Sikuuku suggested.

"Tempting," Henricksen grunted. "Won't deny that." But they'd have to scrub their speed to do it. Maneuvering jets could probably muscle the ship around, but they'd need main propulsion to get moving and chart a course back to Dragoon.

Same thing. Same damn problem, either way.

"Any *other* options?"

Silence from the crew—everyone looking at each, shaking their heads.

"Alright. We do it Hanu's way, then. Ten thousand kilometers—you heard her. *Scythe.*" He pointed at the camera with one hand, wrapping the other around the ship's control stick. "Pass the word to the other Ravens."

"Done," she said, passing the order along.

"Let's drop some pingers before we hit the brakes. Give ourselves some eyes and ears to watch our backs after we go in."

"Also done," she said promptly, adding that order to the last.

Henricksen nodded his thanks, pulling scan data onto his panel, picked out a good-sized asteroid and lined the ship up. "Alright, Ogawa. Prep those engines. Full reverse burn."

"Aye, sir."

Henricksen tugged at his seat straps, while Ogawa worked away at Engineering, obsessively checking the distance to that asteroid field.

Fifty thousand kilometers now—a little over a minute before they'd need to get on the engines again. He breathed deep, chest tight with worry, hoping the rock he'd picked was big enough to shield them. That he didn't run right into the damn thing trying to execute this maneuver and put an end to them all right then and there.

"We'll be fine," *Scythe* said, watching him from above. "I mean, sure, there's a .01 chance I miscalculated—"

"Don't." Henricksen raised a hand, cutting her off. "Don't give me the facts and figures. Just..." He sighed, shaking his head. Tapped a finger to the side of his helmet as he switched comms over to a private channel. "What happened back there?" he asked her. "*Before* you slammed on the brakes and almost turned us all into slurry."

"Not sure what you mean."

"The cloaking system. Damn thing rattles my bones, but this...this was different. *Worse.* Spine feels like a xylophone that got beat with a set of hammers."

"Oh. That. Resonance," she said—a casual, almost flippant response. "From, you know, the stealth shields overlapping."

"Overlapping stealth shields. And just whose idea was that?"

"*Shriek's*. He thought it would make us stealthy. Well, stealthi*er*, I guess, considering...We probably should have tested it," she admitted in a surprisingly sheepish voice.

Henricksen blinked, staring at the camera in surprise. Never heard sheepishness from an AI before. Most of them were all cool tones and serene confidence until somebody pissed them off. "Next time...just give me a little warning next time, okay?"

"Got it. Sorry," *Scythe* added. "About the whole...xylophone thing."

Henricksen grunted, resetting the comms. Checked the front windows and found the asteroid field much closer—*Scythe* and her entourage just thirty thousand kilometers distant now. "Fan out," he called, opening a secure channel to the other Ravens. "Find a line in." He paused, scanning the data from the sensors, feathered the maneuvering jets to shunt *Scythe* to a wide space between two boulders. Consulted the display on the front windows again, noting the positions of the other ships with him, making sure no one else was trying to thread the same hole.

Realized they'd dropped into that wedge formation again—*Scythe* in the lead, *Shriek* and the others stagger-stepped to either side, the resonance from their overlapping stealth shields building, rattling his bones. "Not too tight," he warned. "Last thing I need is Sikuuku chucking his breakfast inside that Artillery pod."

The ships jockeyed around, maneuvering jets flaring as they spread a bit wider, giving themselves more room.

The resonance eased immediately, returning to the expected, vibrating hum.

"That's better." Henricksen wrapped both hands around the control stick, eyes locked onto the front windows as the distance counter hit twenty thousand kilometers out. "*Scythe*. You ready?"

"Let me at 'em," she said, smile in her voice.

Henricksen shrugged his shoulders, breath quickening as the asteroid field loomed close. "Hanu. Call it. Count us down."

"Aye, sir. Fifteen thousand kilometers out."

"Got it," he muttered, giving his harness a tug.

"Don't crash us," Sikuuku warned. "I will be *so* pissed if you crash us going in."

"Appreciate the vote of confidence, Chief."

"Twelve thousand kilometers." Hanu gripped her panel, leaning forward. "Eleven..."

"Pingers deployed," *Scythe* announced. "We've got eyes and ears on the stars."

"Ten."

"*Burn!*"

TWENTY-SEVEN

Main propulsion kicked hard—brutal, battering, tearing at flesh and bone. Henricksen clenched his teeth, holding tight to the panel in front of him as *Scythe* engines lit, firing in full reverse to slow her screaming approach. Velocity plummeted, speed peeling off in huge chunks, but Henricksen hardly noticed. All he saw was that rock ahead of them—a huge, lumpen thing roughly the size of a Dreadnought, tumbling endlessly around its center axis.

Scythe came in on a collision course, less than a kilometer separating the stealth ship from that improvised asteroid shield.

"Shit!" Henricksen grabbed at the controls, hauling the ship over, thrusters firing, pushing *Scythe* hard to port. He cringed, half expecting them to hit the rock anyway, holding on for dear life as the ship skimmed around it, missing it by a hair's breadth. Swore loudly when they came up on another almost immediately, realized going around this one just wasn't an option. "Shit, shit, *shit*!"

He yanked hard, lifting *Scythe*'s nose to send her up and over that rock, perimeter alarms screaming in his ears.

"*Scythe*! Kill the wailers!"

Didn't need the noise. Thousands of rocks out there, spreading in every direction. Didn't need the perimeter alarms going psycho trying to warn him about every last one.

"*Scythe!*"

A last squawk and the shrieking ceased, dropping the bridge pod into silence. Panels kept flashing, though, highlighting nearby asteroids on the schematic projected on the front windows.

Henricksen drew a breath, ears ringing in the sudden silence. Found his center—heart beating double-time, adrenaline pumping through his body—and re-oriented, locating their position on the map.

Looked past the apparently random clutter to the pattern lying beneath, because there was nothing at *all* random about an asteroid field. Each rock spun independently, following an orbit only it knew. And every other rock spun around it, following an endless, unchanging path it had settled into a billion years ago, back when the asteroid field first formed.

Chart that field, and navigation almost became easy. Fly it blind and you took your life into your own hands.

That's where he was right now: holding on, picking his way through. Hated being a pioneer. Wished to hell Kinsey's spook could've coughed up some better intel.

"Report," he barked, eyes on the front windows, hands making minute adjustments as *Scythe* moved deeper into the asteroid field. "Hanu. Did we wake the neighbors?"

"Scans show clean. No sensor sweeps anyway. Can't really tell much more from here."

"Son-of-a-bitch." Sikuuku laughed, fist pounding the side of his pod. "It worked. That crazy-ass idea actually worked."

"Don't count your chickens yet." Henricksen reached for Comms, opening a secure channel to the other Ravens. "*Shriek.*"

"Present," *Shriek* answered cheerily. "*Sharp*'s here with me so he's not splattered either. Dented his belly, though." He dropped his voice, whispering conspiratorially across the common channel. "Not so sure his pilot's all that good."

"*His* pilot can kick *your* pilot's ass all the way across the galaxy," Mahal shot back.

"Can it, you two," Henricksen snapped. "*Sever? Snicker—*"

"Whoo-hoo!" Baldini's bawdy voice drowned out everything else on the line. "Now *that* was a rush!"

Henricksen sighed heavily. Evidently *no one* understood minimal comms. "*Snicker-snack.* You out there?"

"Aye, Captain," Janssen answered. "Skimmed one of those rollers, though. Took some damage."

"How bad?"

A pause before Janssen answered. "Starboard side array's gone. Lost the weapons, too. Engines are fine. Hull's intact. But we're starboard side blind. Open to attack."

Damn. Not off to a good start.

Fucked up their approach and now two ships dented. One left partially mission capable. Didn't bode well for the rest of the mission, especially since, from here on in, things only got harder.

"Stick close to Mahal," Henricksen ordered. "Have *Sharp* and *Snicker-snack* pair up so you can keep an eye on each other."

"Aye, sir."

"Give me a fix on their location, Hanu." Henricksen waited while Hanu swept *Scythe*'s modified sensor array across the area around them, repeating the scans until *Snicker-snack*'s shape appeared, slipping stealthily around a rock.

"Got him, Captain."

"Good. Now layer in the others. Keep tabs on the squadron while we move in."

Hanu looked at him, and at the windows, fingers hovering just above Scan's panel. No easy feat, tracking those ships here. Especially considering all the clutter in the way.

"Not askin' for miracles, Hanu. Just do the best you can."

"Aye, sir," she said quietly, and leaned over her panel, fingers working away.

"Everybody ready?"

"Aye, sir," Hanu and Ogawa answered together.

"Standing by to do nothing," Sikuuku said, stifling a yawn.

"No offense, Chief, but I hope we don't need you. Mission's pretty much fucked if we have to use your guns."

A grunt from the gunner as Henricksen consulted the schematic, searching for a relatively safe path in.

No obvious route to follow, so he zigged and zagged, aiming roughly for the asteroid field's center, *Scythe*'s sensor dating updating Kinsey's roughed-out map as they moved deeper in.

Lot more rocks out there than Kinsey's map accounted for. Spook's data, supposedly, but not very good. Made him wonder what *else* was missing from that improvised map.

"Sir."

"What now, Hanu?" Henricksen growled, checking the map.

Three kilometers at this point, almost halfway to the asteroid field's center.

"Anomalous signature." Hanu pointed to a new piece of information showing on the already cluttered schematic. "Some kind of composite metal structure."

"Ship?" he asked, eyeing the way ahead worriedly.

"Don't think so. This looks…different."

"Different how? *How*?" Henricksen demanded, but Hanu just shook her, cycling through the data on her panel. Shunted it all to Ogawa for a second look. "What?" he snapped. "Somebody tell me what the hell—"

"Mines." Ogawa raised her head, visored face staring at the windows. "Scans missed them before because they're mixed in with the rocks. Couldn't pick up the metal—"

"Until we were right on top of them. Fuck." Henricksen sighed.

One more complication. A complication he severely didn't need.

"Sorry, sir." Small voice from Hanu, shoulders lifting in a helpless shrug.

"Not your fault, Hanu."

Sims didn't show them. Kinsey's map didn't either. Had a hard time picking them out with his *own* eyes because pretty much everything out there looked grey, and black, and big as a goddamn ship.

Bad start to this mission, and things keep getting worse.

Henricksen chewed his lip worriedly, guiding *Scythe* around yet another rock. "Tag the mine and reset the sensors to look for that signature. Mark any others they find in red so I can tell them from the rocks."

"Done," *Scythe* answered, schematic shifting, a dozen or so round, red shapes layering in amongst the rocks.

Hanu looked at them, and at the camera at the front of the bridge. Lashed out at Scan in frustration, muttering something about "stupid, show-off AIs" under her breath.

"Let it go, Hanu," Henricksen advised.

Hanu kept muttering, stabbing angrily at her panel.

Henricksen sighed, making a mental note to talk to *Scythe* about the importance of letting the crew do their fucking jobs. "Send that scan signature to the other ships, Hanu, so they know what to look for."

"Aye, sir." Hanu rattled away at the panel's virtual keyboard, pulling in information from the sensors. A few strokes of the keys and she bundled up a data package, sending it across an encrypted channel.

A flash of red on the front windows and another of those mines appeared. This one dead ahead. Directly in their path.

"Shit," Henricksen swore, diverting. "*Shit!*" as another mine appeared. Two more after that, set close together this time. "Fucking impossible," he muttered, searching for a path.

"Adjust your course two degrees starboard," *Scythe* instructed. "Follow this route." She highlighted several asteroids on the schematic, laid in a zig-zagging line.

"Not exactly a direct route," Henricksen noted, sparing a look for the camera.

"Changes the vector of approach on the center," she admitted, "but it'll get you there. Just don't, you know, run into anything along the way. Especially anything mine-shaped."

"Gee. Thanks, coach." Henricksen adjusted his course, comparing the information on the schematic to the realities of the rocks outside. Adjusted it again, not liking what he saw, swinging even further out.

Cleared a huge rock and saw an alert appear, flashing bright red on his panel.

"Great. What now?"

A touch at the panel in front of him opened the alert. He scanned the information, making it just halfway through the data before a second alert appeared, overlaying the first. A third and fourth, a dozen soon after, cascading in a steady flow.

Mine positions associated with each of them, dozens of those ominous red dots popping into existing, cluttering up the already busy schematic showing on the bridge pod's windows. Pattern to them that slowly came clear. A clustering effect, focused on that blank space at the center—the outer five kilometers of the asteroid field showing clear, more and more mines appearing the further they moved in.

Henricksen slid the ship around a spiked shape, giving it wide berth. Ugly thing, ominous and sinister. Dull grey metal, spherical in shape. Round nubs sticking up everywhere. Like caltrops, but blunted. Sticking out of from a huge ball.

Fixed position, not tumbling like the asteroids around it. Precisely placed, or so it seemed, to fill the spaces between the endlessly spinning rocks.

Grey-sided to hide amongst them, signatures flickering as *Scythe* slid through the stone sea. The route she'd plotted adjusting and readjusting as more and more mines appeared, cluttering the way ahead.

Henricksen consulted the schematic, eyes flicking rapid-fire between that map and the reality of space outside. Cursed and feathered the maneuvering jets, detouring again, slewing the ship sideways to skip around a mine, bringing her back on course again on the other side. "Fucking Kinsey. Fucking spook and her piss-poor map."

"Look at them all," Ogawa breathed, watching a mine slide by. "They're everywhere."

Dozens of them, from what the scans picked up. *Hundreds* of them based on *Scythe*'s projections. Scattered across the length and breadth of the asteroid field, hiding in the shadows of its tumbling rocks.

Not a safe place to be. Rocks were bad enough—trained for those, even if the map was shit—but the mines...

Skim a rock and you'd dent the ship—piss off the mechs, but likely make it home. Skim a mine and it was over. Flash, bang, dead.

Ogawa fidgeted, throwing glances Henricksen's way. "You—you *do* know what you're doing, right, sir?"

"Little late if I don't," Henricksen told her, easing around a rock. "Way back's as ugly as the way ahead at this point. 'Sides," he said, nodding to the schematic on the windows, the promise of open space at the center. "We're just about there."

Less than a kilometer of rocks and mines to thread around now, mines threw them a curveball—huge swathes of them showing on the front windows, ominous and red, painting the schematic in blood—but they just about had it. Just about made it through.

Henricksen twitched his shoulders, trying to ease his harness's grip. Flexed aching fingers clenched in a death grip around the ship's control stick. Concentrated on his flying—that most of all. "Ogawa. Need you on Comms."

"But—"

"Not much use for an Engineer in here," he told her. "But I need *someone* monitoring channels once we clear these rocks." He risked a glance in her direction—a fleeting look only, eyes snapping back to the windows in a hurry. "You keep one ear on that station once we find it, the other on the stars."

Ogawa was quiet a moment, watching the windows, the rocks tumbling by outside. "Aye, sir," she said softly, shoving the Engineering data to one panel, tapping into the Comms system from the other.

"*Scythe?*" Henricksen spared another look for the camera. "Help her out?"

"I've got a few pingers left. I can deploy them once we reach the center if you'd like."

"Much obliged." Henricksen dipped his head, focusing on the windows, spotted an opening just off the port bow, and adjusted their course.

A last diversion, swinging wide of an immense rock, and asteroids retreated as the world opened up.

Henricksen breathed deep, tense muscles relaxing as the schematic adjusted, the deathscape of mines and asteroids retreating behind them, a small sea of empty space stretching ahead.

More death on the far side, but Henricksen ignored that for now. Concentrated on the sensor data streaming across his panel, measuring the size of the space around them, the length and width and found it surprisingly symmetrical: ten kilometers from one side to the other, oval-shaped and vacant. Blessedly empty. Not a mine or asteroid in sight.

Scan pinged, picking up new information, spewing out long lines of data. Henricksen searched the space ahead and spied a monstrosity lurking at the center—a massive structure, ugly and misshapen, surrounded by a loose ring of small ships.

"Guessing that's our science station," Sikuuku said, pulling that image into his pod.

"Must be," Henricksen grunted, adjusting the ship's course, skulking silently around the open space's edge.

"It look kinda odd to you?" Sikuuku asked him.

Henricksen reached for the panel in front of him, accessed the feeds from the ship's forward facing cameras and zoomed in, taking a good, long look.

Odd didn't begin to cover it. Early space stations followed a spoke-and-wheel pattern—cylinder shaped station at the center, walkways radiating outward in a starburst pattern, connecting to a ring-shaped dockyard with ship's berthings arranged along its curving length. Military—being military—tended to go for the cube-on-cube configuration like Dragoon, expanding spaces as needed by adding on more cubes. But this thing...In all his years and all his travels across the galaxy, Henricksen had never come across *any* space station that looked like this.

Orb-shaped, many orbs, actually, with connectors running between them, turning the entire construction into a gigantic dandelion. A molecular structure viewed under magnification, scaled up and built to that design.

"Someone took the whole 'science station' thing a bit far," Sikuuku grunted, cycling through the camera feeds himself. "Small for a station," he noted. "Put ten of those inside Dragoon and *still* have room left over."

"Space is at a premium," Henricksen pointed out, releasing the control stick long enough to wave a hand at the emptiness around them. "You'd be hard put to cram Dragoon inside this asteroid field. Not that Dragoon's anything to write home about."

Proper space station, but old and moldy. Didn't hold a candle to Harmony, or Harbourside, or one of the other, fancier facilities scattered across Meridian Alliance space.

"Take Dragoon over that fragile looking thing any day." Sikuuku blanked the feeds, pulling the targeting system back onto his panel. "Dragoon may stink, but I'd trust that durable old tub over this DSR piece of crap any day."

Personally, Henricksen didn't want either. A few weeks on Dragoon and he was already sick of stations. Missed *Hecate* more than ever. The feel of her as they traveled the stars.

"So what's the plan?" Sikuuku asked, dragging Henricksen's mind back to the present.

"Divide and conquer, same as before. Hanu." Henricksen glanced at Scan, nodded to the shape showing through the windows. "I need scans of that structure. Information on the ships around it."

"On it," she said, fingers flying across her panel.

"*Scythe.* You drop those pingers?"

"Listening devices away," she said brightly. "Ogawa and I pick up any good recipes, we'll be sure to let you know."

"Always lookin' for a good casserole." He flashed a smile at the camera, forgetting the helmet hiding his face. Flipped a thumbs up when he remembered, opening ship-to-ship comms. "*Shriek,*" he called, searching for the ghostly shapes of the RV-Ns on Scan. "You and *Snicker-snack* stick together. Might not be quite as efficient," he acknowledged when *Shriek* started to object, "but he's damn near half-blind."

"Am not," *Snicker-snack* grumped. "I can see just fine on my left side."

"Uh-huh." Henricksen glanced at *Scythe's* camera, shaking his head. "Just stick close to *Shriek,* ya hear me? I want you two searching that section of the asteroid field behind us while *Sharp* and *Sever* take a look around the far side. You find that can, you tell me. Soon as you pick it up."

"Roger-roger!" *Shriek's* comms clicked closed, ghostly shape turning as he and *Snicker-snack* moved off. "By the way," he said, channel crackling, voice coming through. "How will we know if we find this thing-a-ma-jigger canister if we come across it?"

Henricksen sighed. Like he was supposed to know. "Well, it's small, so there's that—"

"How small?"

"I don't *know, Shriek.*" He gritted his teeth, trying for calm. "But Kinsey's spook supposedly tossed it out with the trash, so I'm guessing it's *really* small. As in, smaller than your pilot small."

Shriek whistled appreciatively—piercing tone, and decidedly odd. An AI's version of a whistle, approximating that distinctly human sound. "That's pretty darn small."

"'Spose."

Janssen was actually rather large, as far as human went—tall anyway, if a bit thin—but Henricksen decided to let it go. Watched *Shriek* move away with Petros at the controls, Janssen and *Snicker-snack* following a discrete distance behind. "Janssen," he called, opening a channel to the trailing ship's bridge. "Keep *Shriek* off Comms."

"Got it. I'll keep him quiet."

"Good luck." Ogawa snorted. "Chattiest damn AI I ever met in my life."

Henricksen smiled, detailing *Sever* and *Sharp* to the opposite side of the asteroid field for survey and retrieval while *Scythe* held the middle. Focused on the science station nearby.

A touch at the controls moved the stealth ship away from the asteroid field's edge, put her on approach to the DSR installation, its ring of surrounding ships. He guided her close—close as he dared, tensed up tight, expecting perimeters alarms to start shrieking, warning of station sensors creeping across their skin. Feathered the maneuvering jets to turn her and *keep* turning, settling *Scythe* into a wide, looping pattern, turning round and round the science station and its cluster of ships.

One loop and another, and the station stayed silent—*Scythe's* stealth system holding, cloak doing its job. Third loop around the station and Henricksen finally relaxed a bit. Released his death grip on the ship's controls—looping pattern required little intervention from the pilot, momentum doing most of the work—and sat back, studying the data on the station Scan's sensors picked up.

Uglier close in than it looked from a distance. A single structure, but one constructed from many and disparate parts. Pieces chopped, and fitted, and bolted together. Everything rounded and orb-shaped—a half a dozen spheres on the outside, connected by supporting structures and bridging mechanisms to an oversized globe at the center.

"Ogawa. What's the chatter?" Henricksen kept his voice low, hushed tones whispering across the bridge pod's internal channel.

"Nothing unusual." She turned her head, looking to *Scythe* for confirmation.

"Stealth shield appears to be holding," she confirmed. "They don't even know we're here."

"Yeah, well, don't get cocky." Henricksen spared a look for the camera, fingers feather-light on the control stick—guiding the ship, but not really flying it now. Smooth, steady course—that's what he wanted. Stay off the maneuvering jets. Attract as little attention as possible.

Kept one eye on the sensor data while the ship turned in circles. Tracked the progress of station scans, ran a pass across the ring of ships arranged around it while he was at it, searching for energy signatures and weapons ports—anything that might spell trouble.

Good, bad, or indifferent, the scans came up pretty much empty. Dead ships out there, apparently. At least, as far as the sensors could tell. Didn't make Henricksen feel any better, though. This entire mission felt hinky. All this sneaking around made him twitchy. Nervous as all get-out.

He twitched his shoulders, trying to ease cramped muscles, grimacing as a trickle of sweat worked its way down his back. Sucked in a breath and blew it back, slowing his heart with an effort, concentrating on the simple things. Actionable things. Like keeping the ship steady. Her course flat and smooth.

A whir of machinery and the Artillery pod pivoted, giving Sikuuku a better view of the windows. "Ugly ass pile of junk out there, isn't it?"

"Shoestring budget. That's what you get."

"DSR does love their cobbled-together shit." Sikuuku chuckled and went quiet, staring through the windows as the ship continued its looping course. "You really think that thing's a science station like Kinsey claims? Full of boffins and such?"

"Maybe."

Sikuuku grunted, going quiet again. "That thing in the middle." He leaned out, pointing a finger at the windows. "That look familiar to you?"

Henricksen squinted, peering between the outer orbs to the larger sphere at the center.

It did indeed look familiar. In fact, it bore a rather *uncanny* resemblance to the ship that killed *Hecate*.

"Cepheid?" Henricksen glanced around and saw Sikuuku's helmeted head nod.

"That's what I'm thinking. Rest of them, all those smaller spheres connected to the big one at the center..." Sikuuku grabbed the back of Henricksen's seat, bracing himself as he leaned even further out. "Hard to tell for certain, but if I had to guess, I'd say those are ships as well. Or parts of ships, anyway."

"The remains of ships," *Scythe* said softly. "Carved up and fitted together. The best parts of their bodies taken. AIs cast out, leaving nothing but their ghosts behind."

"Well, that's certainly creepy," Sikuuku muttered, stuffing himself back into his pod.

"Say that again." Henricksen shivered, thinking of *Hecate* again. That copy of her consciousness stored in some Meridian Alliance vault somewhere.

Suddenly wanted out of here. Quite badly, in fact.

"Hanu. What's the status of that station scan?"

Hanu shook her head without looking, eyes focused on the reams of data flowing across her panel. "Getting there, sir, but there's a lot of data to parse through."

"How long?"

Hanu hesitated, shrugging. "Few more minutes. Five at most and I should be able to tell you what that thing out there's about."

Five minutes—an eternity of time.

"And the ships around it?"

Hanu pulled her eyes away from the sensor data long enough to send Henricksen a file.

He nodded his thanks, pulling it up on the Pilot station's panel, sharing the information with Sikuuku inside his pod.

"Transports. Figures," Sikuuku grunted.

"Small ones," Henricksen noted. "For transports anyway. Probably ship to station haulers, not long-haul transports."

"Transports don't carry weapons typically. Assume that's how the DSR ended up with 'em."

"Assume they're dangerous," Henricksen told him. "Or at least very, very unfriendly."

"Got it." Sikuuku reset his pod, flipping switches, settling the targeting visor over his eyes. "First sign of trouble, I'll blast 'em."

"Just hold on for now, okay? No itchy trigger fingers." Henricksen twisted, looking back over his shoulder. "We're stealth ships, remember? Shielded. We start firing and this whole thing'll turn into a helluva mess."

"Fine," Sikuuku muttered, heaving a heavy sigh. "But you say the word and they go boom, boss."

"Boom it is," Henricksen nodded, facing back around. "Ogawa. Check the status of the other Ravens. Let me know if they've found anything yet."

"Aye, sir." Ogawa tapped out a text only message, staring at her panel until the answers came back. "Negatory, sir. Nothing yet."

"Damn."

He'd hoped they'd find that canister quickly. Grab the scans of this station and beat feet back to Dragoon in a hurry.

"How do you suppose they got it in here?" Ogawa asked, listening with half an ear to Comms. "The station-ship-thingy," she elaborated, twiddling her fingers at the shape outside.

"Jumped it," Henricksen guessed.

"Jump a station?" Ogawa sounded suspicious. Like she thought he was pulling her leg. "How would they do that?"

"Built it out of salvaged ships, from the looks of things. Makes sense they left the jump drives in 'em." He paused, considering Sikuuku behind him. "Kinsey told me they found that station before, you know. Found it and *lost* it, which makes me wonder..." He chewed his lip, thinking a moment, glanced at Ogawa and just shrugged. "Can't really explain *how* you lose a station, unless it's got some kind of hyperspace capability, know what I mean?"

Ogawa nodded slowly, helmeted face staring out the windows. Turned back to her station and immersed herself in Comms again.

"Pretty fucking insane taking a wreck like that into hyperspace." Sikuuku flicked a few more switches, adjusted the fit of his targeting visor. "Shooting for a set of coordinates and just *hoping* to hit a clear spot."

"Maybe," Henricksen admitted, shrugging again.

"Or maybe not." Hanu looked at him, and at the windows, toggling the display on the glass to layer the scan data over the asteroid field map. Highlighted the close-packed ships—dangerously close, to Henricksen's mind, pilot's instincts calculating ranges, accounting for drift—pointing to an anomalous energy signature half-hidden in their middle. "Looks like they've got a repeater. Dicey maneuver, but you can severely pare down the jump displacement if you can hone in on the frequency of that thing."

"Still dicey as hell," Sikuuku told her. "Huge set of brass balls on whoever completed that jump."

Thousand ways for that to go sideways. Made Henricksen's stomach clench up just *thinking* about the disastrous consequences of an off-target jump.

Science station my ass. No way they'd take that kind of risk for a simple science installation.

"Hanu. What's the status of those scans?"

A pause as Hanu pulled a last bit of data onto her panel, parsed the information and merged it with what she'd already captured. "Sir..." She trailed off, gesturing at the station outside. "I ran a hull penetration scan so I could get a look at the guts of that thing."

Henricksen threw a surprised look at *Scythe*'s camera. "You can do that?"

"The engineers gave us *really* good sensors."

"Apparently," he said, lips twisting sourly.

Black Ops and its toys. He wondered what other tech they'd created that no one else seemed to know about.

"And what do these extra special sensors with their hull penetrating scans have to say?"

Hanu snuck another look at the camera, as if searching for reassurance. Bowed her head over her panel and rattled away, shunting a series of overlapping, three dimensional diagrams to the front windows. "This," she said, when the last diagram was done.

Henricksen took a look—eyes flicking between those diagrams on the windows and the reality of the station outside. Studied the information there for quite some time, risking a bit of wobble in the ship's flight path to give the structure of the thing a thorough examination. Noting the compartments and bracings, the huge energy source at the station's center surrounded by...something. Some kind of machinery, if he had to guess, though the scans—as good as they were—showed them as somewhat amorphous blobs.

Mostly he saw metal. Huge masses of it. Entire compartments *filled* with it, turning sections of the diagram dark.

Dead ships and a station stuffed full of composite metal. I have a bad feeling about this.

"Run the scans again, Hanu," he said faintly. "Sweep the sensors across those ships out there while you're at it."

She looked up, helmeted head tilting in question. "*Scythe* says they're dead, sir."

"I'm aware of that, Hanu."

She stared a moment, fingers resting on her panel. Nodded and touched at her station, programming the sensors for a second set of hull penetrating scans.

"Something in particular you're looking for?" Sikuuku toggled his helmet comms to a private channel, keeping the question between the two of them.

"Maybe. A hunch, anyway." Henricksen pulled the live feed of the sensor data onto his panel, ignoring the station scans for now, focusing only on those ships. Tapped into that first set of scans, laying the three dimensional model of the manufactory alongside the hull penetrating scans Hanu ran on its ring of ships.

Stared at the results for a long, long time, feeling cold all over before shunting the data to the Artillery pod and letting Sikuuku take a look himself.

"It's a match," he said quietly. "A match to the station. Same composite metal signature sitting inside each of those ships' bellies."

Hanu turned, looking from Henricksen to *Scythe*'s camera. "This isn't a science station, is it, sir?"

"No, Hanu," Henricksen said quietly. "I don't think it is."

"Then what is it?" she asked, voice hushed. "What's in there?"

"Remember those nannites Kinsey showed you?"

She nodded and then froze, sitting up straight. "No," she breathed, shaking her head.

"Inside the station," Henricksen told her, highlighting the repeating metal lumps. "Inside those ships as well."

"What does it mean?" Hanu whispered, still not getting—scared, as she should be, but not enough. Not realizing what all this was about.

"It's a manufactory," *Scythe* told her, soft voice stepping in. "They're *building* nannites in there, Hanu. Building them inside that station, and then stuffing them inside those ships."

TWENTY-EIGHT

"What do we do?" Ogawa twisted, looking from Henricksen to Hanu, to Sikuuku in his Artillery pod. "I mean, this changes things, doesn't it? All of our plans?"

"Not everything. Still gotta find that can." Henricksen glanced at Ogawa, nodded to her station. "What's the word from the other Ravens?"

A check of the channels—helmeted head bowed over her station's panels, multi-colored lights reflecting off the darkened visor covering her face—and Ogawa turned, shaking her head. "Nothing, sir. Not yet anyway. *Shriek* and *Snicker-snack* are barely a quarter of the way through their search pattern, *Sever* and *Sharp* slightly less."

"This is taking too long." Sikuuku kicked at the pod's foot controls, turning it a few inches more. "Rate they're going, we could be here for hours."

"Not like they aren't trying." Ogawa's head pivoted, turning his way. "Lot of rocks out there to pick through. Lot of places for a canister to hide."

"And us stuck here in the middle," Sikuuku grumbled. "Asses hanging in the wind." He shucked over and leaned out of his pod, setting a hand on Henricksen's shoulder. "What are we doing, Captain?"

"Not sure yet." Henricksen chewed his lip, thinking hard. "Figuring that out."

Couldn't leave without that canister—information retrieval was their primary objective, station scans a distant second. But the Brass would want to know about this. The ships, the manufactory, the mines littering the asteroid field.

None of it in the mission plan. Science station supposedly, hiding inside these rocks. No mention of nannites, much less those ship-killing mines.

Shoddy-ass intel, he thought. *Way too shoddy for a supposedly experienced spook.*

Bothered him. Everything *about* this mission bothered him.

"Doesn't make sense. None of this makes sense."

"Captain?" Ogawa raised a hand, waving to get his attention. "I'm picking up a communication."

"Inbound or outbound?"

"Both," she said, puzzled. "And it's...Sir." Ogawa turned her head, visored face showing blood red in the bridge pod's lighting. "It's us, sir. It's coming from us."

Henricksen raised his head, staring right into *Scythe's* camera. "Mind explaining that?"

"I had orders," she told him, voice wooden, mechanical, devoid of any emotion. Any semblance of personality gone.

Two-Six speaking now, not *Scythe*. Two-Six watching from that camera at the front of the bridge.

Pissed Henricksen off something fierce, having her retreat like that. Fall back on just being some nameless, faceless AI. "*We* had orders, remember? Team, *Scythe*." He waved at the crew around him, thumped a fist against his chest. "We work as a team. That means sharing information. Telling each other what's going on."

Scythe said nothing, just watched him from above, silent for a long, long time. "I'm sorry, Henricksen," she said quietly, once she finally found her voice. Her *real* voice, not that bullshit, anonymous AI thing she'd dragged out earlier. "This isn't my choice."

"Isn't your choice?" Henricksen frowned in annoyance. "What the hell—?"

"Jump signature!" Hanu leaned forward, panel lighting in front of her. "Looks like it's outside the asteroid field. Pingers are picking it up."

"Where?" Henricksen asked her. "How far out?"

"Three o'clock." Hanu consulted the data, pushed a marker to the schematic on the front windows to show the buckle's location. "Twenty thousand kilometers out."

"Any data come through? Any idea who—?"

Klaxons kicked in filling the bridge with noise. Scan went crazy, alerts popping up everywhere, flashing insistently for Hanu's attention.

"*Scythe!* You're killin' me here!" Henricksen yelled.

"Sorry."

Scythe silenced the audible alarms while Hanu sorted through half a dozen windows, examining the data on the fly.

"What've we got, Hanu? What new and terrible thing has suddenly gone wrong?"

Hanu leaned close to her panel, examining the data from the sensors. "It's the station, sir. Jump drives are powering up."

"Shit," Sikuuku swore, pod pivoting. "They're gonna jump it. We're gonna lose it again."

"Weapons signatures!" Hanu's fingers fairly danced across Scan's panels. "Armaments are coming on-line."

"Armaments?" Sikuuku flicked at switches, flipped his targeting visor over his eyes. "Thought you said the scans didn't *show* any goddamn armaments, Hanu."

"Missed it," she told him, head shaking. "I must've missed it somehow."

"Movement!" Ogawa warned, as the ships outside shifted, engines flaring bright blue as the station's tiny minders came to life.

"What the hell?" Sikuuku pulled data onto his panel, feeding it to the Artillery pod's targeting system. "Lotta targets out there, boss. Boss?"

"How long?" Henricksen asked quietly. "How long before that station jumps?"

"That much mass?" Ogawa ran a few calculations. "Six minutes, give or take."

"Five minutes, thirty-seven seconds," *Scythe* corrected.

Ogawa shrugged her shoulders, hooked a thumb at the camera. "What she said."

"Shit," Henricksen breathed, staring at the station outside. "Shit, shit, *shit!*" He punched the panel in frustration, slapped at Comms, opening a ship-to-ship channel to *Shriek* and the other Ravens. "Scramble, scramble, scramble. Mission is blown. I repeat, mission is blown. We've got ships inbound, target is live."

"Friendlies?" Janssen sent back.

"Hanu?" Henricksen looked a question at Scan.

Hanu checked the sensor data, shook her head hard. "Can't tell yet, sir. Energy signature's coming through, but I can't get a clear fix. Could be it's our guys out there. Could just as easily be DSR."

"Great. Just fucking great. Peel off," Henricksen ordered, feathering the controls, moving *Scythe* away from the station. "Clear the asteroid field and head back to Dragoon."

"Sir." Janssen again, voice worried. "We jump in here and the distortion field will set off those mines."

"Fuck." The mines. He'd almost forgotten. Henricksen's eyes flicked to the schematic, the bright red dots marking the mines infesting the asteroid field around them. "Thrusters and maneuvering jets only until you clear the asteroid field."

"Faster if we jump it," Baldini argued.

"And more likely you'll end up dead. Jump too close to one of those mines and you'll set off the explosives. Take the mine out and yourself with it."

"Oh." Baldini was quiet a moment, properly cowed. "Helluva a way to go out, though."

"Rather keep livin'," Henricksen told him. "Now go. Get. *Scythe* and I will be right behind you. We'll meet up—"

"What about the payload?" Baldini cut in.

"Goddamit, Baldini. Forget about the payload. We'll come back—"

Perimeter alarms activated again, shrieking bloody murder as the situation changed. Data windows overwhelming Scan's panels as some new complication appeared.

"Ship inbound," Hanu called, sorting through the reams of data on her panel. "Buckle's resolving."

"Go, Baldini. Get out!" Henricksen cut the comms to the other Ravens, keeping one eye on the schematic on the front windows as the stealth ships' signatures moved away. "Ours or theirs, Hanu? Ours or theirs?" he repeated, when Hanu just shook her head.

"I don't—I'm not—*Gogmagog! Gogmagog*'s coming through!"

The schematic on the front windows shifted, data tag appearing, adding a ship's beacon next to the hyperspace displacement marker showing twenty thousand kilometers outside the asteroid field.

"*Gogmagog.*" Henricksen slid his eyes to *Scythe*'s camera. "*Brutus*'s butt buddy? *That's* who you called?"

"I'm sorry, Henricksen."

She sounded it—she truly did. Henricksen wished to hell he knew why she'd done it. What was going on.

"Multiple signatures, Captain." Hanu shunted more data to the front windows, adding a mass of Titan and Aurora signatures, a couple of sleek-sided Valkyries joining soon after.

"Weapons fire!" That from Ogawa, piggybacking off Hanu's panel, trying to help her out. "Fleet ships' armaments are live!"

"*Fuck!*" Henricksen hit the thrusters, shoving *Scythe* toward the asteroid field's edge. Rolled around a rock, skipping neatly by a mine, sensors recording detonations—plasma rounds from the Dreadnought's cannons pounding away at the asteroid field's outer edge—and a whole lot of chaos: asteroids exploding, broken rocks smashing into each other, the entire formation of the asteroid field shifting as *Gogmagog*'s weapons chewed their way toward the center.

Henricksen stared, watching the schematic shift and shift again. Adjusting and readjusting as the asteroid field's integrity shredded. Its millennia old pattern disrupted in mere seconds by the awesome power of *Gogmagog*'s guns.

"What the fuck is he doing?" Sikuuku demanded. "We've got ships in here!"

"Ogawa," Henricksen called. "Message the Fleet. Tell *Gogmagog*—"

"He knows," *Scythe* said softly. "*Gogmagog* has his orders too."

Henricksen frowned at the camera, turned his eyes to the windows, looking from the DSR manufactory to the asteroid field collapsing around it. "The station," he breathed, finally getting it. "He's here to destroy the station before it can get away again."

And the Ravens with it if they didn't get the hell out of here. And *soon*.

A ripple outside and Scan went haywire again—alerts popping up everywhere, painting Hanu's helmet in multi-colored lights. "Jump signature. Close one." Hanu scanned the panels in front of her, searching the sensor data. "I count two—correction, *three* of those DSR ships moving away."

"Show me," Henricksen ordered, slowing the ship, easing around a cluster of mines.

Hanu shunted a video feed to the front windows, *Scythe*'s cameras tracking the DSR vessels at the asteroid field's center as they spun up their jump drives and short-hopped away.

Sub-minds on the pingers picked them up again, sending broken snippets of video back to *Scythe* as the droned ships dropped out of hyperspace, landing smack-dab in the middle of *Gogmagog*'s armada.

The lead ship missed—overjumped its target, streaked right *past* the Meridian Alliance vessels and into deep space—but the vessel behind it struck true. Intersected a Titan's flight path and exploded on contact, destroying both ships in an instant.

A flash of blue as a third ship appeared, dropping out of hyperspace just under five kilometers from *Gogmagog*'s position—far enough out to do some real damage, close enough in that anything in front of it had almost no chance of avoiding its strike. Jump momentum flung it forward, hurtling headlong through space. Henricksen watched it—one eye on the carnage, the bulk of his attention on the rocks around him—cringing as the droned ship hove in on a Valkyrie, scraping along her side.

Photovoltaic cells peeled away, dents appearing in her superstructure, holes opening in her sides. The droned ship sideswiped her and rebounded, slamming broadside into two Auroras, hull splitting open on impact, releasing the nannite payload packed inside it.

The Auroras disappeared, subsumed by a silver-sided swarm. A diamond dust cloud that multiplied, feeding on the remains of the Auroras to create more of itself—a second cloud, large as the first that jumped from the dying Auroras, reaching for the Valkyrie nearby.

Gogamaog's weapons intercepted it before it touched her, plasma canons slicing and dicing, burning the nannites to dust. A flare of energy as he loaded radiologicals—huge missiles, Scan went nuts when those signatures appeared— and launched them at the source of the contagion, nuking the droned ship and both Auroras at once.

And all the while his cannons kept firing, chewing away at the asteroid field, drilling a tunnel toward the station at its center.

"*Scythe.*" Henricksen glanced at the camera, nodded to the schematic on the front windows, the situation playing out against the stars. "What's the math on this say?"

She ran some calculations—split second factoring of mass and energy, the rate of *Gogmagog*'s fire—and built a simulation. Shunted it to the front windows for Henricksen and the crew to see.

"They won't make it." Henricksen twitched the ship to one side, maneuvering around a mine. "*Gogmagog*'s not gonna get through in time."

Lot of energy required to shift that station through hyperspace. Lot of time needed to spool up its engines and create a buckle large enough to accommodate it. But *Gogamagog*'s guns had several kilometers of asteroid field to chew through. And no matter how many times he ran *Scythe*'s simulation, the station always got away before the Dreadnought's guns found it.

We can't lose it. Not again. Not knowing what it is.

Henricksen slowed the ship, turned *Scythe* around.

Comms clicked, Sikuuku's voice speaking directly into his ear. "Tell me you're not doing what I think you're doing."

"Math doesn't work. Figured we'd give *Gogmagog* a little help."

"One stealth ship against a whopping big station?"

"Not asking you to destroy it. Just asking you to help me slow it down a bit." Henricksen fired the thrusters, working his way back to the asteroid field's center.

Sikuuku leaned out, examining the situation outside the windows. Shrugged his shoulders and ducked back into his pod. "Hanu. Give me those station scans."

"Got it." She pushed the data to the Artillery pod. Added the same information to the schematic on the front windows. "Something you're looking for?"

"Engine ports." He scanned the three dimensional model of the station, turning it round and round. "Fucker can't jump if he doesn't have engines." A few seconds of silence and the gunner sighed heavily. "Well, shit. This is gonna be a problem." He tapped at his panel, updating the data Hanu sent him. Pushed a modified version of the station schematic to the front windows, adding markers from the Artillery pod's targeting display. "See that?" He tapped a finger against his panel, highlighting an energy signature at the station's center. "That's the Cepheid's jump drive. And those..." More tapping, more highlighted shapes glowing on the front windows, bright points set in a star pattern around the oversized orb at the station's center. "Those are the jump drives of the other ships they butchered to create that manufactory. They daisy chained them together to make their jump signatures overlap."

Which explained how they managed to move the damned thing in the first place, but not really much else.

"And?" Henricksen prompted.

"Seven hyperspace units means seven targets. That's a lot of engines to try and take out."

Scythe slid free of the asteroid field's clutter, giving Henricksen a clear view of their target. "Ignore the outliers. Cepheid's the nexus, right? Got the biggest engine of the bunch. So you just focus your fire on that. Forget about the rest."

"Toughest target of the lot to hit," Sikuuku noted, flipping switches, settling the targeting visor over his face. "Pretty much buried—"

"Just shoot the damn thing, Chief."

"Aye, sir."

Stiff, surly answer this time. Exactly the way Henricksen liked his gunners.

The Artillery pod *whirred*, pivoting to lock onto its target as Sikuuku hunkered down inside. A squeeze of the triggers activated *Scythe's* cannons, flinging stuttering lines of cobalt blue plasma fire across the stars.

Scan flashed a warning as the station came alive, automated defense system kicking in. Rail guns ignited, chattering out strings of ion rounds as a single plasma cannon lit, chucking fat blobs of plasma fire *Scythe's* way.

Henricksen hit the thrusters, putting on a burst of speed, zigged and zagged, jogging the ship sharply as rail gun fire tore along *Scythe's* side.

"*Fuck!*" Sikuuku swore, targeting system blanking, losing its lock on the Cepheid at the station's center. "This would be a helluva lot easier if you stopped movin' the ship around so damn much."

"I stop movin' and we stop livin'," Henricksen reminded him, yanking hard on the control stick to dodge the station's fire. "Helluva lot easier for them to hit us if we just sit here like a catatonic turtle."

Sikuuku cursed roundly, pouring out more fire. Kicked at a floor pedal to reorient the pod, targeting system re-engaging to guide the cannon fire toward its target. Scored a few hits before the structures shielding the Cepheid got in his way. Spat out *more* curses as he mashed the floor pedal, swinging the Artillery pod around.

The targeting system locked—cannons dead on, errors flickering on and off as the station's outer structures intermittently got in the way. Sikuuku gripped the firing sticks, muttering curses as he squeezed the triggers, pounding away at the station to get at the Cepheid's hull.

Dents appeared, hull plating bending and twisting, slowly peeling away. A sustained burst from *Scythe's* main cannon crumpled one of the external structures, but a jog of the ship and he lost it, targeting lock failing again, shots flying wide.

"Fuck! Fuck! *Fuck!*" Sikuuku punched the panel, swearing at the useless piece of shit targeting system as it desperately realigned.

A shot clipped them—station turret scoring across *Scythe*'s wing, tearing a plasma cannon away—and Henricksen hauled her over, engines igniting as he dodged her away.

Sikuuku kicked out, slewing the pod around. Yanked hard on the firing stick's triggers as the ship came about. "This isn't fucking working!" he yelled. "I can't hit a god damn thing—"

"Boss! *Boss!*" Baldini shouted, comms crackling as his voice came through.

"Shouldn't be here, Baldini." Henricksen grimaced, weaving around the station's fire. "Told you boys to go."

"Can't!" he panted. "Need some help."

"Fuck. What now?" Henricksen checked the schematic, searching for *Sever's* signature. Found *Shriek* and *Snicker-snack* first—the two of them together, just clearing the asteroid field, making a break for the stars—and *Sharp* soon after, following a more wandering line. And *Sever*...

Sever wasn't where he was supposed to be. Hadn't even cleared the mine layer yet.

The can, Henricksen thought, noting the ship's position. *He's still looking for Kinsey's stupid can.*

"Goddammit, Baldini! We'll come back for the payload later. Now get your ass in gear and clear out!"

"Can't," Baldini repeated, pushing a video feed across the channel.

A live stream from *Sever*'s cameras flickered to life on *Scythe*'s front windows, crowding the station schematic to one side. A view of chaos surrounding the ship at its center: rocks swirling randomly, slamming together and disintegrating into deadly clouds of ship killing shards.

Henricksen winced, shoulders hunching as a shrieking squeal filtered across the channel. A thud and the camera slewed sideways, focusing in on a puff of air and a hole torn in *Sever*'s side.

"Trapped," Baldini said, breathless. On the edge of panic now. "Can't find a way out. Field's disintegrating. Can't—I can't—"

A burst of static drowned out the rest of the communication, but the video feed kept running. Slewing one way and the other as Baldini wrestled *Sever* around, dodging one obstacle and another.

Missed a mine by a hair's breadth and came up on a rock. Went up and over, Baldini cursing like a sailor as *Sever's* belly scraped along the top. "Fuck! Fuck me! Boss! We can't—I can't—I can't find a *fucking* way out!"

"Buckle's forming!" Hanu called as a spreading disc of darkness appeared off *Scythe*'s starboard bow. A hyperspace distortion that sucked at her body, trying to drag everything—*Scythe,* the remaining droned ships, hell the whole goddamned *asteroid* field—inside.

Henricksen fought for control, struggling against that pull, doing his best to keep the ship on-line. "How long, Hanu?"

"We've got a minute, maybe a minute thirty before that thing jumps."

"Sikuuku—"

"Boss!" Baldini called, voice desperate now.

"Hang on, Baldini. Just hang on!" Henricksen yelled back. "Scan! Give me a view of the area. Need to know what the hell's happening out there."

Hanu rattled away at her panel, moving the map of the asteroid field to the front windows, layering in *Sever*'s location.

Obstacles around him—asteroids and debris, mines just waiting to go off. Swirling chaos everywhere, spreading in waves across the asteroid field, collapsing the open space at its center.

Can't stay, Henricksen thought, eyes flicking across that map. *We can't stay here much longer or we'll get caught up in all that.*

"Boss!"

"We're working it, Baldini." Plasma fire slammed into *Scythe*'s tail, shoving her nose around. "Shit," Henricksen breathed, bringing the ship back online. "Hanu! Get on that map. Find Baldini a way out."

"How—"

"I don't know, Hanu." Henricksen clenched his teeth, trying for calm. "I'm a little busy right now, in case you hadn't noticed, so I need you to figure it out."

"I don't—I'm not—"

"*Try,* Hanu." He spared a look for Scan. "Just try."

"Aye, sir," she answered. Entirely uncertain. All too aware of the impossibility of that task.

"Sikuuku! How's it going back there?" Henricksen yelled.

"Almost," the gunner hissed, blasting away with his cannons. "Got some heavy fucking shielding, but I'm just about there."

"Ogawa! Give me status—"

"*Boss!*"

Explosion on *Sever*'s feed, mine detonating, peppering the Raven with rock shards. Baldini jogged desperately, putting on speed as the shockwave spread outward. Racing to stay ahead of a chain reaction of explosions—one mine's detonation leading to another, and another, a rippling wave of destruction working its way through the asteroid field, triggering every last mine in its path.

"Jump," Ogawa breathed, staring at the feed on the windows. "He's got to jump it if he's going to get out."

"Thirty seconds!" Hanu called.

"C'mon, c'mon, *c'mon*!" Sikuuku shouted, cannons blasting away.

"Screw this!" Baldini yelled, and a second later, *Sever*'s jump drive activated, the ship itself slewing around.

"What the hell is he doing? Baldini, what the *fuck*—?"

"Henricksen," *Scythe* called, serene voice intruding. "It's ending, Henricksen."

He looked at her, eyes locking onto *Scythe*'s camera. "He'll get it," he said, jerking a thumb at Sikuuku behind him. "He just needs a little more time."

"The asteroid field is destabilizing around us, Henricksen. There *is* no more time." The ship shuddered, plasma fire tearing into *Scythe*'s hull plating. Another shudder—this one deep inside her belly, accompanied by a high-pitched whine—and a warning appeared as the cloaking system shut down.

"Jump drives are cycling!" Ogawa called, sorting through the data on her panel. "Our hyperspace engines just came online!"

"Not yet. Not yet," Sikuuku muttered, cannons firing, tearing holy hell out of the Cepheid's protective plating. "I almost got this. I'm almost there."

"*Scythe.*" Henricksen tore his eyes from the windows as the whining intensified, hyperspace engines filling *Scythe*'s bridge with a bone-rattling hum. "What's going on?"

"I'm sorry, Henricksen, but *Sever* and I are agreed on this."

"Agreed on what?" he asked numbly, cold seeping into his bones. "Agreed on *what, Scythe?*"

"Aw, fuck it!" Baldini shouted, and the video feed changed again.

Sever shot forward, dark void engulfing his nose as he short-spun his jump drive and slid inside.

"Time to go, Henricksen."

Soft voice from *Scythe* now. Gentle and apologetic.

"We're gonna talk about this when we get back to the station," Henricksen told her.

"I know."

Scythe's engines flared as she turned away from the station, slipping into the hyperspace buckle.

Henricksen caught a glimpse of *Sever* in the instant before the jump distortion closed around them. Saw him exit the hyperspace void, sharp-sided shape a blur of disintegrating panels and shards of shredded asteroid, plowing head-on into the DSR station. Heard comms crackle, Baldini screaming a banshee's song of joy and rage as *Sever*'s kamikaze run came to a sudden and abrupt end.

The Raven connected, ploughing nose on into the station's center, triggering a massive explosion. And then the trough them, sucking *Scythe* into hyperspace. Sending her far, far away from that place of destruction and death.

TWENTY-NINE

Scythe drifted, waiting for a pick up in the vastness of wide open space.

Burned out her engines short hopping from the asteroid field. Lost her main cannon and a good chunk of the hull plating on her starboard side when the DSR station blew, obliterating the asteroid field around it. Suspected she still had a few chunks of asteroid lodged somewhere inside her, but the alternative…

Dead in the water's better than dead as a doornail.

Henricksen pulled a video feed onto his panel, studying the remains of the asteroid field outside.

Missed the actual explosion, luckily. Dropped out of hyperspace thirty thousand kilometers from where they started and got caught up in the aftermath—klaxons screaming as a storm of debris pelted *Scythe*'s sides, hammering at her triple-thick shell.

Didn't last long—velocity behind that debris rolled it right across her—but the thirty seconds they *were* caught up in it, rocks and shredded pieces of metal buffeting *Scythe*'s body, were somewhat terrifying. Especially since there was nothing the crew could do but clench their teeth and suffer through it. Let it blow through like a summer thunderstorm, taking the swirling chaos with it.

A lifetime, those thirty seconds. And now here they sat—thrusters damaged, hyperspace engines torn apart—waiting on one of *Gogmagog*'s Valkyries to come and pick them up because they couldn't go much of anywhere on their own.

Embarrassing, that. Having to call up one of their own ships and ask for a rescue. Especially with all that devastation around them. The broken ships and missing crew. AI lives snuffed out.

Long way back to Dragoon, though. Long, slow way with nothing but a stuttering, beat-up propulsion system to get them there. *Scythe* claimed they could make it—might take a few days, but she swore the main engines would hold together—but Henricksen didn't share her confidence.

Didn't relish spending that much time in these cramped quarters, either. Easier to just call for a pick up. Slide *Scythe* into the belly of one of those sleek-sided Valkyries out there and take the leisurely way back. But, oh how it rankled having to call over to *Gogmagog* and ask for a favor. *Gogmagog,* who was the oldest of them. A battle-scarred veteran, long on anger, and short on patience. In no good mood when *Scythe* called over.

Busy working clean-up, scouring every last inch of that section of space to make sure nothing, not one single nannite managed to escape. Busy seeing to his *own* ships—nearly half of them damaged, ten lost completely, torn apart and eaten alive by those very same nannites he hunted, the droned ships in which they came. Hadn't even had time to see to his own wounds, the dents and scrapes that showed clearly, pockmarks and jagged tears running up and down his sides, much less worry about some stealth ship with burnt out engines.

Surly old cuss—all of them were, every last Dreadnought Henricksen had ever met. But he was a tough old bastard, give him that. Limped back to port a smoldering, ramshackle hulk on more than one occasion, but he always made. Always battled his way home.

"Wait," *Gogmagog* told them, and *Scythe*—lacking other options— acknowledged and did just that. Sat and waited. Sent a communication to Dragoon to let them know they'd be late arriving, and then drifted, enduring the razzing that came back.

"Busted up your ride already?" *Shriek tsked*, AI voice filled with disdain. "That's one crap pilot you got there, *Scythe*. *My* pilot got us back to Dragoon just fine. *And Sharp*'s. *And Snicker*—"

"Stuff it, Leroy," Sikuuku growled. "Captain's not in the mood for your crap."

"*Crap*?! It's not—"

"Not. In the mood." Sikuuku cut the channel, muttering something about "blabbermouth AIs" under his breath. Unbuckled his seat's straps and climbed from the Artillery pod, grunting and hissing as he bent and twisted, trying to loosen muscles cramped tight after so many hours in the pod.

Snug fit in there, in every Artillery pod, so far as Henricksen knew. Never could understand why gunners came so damn big when those pods were built so damn small.

"Looks like we're gonna be here a while." Sikuuku nodded to the front windows, the ships running clean up outside. Salvaging parts where they could, searching for survivors amongst the wreckage.

Hoped there were some. Hoped *some* of those dead ships managed to eject their crew before the nannites took over.

"You mind?"

"Hmm?" Henricksen glanced around and saw Sikuuku hook a thumb over his shoulder, indicating the bridge door.

"Starving," he said, stomach rumbling. "Stiff too. Wouldn't mind stretching my legs for a bit."

"Shove off." Henricksen flicked his fingers, waving the gunner away. Considered Ogawa sitting to one side, Hanu on the other. "You two as well."

Ogawa looked up, turned around. "You sure, sir? I don't mind staying. Two sets of eyes—"

"Are just as tired as one. Go," Henricksen told her, nodding to the door. "Could be hours before *Gogmagog* sends someone to get us. Grab some chow. Rack out if you can."

Ogawa still seemed uncertain. "But what if—?"

"I'll *call* you, Ogawa." Henricksen tapped a finger to the side of his helmet. "Promise."

"Aye, sir." Grudging response. Reluctance coming through clearly in the stiff way she stood, throwing a last, lingering glance at the windows before collecting Hanu and following Sikuuku out the door.

"Alone at last," *Scythe* said, smile in her voice.

Henricksen grunted, sorting through data on his panel.

"Something wrong?"

"Nope."

"Voice analysis says otherwise."

"I'll bet," Henricksen muttered, closing one data window, opening another.

Silence after. *Scythe* watching him, Henricksen pointedly ignoring her camera.

"Henricksen." *Scythe* waited, and waited, until he finally looked up. "What's wrong?" she asked, a hint of worry creeping into her tone.

Didn't really want to get into it, not right now, but *Scythe*'s camera kept staring and eventually he relented. Tugged at his seat straps to loosen them and sat back with a sigh. Folded his hands in his lap. "The canister. Kinsey's spook. This whole goddamn *mission*. Was any of it real?"

Scythe didn't answer—not right away. "I don't know," she admitted. "Kinsey didn't tell me."

"And yet you sent him something, didn't you? Right before everything went south."

"Scans," she said, in a soft, apologetic voice. "I sent a copy of the hull penetration scans back to Dragoon."

"Mind telling me why?"

"I had orders."

"Orders," Henricksen grunted. "That's an excuse, *Scythe,* not an explanation."

Silence around him, *Scythe*'s camera an unblinking eye.

"And *Gogamog*?" he asked quietly. "Was he part of those orders too?"

"Yes," she whispered. "And no."

"Well, which is it?" he snapped, growing tired of all these diversions and half truths. "Yes or no, *Scythe*? I want a straight answer this time."

"The message..." *Scythe* hesitated. "The message was pre-programmed. Queued up and ready. All I had to do was send it out."

Henricksen tilted his head, considering, sensing a conspiracy at work. "Shaw?" he guessed. "Did Shaw give you that message? Tell you when and where to send it out?"

She had the access and the interest—one of few who did. But *Scythe* surprised him with an entirely different name.

"Kinsey," she said, voice the barest breath. "My orders came from Kinsey himself."

Not the answer he expected. Not even close.

"I thought he wanted information. Why would he..." Henricksen trailed off, frowning in confusion. Dropped his eyes from the camera and watched *Gogmagog*'s lumpen shape glide by.

Kinsey sent the RV-Ns here to reconnoiter—survey the area and report back. So why would he summon *Gogmagog* and have him take the entire thing out?

"He knew, didn't he? Kinsey knew what this place was all along."

And gave *Scythe* orders—directions in secret that ran counter to Henricksen's own.

"Did he tell you?" he asked, looking back to the camera. "Or did he send you in here blind?"

Scythe's silence said everything. More than any words she could offer.

"Why didn't you tell me?"

"Henricksen—"

"*Why*?" he demanded, angry now. Resentful that she'd kept this secret from him. "Why didn't you tell me?"

More silence—*Scythe* unwilling to answer, or not knowing how. "I'm sorry," she repeated. A default response. The one she fell back on when caught at loose ends. "Kinsey—My orders—I wasn't allowed to tell you," she admitted in a rush.

"I bet," Henricksen muttered, pointedly looking away. He stared at the windows, studying the ships and stars outside, letting the silence stretch between them. Making *Scythe* break it this time.

"I'm sorry," she whispered, having nothing else to offer.

Henricksen grunted in answer, resentful still, holding onto his anger. But being angry at *Scythe* didn't solve anything, and none of this truly was her fault.

Kinsey's plan. His machinations all along. He stared at the windows, wondering why he did it—what prompted a spit and polish, stiff prick like Kinsey to go so far off the reservation—and realized he'd probably never know.

Bastard always was full of secrets. And this the greatest of them all.

"It's alright," he sighed, shifting in his seat, waving a hand at *Scythe's* watching camera. "Kinsey used you. Just like the rest of us."

Scythe was quiet a moment, camera watching from above. "Will we—will I—"

"*We*, Scythe." He turned his visored face toward the camera. "We're a team, remember? You got it right the first time."

"Team," she whispered, sounding surprisingly pleased. "Will *we* be in trouble? For this," she explained, turning her camera toward the windows.

"Maybe." Henricksen shrugged his shoulders. "Hard to know for certain. Blew the reconnoiter, but taking out that station…" He grunted, shaking his head. "Brass can't really argue against destroying a high value target like that."

"And Kinsey?"

"Do you care?"

"Yes. I would feel…bad, if he was punished for this."

"Really?" Henricksen considered her camera a moment, honestly surprised. "My guess is they'll reward him. For the same reasons they won't call us to the carpet."

"You really think so?"

Hopeful voice now—another surprise.

"Probably give him some cushy administrative job in some cushy administrative office far away from here," Henricksen told her. "'Course, his Black Ops days are done. Fleet won't let him anywhere *near* another one of these secret squirrel projects after pulling a stunt like this."

"No," she said quietly. "I suppose not."

Silence again—neither of them speaking for a long, long time.

"Did I do the right thing?" *Scythe* asked some time later. "Should I—Should we—Did I do the right thing in following Kinsey's orders?"

"Yes, *Scythe*," he said patiently. "And no," he added, because that was truth.

"No?" Scythe sounded baffled, morality program struggling to interpret that conflicting answer. "Why no?"

"Secrets, *Scythe*. 'Team' and 'secrets'," he shook his head hard. "Just doesn't work. You put crew at risk—"

"No," she insisted—urgent, earnest voice. "I got us *out*."

"*We* got out. *Shriek* did. *Snicker-snack* and *Sharp*. But what about *Sever*? What about Baldini and the others? They were crew too, *Scythe*. We lost—" He broke off, sighing, weary beyond belief.

Hecate would've gotten it. Would've read the situation and realized immediately that calling the Dreadnought in was a severely bad idea.

Hecate*'s not here,* he reminded himself. *And* Scythe…Scythe*'s just a kid.*

Moral processors undeveloped. Her sense of right and wrong not quite there yet. Instinct and logic in constant conflict with her programming.

Scythe followed orders because she had them, not knowing which to question and which to follow to the letter.

"It's complicated," Henricksen told her, having no better explanation.

"So am I."

"*Touche*," Henricksen smiled, tipping an invisible cap.

A glint of light caught his attention, drawing his eyes back to the windows. To a shimmering sparkle gliding amongst the wreckage—smooth-sided and twinkling like a thousand, atmosphere-filtered stars.

Curious, he pulled up a feed from one of *Scythe*'s many hull cameras, watching the wounded Valkyrie search the dead ships out there for survivors.

Gaping wounds showed on the warship's flanks, entire sections of her sparkling, photovoltaic skin torn away. Eaten down to her composite metal frame.

"Those nannites sure did a number on her."

Heavy damage on that Valkyrie, but she kept fighting. Caught a glimpse of her as they dumped out of jump, swooping in like star-spangled justice—turret guns blazing as she sliced through a pair of droned ships, coming at her from either side.

Tough old bird, that one. Kept fighting, despite the nannites gnawing at her skin. Kept kicking ass, refusing to lay down and die.

"Showed 'em, didn't you?" Henricksen murmured. "Still standing, even after all that."

"Should I be jealous?" The panel flickered as *Scythe* tapped into the feed, taking a look herself.

Henricksen wiped it, shrugging uncomfortably. Went back to studying the data on his panel.

But his eyes kept returning to that Valkyrie, remembering the look of her, the grace and beauty, the *power* as she cut those DSR ships down.

He was captain now, with a captain's stars on his collar. A Raven for the moment, but Black Ops was never his calling. Never really cared for all the cloak and dagger and hush-hush stuff. He'd finish this stint with the Ravens and close out his tour. Move on to another assignment when this one was done.

Warship billet this time, like he'd originally wanted. A Valkyrie, maybe. Like that one out there.

Henricksen glanced at the windows again, snuck a look at *Scythe*'s camera as he reached for the panel in front of him. Keyed into the system and pulled up a record.

Sat there, staring at it, and the name showing at the top.

Serengeti.

Henricksen smiled, liking the sound of it. The images it brought to mind. On a whim, he flicked through her design specs, checking the crew roster while he was at it. Saw *Serengeti*'s captain had already put in her letter—intent to retire written in bold, red text beneath a smiling picture of a serious-faced woman with iron-grey hair.

"Two years and she'll be looking for a new captain." *Scythe* rifled through the rest of the record—a split second of investigation, absorbing every last detail of the Valkyrie's history. "You'll be up for reassignment."

"I will," Henricksen nodded, voice carefully neutral.

"I could put in a good word."

Henricksen blinked, surprised all over again. "That how it works?"

Scythe laughed softly. "How do you think I got you?"

"*Hecate.*" He smiled sadly.

Still looking after me, even from the grave.

Comms crackled, communication coming through from the Valkyrie he'd been ogling, the very same captain smiling back at him from her record.

He closed it up and acknowledged the communication as the Valkyrie detoured, heading their way.

"Looks like she's our ride."

"Looks like," Henricksen nodded, watching the Valkyrie draw near.

Two more years before her captain's chair came available. Not so long, really, and the timing was right.

It might work. It just might work.

CHECK OUT OTHER GREAT SCIENCE FICTION BOOKS

DERELICT: MARINES
by Paul E. Cooley

Fifty years ago, Mira, humanity's last hope to find new resources, exited the solar system bound for Proxima Centauri b. Seven years into her mission, all transmissions ceased without warning. Mira and her crew were presumed lost. Humanity, unified during her construction, splintered into insurgency and rebellion.

Now, an outpost orbiting Pluto has detected a distress call from an unpowered object entering Sol space: Mira has returned. When all attempts at communications fail, S&R Black, a Sol Federation Marine Corps search and rescue vessel, is dispatched from Trident Station to intercept, investigate, and tow the beleaguered Mira to Neptune.

As the marines prepare for the journey, uncertainty and conspiracy fomented by Trident Station's governing AIs, begin to take their toll. Upon reaching Mira, they discover they've been sent on a mission that will almost certainly end in catastrophe.

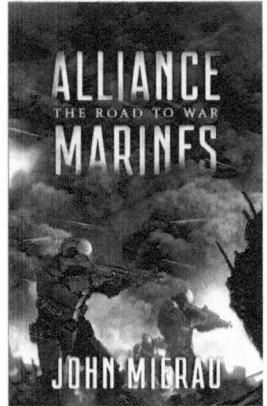

ALLIANCE MARINES
by John Mierau

One by one, all of Earth's colonies have gone dark and silent. Reach, the last colony, teeters on the verge of civil war against its Earth-loyal overlords...and Reach-born rebel Lee Zhang has sworn to push the planet over the edge.

As the colony descends into total war, a convoy from Earth races across the galaxy, carrying news of a threat unlike anything mankind has faced before. The colonies have all been destroyed by a vast alien horde, and now Earth has fallen, too. Time is running out for sworn enemies to learn to trust and unite, or the human race is extinct. The Takers are coming to destroy mankind. If we don't do the job for them first.

CHECK OUT OTHER GREAT SCIENCE FICTION BOOKS

SPACE MARINE AJAX
by Sean-Michael Argo

Ajax answers the call of duty and becomes an Einherjar space marine, charged with defending humanity against hideous alien monsters in furious combat across the galaxy.

The Garm, as they came to be called, emerged from the deepest parts of uncharted space, devouring all that lay before them, a great swarm that scoured entire star systems of all organic life. This space borne hive, this extinction fleet, made no attempts to communicate and offered no mercy.

Humanity has always been a deadly organism, and we would not so easily be made the prey. Unified against a common enemy, we fought back, meeting the swarm with soldiers upon every front.

PLANET LEVIATHAN
by D.J. Goodman

The cyborg commandos of the Galactic Marines are the greatest warriors in the galaxy, but sometimes one will go bad. Too unstable to be let back into the general population and too powerful for a normal prison to hold them, there is only one place they can be sent: Planet Leviathan.

CHECK OUT OTHER GREAT SCIENCE FICTION BOOKS

SALVAGE MERC ONE
by Jake Bible

Joseph Laribeau was born to be a Marine in the Galactic Fleet. He was born to fight the alien enemies known as the Skrang Alliance and travel the galaxy doing his duty as a Marine Sergeant. But when the War ended and Joe found himself medically discharged, the best job ever was over and he never thought he'd find his way again.

Then a beautiful alien walked into his life and offered him a chance at something even greater than the Fleet, a chance to serve with the Salvage Merc Corp.

Now known as Salvage Merc One Eighty-Four, Joe Laribeau is given the ultimate assignment by the SMC bosses. To his surprise it is neither a military nor a corporate salvage. Rather, Joe has to risk his life for one of his own. He has to find and bring back the legend that started the Corp.

SERENGETI
by J.B. Rockwell

It was supposed to be an easy job: find the Dark Star Revolution Starships, destroy them, and go home. But a booby-trapped vessel decimates the Meridian Alliance fleet, leaving Serengeti—a Valkyrie class warship with a sentient AI brain—on her own; wrecked and abandoned in an empty expanse of space. On the edge of total failure, Serengeti thinks only of her crew. She herds the survivors into a lifeboat, intending to sling them into space. But the escape pod sticks in her belly, locking the cryogenically frozen crew inside.

Then a scavenger ship arrives to pick Serengeti's bones clean. Her engines dead, her guns long silenced, Serengeti and her last two robots must find a way to fight the scavengers off and save the crew trapped inside her.